salt

thalassic series
book one

Liz Shipton

This book was previously published under the title *Salt and Fury.*

SALT

New Adult edition. June 01, 2023.

Written by Liz Shipton.

Cover art by Youness Elh.

Tyrannosaurus Yes Media

trigger warning

This book contains scenes depicting explicit sexual activity, scenes depicting underage alcohol abuse, some violence, and discussions of unresolved mental health issues.

It also has swears.
I've been putting dollars in the swear jar, promise.

salt

/sôlt/
NOUN

1. the white crystalline substance that makes seawater undrinkable

2. an experienced sailor

3. the character of someone who is coarse, rude, or spiteful; a bad attitude; sass

chapter
one

"Watch it, Howsley!"

I look up.

A small, white, one-person sailboat is tearing through steel-blue water toward me, less than ten feet away, and closing the gap fast.

"*Shit.*"

Grabbing the tiller, I bank hard to starboard, narrowly dodging the bright green sail passing less than an inch from my nose. The other boat skates by, whips around in a tightly controlled circle and comes right back at me.

Through flecks of spray and shards of sunlight bouncing off the water, I see Electra Nation—aka Miss Perfect, aka My Worst Nightmare—hanging backward over the high side of the boat like a windsurfer, perfectly balanced, and glowering at me.

"Get it together, Howsley!"

Ducking under her mainsail, she tacks away from me, her ponytail swinging like a gold medal as she carves a graceful arc toward the north end of the bay.

My biochip's radio crackles to life and the sailing teacher's voice buzzes through my head. "What's going on out there, Howsley?"

I press a finger to the spot behind my left ear. "Nothing, Sargo, everything's fine."

"Excuse me?!" Electra's outraged voice sizzles over mine through static. "Howsley almost hit me! She wasn't even looking where she was going!"

"You almost hit *me*!"

"I had the right of way!"

"*No, I—*"

Wait. *Did* she have the right of way? I squeeze my eyes shut and try to picture the moment before it happened. But it's blank. Like someone edited out that part of my memory. I must have spaced out for a second. Didn't see Electra coming.

Which is nothing new. When I was a kid my moms had a name for that: a 'blip.' Electra's probably right; she probably had the right of way. And even if she didn't, I can't pretend that I was paying attention.

"Bird, watch out!"

A nervous squeak from behind snaps my head around just in time to see another boat bearing down on me. Cursing, I snatch up the tiller again to veer out of the way.

"Okay, class." Sargo's voice is weary in my ear. "I think that's enough for today. Everyone back to the dock please."

"Oh come *on*!"

"Are you serious?!"

"Way to go, Howsley!"

"We've only been out here thirty minutes!"

Tapping behind my ear to shut out the chorus of complaints from my fellow students, I rip off my beanie and shake out my sweaty hair. My heart is racing, although whether that's because I almost just wrecked two other boats, or because of my fury at Electra and her stupid, perfect ponytail, I don't know.

Ms. Parley, my counselor, told me to take deep breaths when I start to feel angry or like my brain is spinning out of control. Begrudgingly, I take one now and hold it, stretching myself from the inside with the smell of salt and sailcloth.

As my chest expands, the hard edge of something in my inside pocket pokes me in the rib. I jolt with surprise and let out the breath in a rush.

Grog flask.

Whoops. Definitely didn't mean to bring *that* to class. I must have left it in there after last night.

I pull out the little bottle just enough to give it a small shake. A measure of liquid sloshes around inside. Glancing around, I see the rest of the class has already turned downwind and is heading back to the dock.

"Hm," I murmur to myself. "What do we think about this, Bird?"

We think that would be a really bad idea, Bird, my self replies.

Ignoring her and tugging my beanie back on one-handed, I flip open the cap and take a sip. The stuff is astringent. Medicinal. The fumes sting my eyes and rake the inside of my nose as I gulp it down. But the hole it burns in the center of my chest feels good. Feels familiar. I take another sip then wipe the scent of citrus and spice onto the back of my hand and shiver.

Someone will smell it, says self.

Yeah, well, so what? I take another swig, bigger, glaring around, daring someone to spot me. Everything else in my life is on fire, why should I care if I light another one?

You do care. You care what Sargo thinks.

A resigned sigh leaks out of me, the bottle halfway to my lips. I do care what Sargo thinks. If he finds out I was drinking in his class, he'll be pissed.

No, not pissed: *concerned.* Which is worse. Plus, I'd never forgive myself if Sargo got in trouble because of me. He's just a student teacher; he only graduated last year. It's not like he's got job security.

Flipping the cap closed, I tuck the flask back into my pocket, then reach over the side to scoop salt water into my mouth. The sting of salt is like a razor under the ragged edges of my finger-nails. Swishing the abrasive liquid around my mouth for a few seconds, I hold my hand in front of my face, crooking my knuckles to examine them.

Chewed to oblivion. Ugly little bloated corpses at the ends of my fingers. I don't remember when I started chewing them off again. They were starting to grow.

Spitting out the water, I exhale into my palm and sniff—*smells...fine*—then push the tiller of the boat away from me, turning back toward the harbor.

The wind cooperates, for once. It's a perfect day out on the bay —brisk, sunny, the cobalt water of the Salt just starting to whitecap and the sun burning white in the cerulean sky. 'Sporty,' as Sargo would say. I'm sure my classmates were just dying to get out here and show off for each other; it's the first sunny day we've had in months. That's the downside of living in the only place on the New California Coast with water: that water is fog, and it's *always* in the air.

I make it back to the harbor and pull up next to the dock, misjudging the timing and slamming the hull of my boat abruptly against the wood.

"Easy, Howsley!"

Rolling up the sleeves of his school-issued blue button-down, Sargo rushes over, braces both hands on the side of my boat, and shoves me off the dock. He admonishes my carelessness with a stern lift of a single, dark eyebrow, then holds out an olive-brown hand for a dock line.

Other students are already tying up, shooting scathing looks like arrows in my direction. Studiously ignoring them, I toss Sargo a line then jump off the boat with a second line in my hand and kneel to tie it off.

"Bird Howsley!"

Footsteps shake the planks beneath my knee and I look up to see Electra striding past Sargo, her eyes flashing, her ponytail bouncing, the fiber of her expensive waterproof sailing pants *swish-swishing* with every pompous step. Somehow, her crisp white shirt remains unspoiled by sweat or salt stains, even after the two hours of hard sailing we just did. Around her neck, an enormous silver-white pendant flashes in the late afternoon sun.

I turn my attention back to the knot I'm trying to tie. "Wonderful."

Electra draws level and stands over me with her hands on her hips, casting me in shadow. Kneeling on the dock in my leggings, ratty gray beanie, too-short shirt, and the hoodie I've worn so much it has holes in the elbows, I try not to feel like the jester prostrated in front of the queen. I forgot my sailing uniform. Again.

"What is your problem?" she demands.

I ignore her, focusing instead on the knot. *Is it right over left or left over right?* My nails are so chewed down it hurts to use my fingers.

"You're doing that wrong," she says. "Is that supposed to be a cleat hitch?"

Gritting my teeth, I haphazardly sling the line around the cleat, then stand to meet her glare. "What's *your* problem?"

"My problem is that you still don't understand the basic rules of sailing! And on top of that, you weren't even paying attention!"

"I understand the rules! You could have turned. You were coming right at me on purpose!"

"I promise you, I was not."

"Ladies." Sargo steps between us, bringing with him the crisp scent of fogwood trees, sand, and the spray of the Salt. In the pit of my stomach, something flickers around the edges of my anger. *Nerves? Shame?*

"Can we take a breath?" he says. "Please?"

Electra tosses her brassy mane and redirects her glare out over the water, perching a hand on her hip. A metallic glimmer betrays the augmentation in her pin-straight hair, which is actually black, not blonde. No one's really sure why she started augmenting it; it's not like she wasn't pretty before.

The blonde suits her though—of course it does; *everything* suits her. Juxtaposed against the hooded eyes, eggshell skin, and sharp, delicate features of a person from Zhīliú, blonde hair makes Electra Nation the kind of unexpected beautiful that causes most people to do a double take.

Electra's fingers go to her gaudy pendant, twirling it irritatedly. Sargo steps back and turns to me, his dark eyes stern. His clean-shaven jaw and neatly trimmed sable hair remind me acutely of my own scruffy appearance, and I impulsively tuck a rogue clump of mousy frizz up inside my beanie.

"Bird," he says, "I was watching you out there, and Electra's right. In this case, she did have the right of way."

Electra shoots me a triumphant look and turns her million-watt smile toward Sargo. The ponytail bounces. The pendant flashes. My teeth clench.

"But—"

"Electra," Sargo turns to her, "perhaps it would be a good idea to allow Bird a little more room for error out there."

Electra scoffs. "You want me to give her *more* room for error? How about I *stop* leaving her room for error? Maybe then she'll stop making errors."

"How about we stop leaving you room to act like a bitch?" I mutter. "Maybe then you'll stop acting like a bitch."

She rounds on me. "What did you say?"

I flinch, but force myself not to step backward. "I said 'how about you listen to Sargo', since he's the teacher? Or is it hard for you to hear him over the sound of your own ego?"

"Bird, I don't need—"

"*Ego?*" Electra glares at me. "I'm not the one so far up her own ass that she can't see a flogging *boat* coming at her."

"Well maybe if someone wasn't *pointing a flogging boat at me*—"

"I was not pointing my boat at you!"

A small crowd has formed around us as students shuffling past stop to eavesdrop. Sargo moves to shoo them away.

As his attention shifts, Electra, apparently seeing her window, swiftly closes the gap between us. She's in my face so suddenly I have to fight the impulse to step backward again. She lowers her voice to a flinty growl.

"Listen, Howsely. You might have Sargo wrapped around your disgusting chewed-up finger somehow, but I'm not gonna make exceptions for you anymore. You need to start taking responsibility for your shit, or—"

A sudden frown clouds her face. She leans closer to me and sniffs, her frown twisting into a look of horrified disgust.

"Have you been *drinking?*"

The last word rings sharply into the still air, and in the corner of my eye, I see Sargo turn. I send up a half-hearted prayer to whatever alleged gods might still be floating around up there that he didn't actually hear that word, but as his eyes meet mine, his face crumples with disappointment, and I know he did.

Electra's eyes gleam. "Are you *kidding* me, Howsley? You're drunk? In class? You're *eighteen*! That's not even close to legal on so many levels."

"I'm not drunk."

"Whatever you say." She folds her arms. "Wow, you really are just like your brother."

Anger flares like a struck match in the middle of my chest, and without thinking, I shove her hard by the shoulders. Her face twists into a very satisfying 'Oh!' of surprise, and a spike of pure, malevolent glee goes through me as she stumbles backward toward the tied-up boats.

But she's graceful. She regains her balance quickly and lunges at me. Before I can move, she's ripped the beanie from my head and fisted a chunk of my hair. Her grip is like *iron*. I guess I shouldn't be surprised at how strong she is. She's got a year on me and her arms are rippled with muscle from afternoons spent raising sails and pulling lines out on the Salt. The stinging in my scalp makes my eyes water. I can *hear* hairs tearing out of my head.

As she wrenches my head sideways, I glimpse her pendant swinging wildly at her neck, flashing in the sun, and with my free hand, I grab for it. Electra utters a sharp cry as the pendant's chain breaks, scattering fine silver links all over the dock. I make a fist around the stone and prepare to swing.

"Bird! Electra! That is *enough!*"

Someone's hands are around my shoulders. The burning in my scalp eases as Electra releases her grip, and we stumble away from each other. A nervous, bespectacled girl named Polo Parker has Electra's arm. The sudden and overwhelming scent of salt and fogwood tells me it must be Sargo's hands pinning my arms to my sides.

"El, don't! It's not worth it," Polo pleads, pink flushing under her pale, trembling cheeks.

Electra bats away her helping hands with a sharp *tsk* and clutches at her throat for the pendant. Pinpricks of blood bead along the side of her neck where the chain serrated her skin before it broke.

She glares at me. "Give me my necklace."

The sudden urge to fling the necklace off the dock and into the water seizes me, but Sargo's hands are too tight around my biceps.

I twist, furious. "Or *what?*"

Sargo's grip around my arms tightens. "Keep. Still. Howsley," he growls in my ear. When I stop struggling, he says, "Electra, come and get your necklace."

A look of hesitation crosses Electra's face. It's out of place on her; a crack in the visage betraying a chasm of vulnerabilities that might, in fact, comprise a person. But it's a momentary slip; she exhales sharply through her nose and the look vanishes, replaced by her usual carefully-composed smugness.

She tosses her ponytail, marches over in three quick strides, and wrangles the stone from my clenched fist. Then she glares at me one last time, turns, snatches up her pack, and stomps off down the dock. Polo trots after her like an obedient puppy.

Sargo's hands loosen and I pull free, wheeling around to lay into him with all the angry words I didn't get to yell at Electra.

But my vitriol evaporates at the look on his face. Fury, obviously, disbelief, disappointment, but also...yep. *Concern.*

The look seems to get right inside me; I drop my eyes and study my nails.

He sighs. "Shall we take a walk?"

chapter
two

SARGO'S only two years older than me, but I feel so small walking next to him, waiting to be reprimanded like a child.

He walks with his hands behind his back and his tawny face drawn as we round the corner from the Azimuth school dock and step onto Pier Two. Sargo's little thirty-five-foot sailboat is tied up at the end. Her corn-yellow fiberglass hull bobs gently against the jetty, cheerfully juxtaposed against the dark blue water and clear cyan sky. Her dock lines are carefully coiled, her mainsail neatly flaked along the sea-green aluminum boom. On the side of her hull, toward the stern, matching green letters spell the name *Panga*.

We stop on the dock next to the boat, Sargo turning to me as though expecting me to talk first. I stare at the wood planks at my feet in shameful, stubborn silence.

He clears his throat. "Coming to class intoxicated? Nearly causing a wreck? Picking a fight with Electra? That's beyond reckless, even for you."

"I didn't *come* to class intoxicated," I mumble.

"Oh, great, so you were drinking in my class." His voice is so sharp I flinch as if it actually cut me. "Did you think being drunk would make you *less* likely to almost wreck two other boats?"

"I didn't almost wreck those boats because I was drunk. I almost wrecked them because I wasn't paying attention."

Perhaps a bit of a fine hair to split. But I feel it should be on the record.

He drags one hand down his face and stares at me as though he can't quite believe a person as dumb as I am made it this far without dying in a horrible accident. To be fair, he's not wrong to think that.

"Do you understand the danger you put your classmates in today? Do you understand the seriousness of this situation? As your instructor, I have to report this to the school officials." He pauses. "But frankly, as your friend...I'm—"

"*Concerned?*"

His jaw ticks. "Yes. Concerned."

I shift my weight from foot to foot, my fingers impulsively picking at my thumbnail. Why does he have to be concerned? Why can't he just tear me a new one like every other teacher I have and send me on my way?

"Sorry," I mumble. "It was just a...blip. It won't happen again."

"A *blip?* This is not a joke, Bird!" He seems about to lay into me, but catches himself and steps back with a frustrated sigh. "Look. I'm aware that you had a fight with your folks. You won't tell me why. That's fine. But this is...not a good way of dealing with that."

I scowl at the dock. Sargo doesn't put a lot of stock in people who drink. His uncle Blenny is a grog blossom. He's never flat-out told me not to do it, but today wasn't the first time I'd seen that look of disappointment on his face. I brace for a lecture.

"Have you spoken to your moms yet?" he asks instead.

The ember of anger lights in my chest again. It glows with a dull heat.

"No."

"Okay." He observes me quietly. "Will you be staying at our place again tonight?"

"Is...that alright?" I peek into his face to see if I can discern what he's thinking, but he's recovered some of his usual composure and become inscrutable. He's always inscrutable, unless I've done something *really* obnoxious.

"Of course," he sighs, and shrugs his wide shoulders. "You're always welcome. Blenny says you can stay as long as you want."

I haven't told Sargo why I'm fighting with my moms. Why I've been crashing at his uncle Blenny's house for the last three days. And he hasn't asked. That's why I like Sargo: he doesn't pry. You could call us friends, but at the end of the day, he's more like a counselor. A *concerned* counselor, but not a prying one. He has his own problems to deal with.

A gust of wind rips through the harbor, setting carelessly untied lines clanging against their masts. Sargo looks up instinctively to check the lines running up *Panga's* mast, but of course, they're all neatly secured and make no sound at all. That's the kind of sailor Sargo is: tidy. Methodical. Everything in its place.

His gaze sticks on the mast and he contemplates it for a long moment as though lost in thought. I decide to prod him, glad to turn the tables, eager to move the conversation onto something else.

"Something on your mind?"

He doesn't answer right away, his thoughtful gaze still skyward. "Today is the anniversary of the day my folks died," he says finally.

My gut twists. *Right.* I follow his gaze to *Panga's* mast. She was their boat. I'm sure everything about her reminds him of them.

"I forgot."

"It's okay," he says. "It's not your job to remember."

"Yeah, but we've just been going on about me—"

"Truly, Bird. It's okay. It was a long time ago."

I sigh, feeling small and selfish and stupid. He may be just a counselor, but at the end of the day...you could also call us friends. "I'm sorry. I'm an asshole."

"You're not an asshole." He touches his palm to *Panga's* hull.

"You're...salty. But I do think you should talk to your folks. You may regret it if you don't."

A flicker of irritation. *Is he really using his dead moms to guilt-trip me?*

"Yeah," I say bitterly, "maybe."

"And I think you should give Electra a break."

"Give *her* a break? How about she gives *me* a break?"

Sargo eyes me silently.

I fold my arms. "Not gonna happen. She's intolerable."

"Intolerable?" He lifts an eyebrow. "If by that you mean she's headstrong and intelligent, then yes, I suppose she is intolerable. Like you."

"I'm not like her."

"Actually, you're right." He smirks. "*She* knows how to sail."

I curl my lip. "Very funny. She's also entitled and rude."

"You're rude."

"Yeah—wait, no..." I scowl. "I'm not rude. I'm salty, remember?"

"Mm."

"Anyway, she *is* entitled. Did you see the size of the stone in that necklace?"

He sighs. "Does having nice things make her a bad person?"

"No. Being a bad person makes her a bad person."

"She's not a bad person. Her family has coin. Those are different things."

I roll my eyes. "'Has coin' is a *massive* understatement."

Electra's mom, Axioma Nation, is the founder and CEO of Zenith Biotech, the largest of the Big Four and the company that privatized the State and brought biochip technology to the world.

Axioma Nation is one of the most powerful people on the planet—not that there's much of a planet left to be powerful on. It was Axioma Nation and Zenith that ended the last pandemic and brought the world back from collapse twenty years ago. They took over from the governments and they pretty much run everything now. Zenith's headquarters are in Brume, and anyone in town who isn't fixing shit or shucking oysters works for them. My mom shucks oysters. My other mom fixes shit.

I scowl at Sargo. "I just don't know how you can be friends with her."

He shrugs. "Our families go back a long way. My family owes them a lot. And we have a lot in common. Brume is in our blood."

"Then I don't know how you can be friends with *me*."

"Brume is in your blood too," he sighs, pulling the key to *Panga's* main hatch from his pocket.

"It sure as Salt doesn't feel like it."

I stoop to pick up my pack and a question pops into my head.

"Hey, why did you trap me on the dock and make Electra take the necklace out of my hand? Why didn't you just let me give it back to her? I was totally defenseless. She could have attacked me again."

"She wouldn't do that." Sargo shakes his head sagely. "It's not who she is. Fighting is very out of character for her."

I narrow my eyes. *Seemed pretty in character today.* "You're sure about that, are you?"

"Quite sure. *You*, on the other hand…"

"What *about* me? You think I'm the kind of person that hits someone when they can't fight back?"

He narrows his eyes. "Maybe. I'm never really sure what you're going to do. Except today: today I was pretty sure that if I let go of you, you were going to throw that necklace right into the Salt."

I grin. "You got me."

Sargo shakes his head again. "You see? Reckless. You don't think before you act. So after you threw it in the Salt, then what would you have done? You said yourself that stone was enormous. Can you afford to replace it?"

I sigh and turn my gaze out over the water.

"I have to writ~~~ ~~~~ ~~~ ays. "I don't know what the ~~~~~~~~~~~~~~~~~~~~~~ t be a suspension. I'll put in a ~~~~~~~~~~~~~~~~~~~ ı soft spot for you, so maybe you'll get off easy. Please, just...don't do it again. Not in my class, at least."

I feel the last words like a needle in my side. He's hurt that I don't take his class seriously. Sailing is a big deal to Sargo. It's a big deal to Brume: this town only weathered the last pandemic because the citizens had access to boats. When the virus decimated the city, they fled into the bay and anchored just offshore. It was the safest way to isolate. Some people were out there for *years*. Sargo was *born* out there.

Not to take anything away from him, but it's no wonder he's so good at sailing. Born on a boat? Feels like a bit of an unfair advantage.

"I know you think this class is a joke," Sargo continues, "but you need to take it seriously. It's the law, Bird."

"It's a dumb law."

He sets his jaw. "You need to know how to sail. You need to be prepared to quarantine out there in the event of another pandemic, and you need to be able to survive as the Salt keeps rising. You'll be evaluated when you turn nineteen and if your skills aren't up to Zenith standards, you won't be allowed to graduate. And not only that—"

He stops himself and sighs again, but I know what he hasn't said. Sargo only turned nineteen a year and a half ago. This is the first time Zenith has let anyone so young teach this class. And if I fail, it doesn't just reflect poorly on me...

I nudge a nail sticking out of the dock with my toe. "Will they...reprimand you? For what I did today?"

"*Me?*" Sargo's voice is incredulous, but then he hesitates, falling silent for a moment, as though he hadn't considered this possibility.

Finally, he says, "I don't think so. But...if you can't take care of yourself, you create work for everyone around you. The community is only as strong as its weakest link. We're all in this, right? Brume pride?"

"Yup," I mumble. "Brume pride."

Brume pride.

An intolerable Zenith slogan that everyone in this town seems to cling to. As if *we* made Brume what it is. We didn't make Brume. Or at least, *I* didn't. I was just lucky enough to be born here. In a bubble that wasn't totally devastated by climate disasters. In a bubble that survived the pandemic, when billions of others did not. Maybe for everyone else that's a source of pride, but for me, it just feels like dumb luck. Not exactly something to be proud of.

"Look," he says, "I don't want to go on at you about this. Can you please just make an effort not to derail my class in the future?"

I nod, my eyes still on the dock.

"Okay." He hesitates. "Are you...sticking around to help me out today?"

I shrug. "I guess."

"Great." His tone brightens, and I look up to find him grinning. "Do you want to see what I did yesterday?"

He hops over the rail onto *Panga's* deck, and I follow him to discover he's torn up the rotten old wood that used to be there. In place of the splintered, graying planks he's laid beautiful, honey-colored teak in a neatly-interlocking pattern that reminds me of a woven basket.

All thoughts of Brume, of sailing, of Electra and her necklace and her stupid, perfect ponytail evaporate. I stare around with my mouth open.

"Did you do all this yourself?"

"I did," he says, and though he tries to temper it, I sense his pride. "I finished it last night."

"It's beautiful. But you should have waited for me! I would have helped."

"Oh, don't worry." He ducks into the boat's covered cockpit, returning moments later with a jar of teak varnish, two brushes, and a sly smile. "There's still plenty to do."

We sit on the bow, our legs dangling over the sides, deep in the repetitive, painstaking job of working the varnish into every plank of the new deck. The sun is getting low and heat rises from the wood, drawing the rich, chemical smell of the black pitch into my nose. Even with my bandana pulled over my face, the fumes are pretty overpowering.

To be honest, I don't mind it. The smell or the work. Helping Sargo fix up *Panga* has always felt weirdly soothing. Possibly because I know I won't cause a disaster if I zone out while I'm doing it. I can disappear into this work, channel the constant buzzing of my mind into it. It feels almost meditative.

Or maybe I'm just high on fumes.

Either way, after the last three days, I welcome the calm with open arms.

"You know tomorrow it will have been a year since we met?" says Sargo, his eyes on the end of his brush as he works it into a crack in the wood.

I grin sideways at him. "Oh really? Sooo, can I invoice you for all this manual labor I've done yet, or…"

He snorts. "Sure, Howsley. Bill my secretary."

The sound of his laugh makes my heart jump a little. Sargo doesn't laugh a lot, so it feels like a big win when you're the one that makes it happen. But it also feels like a fragile, fleeting thing.

"It's weird that you remember how long it's been since we met," I say, keeping my eyes on my brush.

He frowns at me. "Is it?"

"Yeah. What, are you planning on celebrating? Or…commiserating?"

He scoffs, shaking his head. "No, I just have a log in my chip of the day you started detention." He taps the side of his head and reads words I can't see out of the air in front of him. "April third, twenty-one ninety-two. Detention with Howsley."

"Jesus, have I really been helping you fix up this wreck for a *year*?"

He flinches. "Don't say *Jesus*, Howsley. And yes. You have." He taps his temple to clear the log from his chip. "Which is interesting, because Fen told me your detention was only supposed to be a week. So I'm not really sure what you're still doing here."

"*You* seemed like you needed help." I counter, defensively. "This boat was a piece of junk when I started."

"Oh, is *that* what it is? I thought you just didn't have anything else going on."

My face flushes. He's right. I don't have any friends at this school. When Mr. Fen, the old sailing teacher, gave me a week of detention helping Sargo fix up *Panga*, I *didn't* have much else going on. A week turned into a month, and a month turned into six, and six months turned into a year. The patient sailor and his rotten little sloop became like a life raft in a school where I was drowning, and I've clung to them ever since.

Not that I would ever admit that.

Honestly, I don't know why Sargo still lets me hang around with him. When we first met, we bonded over the fact that we both have two moms. Well...I have two moms; Sargo *had* two moms. But apart from that, we don't exactly have a lot in common. Maybe he feels obligated to be nice to me now that he's a teacher. Maybe he's just a really nice person. Sometimes I suspect he just keeps me around for the free labor.

I push itchy hair out of my sticky face with the back of my arm, sink my brush back into the thick, black varnish and pull it out, dripping.

"That looks good." Sargo says as I lay the brush back against the plank I've been painting.

"Thanks."

His gaze seems to stick on the movement of my brush. I try to ignore it, but the feeling of his eyes on me makes my skin prickle, and finally, unable to stand it anymore, I set my brush down and turn to him.

"What's up? Am I doing something wrong?"

He blinks. "No. Sorry. Just thinking about my folks." He returns to his work. "They always dreamed about sailing this boat somewhere."

"Oh." I frown. "I didn't know that."

"They used to talk about it a lot when I was a kid. Mama Marlin wanted to go south, to see if she could find her family. She used to tell me about delfíns and archipelicans; about diving off the boat in the middle of open water, no land in sight, nothing below you for a thousand feet. She had me convinced we were going to sail to Pocosín. I used to dream about it."

"What's in Pocosín?"

"It's the closest Harbor City to where she was born. She seemed to think we would find something there. Something she felt she lost when she came here."

"What?"

He shrugs. "Our roots. People who look like us."

Discomfort prickles my skin like a chilly breeze. He doesn't talk about it much, but not many people in Brume look like Sargo. Sandy-brown skin, black hair. Foreign, like his name: Sargo Paz. There aren't a lot of people from Pocosín in Brume. They were priced out a long time ago. Before the pandemic. Before the Salt even really started to rise; back when the New American West Coast was still just the West Coast, and the Central American Strait was just a canal.

I pick up my brush, acutely aware of my own pale hands. My blue eyes and frizzy brown hair. I may *feel* like I don't belong in Brume, but no one would ever tell me that I *look* like I don't belong here.

I put my eyes back on my work. "What about your other mom? Gnamma? Did she want to go too?"

"Mama G..." Sargo's voice hardens. He picks up his brush again. "She just wanted to get out of trouble."

I hesitate. He's never talked about how his moms died before. "What…kind of trouble?"

He seems not to have heard me, keeping his eyes on the end of his brush. Finally, he says, "My uncle Blenny got her in on some kind of job. It went wrong, and Gnamma ended up owing someone money. When she couldn't pay, they came after her. Marlin tried to intervene. They were both killed."

"How old were you?"

"Eleven."

I nod slowly, still staring at my brush. I don't know what to say. So I do what I usually do when that happens and make a stupid joke.

"You'd think, having barely survived a pandemic and running out of habitable space on the planet, that people would have figured out how to pull together and love each other by now. But I guess deep down we're still a bunch of petty, murdering assholes."

He almost smiles.

"After they died," he continues, dipping his brush back into the varnish, "Uncle Blenny took on Gnamma's debt. But…" He sighs. "But Blenny's too sozzled on grog most of the time to be of much use to anyone, so he's still paying it off. Well…I guess I'm paying it off."

I frown. "*You're* paying it off?"

"Where do you think all the coin from this teaching job is going? You think I'd be sitting here painting this boat with you if I had it? No way, Howsley. I'd be sitting here surrounded by naked girls, watching *them* paint it for me."

I roll my eyes. "*That's* what you'd do with a bunch of naked girls?"

He flashes a small smile. "To start."

"Spare me."

Still smiling, he dips his brush back into the varnish. "Anyway, it is what it is. Pocosín was a nice dream. But it was a dream."

"That doesn't have to be true. Maybe one day you'll sail out of here instead. Make it to Pocosín. Find your people."

He shoots me a look. "Come on, Howsley. Nobody leaves Brume."

We paint in silence until the newly varnished deck gleams dark and sticky and the air is damp and cold. Sargo stands and stretches. He packs up the nearly empty jar of varnish, takes my brush, and ducks down the three companionway steps to wash up in the galley below deck.

I peek down the steps after him. He stands with his back to me, washing our brushes in a small metal sink at the bottom of the stairs, his head nearly touching the low ceiling. Beyond the sink, two faded, threadbare sofas run along either side of the narrow cabin, with a small table set between them. Just beyond that, a door leading to the head, and another to the bunk in the bow where Sargo sometimes sleeps if he's here working late.

The work that Sargo has done on the boat shines through here too—the patch jobs he's done on the sofas and the floorboards he's replaced. Everything worn but clean, the wood old but polished, the space small but tidy. Methodical. Everything in its place.

I climb out of the cockpit to sit with my legs over the side and my arms over the rail, mulling our conversation over in my mind, watching the last fiery sliver of sun extinguish itself in the distant silver horizon.

That night, I toss and turn on Blenny's living room sofa.

The blanket I borrowed from Sargo seems itchier than usual. The sound of Blenny and Sargo snoring away upstairs grates against my nerves like the droning of enormous insects. My eyes burn with tiredness. I glare at the ceiling like it's the ceiling's fault I can't sleep. For the first time since storming out of my folks' house three nights ago, I miss my bed.

Out of the jangling carousel of thoughts rolling around in my skull, a single one shakes loose and comes to the surface.

You should check Shale's message again.

I roll onto my other side, trying to ignore it.

Maybe he's replied.

He hasn't.

But what if he has? What if he has and you missed it? Just check, just in case.

I don't want to check. If I check, I'll be all the way awake. If I'm all the way awake, I won't go back to sleep.

You're already awake. Just check.

Throwing off the blanket, I sit up.

I tap my right temple to pull up Shale's message on my biochip. The text augments my vision, glowing jade-green in front of the dusky-orange backdrop of Blenny's living room. Dusky orange because the room is lit by the eerie glow from the blood-red moon hanging like a perverted sun in the dark sky outside the window. Even in Brume, where the air is relatively clear, the moon is never white.

I squint at the message text.

>>> *Birb! It's me. Come to Alluvium. I have a jib for you.*

>>> **job*

'Birb.' The word that blew my life apart. Ten years of silence, and then 'Birb.' Beneath his message, my reply glows, unanswered.

>>> *Shale?*

It's been three days. Why hasn't he written back? I swipe through the air to pull up his message's metadata, even though I've looked at it a thousand times already.

>>> *Time sent: 1700. Sat Apr 1. 2192*

>>> *Sent from: Alluvium, New Central America*

>>> *Name of sender: undefined.*

Sender undefined. But I don't need metadata to tell me it's Shale. No one else ever called me 'Birb.'

I swipe the message closed and tap my left temple to check the time. The numbers hang in the air in front of the window.

>>> *0400*

Sighing, I the clock by tapping my left temple again, then fling myself back onto the cushions and roll onto my side. Too early to get up, too late to go to sleep.

Across the room, Blenny's grog cabinet squats in front of the window in a shaft of orange moonlight. Two rectangular doors and a janky old knob give the cabinet an ugly, leering face. I stare into its eyes.

It's not as though I'm some kind of lush like Blenny—until two days ago, when Shale's message came through and my life blew up, I only drank at parties. And even *I* can admit that drinking grog in class is a bridge too far.

I would like to go to sleep, though...

Rolling off the couch, I pad across the room, swift and quiet as a cat on bare feet. I pull the cabinet's key from its 'hiding place' on the windowsill.

Blenny was the one who first gave me grog: last year, at Sargo's birthday party. I barely knew Sargo then, let alone all his friends, including Electra and her whole crew. After an hour of standing around with them in the living room, talking to no one, feeling like an injured fly at a spider party, I wandered into the kitchen and found Blenny, halfway to Fiddler's Green on grog.

I don't really know what made me sit down and ask him to let me try some. I guess I'm just no good at parties. Grog makes me better at parties. It gives me something to do with my hands. If I wasn't drinking, I'd be chewing my nails down to the quick, and for some reason, people seem to find that more unpleasant than watching me get drunk.

I pull a mug from a kitchen cupboard and slosh a measure of liquid into it. Then I pad back to the cabinet, replace the bottle, and lock the door. I used to top up the bottle with water so it wouldn't be so obvious that I'd been sneaking it, but it turns out that diluting grog with water actually makes that *more* obvious. Blenny knew immediately. He said, "Stealing half of it is bad. Ruining the rest is worse."

Settling back onto the sofa, I take a sip and stare through the window.

The great thing about grog is that it works quickly. Like, really quickly. Especially if you're an eighteen-year-old girl who weighs a hundred and ten pounds. It's not like we have companies distributing carefully-regulated substances in this post-apocalyptic nightmare of a world. None of the Big Four corporations deals in liquor—although I bet they'd make killing if they did. People basically make it in their bathtubs. The only reason I know it's not *actually* rocket fuel is because there isn't any rocket fuel left in the world anymore.

A few sips in, the relentless loop of thoughts in my head begins to unwind. I set the half-full mug on the floor and close my eyes.

"Wow, you really are just like your brother."

My eyes snap open. What did Electra mean by that? She didn't even *know* Shale. The thought carousel begins jangling around again. I sit up, snatching the mug off the floor, and down it.

I find myself at the cabinet again, pouring another mug. This time, I let the mug fill a bit longer before I put the bottle back. I sit on the sofa again, pulling up Shale's message, and stare through it, letting the letters blur and duplicate across my vision.

>>> *I HAVE A JIB FOR YOU.*

>>> * *JOB*

I should be happy to hear from him. Elated. I should be sobbing with joy and celebrating with my moms. Instead I just feel pissed.

I find myself at the cabinet again, pouring a third mug.

Ten years. Where has he been? Why didn't he try to contact me before? What is he doing in *Alluvium?* How did he even get all the way to New Central America? And what the hell does he mean 'a job'? He wants me to come to Alluvium for a *job?* As if I could just up and leave?

I scoff, shaking my head, and shove the bottle back into the cabinet.

Like Sargo said: nobody leaves Brume.

chapter
three

S<small>ARGO FOLDS</small> his arms and surveys me frankly. "Drunk?" he says. "In my class. Again."

I shrink, dropping my gaze, and nudge at the dock with my toe. "I wasn't *drunk*..."

"Drinking, then."

"It was, like, *two* sips."

I hear a long, angry exhale deep in the back of his throat. When I peek up to meet his eyes, they are stern.

"And you think this is acceptable behavior?"

I shrug. "I guess not?"

"You *guess* not?"

"Fine—no. Okay? You're right. It's not."

"Do you think I can afford to have you jeopardizing my class like that?"

"No," I mumble, skirting his eyes.

"Do you think I can afford to have you causing accidents?"

"No."

"No what?"

I look up, frowning. "What?"

"No," he says softly, "what?"

"No...way?"

His eyes flash. A muscle in his jaw ticks.

"Uh…" I smile hesitantly, confused. *No what?* What does he want me to say? "No…of course not? No…and…I'm sorry?"

His hand flicks up so fast I don't have time to move before it's around my jaw. My breath stills.

"What are you doing?" I whisper.

He tightens his grip to just this side of too hard and pulls me toward him. My chest comes up against his, and the scent of him floods my nose—salt and sand, and fogwood trees. The fabric of his shirt is so close I can see the individual fibers weaving over and under each other. His body firm and warm inside it. He tips my chin up so that he can glare at me a moment longer, then puts his lips against my ear.

"No," he repeats, "what?"

The words ripple down the back of my neck. My pulse throbs under his fingertips.

"I don't know what you want me to say," I whisper to the sky.

A sigh of frustration against my ear. "Come on, Howsley," he mutters, "you're a smart girl."

Being this close to him is…disorienting. The brush of his shirt and the press of the body inside it. His fingertips on my neck. That this is happening *here*, on the public dock, of all places. That this is happening…at *all*.

What is happening?

The tips of my ears buzz. Heat blooms like a rose across my throat. It rolls like honey down my arms and into the tips of my fingers.

His lips move in the hollow below my ear. "Your heart is beating fast. Are you nervous, Howsley?"

I manage to nod, my eyes still on the sky.

"I'm going to ask you one more time," he says, and he's so close to me I feel the words inside my own chest. "No…what?"

"No…Sargo."

He smiles against my neck. "Almost."

The hand around my jaw releases, and he brushes the front of my throat with his fingertips. I close my eyes as he trails them lower, drawing a feather-light line down the center of my chest.

His lips move against my ear again. "Do you want to know what I do to girls who—"

I wake with a gasp and blink at the ceiling.

Blenny's ceiling. I'm on the couch at Sargo's. It's early morning —the light coming through the window is weak and gray. I lift my hands and put the backs of them against my cheeks.

Jesus, what the hell was that?

A creak on the floor above me. Snatching up the blanket, I yank it over my head, closing my eyes, and lie perfectly still as footsteps come down the stairs, quietly pass the couch, and head into the kitchen.

Sargo. Up to teach an early class.

I pretend to sleep while he creeps around, making quiet sounds with the kettle and filling the house with the bitter-orange smell of black tea.

For a long time after he softly closes the front door behind him, I don't move. Or at least, the *outside* of me doesn't move. *Inside*, my heart is still crashing around like a panicked animal, looking for somewhere to hide.

It was a dream, I tell myself.

It was a hell of a dream, my self replies.

Throwing off the blanket, I roll off the couch. I pat my face. I shake my arms and legs like some kind of possessed marionette, trying to rid myself of the shivery, unsettled feeling. I blow air through my cheeks and stare through the window.

People have dreams like that all the time. It doesn't mean anything.

Folding up the itchy blanket, I head upstairs to get ready for class. Glare at myself in Blenny's bathroom mirror as I wash my face. Chew my nail while I wait for the kettle to boil. I sit on the couch to drink my tea, staring at the grog cabinet through the steam coming off the top. I can feel a hangover banging on the cranial gates. I didn't realize I drank that much last night.

The hangover is still banging on the back of my head an hour later as I sit in the back of history class at Azimuth, staring into space.

"…was outlawed by Zenith," someone is saying. "Can you tell me what year that was?"

Something pointy digs into my shoulder. I blink and turn around.

"What?"

Raven Tarbuckle, the girl who sits behind me, raises her eyebrows over my shoulder, to where Ms. Dawley, the history teacher, is peering at me expectantly over the top of her wire-rimmed spex.

"Oh…uh, what?"

She sighs. "Please try to pay attention, Miss Howsley. I'll ask again. In what year did Zenith make it a crime to leave Harbor Cities?"

"Uh…" I dig through my mind and find nothing. "Twenty-one-eighty?"

She sighs through her nose. "Try again. This test review is meant to benefit *you*, not me."

"Twenty…one…" I shrug. "I don't know."

"Twenty-on-seventy-three," she says. "Can you tell me *why* they made it a crime?"

"Uh…the pandemic," I recite.

"Yes," she sighs, "but I'm looking for specifics."

"They did it to prevent transmission of disease between cities," pipes up Raven. "Before the pandemic, Harbor Cities like Brume and Alluvium were full of refugees fleeing natural disasters. That's partly why the virus was so devastating—the overcrowding. When the governments collapsed during the pandemic, the Big Four rose to power and Zenith made it illegal for any Citizen to leave a Harbor City so that disease could never be spread like that again. The only ships transiting the Salt now are automated freighters carrying parts for Big Four companies."

I resist the urge to turn around in my seat and glare at her.

"What about Reckoners?" says someone behind me. "Don't they still live on the Salt?"

"The Dead Reckoners were lawless pirates and most of them are presumed dead," says Ms. Dawley briskly. "You do still hear the occasional report of a Reckoner sailing ship turning up in Alluvium or Pocosín, but it's rare. The few that remain operate outside the law and do not adhere to Zenith's policies. We won't spend too much time on them in this class."

She taps her temple and swipes through the air to pull up the next page of notes on her biochip.

"Moving on. Can anyone tell me what year Fire Season ended? Miss Howsley? Want to give it another shot?"

I restrain a frustrated sigh. "I don't know…twenty-one-thirty-nine?"

"Incorrect. Miss Tarbuckle?"

"Twenty-one-twenty-three," says Raven promptly. "It started in twenty-twenty-three and lasted for a century."

"Correct," says Miss Dawley. "And can anyone tell me in what year the Gas Wars started?"

"Twenty-one-thirty-nine," says Raven. "The same year the first Reckoners fled to Île Tor to dodge the draft."

"Correct again, Raven," says Miss Dawley. "Everyone please take out your slates and pull up the map of the New Pacific."

I reach into my pack and find the canvas cloth that wraps my slate buried in the bottom. Unwrapping the slender stone rectangle, I lay it on my desk and tap my right brow to pull up the materials for this course on the Net.

"Incidentally," Miss Dawley says as I swipe through the air to find the map, "can anyone tell me why the Net was one of the few systems not affected by the collapse?"

"Satellites," says someone behind me. "It runs on satellites and the satellites never came down."

"Correct," says Miss Dawley. "Miss Howsley, are you taking notes? The test is in two days."

I scowl at my slate, adjusting the size and focus of the map by dragging my finger across my brow, and aiming the projection at the dark stone.

The shapes of the New California Coast, La Federación de Nuevo Centroamérica y México, and the Salt glow crisply against the smooth, black surface of the slate. I stare at them, trying to burn the names into my brain. There are only seven cities left in the world, so you'd think I'd be able to remember where all of them are, but somehow I still struggle with the geography.

"Since we mentioned Dead Reckoners," says Ms. Dawley, "it's worth noting that when the Reckoners left the mainlands fifty years ago, the Salt was less volatile than it is today. After the Reckoners settled on Île Tor, the island received Harbor City status because, like the Harbor Cities, its climate had remained temperate enough to be habitable. However, unlike Brume, Alluvium, Pocosín, Grike, Zhīliú, Krepost' and Qanat, Île Tor did not have its own fresh water source. Reckoners were heavily dependent on their desalinators to make fresh water from the Salt."

Her voice fades into the background as I study the shape of the map: Brume, tucked like a green jewel into the New California coast, and thousands of miles south, Alluvium, set into what remains of New Central America. It suddenly strikes me as *impossible* that my brother could have made it all the way from one city to the other. Travel between cities is illegal. How the hell did he *get* there?

I raise my hand. Ms. Dawley arches her eyebrows at my unexpected voluntary participation.

"Does Zenith ever make exceptions to people sailing between cities?" I ask.

Ms. Dawley shakes her head. "No. And even if they did, these days the Salt is so dangerous that you would need incredible skill to navigate it."

"Even to Alluvium?" I ask.

Someone snickers. "You gonna sail to Alluvium, Howsley? Didn't you almost wreck your boat yesterday?"

"That's enough." Ms. Dawley taps her temple again. "No one's sailing to Alluvium. Let's move on."

The bell rings thirty minutes later. I decide to go down to the harbor during break. I still don't have a good answer to my question about how someone might get from Brume to Alluvium, and I feel like Sargo might be more willing to entertain the question than Ms. Dawley.

A thick blanket of fog hangs low over the still, gray water. I spot Sargo sitting on the dock next to *Panga*, a jumble of tools spread around him, and a flash of nervousness halts me. As though, if I get to close, he might somehow know what I dreamed about this morning. Like he'll give me one of those looks that gets right inside me and see everything that's in my head.

He glances up and sees me, anxiously hovering, and offers a small wave and a confused frown. I silently curse myself. Now he's going to think I'm acting weird. And besides, it's not like it meant anything. That person in the dream wasn't even anything like him. He's not some domineering asshole, he's flogging *Sargo*, for flog's flogging sake.

His hands are covered in grease, the sleeves of his blue button-down rolled up to the elbows. His pants are cuffed to expose about three inches of brown ankle, his shoes neatly lined up at the edge of the dock, socks tucked into them. I've never understood it, but despite his rigidity, neatness, and love of order, Sargo is not a fan of shoes.

"Oh boy." I stop in front of him. "What's going on here?"

He squints at me and holds up a rod of metal, shiny with oil.

"Fixing the autopilot. So I'll be able to sleep while *Panga* steers herself."

"Where are you sailing to, that you'll need to sleep before you get there?"

He shrugs. "Probably nowhere. But it's pretty cool, right?"

I shake my head and sigh. Sargo's always working on something. I swear he could find something to fix on a perfect circle. I watch him work for a minute, chewing my thumbnail, not sure how to broach the question I want to ask.

"Sargo…" I say finally, tentatively.

"Mm?" He's completely absorbed in tweaking something on the side of the autopilot and doesn't look up.

"What's the furthest you've ever sailed *Panga*?"

He squints up at me again. "Why?"

"I was just wondering…theoretically, could you make it to Alluvium on *Panga*?"

"Alluvium?" He frowns. "Why?"

I shrug and nudge a barnacle on the dock with my toe. "Just curious. You got me thinking after you said all that stuff about your moms yesterday."

He eyes me. "Thinking, huh? That doesn't sound like you."

"I'm always thinking, asshole. Just not about anything useful. You didn't answer my question."

He turns his attention back to the greasy metal rod. "No. I don't think so. The Salt has claimed the lives—"

"Yeah, yeah, I know, claimed the lives of thousands of sailors."

He raises his eyebrows. "Yes. And even if that wasn't the case, it's illegal. And anyway, *Panga's* not ready."

"What do you mean 'not ready'?"

"There's still a lot of work that needs to be done before she's Salt-worthy."

I frown. "But you've been fixing up *Panga* for…a long time now. Like, since before I met you. What else is left to do?"

I don't mean for the question to sound sarcastic, but I guess it comes out that way. Sargo looks annoyed.

"This stuff takes a long time," he says impatiently, "if you want to do it right."

"Okay," I say, equally impatiently, "*what stuff*?"

He doesn't say anything for several moments, returning his attention to the autopilot. Finally, he says, "I suppose the biggest thing is the sail."

"The mainsail?"

He nods. "It's old. In bad shape. I could sail under it, but eventually, it will fail."

"Fail how?"

"Tear. Sag. Just generally fall apart."

"How long would it take you to fix?"

He rubs the top of his head with a distracted hand, leaving grease in his hair. "It's not something you fix. It needs to be replaced. And that takes coin. A lot of coin."

"How much?"

"I don't know, Bird—twenty thousand Ubicoin? Thirty thousand? Maybe more? Where are you going with this?"

"I don't know. Just curious I guess."

"Mm." He narrows his eyes at me and I look away. Then he picks up a rag and turns his attention back to the greasy chunk of metal.

Somewhere up on the hill, the bell rings. Sargo doesn't look at me as he says, "Better get going, Howsley."

I turn up the dock and head toward the path that will take me back up the hill to the campus, my mind turning over our conversation like the pieces of a puzzle.

———————

My summons to the principal's office to discuss the incident in Sargo's class yesterday comes as I'm finishing fourth session. I'm stepping out of the classroom into the cool, foggy forest of Azimuth's outdoor campus when a ding fires off inside my head and a new message alert slides in front of my eyes. I swipe through the air to open it.

>>> BIRD HOWSLEY. REPORT TO PRINCIPAL YIP NO LATER THAN 1145.

I close the message and tap my left temple to check the time.

>>> 1130

Better get going, then.

The walk to Principle Yip's office seems longer than usual today. My feet feel as though they're made of lead. Of all the times I've been to Yip's office—which is many—I've never been in for such a serious infraction before. If I get suspended, will it be my third this year, or fourth? I forget what's supposed to happen after three suspensions. Something bad, I suspect.

I pick my way over the broken concrete and exposed roots of the abandoned second quad, slowly being reclaimed by trees and heaps of crawling vines. Most of the campus buildings have been unused since the majority of Brume's population was wiped out twenty years ago. Some have been repurposed to serve as Zenith's headquarters, which takes up almost a quarter of the main campus now.

A poster on the door to Yip's office instructs me to '*Put on your own mask first.*' A well-worn Zenith slogan drilled into my generation since the day we were born. Personally, I think it's probably safe to assume that anyone who was carrying the virus is long dead. But what do I know? I tug my bandana up from its near-permanent position around my neck and pull it over my nose.

'*Put on your own mask first.*' It sounds sensible, but it's really depressing if you think about what it actually means. It goes hand in hand with '*Brume pride.*' Brume first. Me first. That's what it actually means.

With my bandana on, reeling from the sickly smell of last night's grog on my breath, I steel myself and knock.

"Enter."

Calypso Yip's crisp soprano rings through the door. I push it open to reveal a small, neat office, filled with light, glass, and green plants. Yip sits behind an oak desk, her steely hair wound tightly into a little pile on top of her head. She peers through her spex at a slate, acknowledging me with a bony finger and not looking up as I enter. She sips from a cup of brew, then pulls a silk handkerchief up over her nose.

Yip has coin. You can tell by the cut of her clothes and the fineness of that handkerchief. Not Axioma Nation-level coin, but more than most. Her family owns a massive estate out by the wind farm. They've been there for generations. That's how they survived the pandemic: holed up on their property and waited it out. Put up an electric fence. Killed all their horses for food and set the dogs on anyone who tried to come in. Most of the people who survived the pandemic were wealthy. They either owned land or had boats.

Yip sets down her slate and taps a finger to her temple, then turns her tired eyes to me.

"Bird."

"Ms. Yip."

We sit in silence while she observes me through her tiny spex then arches a questioning eyebrow. "Well? What do you have to say for yourself?"

I shrug, picking at my nails. "Sorry, I guess."

"Intoxicated on school property. In a school boat. Nearly caused the wrecks of two other vessels and then," her already sharp voice pitches up a few steps, "starting a physical altercation with another student!"

"I didn't start it! She provoked me!"

Yip *tuts* impatiently. "Yes, well I have spoken to Miss Nation about her involvement in the incident, and rest assured, she will be reprimanded as well. But regardless of who said what, I have several witnesses who all attest that it was you who threw the first punch."

She leans back in her chair, pushing her spex to the top of her head and rubbing her eyes.

"How many times have we been here, Bird?"

"This year?" I want to say, *"three or four."* But I sense the question is rhetorical and hold my tongue.

She puts the spex back on and looks at me. "Ms. Parley says you haven't been showing up for counseling."

I exhale sharply and glare at my feet. "I don't like talking to her."

"We can't help you if you won't help yourself, Bird."

Silence settles.

"I'm sorry," I repeat, not sure what else to say. "It won't happen again."

Yip sighs. "No," she says heavily, picking up the slate. "Indeed it won't. Because I'm afraid, Bird, that you're being expelled."

My stomach drops. *Expelled?*

Looks like you figured out what happens after three suspensions.

Yip touches two fingers to her left brow and then swipes them through the air toward me. A file transfer pops up on my chip. She turns the slate around and holds it out to me. I take it, my chest hollow, my arms oddly weightless.

I hold up the slate, twisting two fingers against my left brow to adjust the file's font size and focus the bright glow of the words against the stone's smooth, dark surface.

Tues. April 4

To Ms. Jade Shorbe and Ms. Kestrel Howsley,

This letter serves to inform you of the expulsion of your daughter, Bird Howsley, from Azimuth All-Levels School, effective immediately. Bird seems resistant to the help she has been offered by the school's counselor, and appears to be making no effort to change. Her behavior has escalated to the point that the staff believe she poses a legitimate threat to her fellow students. In the interest of their safety, we must recommend her immediate removal from the school.

In accordance with Zenith policies, it is Azimuth's duty to do 'the most good for the most people.' As I'm sure you are aware, resources are scarce. We are obligated to funnel those resources toward the well-being of our student majority, not toward a single special case.

Please do not hesitate to contact the school administrator should you have any questions.

Sincerely,

Harding Shores

HEAD DIRECTOR, AZIMUTH EDU

I stare at the words for a long time. *'The most good for the most people.'* There's another one of those delightful Zenith aphorisms. *Legitimate threat.* Who is this person they're talking about? That can't be me. The hangover begins to pound on the back door again.

Through the buzzing in my ears, I become aware that Yip is speaking.

"…has already been sent to your mothers. I've been instructed to escort you from the premises. Do you have any possessions in your locker?"

I blink and look up, the text of the file still glowing before my eyes—bright green font, too small to read, overlaid against the room. The clutter in my vision only increases my wooziness.

"Uh—no." I touch my fingers to my brow and the letters disappear.

"Okay."

Yip holds out her hand for the slate and numbly, I hand it over. She sets it in a drawer and stands, bracing her fingers on the desk, her back straight, her tiny frame and thin skirt like another neatly-trimmed plant in this room full of green.

"If you don't have any questions for me then I'll walk you to the gate."

She pauses, a sad look passing behind her eyes. Disappointment? Pity?

"I'm sorry, Bird," she says quietly. "If it were up to me, it wouldn't be happening this way. But the director," she sighs, "was adamant, and I can't go against Zenith's dictums. I was at least able to get Shores to drop formal charges against you. You'll be expelled, but you're not facing proper authorities."

"You already sent this to my moms?" is all I can think to ask.

She nods.

Great.

I stand and turn to leave. My legs feel like water. The bandana around my face is stifling, the sourness of old grog on my breath nauseating. Yip hurries around her desk to open the door for me and I bristle, annoyed by the exaggerated show of cordiality.

"I got it, thanks."

"I have to escort you from the premises," she reminds me quietly, standing aside and holding the door open.

"Oh. Right."

Blushing furiously, I duck across the threshold and into the blissfully cool, damp air outside, tugging the suffocating cloth away from my face. Almost immediately, I feel eyes on me.

A cluster of girls my age parts to let us pass. Just beyond, a little boy stares up at me, wide-eyed, clutching his pack to his chest with both arms. A student teacher that I recognize as a friend of Sargo's ducks his head as he walks by, avoiding eye contact.

How does everyone in the school somehow already know about this? I keep my eyes down and resist the urge to pull the bandana up again to hide. I need a disguise. A pair of darx and a fake mustache.

My head is pounding by the time we pass the girl's bathroom near the campus's west gate. I feel sick. I really don't want to throw up here, in front of everyone. If I'm going down in front of all these assholes, it's sure as Salt not going to be while also puking my guts out.

I stop in front of the bathroom door. "I need to use the bathroom."

Yip trips to a halt. "Ah—oh," she adjusts her spex, "well, yes okay. Be quick."

I don't bother putting the bandana back on. I barely make it into the last stall, where I stand over the toilet with my hands on my knees and eject a vile brown liquid into it with gut-wrenching force, dodging splatter. Then I flip the lid closed and sit on it, propping my head in my hands and staring through the open stall door at my reflection in the mirror on the opposite wall. My head spins.

A legitimate threat to her fellow students.

You know what?

Fine.

It's not as though I had any great love for this school or anyone in it. It's not as though I was a great scholar, or a stellar athlete, or even friends with anyone. Except for Sargo, and he's probably only nice to me because he's my teacher.

Maybe I *will* take up Shale's insane offer and go to Alluvium. If he figured out how to get there, so can I. No point sticking around here. At least in Alluvium, there might be a job waiting for me.

And you know what else?

I reach into my pack and feel around for the little grog flask, which I topped up from Blenny's cabinet before I left this morning. As long as everyone thinks I'm trash and I'm never coming back, might as well send myself off right.

I take a big swig. *To failure!*

The bathroom door swings open and voices ring into the tiled space.

"I think they're expelling her."

"I heard she's legitimately crazy."

"So did she hit you, or what?"

"No, but she was going to."

My blood freezes at the sound of Electra's unmistakably smug voice. I nudge the door of my stall shut with my toe and sip from the flask again.

"She broke the necklace my mom gave me too."

"Oh no!"

"Yeah." I hear a pack rustling. "See? I brought it today to show Mr. Balso to see if he can fix the chain."

"Ugh, that bitch is so *stray!* I'm so glad they're kicking her out."

Stray? I'm not flogging stray, thank you very much.

I let the door open ever so slightly and put one eye to the crack. Electra, Polo, and Raven stand at the mirror, preening and talking to each other's reflections. They don't bother to mask up. No one does when they think no one's looking.

"Honestly," says Electra, tucking the pendant back into her pack, "I feel bad for her. It's kind of sad, you know?"

"Whatever, it's not like she has some traumatic life. She just wants attention," says Raven, turning away from the glass and going into the stall next to me.

"I guess." Electra pouts at herself. "Didn't her brother die or something?" She sets her pack on the floor and goes into another stall. Polo, silent, follows suit.

I eye Electra's pack. I don't know if it's the grog, the expulsion, the feeling that my life is spinning out of control, or just hearing that smug cow call me *stray* behind my back, but every fiber of my being is suddenly seized by the impulse to walk out there, fish that stupid pendant out of her bag, and make a run for it.

"What I don't get," Raven continues loudly from inside her stall, "is why Sargo hangs out with her. He's so much better than that."

"Ugh, I know," Electra agrees. "He's just nice."

Okay, that's it.

Trembling with rage, I push open the door and take two quick, silent steps to the pack.

What are you doing, Bird?! says self in the back of my head. *This is crazy.*

It'll be fine, I tell her. *I know what I'm doing.*

I don't know what I'm doing. Yip is right outside. It's not as though I have anywhere to run. But I've already been expelled. Does Yip even have any authority over me any more? How does that work?

Pushing the questions aside, I squat down and grab Electra's pack. I have no idea which pocket the stone is in, so I start feeling all over the outside, squeezing the pockets to find a lump.

"Is someone there?"

Electra's voice rings through the stall door. I freeze. Cold sweat leaps out along my hairline as I frantically squeeze the remaining pockets. *Where is it, for flog's sake?!*

"Hello?"

Abandoning the squeeze method, I throw quiet caution to the wind and unzip the pack.

"Excuse me? Is someone out there? What are you doing?"

I hear the sound of a toilet flush and feel panic rising in my chest. If I don't find it soon I'm going to have to abort and get out of here, fast.

Just a few more seconds.

I feel the lump of the pendant through the fabric of a side pocket. Grinning with relief, I zip open the pocket, stick my hand in, feel my trembling fingers close around the smooth, cold stone, and—

Everything goes black.

chapter
four

"YOU DO IT!"

"No, you do it!"

"No way!"

"I can't go out there!"

"Fife, come on!"

The giggled whispers of two little girls emanated from behind a tall patch of dry brush. It was early morning, and the sun was only just beginning to bake the hard, red earth. The younger of the two girls peeked through the bare branches of the brush at a lanky thirteen-year-old boy about twenty feet away. He scuffed his bare feet in the dirt and whistled.

"He's *your* brother," whispered Fife.

"Fine," the girl hissed to her friend, tightening her grip around the big, wriggling jackrat in her small hands, "I'll do it."

She exploded out of the brush in a shower of dry leaves and charged toward her brother. At the very last moment, however, as she raised her arms over her head and prepared to stuff the jackrat down the back of his filthy, ragged shirt, he ducked, catching her so off guard that she stumbled.

The world went upside down as he scooped her up and flipped her, and she dropped the jackrat with an ear-splitting squeal. She heard Fife utter a whooping cry of war from inside the bush, and the world went roughly right-side-up again as her brother dumped her in the dirt, spun around and prepared himself for the second attack. Fife came running out of the bush as the girl launched herself at her brother's legs, toppling him. They wrestled, and she quickly found herself pinned.

"You stray sonofabitch!" she screamed, kicking and twisting in the dirt. "You let me go or I'm telling Mom!"

"Language!" her brother sang, sitting on her chest and catching her wrists in his hands.

"Fife! Help!"

Fife threw herself across the boy's shoulders and began pummeling him with little fists, but he shrugged her off with ease and trapped her too with an arm around her skinny waist. Fife shrieked with delight and clutched at him.

It didn't take long for the girl to tire herself out. The sun was creeping up in the sky and it was getting too hot for this kind of thing. Eventually, they called a truce, and the three of them sat in the anemic shade of a bare tree, wiping sweat from their faces and smacking dry, thirsty lips.

"Let's go to the creek," said the boy, slapping his knees as he stood, like he'd seen a grown-up do once. "I'm thirsty."

"We can't drink creekwater," his sister whispered. "It's not safe."

He grinned a sly grin. "It is if you have a brackish pot."

She goggled. "You don't have one."

"Do so."

"From where?"

"I made it."

"Did not."

"Did so. Mom says I'm old enough to use one now."

Fife narrowed her eyes. "Old enough to make a fire?"

"Yup!" The boy puffed his chest. "I made a fire yesterday."

"By yourself?" said Fife.

"Yes, Fife," said the boy. "By myself."

His sister glanced at Fife. Fife looked impressed. Making

brackish was a big deal. It was a rite of passage that meant you
were capable of surviving on your own. The girl folded her arms
and fixed her brother with a defiant stare.

"Okay," she said, "prove it."

They rounded the last bend and sighted the creek ten minutes
later. The girl's brother carried a small pack over his shoulder,
which she supposed must contain the alleged brackish pot. He
handled the pack as if it were made of glass, carrying it delicately over his shoulder without even letting her or Fife see
inside.

The girl trailed her brother and Fife, kicking dust and dragging her feet. Up ahead, her brother said something she couldn't
hear and Fife burst into giggles. She perked up and trotted a few
steps.

"What's so funny?"

"Nothing." Fife tossed her hair.

The girl rolled her eyes. It didn't use to be like this. The three
of them used to do everything together. Now it seemed like it was
always her brother and Fife walking together a few steps ahead.

They came to the edge of the creek—or what passed for a creek
—and her brother gently removed his pack and set it on the
ground. As he kneeled to open it, Fife uttered a little cry and
pointed.

"Look! There's a man! A man in the creek."

The girl looked. Standing in the middle of the creek, ankle-
deep in the murky water, was an old man she had never seen
before. The girl froze. There were only ten people in their part of
the Settlement and she knew every one of them like family.
Strangers were a rare occurrence. Strangers came from Outside.

Her brother stood, clenching his fists tightly at his sides. He stepped forward and spoke with a slight tremble in his voice.

"Hello?"

The old man didn't seem to hear him. He was staring around through one cloudy eye, but at what, the girl couldn't be sure. Where his other eye should be was just an empty hole. The top of his head was bald and red from the sun, scabbed and peeling. A few oily strings of hair hung around his face and a gnarled gray beard sprang like foliage from his chin. His body rattled with a violent cough that turned into a long, wheezed exhalation.

"Sir?"

Her brother pulled a bandana over his mouth and goggles from the top of his head over his eyes. He pulled gloves from his pocket and donned them, then took another step forward, touching the two middle fingers of his left hand to the center of his brow, as they'd all been taught to do when greeting an elder. The old man ignored him. Then, to the girl's horror, he stooped and cupped his hands in the creek water, scooped up a handful, and drank.

"Sir!" Her brother ran now, wading into the water, stretching a gloved hand toward the man. "You can't drink the water! It isn't safe!"

The man dropped to his knees in the middle of the creek and put his face in the water. He sucked it down, gurgling and gasping, as though he'd never slake the thirst consuming him. Fife gave a little cry and put her hands over her face as the boy reached him.

"Sir, please," he cried, "you can't drink that!"

He put a hand on the man's shoulder, and the touch seemed to ignite something in the man. He snarled and flung his arm violently, catching the boy on the side of his head and sending him staggering sideways. His sister stood paralyzed, frightened tears clenching her chest. The man bent back to the water. Her brother, afraid to interfere again, looked around helplessly.

"Fife!" he cried. "Go and get help!"

Fife turned and bolted. The girl watched her go, then turned just in time to see the old man circle on her brother like a monster, screaming unintelligibly and shoving him with all his might. Her brother stumbled, tripped, and fell backward into the creek.

Her heart lurched and she plunged in after him, the filthy water coming almost to her knees. She grabbed hold of her brother's arm and helped him struggle to his feet. They stood, dripping, helpless, as the man dropped to his knees again and continued to suck down the creek water.

Their parents had always said—everyone in the Settlement said—that the creek water wasn't safe to drink. Too much salt, too many minerals. 'Microplastics.' That's why the older people in the Settlement made brackish. Brackish made the water drinkable.

But the little girl realized now that she had never actually been told what would happen if she *did* drink the water straight. She'd never seen anyone do it. Never, until this stranger. Would it kill him right away? Would he fall on his face, clutching his throat and gasping his last breath, right there in front of them? She couldn't bear the thought of it, and yet she couldn't look away.

"Gods almighty!"

A cry went up behind her. She recognized her mother and two of the strongest older men from the Settlement, dressed in masks, goggles and gloves like her brother. They sprinted past the children, caught the old man under his arms, and pulled him to his feet. He spit and snarled like a sandcat, flung his arms in all directions, and kicked at them with his gnarled old feet.

"It only makes you thirstier! You'll drink yourself to death!" one of the men yelled, struggling to pin the old man's arms.

"Get him to the med tent!" the girl's mother yelled, and then seemed to see the children for the first time. "And for gods' sakes get my children out of here!"

Someone grabbed the girl from behind and the world went sideways as she was tucked tightly between a fat, strong arm and a large, round bosom. A woman's deep, familiar voice vibrated through the tight squeeze.

"Come on little one. Let's get you inside the perimeter."

The girl watched the ground move as she was carried away. Behind her, the continued shouts and splashing of her mother and the two men wrestling with the old man faded as she rounded the bend and left the creek behind.

That night the girl huddled with Fife and her brother around a small fire in the center of the Settlement. Her brother had spent all afternoon getting it going, talking very quickly and animatedly with a brave but trembling voice, showing the girls everything he was doing, making jokes, until they had almost forgotten about the old man in the creek.

The fire was small and smoky because he had used the wrong kind of kindling, but Fife had oohed and ahhed enough to elicit a shy smile from her brother, which in turn elicited a monstrous eye roll from the little girl.

Fife hugged her knees to her chest, resting her chin on them and poking at the fire with a long stick. "What do you think will happen to that man?"

"They probably sent him off," the boy said.

Fife looked alarmed. "What do you mean?"

The boy twisted and broke a twig between his fingers and tossed the two halves into the flames. "He can't stay around here."

"Did he die?" asked the little girl.

Her brother shook his head. "You don't die right away. You have to drink a lot before it kills you. Years and years. I bet the elders sent him off."

"But what do you mean 'off'?" Fife repeated.

"Away. Out." The boy gestured toward the dark outside the

perimeter. "Somewhere else."

"But there is nowhere else," said Fife. The boy shrugged again. Fife's eyes went momentarily wide, and then she fell silent, gazing into the fire.

"Why can't he stay here?" demanded the girl, because she was only seven and too young to understand what Fife apparently had.

"We don't have enough food and water for another person here," said her brother. "And he's a crazy old man. What use is he?"

"But shouldn't we help him?"

The boy shook his head. "That's not the way. You have to drink from your own creek. This is our creek. It's all we've got. We have to make do. He has to make do with his lot. That's just the way it is."

The girl fell silent. She was only seven, and her brother was thirteen, so she knew he was right. But it certainly didn't feel right. She felt the tightness of tears in her chest and turned to hide her face. Fife opened her arm and pulled the little girl close.

"It's not fair," sniffed the girl.

"I know," agreed Fife. "But it's the way."

chapter
five

I STUMBLE TO MY KNEES, throwing out a hand to catch myself.

I can't see.

My hand lands hard on slick wood. I smell clean, salty air and grease and diesel. I hear the shush of rolling water and the cry of a gull.

A pinprick of light appears at the center of my vision, rapidly expanding like an aperture. I set my other hand down next to the first. I'm holding something. A stone.

Blurry shapes appear as the aperture of light expands, filling my eyes, dazzling me. Masts; the glint of sun on water. *Panga's* cheerful yellow hull emerges from the haze, in triplicate, then doubled, then one. I'm at the harbor. On the public dock.

Wasn't I just in the bathroom?

Blinking hard, I struggle to my feet. As my vision clears, I see the windows of Azimuth campus, glinting in the sun halfway up the hill behind the harbor. Somehow I managed to get off-campus. Somehow I got off-campus and all the way to the harbor. How the hell did that happen?

The sound of footsteps turns my head. An old fisherman is shuffling along the dock toward me. He gives me a quizzical look as I step aside to let him pass.

"What are you doing here?"

"Uh…" I blink. "Good question."

"Shouldn't you be in class?"

"I— No. Not…anymore."

Frowning, he shuffles off down the dock. I stare after him, still blinking, my mind spinning.

What just happened? What the hell just happened?

I was in the girl's bathroom, kneeling on the floor, looking through Electra's pack. I heard a toilet flush. I heard Electra's voice. And then…nothing.

Did she hit me? Render me unconscious? Did someone bring me down here? Is this some kind of prank? Should I go back?

I become aware of the cool weight of the stone in my hand, and I hold it up and turn it over. The jumble of questions in my head abruptly clears. I can't go back. I just *stole* this. Somehow I made it out without being caught. Going back seems like a pretty stupid idea.

Tucking the stone into my pocket, I look up and down the dock.

Okay, Bird. So you have no idea how you got here. Maybe let's focus on where you're going to go.

I can't go back to campus—I was just expelled and now I'm also a thief. I can't go home—Mama K usually comes home at lunch, and after our fight, then me going AWOL for three days and being expelled, I'm in no rush to bump into her.

I flip my hood up and adjust my pack on my shoulders. Sargo's. I'll go to Sargo's.

Blenny's sofa is as scratchy as ever. I flop onto it and pull the flask from my pack. There are a few dregs left in the bottom, and I tip them back with trembling hands. A familiar warmth pools in the center of my chest and then disperses, diluting the adrenaline, washing it away, down my arms, out of my fingertips. I squeeze my eyes shut and rub my forehead with my palm.

How the hell did I get out of that bathroom?

It's been a rough couple of days. I haven't been sleeping well. My brain is fried. I'm hallucinating or something.

I probably just spaced out and don't remember walking off campus. It wouldn't be the first time. Sometimes I get so lost in thought walking between places that I get to where I'm going and have no memory of how I got there.

A *blip*, as the moms would call it.

Unless…

My eye lands on Electra's stone, perched on the edge of the low wooden table in front of me. I pick it up.

Unless the stone somehow transported me.

My pulse ticks up as I hold the stone up to the light. Slicks of green and purple on its glossy white surface catch the light like oil on water; ephemeral, almost invisible. It's perfectly oval and so smooth it's hard to know where my fingertips end and the stone begins. On an impulse, I tap it against my teeth.

What is this thing?

Opening my pack, I dig out my slate, then sit back into the cushions and tap my right brow with two fingers to pull up the Net.

Finding information about the stone proves more difficult than I thought it would be. Page after page turns up nothing. My eyes start to itch. I'm chewing my thumbnail and I've read the same paragraph at least four times by the time I realize that an hour has gone by. Pinning my hand under my leg to stop myself gnawing on it, I set down my slate.

This is ridiculous. However I got from Azimuth to the dock, it almost certainly wasn't a *magic rock.*

I rub my eyes and check the time. 1315. Sargo will be home in less than an hour. I'm sure he knows by now that I've been kicked out of Azimuth. The thought of facing him appeals about as much as the thought of facing my moms.

With a sigh, I pick up the slate and am about to shut down the Net when a link catches my eye.

I open it and find myself in some kind of forum. Scrolling through the entries, I can tell it's pre-pandemic—the goofy styling gives it away. There's a lot of nerdy stuff going on in here.

A lot of talk about rocks. I gesture in the air to compose a new question.

>>> *Hello! Newbie here. I'm looking for information about a stone. It's about the size of a girl's palm, pearly white with kind of a green and purple sheen. Any info, please dm!*

I scroll through a few more pages before I remember the time. 1320 now. I should get moving if I want to get out before Sargo gets home.

A ping in my ear alerts me that a private message request has come through from the forum. *That was quick.* I swipe it open.

>>> *u got frennonite?*

I squint at the name of the sender—*V*—then compose and send a reply.

>>> *What's frennonite?*

Their response comes almost immediately. It's text copied from an online encyclopedia.

>>> *Frennonite: Engineered for use in tech manufacturing. Replaced cobalt, gold, tellurium, and lithium as the primary element in electronic devices. Critical in the development of biochip technology.*

Underneath is a picture of a stone that looks exactly like Electra's. My heart skips.

>>> *Yes, that's it!*

So it's not a natural stone at all. It's an engineered pre-pandemic hybrid of some kind. Probably made by Zenith. Probably not magic, then. There's a ping in my ear as the next message comes through.

>>> *u selling?*

Selling? I frown at the words. No, I'm not selling. I'm trying to find out how I got from the girl's bathroom to the public dock with no memory of how it happened.

I begin to compose a reply and hesitate, my fingers hovering in the air. *Selling…*

Is there any reason *not* to sell the stone? Honestly, it would probably be better if I did. Get it off my hands. If Electra saw me take it, I'm already flogged. If she didn't, then she's had two hours to realize it's missing and I'm willing to bet I'm her prime suspect.

Squeezing my eyes shut, I rub my face with both hands. I've been expelled from the only school in Brume and now I'm probably wanted for theft. I can practically *see* my future spiraling down the toilet. Let's face it: it wouldn't hurt to have some extra coin. It's not like I have a job, and at this rate, the odds that anyone would ever give me one are slim to—

My eyes snap open. Shale. *I have a job for you.*

If I sell this thing, I could use the coin to buy Sargo a new mainsail. And if Sargo had a new mainsail, he'd be able to sail to Pocosín. And if he was already going to Pocosín…maybe I could convince him to go to Alluvium on the way. Where my brother has a job for me. Where *maybe* I have a future.

Is that crazy?

Yes, very.

Okay, but let's look at it objectively: Sargo's been out of Azimuth for a year now and as far as I can tell, the only thing keeping him there is teaching that class. He has no family in Brume, except for Blenny, and after what he was saying the other day, about his folks sailing away on *Panga*, about going to Pocosín…I *know* that was more than a childhood dream. It has to be. What else is he busy fixing the autopilot for? He *wants* to go. He's just worried that the boat isn't ready. But with a new sail?

Maybe. Maybe I could convince him.

Convince him to embark on a highly illegal suicide mission into the body of water that has 'claimed the lives of thousands of sailors'? Sure, Bird. You go right ahead and try that. Sargo is definitely the kind of person that would think that's a good idea.

Blocking out the unhelpful voice in the back of my head, I turn back to the slate.

Whoever this *V* person is, they replied quickly. What are the odds that someone else is on the Net researching the same thing I am at the same exact moment? I don't know. I was never very good at working out odds. I compose another message.

>>> *WHO IS THIS?*

>>> *DON'T WORRY ABOUT IT U SELLING OR NO?*

I take a breath.

>>> *I'M SELLING*

>>> *HOW MUCH U WANT*

How much do I want? I have no idea. How much is it worth? I twist my mouth and chew my nail while I try to think of a response that doesn't give me away as a total rube, and finally go with

>>> *HOW MUCH YOU GOT?*

The cursor blinks for what feels like an eternity, then the reply comes, short and sweet.

>>> *20K UBC*

Flogging Molly! Twenty thousand Ubicoin?! Twenty thousand is more coin than I've even tried to imagine before. And all I have to do is type *yes* and I'll have it! I've never felt so close to something so massive. I can't believe it was that easy.

I'm sending my response before I can stop myself.

>>> *MAKE IT 30*

What am I doing?! *Jesus, just say yes you lunatic!*

An eternity passes with nothing but the sound of my heart in my ears. Then, a *ping*. The reply blinks back.

>>> *25. MEET AT THE WATERHOUSE. 2200*

Twenty-five! Flogging Molly, I can't believe that *worked!* Holy shit...did I just negotiate? Wait. The Waterhouse? That's all the way in the Flats. I don't have coin for a water taxi.

Unless...

Sargo has a second boat besides *Panga*—a little dinghy with an electric motor that he uses to run errands around the harbor. He calls it 'the skiff.' Technically, it's Blenny's, but Blenny lets Sargo use it whenever he wants. No sail, big enough for two people, and super fast...

I've never driven the skiff by myself. I'd usually never dream of taking it without Sargo's permission. But something tells me

Sargo won't approve of my plan to meet a stranger I met on the Net at a sketchy bar in the Flats to sell stolen goods—

Seriously though, who are you?

—better to keep him in the dark until after I get the coin. At 2200 Sargo should be asleep. He's a pretty early-to-bed kind of guy. It shouldn't be too hard to…borrow the skiff.

Steal the skiff. You mean 'steal the skiff.'

Don't think of it as stealing, I tell myself. Think of it as doing what's necessary.

Picturing what Sargo's face will look like tomorrow when I transfer him twenty-five thousand Ubicoin and tell him it's for the sail is a lot more fun than imagining the lecture he's probably going to give me about being expelled.

I bolt upstairs to his room and grab the skiff key from its hook by the door, shoving down a twinge of guilt as I hang it around my neck.

Downstairs, I tuck the stone into the pocket of my hoodie and leave my pack on the sofa. Then I lock the door behind me and head to the Green to kill time until 2200.

chapter
six

THE SLICK WOOD planks of Pier Two creak and groan under my feet. It's 2130—dark, damp and chilly; the air so thick with fog that I can't see the end of the dock. The harbor is silent and empty, the water still. Not even the cry of a bird disturbs the quiet.

Panga emerges from the mist like a ghost ship. At night she looks like a different boat; the bright yellow hull and striking green letters that spell out her name are just shades of gray in the dark.

The skiff is tied up next to her. I drop to my knees to untie the line, then fling myself into it, kicking off the dock and using my momentum to propel the little boat out into the harbor channel. It takes me three tries to start the motor, and when it finally kicks on, it happens so suddenly it almost knocks me down.

The skiff lurches forward and I snatch up the tiller, pulling hard to the left and sending the boat careening in a wide arc towards the south end of the bay. It goes faster than I thought it would, and it takes me a few minutes to get used to the steering.

Left a bit. Right a bit. Not too hard! Easy now.

A tangle of frizzy curls whips across my face from under my beanie, and I inhale the salty night air. As I near the south end of the bay, a channel opens up in the breakwater. I swing the skiff into the channel and under Fisherman's Bridge, cutting up toward the Flats.

On the other side of the bridge is a small stretch of sand where I can land the skiff. I circle and kill the motor, letting the boat drift slowly to shore while I pull off my shoes and socks and roll up my pants. I'm actually not terrible at landing the skiff: the few times I've used it with Sargo, I'm usually the one who has to hop out and haul it ashore while he drives. He doesn't trust me to drive.

As the bottom of the little boat bumps against the sand, I hop over the bow with a line in my hand, landing ankle-deep in chilly water, and heave with all my might to pull it out of the tide.

Putting the key back around my neck, I double-check that I still have the stone, panic when it isn't where I put it, remember that I put it in my *other* pocket, and hop to pull my shoes on over bare, sandy feet as I trot away from the shore and toward the road. At the top of the beach, I look left, then right down the quiet, unfamiliar street. I've never been to this sketchy part of town before.

Maybe you should start hanging out here. Embrace your new persona as a total degenerate.

Funny.

Tapping my left brow to augment the scene in front of me with a map, I gesture in the air to input the location. A moment later the ground in front of me illuminates with a glowing, green arrow. It leads away from my feet to the left and down the street, then bends and disappears around a corner.

I follow the arrow through the grungy streets of the Flats for about ten minutes, eventually landing in front of a dark, shabby-looking warehouse. It sits on the corner of a scruffy patch of beach, the muffled thump of music from inside punctuated by the shrieks of gulls and the barking of Salt dogs in the bay.

A few people mill around the entrance, chatting in low voices and taking long puffs from a shared dart. The dart's slender metal case glows through a rainbow of neon colors as the smokers drag on it, exhaling thick, floral-smelling plumes into the air. The women shiver in their too-small clothes. A girl with flinty eyes and sallow skin glares at me as I approach.

I tap my right temple to pull up the chat log from earlier and send a message.

>>> *HERE*

>>> *RED SCARF*, V replies. *BLUE HAT*

Scanning the meandering waifs in front of me, I spot a blue hat on a man leaning against the corner of the club, obscured by shadow and facing away from me.

>>> *I SEE YOU*

The man in the blue hat lifts his head but doesn't turn. He gestures in the air in a way that I recognize as composing a message, and a moment later I receive

>>> *GREET ME LIKE A FRIEND*

As I steel myself and walk to him, I suddenly wonder if V is even his real name. I suddenly wonder why he's so interested in buying this stone at all. I suddenly wonder what the hell I think I'm doing at a sketchy warehouse in the Flats in the middle of the night on a flogging Tuesday.

I watch my hand clapping him on the shoulder as if it isn't part of my body.

I hear myself say, "Hey, man!"

Hey man? Since when do you say 'hey man'?

V turns. He's older than me—I would guess in his thirties—and I'm immediately struck by the incredible thinness of his face, the whiteness of his skin, and the weirdly metallic quality of his gray eyes. His hair has been augmented. Under the sad neon light from the sign above the warehouse door, it shimmers with a kaleidoscope of different colors.

"How are you?" he says with a thin-lipped smile.

"Doing well, doing well," I hear myself say. I attempt a casual smile but I can feel myself nodding too much. When I'm nervous, my head bobs like a buoy in chop.

The door of the club bursts open, splitting the still air with music and voices. I jump sideways as a couple in matching orange leather jumpsuits stumbles out into the street.

V watches the couple pass, his smile frozen in place, then catches the closing door with his foot. On the other side, a bald man with his arms folded across a barrel chest steps in front of the door, but V waves him away.

"She's with me."

My eyes struggle to adjust as I find myself dumped into a dark, humid sea of bodies. I quickly pull my bandana up to cover my nose and mouth; no one else in here is masked up, and it makes my skin crawl. I may be on the fence about the *'Put on your own mask first'* thing, but even I can see this is bananas. So many sweaty humans. So little fresh air. Where did all these people even come from? This must be, like, half of Brume.

The floor beneath my feet is sticky and the air is filled with the pungent odors of booze, dart smoke, and sweat. In cages above me, men and women fling their half-naked—nope, fully naked—bodies around as though possessed. V pushes me through a small door next to the bar.

The raucous assault of light and noise abruptly ceases as we step into a quiet room lit with dim red light. Cushions and low couches are flung about the plush carpet, and a thick curtain of smoke hangs just below the low ceiling. A few people are sprawled on the cushions, looking half-asleep or half-dead. A couple of them nod at V as he steers me to a booth at the back of the room. As we sit, over the thump of the muffled music, he says quietly, "You have the item?"

I scoot sideways to wriggle the stone out of my back pocket and slide it onto the table. V surveys me, then leans forward and picks it up, holding it between two fingers to catch the light.

"Okay?" I say.

He sits back, dropping the stone into his palm and holding it flat.

"Very nice." He sets it on the table.

"And you'll pay?"

"Yes, yes, we'll get to that." He waves his hand. "How about a drink? We should celebrate."

He pulls a slender glass pipe and a leather pouch from inside his coat, opens the pouch with two fingers, and extracts a pinch of sticky black gunk.

"I don't think—"

"Relax." He presses the gunk into the end of the pipe and reaches back into his coat for matches. *Matches.* Who uses those anymore? Where did he even get them? He strikes one and holds it under the pipe while he puffs a few times until a thin tendril of smoke curls from the black gunk. The overwhelming smell of spray paint and barbecue sauce assaults my nostrils.

Shaking the match to extinguish it with one hand, V beckons to a bored-looking girl behind the nearly empty bar with the other. She skulks across the room with the alacrity of someone who truly hates her job. I notice bruises on her thighs.

"Two," says V, exhaling a cloud of smoke into her face. The girl gives no indication that she's heard him and saunters unhurriedly back to the bar as the smoke dissipates across the table. It's thick and somehow greasy, and even with the bandana on, it chokes me.

I glance nervously at the other patrons slouched around the room.

"Look, I really just want my coin. I'm not looking for a date."

He laughs, a single short bark, and waves an amused finger at me. His hands are smooth and very pale, almost luminescent in the dim red light. The tips of the three fingers he used to handle the pipe are black and shiny.

"Funny," he says as he drags on the pipe and exhales another cloud of oily, evil-smelling smoke. "That's funny. What's your name?"

"Why do you need to know that?"

"I like to know the names of the people I'm doing business with." He turns the pipe toward me and offers it.

I eye the black gunk. "What is it?"

"Haar."

Haar?! Jack's ass, Bird, you really are in deep.

For once in my life, I exercise caution. Haar is about the worst thing you can put in your body. Grog might make you forget stuff, but at least you get to keep your teeth. I shake my head.

"Suit yourself," he says. "I'm Five."

"I thought your name was V."

He regards me with an irritating smirk. "It is."

What is that? Some kind of pun?

"Clever," I say, flatly.

He drags on the pipe again, his eyes crawling over my body. "Is this your first time in a club like this?"

I fold my arms across my chest, my skin prickling under his creepy leer, and look for the bar girl. She's chatting to her coworker and hasn't started making our drinks.

"Yes," I say.

"And what do you think?"

"About what?"

"The club. You like it?"

"Oh, uh—" Across the room, the bar girl checks her slate. Inside my head, I scream at her to hurry up. "Sure, it's fine."

Five surveys the room with a kind of bored amusement. "To be honest, I'm surprised Zenith hasn't shut it down. It's exactly the kind of thing those hags hate. But I guess they can't be in control of everything, as much as they'd like you to think they are. They just don't have the manpower—uh, *woman*power." He smiles, another creepy leer that makes my skin crawl.

That word—*hags*—sticks in my mind like a foxtail. It's a word a particular kind of person, usually a dude, uses to refer to the women at Zenith. You don't hear it around here very much—you don't get a lot of Zenith dissenters in Brume, because basically everyone here works for them. Brume pride and love for Zenith go pretty much hand in hand. But apparently not for this guy.

"You're not a fan of Zenith?" I ask.

Five curls a lip. "The Fat Sallies? No, can't say I am."

Fat Sallies. That's another one. A term mostly used by angry little men who can't deal with the fact that the world's governing corporation is made up entirely of women.

I don't really care for politics—that's more Sargo's thing—but I do think it's pretty cool that after the pandemic, people crawled out of the wreckage, looked around at the mess they'd made, and basically thought, "You know what? The men had their chance. Let's see how the women do for a while."

The girl returns with the drinks; two tiny glasses of slick red liquid, steaming gently. Their spicy smell pricks the inside of my nose as she sets them down between us. I eye the glass nearest me.

Five is already scooping his up, holding it to his nose. "You ever have pyrewater?" I shake my head. "And I bet this is your first black market trade too?" He gestures at the stone on the table.

Black market trade? Is that what this is? Is that what you're doing on a Tuesday night, Howsley?

I nod.

"In that case, a toast." He holds his glass aloft and winks. "To trying new things."

"And then you'll give me my coin?"

"Yes, yes." He *tsks* with frustration, waving a hand. "Like I said, we'll get to it. Let's talk a little first."

His eyes crawl over me again and I cross my arms almost involuntarily. Of course this couldn't just be a simple transaction. Of course he's the kind of creep who wants to trap me here and make me have a drink with him. Because he can. Because right now, he has my coin, and the only way for me to get it is to play along. Because I'm too small and too weak to crack him upside the head and take it from him. I swallow my irritation and reach for the glass.

"To your first pyrewater." Five tilts his glass toward me. "And your first black market trade."

Sighing, I hold up my glass. He clinks it and tosses his back, gasps, and sets the glass down on the table as I sniff mine. It smells like smoke and cinnamon. Tilting my head back, I down as much as I can, choking on the unexpected rush of chilling, sticky sweetness. I cough and set the glass down, my eyes watering.

Five chuckles. "Not a drinker?"

"Not this stuff."

I wipe my eyes on the back of my hand. Five has picked up the stone again and is holding it up to the light. I'm starting to feel a bit itchy at seeing it in his hands without having my hands on the coin.

Actually...I think I'm just starting to feel...itchy?

"S'what're y'gonna do withit?" I slur. *Wow, pyrewater works fast.* My tongue feels thick. An icy sensation is creeping outward from my chest.

"Sell it," he shrugs. "I know a guy. He works for some people. They're working on a thing. Did you know that Zenith uses these stones to make biochips? Not just beautiful, you see. Functional too. Very valuable."

"Isitmagic?" I slur.

"*Magic?*" He shoots me an incredulous look. "What is this, a fantasy book?"

He pulls his sleeve back and presses a finger to his temple while he looks at his wrist, checking a watch I can't see. Then he looks back at me, his eyes suddenly bright with malice.

"I imagine you're feeling rather unwell by now, yes?"

"What?"

I can't keep Five still in my vision. He jumps from side to side as the rest of the room swims behind him. This is nothing like grog. The cool rush from the pyrewater has become a numbness that radiates from my chest into my arms, my legs, my fingers.

"I feel—funny," I try to say, but rather than forming words, my tongue just flops around uselessly. Why isn't Five having the same trouble with this that I am? I feel a string of saliva slip from the corner of my mouth, and then I lose control of my neck entirely and slump onto the table.

From the corner of my eye, I see Five stand, pocketing the stone. I try to reach for him, but my hand weighs a thousand pounds. He picks up the glass pipe again, drags on it, and squats next to me, blowing oily smoke into my face.

"Sorry about that," he says, looking unapologetic. "That wasn't just pyrewater. But you'll be fine. A mild sedative."

All I can manage is, "Why?"

"I couldn't really afford to part with twenty-five K. Everyone's trying to make coin. You understand." He pats my cheek with his gross, smooth hand and winks. "I'd better get out of here before the haar kicks in."

Standing, he adjusts his scarf and slips away from the table. I stare after him as darkness crowds the edges of my vision. He stops at the bar just long enough to press something into the hand of the girl who served us the drinks. She glances in my direction, then pockets it, and retreats to a back room.

That stray flogging bitch.

At the door, Five turns, touches two fingers to the brim of his hat, and ducks out. The darkness in the corners of my vision spreads, blossoms like squid ink, clouds my eyes, and shrouds me in blackness.

chapter
seven

THE LITTLE GIRL sat in the saltnut tree by the creek, stripping the leaves off small branches and collecting them in a hemp sack so her family could pound them for mash.

The hot summer sun dappled spots onto her bare arms and legs through the leaves, and sweat poured from her skinny body. Her ears rang with the buzzing of insects. Below her, the hard red earth radiated heat, and patches of brown grass looked dry enough to burst into flames.

On the branch above, her brother swung his feet as he whistled, filling his own sack. He was halfway into fourteen now, and he had an easy way about him despite the gangly nature of his arms and legs. He finished stripping a branch and flicked it at the girl's head.

"Stop it!"

"Oh sorry." His eyes crinkled down at her. "Was that in your hair?"

"Don't drop sticks on my head."

"Sorry. Accident." He shrugged and flicked another one at her. "Oops. Did it again."

The little girl set her knife carefully on the branch and aimed a stick at her brother's head. It hit him squarely in the eye.

"God dammit!"

"I told you not to drop sticks on me. And don't say 'God'."

"Don't tell me what to say!" He rubbed his eye. Then, begrudgingly, he mumbled, "Good shot."

She snuck a grin up at him. They worked in silence for a few minutes, then the boy set down his knife and stared through his swinging feet at the creek below.

"I'm thirsty," he announced.

"Me too," his sister admitted. "Can you make some brackish?"

The boy pulled a face. "I'm sick of brackish." He snapped a twig between his fingers and tossed the pieces into the creek, his brow knitted in thought. "What do you think fogwater tastes like?" he said.

The little girl frowned. "What's fogwater?"

"It's what they have in the City."

His sister rolled her eyes. The City again.

A week ago, a group of strangers had arrived in the Settlement. These strangers weren't all burnt up and stringy and crazy like the old man they had found in the creek last year. These strangers were clean. So clean they smelled good. And there were a lot of them, at least five. They had come in some kind of EV. Electric vehicle. But an EV unlike any the girl had ever seen. A big, shiny thing on large, knobbly wheels that rolled over the red earth so easily the girl thought it must be floating.

They had come to congratulate them, the strangers said. Their Settlement had been chosen to take part in this year's Lottery. One family would be chosen to win. The little girl didn't know what that meant, but her parents had gotten very excited. It was a chance, they said, a chance to get out. The girl wasn't sure if she liked that. 'Out' was where they sent the old man. 'Out' wasn't safe.

"I don't know," she said eventually, turning away from her brother and back to her work. "I guess it tastes like water."

"Not like this water." The boy gestured at the creek in disgust. "It's pure. Comes out of the sky."

"It's still just water."

"I bet it tastes better. I bet everything in the City is better." He picked up his knife again and began working on another branch. "It's gonna be amazing. There's gonna be electric bikes and boats and fresh, clean water. We're gonna get chipped."

"We have to win first."

"Of course we'll win," he scoffed. "They only want one family, and they want a family with kids. We're the only kids in the Settlement."

"What about Fife?"

Her brother paused. In all his excitement had he forgotten about Fife? The girl wrinkled her nose. She hadn't forgotten.

"She can come later," the boy reasoned. "They said they do the Lottery every year. I bet it comes here again soon."

But he was quiet for a long time after that, and the girl knew he was thinking deeply.

chapter
eight

My eyes snap open, and dawn clamors into them like an interrogation.

I squeeze them shut again. They feel swollen and crusty. The inside of my mouth is sticky. My throat like sandpaper. I lie very still and wait for my head to stop spinning, then make one eye into a tiny slit. Slowly, carefully, I do the same with the other eye, scrunching up my face against the invasive daylight until I can open them both.

I'm outside. A chilly, damp fog has pulled the sky down on top of me, and the air is salty and punctured by the cries of gulls. Sitting up in cold sand, feeling stiffness in my neck and shoulders, I look around. I'm on the beach—I guess by the black sand and trash everywhere that it must be somewhere in the Flats.

The stone.

I scramble to my knees, digging my hands into my pockets. But of course, it isn't there. *Stupid.* Stupid brain. Stupid Bird. That stray sonofabitch drugged me and left me in that bar. He gave something to our server on his way out. Haar, maybe? He paid her off to put something in my drink.

Squeezing my head between my hands, I frown. *If he left you there,* says self, *then…how did you get out here?*

Someone must have found me slumped over that table and moved me out here.

But...if they had done that, they would have scanned my retinas and gotten my ID from my chip. If *that* had happened, they would have called my moms and my moms would have murdered me. So I'd be dead already. So that can't be it.

So what happened?

I spit out a piece of thumbnail, tasting blood, and realize I'm chewing my nails again. I pull my hat back on. This is the second time now that I've blacked out somewhere and woken up somewhere else with no idea how I got there. If I'm not careful I'm going to end up like Sargo's uncle Blenny, blacking out all the time, shambling around in my pajamas, forgetting—

With a jolt, I remember the skiff. Blenny's skiff. I look around and see it still pulled up, halfway down the beach where I left it, the rising tide just starting to lap around the bottom. If I don't get it back before Sargo gets to the dock to teach his early class, he'll know something's up.

Do I still have the key? Squeezed by sudden panic, I shove my hand into the front of my shirt and feel my fingers close around it, gritty with sand. Heaving a sigh of relief, I scramble to my feet while I pull up directions on my chip and check the time.

>>> *0553*

If I sprint, I can make it.

———————

An hour later, with the skiff returned in the nick of time and my head pounding like a ship's bell, I skulk back across Fisherman's Bridge toward home. I know it's not *great* that I was expelled, but seriously...thank *flog* I don't have school today.

The fog is burning off. Tendrils of it wind through the

fogwood trees and out toward the Salt. I stop in the middle of
the bridge and lean my elbows on the rail to look out over
Brume. A few small white birds swoop from under the bridge
across the bay. They catch the wind and bank right, over the
solar-paneled rooftops of Midtown. Fog traps stretch between
the roofs, soaked with fresh drinking water, glistening like enormous spiderwebs in the cold morning sun. The birds wheel out
across the crumbling, unused neighborhoods of the rest of the
city, toward the perpetually turning white windmills of the
Farm.

I can hear the occasional shout from the harbor, where daily
harvest will have already started, and Mama K is likely shucking
oysters. A lead weight settles in the pit of my stomach. *The moms.*
Sooner or later, I'm going to have to talk to them.

The six flights of steps up to my family's apartment are brutal
today. The woman in the faded Zenith poster that's plastered on
the wall halfway up beams down at me, and I want to punch a
hole in her face.

"Climb into your future!"

Most days, I don't mind walking up and down stairs. I'm in
good shape, if a little skinny, and I find that walking helps to quiet
my mind. But some days you wake up on a garbage-covered
beach in the Flats, after having been drugged and robbed the
night before, and you just need, you know, a break.

I stumble through the front door, gasping and sweating out
grog and pyrewater. The kitchen is mercifully cool and dark. The
smell of damp earth tells me Mama K recently watered the veg.
Her tomato vines climb around the kitchen window, the morning
sun filtering in through their bright green leaves like stained glass.

I beeline to the sink and gulp crisp, cold water straight from
the tap until I feel like I might throw up. Then I pluck a big red
tomato off the vine and walk down the hall to my room.

My bed has been made, which means Mama K was in here
without my permission, but I'm too tired to care. Fresh air and
early morning sun pour through the open window. I lean on the

sill and look out. A patchwork of fog traps and solar-panels gleams in the bright morning air.

The aloe plant on my windowsill has been watered too. With a sigh, I set the tomato next to it, then kick off my shoes, flop onto the bed, and tug off my itchy beanie. Shaking out my hair, I peek at my face in the mirror that leans against the opposite wall. It's pale and thin, my eyes wild with lack of sleep, the pupils the size of dinner plates. My hair looks like it's having a party.

So at least somebody's having a good time.

The front door opens and closes with a soft click and I hear the unmistakable tapping of Mama K's shoes across the tile in the kitchen. I frown at myself in the glass. She should be at work.

Hopping up, I pad swiftly across the room on bare feet to gently push my bedroom door closed.

"Hello?" Mama K's voice floats through from the kitchen. *Seriously? That woman has the ears of a bat.* "Hello? Bird?"

I sigh heavily and open the door. "Yeah?"

The rapid *tap-tap-tap* of her shoes marching briskly across the kitchen floor turns into the subdued sound of them on the carpet in the hall, and then she appears around the corner. She somehow looks even tinier than I remember her; taut and shrunken. She pauses, taking me in, and I brace myself for an angry tirade.

Instead, she wordlessly strides down the hall and grabs me in a painfully tight hug. The stab of her bones against my skin alarms me.

"Where have you been?"

Her voice is sharp but not angry, and as she steps back I note the dark circles under her eyes, the unkempt tangle of graying reddish hair, even frizzier than mine.

"Gods, Bird, you look awful, what have you—" She stops suddenly, grabs me by the shoulders and pulls me closer, sniffing. "Have you been *drinking?*"

I try to shrug her off, to sidestep around her, but she blocks me, her eyes fierce.

"I'm talking to you!"

"No! I mean…it—it wasn't my fault." I fold my arms and look at the floor.

"Wasn't your fault?" She tips a finger under my chin to pull my face back up to hers. Her expression has morphed from worry to fury in a heartbeat. "What happened, then? Someone held your mouth open and poured it in, did they?"

I roll my eyes and turn to go back into my room.

"I'm *talking* to you!"

"No, Mom!" I spin to face her. "Obviously no one held my mouth open and poured it in! I can't…explain it right now. Why aren't you at work?"

"Excuse me?"

That was the wrong thing to ask. I knew before I said it, but for some reason, it just popped out.

She exhales through wide nostrils. "Your mom forgot her slate. I came to get it and drop it by the Farm for her." She pauses. "No need to ask why you're not in class, I suppose."

I hold her glare, defiance, shame, and fury fighting for space in my brain. I really wasn't prepared to talk about the expulsion right now, but it looks like that's what we're doing. So be it. If she's going to murder me, might as well get it over with. She exhales again through her nose, her lips drawn into a hard line, and I brace myself for shouting.

Instead, her eyes brim with tears. She covers her mouth with her hand as if to hold them back, but a single sob escapes. The sound of it is so jarring and alien I flinch. Mama J's a softy—she'll cry at the drop of a hat. But Mama K doesn't cry.

I don't know where to look, and decide on my feet. My toes are filthy. I wiggle them as Mama K heaves another gut-wrenching sob and pulls me in for another bony hug. This time I let her hold me for a long time, staring at the wall over her shoulder, her wiry hair poking me in the eyes and cheeks, her familiar smell of leather and fermented tea filling my nose.

Finally, she steps back, wiping her eyes with the heel of her hand.

"I'm sorry," she says.

"It's okay." I keep my eyes on my toes, not sure what she's apologizing for.

"I was so worried about you."

We stand awkwardly in the doorway while she pulls a faded yellow bandana from her sleeve and loudly blows her nose. She pats her wild hair as though that will tame it.

"Can we talk?"

I shrug and step aside to let her into my room. We sit side by side on the bed. For a long time, neither of us says anything. She sniffs and dabs her face.

"I'm sorry we didn't tell you about Shale," she says.

What? She wants to talk about *Shale?* She's apologizing to *me?* Where's the reaming about getting kicked out of Azimuth? About going AWOL for three days? About showing up reeking of grog? I was expecting to be murdered. Is she trying to lull me into a false sense of security?

I decide to go with it. "You *lied* to me about Shale."

"Yes, okay. I'm sorry we lied to you about Shale."

"Why did you do that?" An unexpected knot of tears clogs my throat as the anger of the last three days wells up inside me all at once. I clamp my mouth shut against it and wait for her reply. It takes a long time to come.

"I was afraid," she says. "I was afraid that if you thought he was alive, you would try to go after him. I was afraid I would lose you, too."

"So you told me he *died?* You told me my brother died."

Her voice rises. "If I had told you he went missing, you would have been out there after him. I knew you would. It's one thing for a sixteen-year-old boy to be out in the State, on his own, doing gods know what with gods know who, but you were nine years old!" Her voice cracks. "And—your mom and I knew the odds of him surviving out there. When two months had gone by and there was no trace of him, we—"

She stops and presses the bandana against her mouth.

"You figured it wasn't a lie," I finish for her. She nods silently. I stare at the floor in front of me, wishing she would stop crying. "You gave up."

"The peace force gave up," she says. She takes a deep breath and sits up straight. "Everything felt out of control. Your mom and I were fighting all the time. It felt like everything was…shattering, all around us. It felt like everything was falling apart. If I had lost you too…"

I pick viciously at my thumbnail, as if getting that one uneven bit off it will somehow smooth everything out. As if, by working at it hard enough, I could smooth down the roughness, fix that little bit of ragged edge. In the back of my mind, I know it's impossible. Picking at it only makes it worse.

So why can't you stop doing it?

Mama K puts her hand over mine to stop me, and I yank my hand away. She sighs.

"I understand that you're upset. I think you have every right to be. We should have told you he left—"

"Why did he leave?"

I don't want to hear her excuses and apologies. I want to know what happened. I want to know *why*.

Shale wasn't like me. There was no reason for him to want to leave Brume. He was popular, doing well in his classes. He loved sailing. Of all the questions that have been banging around my head for the last three days, this is the one that's been banging the loudest. It doesn't make sense.

Mama K fiddles with her sleeve. "I don't know. He was sixteen. He was impulsive."

He left the only habitable place for thousands of miles and risked his life crossing a deadly body of water on a *whim?* How did he even pay for the passage? Whose boat did he go on? Who in Brume even has the capacity to make a journey like that? How did he *survive?* New questions are forming and the old questions haven't even been answered.

I frown at her. "But he loved it here."

"Like I said, Bird," she sighs, "I don't know. I don't know what he was thinking, okay? He wasn't thinking. You were too young to know what was going on with him. He was hanging around with a bad crowd. Drinking. He wasn't the same."

"Drinking?"

"That shit the old sailing lushes drink. Grok or gunk or something."

"Grog?"

She looks at me sharply. "Yes. That's it."

I shift, averting my eyes.

She's quiet for a long, brittle moment. Then says, "Listen to me, Bird. I…understand it's been a tough couple of days. I'm not —I'm not going to ask what you've been doing. I don't want to know. But if I ever find out that you're getting into that—"

"Okay! I get it."

Silence again. We both stare out of the window. Electra's words float through my head. *Just like your brother.*

So she knew. She knew Shale was drinking. Electra has an older sister, Paradi, who would be close to Shale's age. If Paradi knew Shale was into that stuff, it's not a stretch to imagine she would have told her sister.

"Bird?"

I turn away from the window. Mama K is smiling gently.

"Did you blip? I asked you a question."

"I was just thinking."

"About what?"

"It doesn't matter." I sigh through my nose. "So what are you going to do about Shale? Are you going to try and find him?"

To my surprise, she laughs bitterly. "He doesn't want to talk to me, Bird. He contacted you. If he wanted me and Mama J to find him he would have reached out to us a long time ago."

I stare at her. "So, what, you're just gonna…do nothing? Don't you even want to…tell him off for running away?"

She smiles sadly. "He's not a boy anymore. I can't tell him off. I can't tell him to do anything. I never could. Besides, he can clearly take care of himself."

She stands, her knees popping. I watch her cross to the door with a confused scowl. She stops in the doorway and turns. Her face is anxious as she asks, "Have you responded to his message?"

I hold her gaze, my mind turning over. She doesn't want to find him. Doesn't even want to talk to him. Why? How can she not want to see her own son?

"No," I lie, "I haven't."

"Please, just—please don't do anything...stupid. Please just... come home tonight? We'll have dinner. Mama J too. We can talk about it some more. We can talk about *everything*." She looks at me pointedly. "Expulsion included."

Cool, so you're definitely still in trouble. Murder is not off the table.

I sigh and look out the window. I guess I might as well come home for dinner. See what my folks have to say.

"Sure," I say. "I'll be here."

She smiles. "I love you, Birdie."

I roll my eyes. "Love you too."

She turns, closing the door softly behind her. I hear her footsteps in the hallway, then in the kitchen, then the quiet click of the front door. The silence she leaves in her wake makes my ears ring.

I sit, immobilized on the bed, the events of the past twenty-four hours converging on me all at once, crushing me. Flopping backward, I relish the softness of the pillows, the coolness of the sheets. My eyes begin to close.

chapter
nine

"WAKE UP."

A ceiling flutters in front of my eyes. A wood ceiling with a single paper-covered lightbulb in the center of it. It's a familiar ceiling. My ceiling.

My eyes feel sticky. They want to close again. I turn my head to one side.

"I'm tryna sleep."

"Wake up." It's a deep, unfamiliar voice. A man's voice. I open my eyes.

A body looms over me. A weight pins my chest, crushing the air out of me. I try to scream, but the sound is muffled against the leather of a gloved hand.

"Stop screaming."

The gloved hand releases my mouth and I manage to draw a single breath before it cuffs me hard across the face. Light explodes inside my head and cold, stinging pain blooms from my nose.

"Am I gonna have to tell you again?"

I feel blood in my nose. I shake my head.

"Good."

The weight on my chest lifts and I struggle upright. In front of me, a brute of a man is cracking the knuckles on his gnarled, hairy hands. His stiff wax jacket and knee-high boots seem to barely contain his barrel chest and bulging calves. But it's the sight of his face that freezes the breath in my throat.

This man has no face.

The front of his head is a smooth, pixelated blur, the eyes, nose, and mouth nothing more than dark smudges, stretched and warped into a permanent scream. It flickers and twitches like a broken screen, the smudges rearranging themselves into ever more grotesque configurations. The smudge of the nose moving to the forehead. The eyes creeping down the cheeks.

"She cooperating?" says a voice from across the room. A stocky man in a smaller wax jacket and matching knee-high boots stands in the doorway. He has no face either.

"Bird Howsley?" he says.

I'm so stunned to hear my name in this monster's mouth that I don't even think to lie. I nod once.

"She's cooperating," says the big man.

The little man walks across the room, his boots squeaking, the dissolved features of his faceless blur shifting and flickering as he moves, so that I always see the same angle, no matter what direction I'm looking from. It's like watching an eerie painting dissolve and reform.

"How do you know my name?" I feel blood from my nose pooling on top of my lip. I lift my hand to stop it dripping.

"A concerned citizen provided us with all the information we needed to find you, Miss Howsley," says the small man, standing next to his partner.

I shrink back into my bed, the soft, familiar sheets feeling suddenly bizarre and out of place. "What do you want?"

"I imagine a bright girl like you can work that out on her own." The small man produces a slate from an inside coat pocket and taps the side of his head with a long finger. "Where's the stone?"

My stomach drops. I try to keep my face impassive. "What stone?"

"I'd advise you not to play games with me, Miss Howsley. You are unlikely to win. Now I'll ask again: where is the stone that you stole from Axioma Nation's daughter yesterday?"

I must be taking too long to answer because the big man takes a swift step toward me and grabs my chin in his hand.

"I don't have it," I gasp. "It's gone."

His grip tightens. "Gone where?"

"I don't know!"

The big man turns my head to one side and backhands me with his other hand, sending me sprawling onto the bizarrely soft, familiar bed. Bright red spots appear on my white sheets as the blood already running from my nose splatters. Before I can right myself, his hand is around my face again.

"Gone where?"

"I don't know."

This time, he does me the courtesy of hitting the other side of my face.

"Alright, alright," says the little man. "Give it a minute. We're here to shake her up, not beat her to death."

I blink woozily. It feels as though my eyelids are operating independently from one another.

"Someone took it," I say through the blood in my mouth. A tooth near the back of my upper jaw wiggles.

"Who?" the little man asks sharply.

"His name was V."

"V?"

"No—wait, it was something else—" My mind swims feebly back to the night before.

Three? Four?

"Five."

"Five what?"

It sounds like the setup to some kind of joke. Knock knock. Who's there? Five. Five what? Fish alive? I shake my head, struggling to focus.

"I don't know. I was going to sell him the stone, but he stole it." The room sways nauseatingly around me.

"Where was this?"

"At the Waterhouse."

"And how do you know this 'Five'?"

"I don't."

The little man makes a few quick gestures at his slate, then turns his faceless head back up to me.

"Well, I'd say you are in a pretty bad spot, Miss Howsley."

I search for a trace of humanity in his blank, featureless void and find none.

"Our organization was hired to retrieve Miss Nation's necklace," he continues, "and unfortunately, we won't get paid unless we do. Miss Nation claims to have entered into an altercation with you at the docks two days ago, during which time you attempted to steal the necklace."

"I wasn't trying to steal it—"

The little man holds up a finger. "Additionally, we found a post linked to your biochip in an online forum, seeking information about the stone."

Shit. Stupid, stupid, stupid Bird.

"So it seems clear that you took it. And if what you say is true," he continues, "and you're unable to produce the stone... well, the way we see it, you have limited options."

Oh good. You have options.

"Option one: you find the item and return it to us. It seems unlikely that you'll be able to do that, as you have no idea who took it or how to find him." He makes another gesture at his slate. "Option two: you repay Miss Nation the full amount of the item. This comes to—" he consults his slate, "—fifty thousand UBC."

Fifty thousand?! I barely have time to register the shock of the number before he plows on.

"Option three—and this is where I imagine we'll be most likely to find a harmonious solution to this problem—we recoup payment from you in another form and transfer that to our employer."

I swallow hard. "What other form?"

He waves his hand dismissively. "Girl like you, young, in decent shape...sells quickly. And if not, well—" he steps back, and even through his faceless smear, I can tell he's looking me up and down, "—the parts look good. Could be sold separately."

The big man chuckles.

"So," says the little man, clasping his hands in front of him like he's finishing a meeting, "what will it be?"

I'm overwhelmed by the sudden feeling of falling, as though I was clinging to a cliff edge and my grip failed. This can't be happening. The Nations hired thugs to beat up a little girl? The room tilts sideways. A queasy feeling in my stomach wells up into my throat. I lean forward with my hands on my knees and vomit between my bare feet.

"Gods!" The little man jumps backward as it splatters onto his shoe. The big man says nothing, but as he steps away, I hear him retching.

And as they retreat, a clear path to the door opens up between them.

Without so much as pausing to wipe my mouth, I lunge toward it.

I don't remember running through the door, but I must have, because I'm over the threshold and barreling toward the kitchen, my bare feet pounding like a drum on the carpet in the hall. I hear shouting.

Flinging open the kitchen door, I take the outside stairs two at a time, past the smiling Zenith poster, feeling, rather than hearing, the big man behind me, gaining on me, reaching out to catch hold of my coat.

I fling myself over the edge of the last flight of stairs and drop six feet onto the street.

Shoes. Where are your shoes?

Splintering pain shoots up my legs as I land on bare feet, and I catch myself with one hand against the pavement. Limping, I turn right, away from the harbor, and begin shoving my way through the crowd of morning commuters until I reach the little bakery on the corner. I glance back over my shoulder, scanning for the creeps, then duck into the shop, pulling my bandana over my nose, my collar up, and my hood on.

The heat and smell of warm bread overwhelm me as I walk in. I turn my face away from the girl behind the counter, who doesn't bother to look up from her slate, and walk briskly to the back. Squatting behind a tall wooden shelf piled high with loaves so fresh I can feel the heat still radiating off them, I heave in great lungfuls of yeasty air and strain to hear over the muffled pounding of rolling pins and the roaring of massive oven fires in the kitchen behind me.

A minute passes. Two minutes. The pain in my shins recedes. I stand up and slowly peer around the shelf. The girl behind the counter is still absorbed in her slate. There's no one else in the shop.

Back in the brisk air of the street, I glance in both directions. Seeing no trace of the creeps, I turn left, toward the harbor, my bare feet tender on the cold, hard concrete.

I keep my head down and my bandana on, pulling my collar higher and my hood closer around my battered face as I walk. Blood is still pouring from my nose, and my left eye stings in the cold air. I remember how terrible I thought I looked in the mirror this morning and almost laugh out loud.

Sargo's house comes into view as I round the last corner by the harbor. I check the time.

>>> *1007*

He should be teaching. Glancing over my shoulder, I step over the low wall into Blenny's scraggly veg patch and slip around the side of the house to the back door. Blenny usually leaves it unlocked, and I heave a sigh of relief as the knob turns easily in my hand.

The house is dim, the smell of old cooking and spilled grog

leaching out of every soft surface. I pause, listening. No sound of Blenny's shambling footsteps, no sign of Sargo. I walk quietly to the front room and scoop up my pack, still on the floor by the sofa where I left it less than twelve hours ago. Then I head upstairs to Sargo's room.

I open the door and nearly drop my pack as I come face-to-face with him.

"Bird!" he says in surprise, "What're you—" His eyes widen. "Your face."

"I—I didn't think you'd be here. Why aren't you teaching?"

"The conditions weren't good. Too windy. We canceled class." He stares at me. "What…happened?"

I let go of my pack. I'm going to have to tell Sargo what I've done. More than anything else that's happened today, this frightens me. I feel a drop of blood trembling at the top of my lip and bring my hand up to stop it, too late. It lands on the floor between our feet with an almost inaudible plop.

"Sorry," I murmur, looking down and noting my filthy bare feet for the second time that morning.

"What happened to your shoes?" The alarm in his voice mounts.

All I can do is shrug.

"Bathroom," he says, and I feel his firm hand on my shoulder. "Now."

chapter
ten

SITTING on the edge of Blenny's scrap metal bathtub, I try not to look at my face in the mirror on the opposite wall.

My left eye, already swelling shut, is blossoming an extravagant green and purple bruise. My eyebrow is split, and I hold toilet paper to my nose to stop the blood from seeping from one nostril. I'm too scared to tongue the loose tooth in the back of my mouth, but the dull ache in my jaw tells me it probably doesn't look good back there.

Sargo gently dabs my split eyebrow with something cool that smells so strongly of mint and citrus it make my eyes water. Everywhere he dabs, my skin prickles. I flinch as he touches a tender spot.

"Sorry," he says softly.

"It's okay." My voice comes out in a hoarse whisper. I don't know why we're both whispering. The only other sounds in the room are our quiet breathing and the slow and steady plink of water from a tap.

I focus on the wall behind his shoulder. "I'm in trouble, Sargo."

"That seems clear," he says. "Close your eyes."

I do, wincing.

"Hurts?"

I nod.

"I'm going to put some ice on it."

I hear the soft clink of ice in a fabric bag, then feel his breath close to my face. I imagine his brow furrowing as he touches the pack to my cheek. The cold sends a shiver through me and I pull away.

"Okay?"

I nod, sitting up straighter. "Just startled me."

He gently places the pack against my face again and I reach up my hand to hold it there. I sit with my eyes closed, listening to the soft rustle and clink of Sargo putting away the first aid kit.

"How do you know how to do all this stuff?" I ask.

"I had to get trained in first aid when I started teaching."

I hear the click of a cabinet door closing, then I sense him sitting next to me on the tub.

"What happened?" he asks finally. "Who...did this?"

I can feel his eyes on the side of my face, but I can't look at him. Keeping my eyes closed, I mumble my way through the events of the last twenty-four hours. Shale. My plan to get coin for the mainsail. Stealing the stone, Five, the club in the Flats, the two men. Everything.

Well, not everything. I leave out exactly how much grog I've been drinking, and that I've blacked out and woken up in a new place twice in the last week. I'm sure it's pretty self-evident that these were not the decisions of a sober person. Sargo is so quiet by the time I finish that I wonder if he's still there.

Finally, he speaks. "These men," he asks slowly, "did they... have faces?"

I snap open my eyes—well, the one that will open—and turn to him. "How did you know—?"

His jaw locks. "We have to go," he says.

"What?"

"We have to go." He stands up, throwing the bathroom door open. "Now!"

He's through the door before I can say anything else. My legs stand as though commanded by his voice and I stumble after him.

"Sargo, wait!" I follow him down the hall, still clutching the ice pack to my face, feeling like I'm in some kind of weird nightmare. "What's going on?"

"They'll follow you here." He ducks through the door into his room. "They're probably already on the way."

"Who?" I trip to a halt at his door and lean against the doorframe.

Sargo doesn't answer. He's on his knees, rifling through a large hamper in the corner of his room, stuffing clothes into his pack.

"They'll figure out we're friends," he says, "they'll come here."

"Who?! Who will come here?"

He glances over his shoulder at me and I see panic in his eyes. True fear. I've never seen Sargo look like that, ever. It's surreal and unsettling; like seeing Mama K cry.

"The Anonymity."

He snatches up his pack and goes to the bed, lies flat on his stomach, and pulls out a small box. "They control the black market in Brume. Haar dealers. Murderers. Really...just really bad guys, okay?" He rifles through the box, throwing a few more things into the pack.

"How do you know—"

"Just trust me! I know. My mom—Mama Gnamma owed them money. My uncle still does."

Mama G. Sargo's mom died because she owed someone money. She owed *these* guys money. She owed these guys money and they killed her. Her and Marlin.

The parts look good.

I swallow. "Blenny's debt. It's...with them?"

"Yeah. And they know who I am. They know where I live. They know everything about me. And if they find out I helped you—"

"Just tell them you haven't seen me!"

"They'll know, Bird. They always know."

"Tell them I took off! You don't need to be involved in this! I'm sorry I came here. I shouldn't have done, it was stupid."

"It's not your fault." His voice is shaking. "You didn't know."

I stand frozen in the doorway while he continues ransacking his room, stuffing things into his pack.

"This doesn't make sense," I say, "Electra's *mom* sent them."

His head whips around. "What? No. No way."

"They said they had an employer."

"I don't think Axioma Nation would do that. They probably just saw that post you made on the Net and decided to come after you. They're always skulking around the Net looking for some opportunity."

He continues throwing things into his pack. His alarm is beyond unsettling.

"Sargo, you're not listening to me. This doesn't need to involve you. I'll hide out at the Green, I'll figure something out. If they come here, just lie—"

"You can't lie to these guys," he mutters. "They always get the truth. You think your face looks bad?" He shakes his head. "Do you have everything you need?"

I look around, dazed, and spot my pack on the floor where I dropped it earlier. My hand goes to my hair. "My hat," I murmur.

"Your *hat?* Come on Bird, focus. Do you have your pack? Your slate?"

Holding the ice pack to my face with one hand, I struggle into my pack with the other. Sargo flings a pair of shoes at me, and I barely catch them one-handed.

"Where are we going?"

"I don't know. We just need to get somewhere safe for a while. I need to think."

I put down the ice pack and pull the too-big shoes on, my mind racing. We can't go back to my house. There's no way I can go back to campus, and finding either of my moms at work is out of the question. Where can we go? Where is safe?

Panga.

"Sargo!" I gasp.

But Sargo is shaking his head as though he knows what I'm about to say.

"I already thought about it, Bird. Blenny would know that's where we'll go. And if the Anonymity comes here, he won't cover for us. He'll send them right to the harbor."

"What if we're not *in* the harbor?" I press, the idea forming in my mind as I speak, the pieces of my shattered plan reassembling themselves in real time. "What if we leave? On *Panga*. If we go now, we'll have a decent head start."

Sargo is shaking his head again. "No, Bird. No! Are you listening to yourself? What you're suggesting is illegal."

"And what *you're* suggesting is that we wait around to get murdered!"

He shakes his head. "Even if I was going to entertain the notion of breaking the law, leaving would be incredibly stupid. The mainsail is not reliable—"

I toss my head impatiently. "You use that sail all the time! How many times have you sailed *Panga* around the bay? Fifty? A hundred? You've taken her out sailing almost every weekend since I met you! Why should this be any different?"

"Because sailing around the bay isn't the same as sailing across the Salt!" he exclaims. "Think, Bird! This isn't like going out for a day sail and sandwiches! You can't just decide to cross the Salt on a whim! If the mainsail fails here we're close to home. Close to the harbor. We can call for help, come back to safety. Out there—" he waves an arm in the direction of the Salt, "—if something goes wrong, we have nowhere to go!"

"We already have nowhere to go! Those guys are coming *here!* What choice do we have? Where else can we go?"

Sargo seems adrift in the middle of the room. He clasps his hands on top of his head, looking around as though he might find an answer amongst his strewn possessions.

I catch his eye. "You know I'm right. If these guys are as bad as you say they are, then we can't stay in Brume."

A thousand thoughts fly behind his eyes. I remember the conversation we had two days ago. How his folks wanted to sail to Pocosín. How it was his dream as a kid. Finding his people. Deep down, deep deep down, I know he wants to go.

He stares at me for a long moment. "There's a point seventy miles south of here," he says finally. My heart skips. "With a cove on the other side. Naze. Where the old climate Settlement used to be. We could make for that. Anchor there. Hide out for a few days, I don't know. Have some time to think."

"And then what? We just...come back? Don't you think—"

"I don't know, Bird! This isn't some lark you can just...casually undertake. This is *serious.*"

"Have you *looked* at my face? I'm not a child. I don't need you to tell me when things are serious." I take a deep breath. "We should go to Alluvium."

"Alluvium?" He raises his eyebrows. "That's over two thousand miles from here."

Two thousand? I didn't know that, but I keep my face from showing my surprise.

"The further away the better."

His eyes narrow. For a long moment, we watch each other. Then he says, "We'll make for Naze. And then...we'll talk." He slings his pack over his shoulder and walks silently out of the room.

Even though nobody else is home, I find myself holding my breath as we creep down the stairs. The house is quiet but for the creaking of our steps. I'm halfway to the bottom when the front door shakes with three loud knocks.

"Blenny Farr!" It's the voice of the man who feng-shuid my face. He pounds on the door again.

I freeze. Sargo puts a finger to his lips and gestures at me to keep going. I creep down the last five steps like I'm trying not to wake the dead, crouching to stay out of sight below the front window. At the bottom of the stairs, we turn right and, staying low, slink to the kitchen. The door knob rattles behind us.

"Blenny Farr! We have some questions for you regarding the whereabouts of Miss Bird Howsley." The reedy voice of the big man's little partner. "Our sources indicate that she is friends with your nephew, Sargo Paz."

"Come on, Blenny. Open the door. We know who you are."

In the kitchen, Sargo and I gently turn the knob on the back door. It opens with a squeak, and I flinch, listening over the pounding of blood in my ears for some indication that we've been heard. It doesn't come.

My nerves sizzle as we step into the alley behind the house, turn right and head for the main street. At any moment, those faceless creeps will hear us. At any moment, they'll appear around the corner. Every step seems to echo tenfold as we slink down the alley, hugging the fence. They'll hear us. There's no way they won't hear us.

We make it to the street, glance in both directions, and run.

The docks are quiet except for a few oyster farmers hauling in their morning catch. Walking down the pier toward *Panga* as quickly as we can, we try not to glance over our shoulders, try not to call attention to ourselves. The skiff has been hauled out of the water and stowed on *Panga*'s bow.

"Should we leave the skiff?" I whisper.

Sargo shakes his head. "We'll take it with us. There's no dock at Naze. It's just a cove. If we need to go ashore, we'll need the skiff."

He swings himself over the rail and flips on *Panga*'s motor wordlessly, while I untie the dock lines with trembling hands. I'm so filled with adrenaline I barely register the pain in my chewed-up fingertips. I lean back on the stern line with all my weight to point *Panga's* bow out into the channel, then give the boat a hard push and hop over the rail onto her deck as she glides away from the dock.

When we come to the end of the channel and reach open water, I clamber onto the bow and pull down on the main halyard as hard as I can to raise the mainsail. I keep pulling, hand over hand as the sail slowly ascends the mast, a huge white canvas, translucent in the sunlight, curved like a wing against the sky.

Sargo is steering with one hand and loosening the main sheet with the other when I climb back into the cockpit. The boom swings to starboard and the mainsail snaps open.

Sudden quiet envelops us as Sargo flips off the motor and the boat becomes sail-powered. I gaze back over the stern at Brume diminishing behind us, the hush of water against the hull and the creak of the mast the only sounds. The masts in the harbor grow smaller and smaller, until they look like matchsticks against the green hills. The solar panels and fog traps and little houses blur together and fade into the trees. Way up in the hill behind the harbor, the buildings of Azimuth campus and Zenith glint in the sun. Kids are in class up there right now. People are at work. I feel like I'm looking back at Brume through a window.

Mama K's face appears before my eyes.

"Oh!" I cover my mouth with my hand. "I was supposed to be home for dinner."

Sargo snorts. "You're welcome to swim," he says from the helm, not taking his eyes off the horizon.

A wave of cold panic. My moms. Those men. Will they go after my moms? Instinctively, I tap my temple to pull up Messenger and compose a hasty message.

>>> GONE TO FIND SHALE. I'M OKAY. PLEASE LEAVE THE HOUSE. YOU ARE NOT SAFE THERE.

My fingers are about to make the send gesture when something stops me. I can't send this. It contains location metadata. If those Anonymity guys come for my moms, this message will give them the exact coordinates of my last known location and the exact time I was there. I stare at the blinking cursor.

I can't just leave without telling my moms. Can I? What will they do when I don't come home?

What would the Anonymity do to them to get information about your whereabouts?

My fingers hover in the air. Then I delete the message and close Messenger. It's safer for them if they don't know. I pull my hood on and turn to face the bow. In front of the boat, the Salt stretches to the horizon like a glittering, silver wasteland.

We're leaving Brume. My mind bends to accept that new reality. I won't be going home for dinner, not for a long time.

chapter
eleven

NIGHT IS FALLING, and waves have been building since we left Brume. The Salt, violet in the fading light, roils with confused swells that pick us up, turn us sideways, and throw us down, over, and over, and over. There's no rhythm to it, no rhyme or reason. The chaos is almost monotonous.

My stomach heaves with each queasy tilt of the ship. My head aches and my eyes feel heavy. A kind of malaise is settling over me, a heaviness like the flu. I slump in the cockpit, staring over the side at the horizon. Sargo told me if I keep my eye on the horizon, I won't get sick. It doesn't seem to be working.

The swell is big out here; *Panga* feels like a toy duck in a bathtub. We're twenty miles from Brume now, and ten miles offshore. Further into the Salt than I've ever been. There's nowhere to anchor between here and Naze, another fifty miles south. Nowhere to stop. No turning back. I feel helpless, at the mercy of the water. I eye the rapidly sinking sun with apprehension and turn over my shoulder to Sargo.

"Is this...safe? I've never sailed at night before."

His face is determined. He readjusts his grip on the helm. "Como la Sal, por lo que el marinero," he says.

I blink. "What does that mean?"

"'As the Salt, so the sailor.' Something Mama Marlin used to tell me. When the weather was bad and I was scared, or if the wind died completely and I was frustrated, she would say 'como la Sal, por lo que el marinero, mijo.' It means…you can't change the wind. You can't change the waves. You can only change yourself and your ship. You have to sail in the conditions you're given. You have to find a way to make it work."

I've never heard him speak the southern language before. I let the words sink in as I turn my gaze back over the water. *As the Salt, so the sailor.* It reminds me of something. Something my mom used to say, but I can't remember the exact phrasing.

"I didn't know you spoke the southern language," I say finally.

"I don't. It's the only thing I know how to say. Well…that and one other thing."

"What's that?"

"*'Te tengo.'* Means *'I've got you.'* That's what she would say when I was scared. *'Te tengo, mijo.'*"

A phrase pops into my head as if from nowhere, bringing with it an unsettling sense of deja vu.

We drink from our own creek.

That's the phrase I was trying to remember—it's something Mama K used to say. But I'm sure I've heard it somewhere else recently. Where? In a dream? The image of a boy swims before my eyes. A boy in a creek. I blink, and it's gone.

"Mama K used to say *'We drink from our own creek.'*" I tell Sargo. "I guess it's kind of the same as your *'As the Salt'* thing. Only less…uplifting."

"Less uplifting? Why's that?"

"Just kind of always felt like she was saying 'you get what you get.' Like you're stuck with whatever you start with. You can't change it. Maybe that's why I always felt so stuck in Brume."

"Brume's not such a bad place to be stuck."

I look over the side at the roiling swell, feeling tiny and fragile and already far from home.

"Yeah…I know."

The boat rolls again and my stomach heaves. I quickly turn around and focus my eyes straight out, but it's so dark now I can't even make out the horizon. With nothing to anchor me, there's no way to combat the nausea.

"Anyway, what I was trying to say is I think we'll be fine," Sargo says. "The waves won't get worse just because it's dark."

He's right, like he usually is. The Salt doesn't care if it's day or night. Nothing changes as the light disappears except that now we can't *see* the massive waves barreling all around us. In a way, it's almost better.

Almost.

We pull our hoods tight against the chilly fog and huddle in *Panga's* tiny cockpit, wedging ourselves into the corners, bracing our feet against winches and cleats, fighting off sleep. It's so dark, I can't even see my own hands. I feel completely untethered from reality, like I'm tumbling through a void. For a long time, the roar of wind and rushing water against the hull is the only indication that anything is out there at all.

In the early hours of the morning, the wind begins to drop, and the swell calms. *Panga* rolls more gently, almost predictably, over the waves. Now that we're away from Brume, the air is fogless, but a murky brown smog is beginning to creep around its edges.

"We'll be around the point by sunrise," croaks Sargo.

I struggle to make out his face in the graying dawn light. I suppose he must look as tired as I feel. He touches his brow to check a map.

"There's a cove on the other side of the point. We can drop anchor and rest for a few hours."

"What about those guys? The...Anonymity guys. Won't they catch up?"

"They probably haven't figured out we've left yet. And *Panga* is quick. I think we'll be safe for a little while."

Dawn is breaking as we round the tip of the point at Naze and tuck into the protected cove just beyond. I stretch the ache of cold and tiredness out of my limbs and touch my injured face gingerly with my fingertips. It's stiff and sore, my eye swollen nearly shut. My stomach feels more settled, but the seasickness has left me with a flu-like feeling that I can't shake.

We climb onto the bow to put the sails away and drop the anchor, then Sargo wordlessly retreats to the cockpit. Something's wrong—he's tense and silent—but I too feel weak and exhausted to find out what.

Instead, I stand on the bow and look around. We're surrounded on three sides by a steep ridge of rock, bare but for a few cacti and Salt scrubs clinging to life against the cliff. Inside the lee of the point, the water is as smooth as glass. Except for the call of one lonely bird, the air is still.

I turn around and scan the open water behind us. I see no sails on the horizon, no skiffs in pursuit. The sky is a sickly yellow-brown. Hard to believe that less than a hundred miles south of Brume, this is what it's like. And this isn't even the worst of it.

I run my index fingers over the gnawed-up skin around my thumbnails, then shove my hand into my pocket to keep myself from chewing them. Calm settles over me like a gentle gray fog. *Is it calm?* I ask myself, *or is it exhaustion?* Probably exhaustion.

On the bow, next to the skiff, there's a big canvas bag with a spare sail stuffed inside it. I curl myself into it and close my eyes.

In my dreams, men without faces climb out of the water and drag me over the side of the boat, pulling me down into the black, cold squeeze of the deep.

I doze in snatches as the sun slowly warms the deck and begins its slow progress across the sky. When, by mid-morning, the heat becomes too much to bear I wake, sweating through my clothes. I roll out of the sail bag and stagger back to the cockpit, my swollen-shut eye wreaking havoc on my depth perception. Sargo is asleep on the starboard sofa in the main cabin below.

I fill the kettle and make some tea. It's the only thing we have on board that even remotely resembles food, and the smell of orange and cinnamon twists my stomach into grumbling knots.

When was the last time you ate? I'm pretty sure you've been running on booze for three strait days.

Sargo stirs as I'm pouring two cups of tea. I hand one to him and greet him with, "We need food."

He sips his tea, his face hollow. "I'll put the fishing line out."

I scrunch my face. For all his skills as a sailor, I know for a fact that Sargo has never caught a fish. It's not his fault. There are barely any fish left in the Salt to catch.

"I was thinking we should go ashore," I say. "We might find some edible plants or something. Or...jackrats, maybe."

He makes a face. *"Jackrats?* You're going to *eat* jackrats?"

"I don't know! I'm trying to be proactive here."

He shakes his head. "We can't go ashore. We don't know what might be up there."

"What are you *talking* about?" I shake my head, incredulous. "There's *nothing* up there. The remains of the climate Settlement, and everyone who lived in that died in the pandemic."

"I said *no*, Bird." His tone is so sharp it jolts me into silence. He eyes me for a long moment. "We should fish first," he says finally. "If that doesn't work...then we'll talk."

I breathe out hard and slow through my nose. I don't like the idea of sitting around here, wasting time, trying to catch fish that don't exist. But I can tell Sargo's not budging on this.

"Fine. One hour."

Sargo sets the fishing pole with a weighted lure and casts it over the side of the boat. With the sun beating down, it's too hot for me in the cockpit, so I go below to find something to do. I spot our packs lying by the navigation table. If we end up going ashore —*when* we end up going ashore—we'll need them, so I dump out what's in them and try to think about what might be useful to take with us. I dig a couple of short knives out of a drawer in the galley. I'm not sure yet what I plan to do with them. Harvest cactus, I suppose. Or...murder jackrats.

I find Sargo's pair of nox in a drawer at the navigation table. They look old—probably belonged to his great-great-grandfather.

Big, heavy things with glass lenses and a canvas neck strap. Not terribly easy to carry, but necessary if you want to see stuff that's far away. For all the advances in biochip technology that were made before the pandemic, they never figured out how to manipulate eyesight. No zooming in or 'enhancing.' I'm not sure why. We learned about it at Azimuth, but I wasn't really paying attention. In order to get that stuff to work you'd need to hook up ocular nerves to...other nerves and...stuff like that...

You're out of your element here.

Anyway, nox are useful.

I tuck them into Sargo's pack and close the navigation table drawer.

An hour later I pop my head back up into the cockpit. Sargo sits with the rod across his lap, looking murderous. The hook is empty.

"Get anything?"

He glares at me in silence.

The air between us crackles as we prepare to go ashore. Sargo is still moody. We move silently around each other in a cabin that's too small for two people who aren't speaking to each other. I hand Sargo his pack, and he takes it wordlessly. Together we lift the skiff from the bow and drop it over the side into the water, then hop into it.

Glancing back at *Panga* as we speed away from her in the skiff, I feel a wave of apprehension. She's just sitting in the middle of the bay, completely exposed.

How the hell do you hide a sailboat?

If the Anonymity catches up to us before we get back, they'll find *Panga* and that will be it. They could board her and wait to ambush us, or worse, sink her. The look on Sargo's face tells me he's thinking the same thing.

"We'll be quick," I say, peeking at him.

He doesn't respond.

We land the skiff on a small spit of sand at the top of the bay and haul it up the beach to keep it out of the rising tide. It's a steep climb from the beach to the top of the surrounding ridge and we stop several times to rest. I use my short kitchen knife to cut a few leaves from a cactus. The spines are lethal, but when I snap open the thick, tough hide, the flesh inside is green and juicy. I put the leaves in my pack.

"You sure we can eat that?" asks Sargo bluntly.

I shrug. "I think so."

I don't know what makes me think that. Maybe it's residual knowledge from watching Mama K in the garden? She was always nagging me about how important it is to learn how to grow your own food. *'Dig into the future!'* Another Zenith aphorism.

Everyone in Brume has a garden or a spot in the community plot. Everyone provides at least a portion of their own food. Mama K used to teach horticulture classes during the summer at Azimuth. I never paid much attention, but I guess some of it must have gotten through.

I feel a pang in my chest and realize I'm chewing my thumbnail again.

Stop thinking about your moms.

We stop at a small outcropping near the top of the ridge to look back across the Salt for pursuing boats. I feel a small knot loosen in my chest when there are no other sails on the Salt that we can see.

I squint the other way: inland, across the hard, red earth. Looking for...what, exactly? Dust clouds, I suppose. Some indicator that someone is following us by land.

"They won't come by land," says Sargo, as though reading my thoughts.

I turn to him. "You sure?"

"There's no infrastructure anymore for travel by land or air. It was all either destroyed by climate disasters or never got finished before the pandemic. And there's no fresh water on land. Hasn't been for almost a century. At least on the Salt, if you have a watermaker, you can desalinate the saltwater to make desal. In the State, there's nothing."

We reach the top of the hill and crest the ridge. It feels like a thousand degrees, but it's probably only a hundred. The red, rocky earth radiates heat and the only other signs of life apart from the bugs zinging in and out of our ears are the leathery cacti and some scraggly Salt scrubs. We haven't so much as heard a jackrat.

I take a seat against a rock, turn my head and look south. The coastline turns black and ugly pretty quickly after Naze. A bleak, charred stretch of cliff, barely recovered from the fires that burned this part of the world for almost a century. Fire Season.

"Bird!"

Sargo's voice is urgent. I crane my neck to squint up at him. He's looking over the top of the ridge and down the other side into the inland valley. I scramble up next to him and follow his pointed finger.

"Is that...?"

"The old Settlement." He hands me the nox and I lift them to my eyes.

Sprawling across the valley floor like junk spilled from a box is the remains of the Naze climate settlement. Miles and miles of tents, shacks, and lean-tos assembled from scrap; thousands of those big old electric vehicles that people used to live in. All of it run-down, covered in sand, and falling apart. Salt scrubs and saltnut trees have reclaimed parts of the space, sprouting through the windows of EVs, and splitting the fabric of tents. It stretches all the way to the horizon at the bottom of the valley, a river of scrap metal, wood, and canvas.

"I can't believe all this stuff is still here," I murmur.

"Yeah," he says quietly. "It's bigger than I thought."

"How many refugees were here? Before the pandemic"

"You're supposed to call them 'Settlers,' not refugees. And...I don't know. Millions?"

"Jesus."

"*Gods*," Sargo corrects me.

I shoot him a look. "Seriously? You're looking at a graveyard millions of people deep, and you're going to be pedantic about political correctness?"

"Words matter, Bird."

"Jesus, Allah, Buddha, what's the difference? It's not like any of them are actually up there. And if they are, they clearly don't give a shit about any of us."

He observes the valley quietly. "It's not about whether they're up there. It's about respecting other people's beliefs. That's what the Polytheistic Revolution was about."

I take back the nox. "I'll respect the 'gods' when they do something to earn my respect."

"It doesn't matter if you respect the gods," says Sargo. "It's about respecting the people who believe in them. By singling out Jesus as an expletive, you're actually disrespecting people who believe in other deities. It belittles the—"

I lift a hand to shut him up. "I'm gonna be honest: they're just words to me. And 'God dammit' is a lot more satisfying to say out loud when you stub your toe than 'gods'."

Lifting the nox to my eyes and surveying the ruined settlement, I feel a kind of deep, terrifying sadness. It's just so big. We learned about climate settlements at Azimuth. But seeing it right in front of you like this, the scale kind of knocks you back. Millions of people. Living on top of each other. No way to quarantine. No boats to escape into the Salt. The virus decimated places like this.

I lower the nox. "Is it disrespectful to scavenge shit from the dead?"

"Yes. Hugely."

"Do we have a choice?"

Sargo scratches at the shadow of hair coming in around his jaw, looking hesitant.

"Maybe there's cans of food or something," I prod.

He sighs and nods slowly. "Okay."

We're halfway down the ridge into the valley when something catches my eye. A flash of light from one of the huts closest to the perimeter of the settlement, so brief that I'm sure I've imagined it. A few paces later, it happens again.

I pause. It's probably just the sun reflecting off an old window. Keeping still, I watch the spot where I thought I saw the light. Another flash.

"Sargo," I whisper, "give me the nox."

He hands them over and I press them to my eyes and focus them on the spot. My stomach drops.

"There's a person."

"*What?* No. No there isn't."

"Yes there is! Next to that hut, behind the barrel. They're using nox. I can see the sun reflecting off the lenses."

I hand the nox back to Sargo. He presses them to his eyes and I direct him to the spot.

He goes still. "We should get out of here."

"Wait."

"Bird—"

"Just wait!" I hiss. "Something about that person seemed off to me."

I hold my hand out again for the nox and Sargo hands them over with an irritated sigh. I scan back down to the hut.

"It's a kid!"

"A kid?"

"Yeah. A little boy. He's really small. He doesn't exactly look...threatening."

I scan the tents and huts closest to us, taking each one in more carefully this time. About twenty yards from the perimeter of the Settlement, there's a small circle of dwellings that catches my eye. The dwellings are different from the others around them. Less falling apart, less covered in sand. My eyes come to rest on a hut on the far side of the circle. It's slightly larger than the others, with a fence of sticks and barbed wire around it. On the back side of the hut, partially obscured, I catch a glimpse of green leaves.

"There's *people* down there," I murmur. "Look." I had Sargo the nox. "I think they have a garden."

"That's not possible." He squints through the lenses. "There's no people here. Everyone died. And there's no water. You can't have a garden without water."

"Well, it looks like they do. Maybe they have veg. Maybe they'd be willing to trade."

"Trade? No way. Trade what?" He stuffs the nox into his pack and hoists it onto his shoulders. "This is crazy. I'm going back to the boat."

My irritation at his cautious behavior resurfaces. *Typical Sargo.* "Why do you just assume these people are dangerous? We don't know anything about them."

"I don't know, Bird, but it doesn't seem like a terrible idea to be careful, does it?" His tone rises to match mine.

"I have a good feeling about it."

"A *feeling?* We can't make decisions based on your feelings."

"Oh, but we can make them based on yours?"

"I don't make decisions based on my feelings, Bird. But if I did, you know what? It would be fine. Because my feelings are sound. Your feelings are unreliable. *You* are unreliable."

I stare at him in disbelief. Then I hitch my pack higher on my shoulders. "You know what? Fine. Go back. But I don't think these people are going to hurt us. I'm going down there." I shove him out of my way.

"Bird. *Bird!*" His hissed cries fade over my shoulder as I stalk furiously down the ridge.

A few people come out of their homes as I approach, shielding their eyes from the sun and watching me with silent, expression-less faces. My pulse begins to quicken. This is supposed to be a ghost town. I sure as Salt hope the ghosts are friendly.

Instinctively, I pull my bandana up to cover the lower half of my face. At the edge of the circle of huts, I stop. Four or five people, including the little boy with the nox, stand in front of me. I begin to raise my hand in greeting, but something stops me. A feeling. Instead, I touch my two middle fingers to my brow. To my surprise, they all return the gesture.

Where did that come from?

It's not a greeting we use in Brume. I must have read about it somewhere. A history class at Azimuth maybe.

"Uh, sorry for…intruding," I say. "We're in need of food."

The sun-beaten faces remain expressionless, hard, and unreadable.

"We're able to trade," I continue hesitantly.

"Trade what?" A small man steps forward from the middle of the group. He's shorter than me, with a spare frame and a ruddy face flecked with white sunspots.

Good question.

"We have parts," I say, thinking fast. "Spare parts for a sailboat."

"No sailboats here," says the man. "What else you got?"

"Well, not just parts for boats. We have…" I rack my brain. What does Sargo keep aboard *Panga*? Lots of stuff. He has at least two of every nut, bolt, and screw.

"Pumps, hoses, lines, filters," I continue, "uh, a desalinator—"

The man perks up. "What kind of desalinator?"

"A…small one?" I have no idea. "Wait!" I hold up my finger to him and tap behind my ear to activate the radio in my chip. "Sargo?"

The man narrows his eyes at me and I give him an apologetic smile. "Just wait one second."

"Bird?" Sargo's voice buzzes in my ear.

"Hey! Sargo, they want to trade. They want to know what kind of desalinator we have."

"We're not giving them our desalinator!"

"No, obviously not! But what about spare parts?"

He's quiet. Then, "It's a 10L. I made it out of scrap. I have a spare filter and a pump."

I relay this information to the man, who nods. "We can offer bread and a few veg in exchange for the filter," he says. "Don't have much more'n that."

"That filter is worth at least a hundred coin!" says Sargo when I tell him this.

"Well, it's all they've got. Look," I whisper, turning my back to the man again, "we're not exactly in a position to be demanding here. Either we take what they have, or we live on tea for the next week."

"We can fish!" Sargo exclaims impatiently.

"Come on, Sargo!" I fire back. "Do you really think we're going to catch anything?"

He's silent. I turn around and address the man again. "We'll take whatever you've got. Thank you."

chapter
twelve

SARGO and I climb down the ridge toward the Settlement with *Panga's* spare desalinator filter in Sargo's pack. It was over an hour of trudging in the baking sun all the way to *Panga* and back, and I feel lightheaded and hollow.

The small man I spoke to earlier meets us at the perimeter, and we cross through the circle of dwellings toward the hut with the garden on the other side of the compound.

We're nearly to the fence when the air rends with a cannonade of barking and a flash of brown and white shoots from under the hut like a bullet. An enormous doggerel tears toward us, its eyes rimmed white, a ridge of hair bristling like a mohawk from the top of its massive head to the tip of its tail.

My insides become water. I stumble backward and feel Sargo catch me under the elbow. At the fence, the doggerel stops short, yanked back on its hind legs by a length of heavy chain around its neck. It stands as tall as me, clawing at the fence with paws the size of my hand, flecks of white spittle spattering from its jaws. Its eyes, I can see now, are startling. Not *rimmed* with white: so blue they *are* almost white.

"Git back!"

The man grabs a hefty stick that's leaning against the fence and clobbers the doggerel around the head with it. It yelps and scurries away from the fence. Apparently not satisfied, the man flings the stick after it, catching it on the hindquarters and eliciting another yelp as it slinks under the hut with its tail tucked. He stalks through a gap in the fence and motions for us to follow him.

I hesitate. "Can it…get us?"

Shaking his head, he holds out his hand for our packs. I carefully step through the fence and hand mine over, and he wordlessly stoops and begins to fill it with greens. I glance at the dog. It lies flat against the ground under the hut, its wide, fearful eyes fixed on the man.

"Your doggerel?"

He grunts and shakes his head, pulling an anemic carrot up out of the dirt. "Belonged to the girl who used to live here." He indicates the hut.

"Where is she?"

"Died six days ago. Shame. Wasn't much older than you. She used to tend the garden. Dog's always been a menace, but the girl did a fine job with the veg so we let it slide. Now she's gone, all anyone wants to do is put the damn thing out of its misery, but no one can get near enough to get it done."

"You mean kill it?" Sargo's voice is disturbed.

The man nods.

I can't say I'm surprised. No one keeps pets, even in Harbor Cities; the cost to feed and water them is just too high. I'm actually surprised to see a dog at all; I thought they had all died in the pandemic. Most of the domesticated animals did. Most of the wild ones went extinct long before that.

"What'll happen to it?" asks Sargo.

"Well, we stopped feeding her four days ago," says the man matter-of-factly. "Only a matter of time til she starves."

I watch the miserable thing cowering under the hut. "Couldn't she be useful as a guard dog?"

"A guard against what?" The man gestures at the wasted red terrain around us. "No one bothering us out here. 'Cept you two."

He disappears into the hut. I gaze at the dog, noting the ribs and hips poking through her filthy coat. The sadness in her blue-white eyes is so profound that I have to look away.

The man emerges with two bundles of cloth and pulls back a corner of one to show me a loaf of bread. I don't recognize it as the bread from home—it's almost flat and looks pale and spongy. Still, it's warm, and the steam that rises from it is rich.

"Thank you."

I tuck the bundle into my pack along with the carrots, the greens, and a bunch of scraggly orange things that I don't recognize. It's more than I thought we would get. Sargo seems somewhat placated, nodding gratefully as he hands over the filter.

The man turns it over in his hands, inspecting it. "Looks to be in good shape."

"It is," says Sargo.

More people have joined the small crowd to watch us leave by the time we walk back to the other side of the Settlement. I stop at the perimeter and turn back toward the assembled Settlers. I don't know why, but I feel compelled to perform the gesture again—touching my fingers to my brow and bowing my head. Again, they all return it. The back of my neck prickles with a bizarre sense of deja vu.

Sargo gives me a quizzical look. "What's that all about?"

"I don't...know," I say under my breath. Sweat trickles down the center of my chest. I drag my forearm across my head. Too hot.

"Where'd you learn that?"

I can't help but give him some snark. "I guess it was just...a feeling."

My eyes meet those of a woman standing near the front of the crowd. She has the squat, saggy-skinned figure of a woman who was once very plump. Big, strong arms and a red, sweaty face surrounded by a spray of frizzy, graying hair. Something about her is familiar. As our eyes meet, a spark passes between us. She's looking at me like she knows me.

I dart my eyes away, taking in the rest of the faces, the tents and huts, the EVs. A twisted old saltnut tree, a creek. Familiar. All of it. Where have I seen this all before?

Fife.

The name comes to me from nowhere. My mind clutches at it, tries to grasp it, to turn it over and examine it, but like a dream, it's already evaporating. It slips away like water through my fingers. Blue eyes. A little girl. I'm leaving something very important behind—

The heat beating through my thick hood is suddenly unbearable. I can't breathe. I tug the bandana away from my nose and mouth and double over with my hands on my knees, spinning. I close my eyes, but I can't shut that image out of my head. Blue eyes. A little girl. A profound sadness.

You left her behind.

The crowd parts to let me through as I stride back across the perimeter. The man we traded the filter to stands exactly where we left him, the filter still in his hand. He watches me approach the garden with a wary eye. I stop well back from the fence. From under the hut comes a low, menacing growl. I hear Sargo's footsteps pounding up behind me.

"Forget something?" says the man.

"I'll take the dog."

The man tilts up his chin, regarding me with unmitigated suspicion.

"She's a burden to you," I continue. "You said so yourself. If you're just going to let her starve, you might as well give her to me. I'd be doing you a favor."

"Bird, what are you doing?" Sargo grabs me hard by the shoulder and pulls me around.

"I'm taking the dog."

"What?! No way. This is not our problem. Just let it go."

I shake my head. "I'm making it my problem."

"No, Bird, this is crazy."

"I'm not leaving her behind!" A confusing ball of tears rises behind my face and I whirl around and face the man to keep Sargo from seeing them.

I left her behind. I left Fife behind. I don't know what it means but suddenly I know it as certainly as I know my own name. I left her behind.

The man is still watching me with narrow eyes.

"Do we have a deal?" I demand.

He shrugs. "Her chain hooks up in the back. Good luck."

Sargo grabs at my arm but I shake him off and march around the fence to the back of the hut.

"Bird, what the hell are you doing?" he hisses, keeping step with me. "Be sensible! What are we going to do with a dog? How will we feed it? We can barely feed ourselves."

Ignoring him, I look around for the end of the chain. I spot it looped around a metal pole sticking out of the ground and stoop to pick it up.

"I don't know. But we'll figure it out. We have transport. We have coin. We can take her off these people's hands. We'd be helping them and helping her."

"We don't need to be helping anyone! We need to help ourselves! Put on your own mask first, remember?"

"Don't quote that shit at me! *'Brume Pride.' 'Put on your own mask first.'* I'm so tired of hearing it!"

"You're acting insane. I get that you're trying to do something nice, but…" he lowers his voice, "*think* for a minute. This is reckless. This is exactly the kind of thing that got you into trouble with the Anonymity in the first place! This is what got you kicked out of Azimuth."

I glare at him, angry heat rising in my cheeks, furious that he would bring that up. Furious that he would throw that in my face.

Furious that he's right?

"These people have to drink from their own creek," he says quietly. "You can't change that."

The words stop the air in my chest. It's like hearing Mama K's voice channeled through him. *'We drink from our own creek.' 'Put on your own mask first.'* They're not just slogans. That's how we survive. By putting ourselves first. I know that. But standing here, with those pitiful blue eyes swimming around in my head, with that deep, confusing, familiar sense of loss like an open, salted wound in my chest, I can't just walk away.

I left Fife behind. I'm not leaving this dog too.

"You're right," I say, "I can't change these people's lives. But I can change *this.*" I shake the chain. I point under the hut. "I can fix *this.*"

He scoffs. "Oh, so now you want to fix things?"

"What is *that* supposed to mean?"

"When you were running around Brume, getting drunk, stealing from my friends, dragging me into your mess with the Anonymity, it seemed like you were hell-bent on destroying everything! But now, *now* you want to fix something?"

I stare at him. So *that's* what's been pissing him off all morning. "I said I was sorry! I know I screwed up! I only did it to get the coin for *your* mainsail! I was trying to help!"

"I never asked for your help!" he snaps. "And neither did these people. Look at where you are, Bird! You were expelled for reckless endangerment and intoxication! You're on the run from a criminal organization! You can't help anyone. You can't even help yourself! Who do you think you are?"

Angry tears choke me. "I'm someone who's trying to do the right thing!"

"Well, this isn't it!"

I wheel around and stalk away from him, but his words follow me like a toxic cloud.

Can't even help yourself.

When I drop to my hands and knees and peer under the hut, I see the chain snaking from my hand to the other side, where the dog lies facing away from me. Apparently, she hasn't noticed we're back here yet, or she's just too weak and tired to care anymore. I pull my pack off, dig out a bundle of bread, open it, and tear off a chunk.

"You're giving it our food?!" Sargo storms up behind me and snatches the loaf out of my hands. "My desal filter paid for this!"

I scramble to my feet and try to grab the bread back from him. "Do you hear yourself? *My* filter! *My* food! *'Brume pride.' 'Me first.'*"

His brow creases incredulously. "But it *was* my filter! This isn't the time to be having some existential crisis, Bird! This is about survival. You have to take this seriously! For once in your life, take something seriously!"

I pause, my hands around the loaf. "What do you mean, 'for once in my life'?"

"Oh come on! You know exactly what I mean."

"No..." I tilt my head and glare at him. "I don't."

"You treat everything like a joke! You make dumb mistakes all the time because you don't *think*. Maybe you got away with it in Brume, but you can't do that stuff out here. You have to think before you act. If you don't, the Salt will kill you. And if it doesn't, the Anonymity will. And frankly, right now, I don't care if they do."

I gape, stunned into silence. His words hang in the air between us like haar. He drops his hands, letting go of the bread. "I didn't mean—"

"You know what?" I shove the remains of the loaf hard into his chest. "I never asked for your help either. I told you in Brume that I would handle this on my own. You didn't have to come with me. *You* chose to leave. If you don't want to be here, why don't you take *your* food and get back on *your* boat and go home!"

He stares at me. I glare back. Then his eyes harden. "Fine." He shoves the loaf into his pack. "Fine." He swings the pack onto his shoulder. "Fine." He turns, and storms across the compound.

I stare after him. My hands, still clutching the chunk of bread, drop limply to my sides. The air leaves me in a rush.

What the hell are you going to do now?

Something cold and wet presses gently against the back of my hand, and I nearly jump out of my skin. The dog sits next to me,

her massive head level with my hips, face upturned, blue eyes
blazing out of her gaunt face like dying stars. Around one eye is a
large black and brown patch like some kind of mockery of a pirate
costume. The other side of her face is white, I assume, under the
filth. Her ears lay loose against the sides of her head. Big brown
splotches paint the rest of her skinny, grubby body. Up close, she's
actually kind of cute. Big. Scary. But cute.

She nudges my hand again and I let the chunk of bread fall to
the ground. She pounces on it, snarfs it down, and looks back up
at me, licking her chops. A small smile turns the corners of my
lips as I stretch out my hand to pet the top of her head.

With a snarl, she lunges.

"Jesus!"

Her jaws close around my hand, and I wrench it away and
hold it up to my face. Two dots of blood bloom from the meat
below my thumb. The dog lowers her head between her ragged
shoulder blades and eyes me, the patch around her eye suddenly
menacing, like a black eye she earned in some brawl.

You should see the other guy, mutters self in the back of my head.

Glancing over my shoulder, I take two very slow steps backward. Sargo is just a speck making his way up the ridge toward
the Salt. Is he actually going to leave me here? Is it too late to catch
up with him? I put one eye back on the dog. Is she fast enough to
catch me if I try?

Only one way to find out.

Slinging the pack over my shoulder, I duck under the fence
and run.

Halfway up the ridge I collapse onto my hands and knees. I can't
run anymore. I need food. And water. The doggerel, skulking

about twenty paces behind me, looks to be in even worse shape than I am. Her head sags, her legs trembling. The chain around her neck leaves a wide trail as it drags through the dirt behind her. Neither of us have it in us to keep this chase up. I roll onto my back and lie in the dirt, sweat trickling down my temples, dry, red dust clouds settling on my skin like paint.

When I finally get my breath and stand, the dog is sitting ten feet away, staring at me with big, hungry eyes.

"First I feed you, then you bite me, then you chase me, and now you want me to feed you again?" I gasp, wiping my arm across my face.

She licks her chops and doesn't move. I shake my head, doubling over with my hands on my knees. The heat, the thirst, the throbbing of my wounded hand, and those sad, hungry eyes are too much. I can't stand it. I scoop up a rock.

"Didn't you learn not to bite the hand that feeds you? I set you free. The way I see it, we're square." I half-heartedly toss it at her. "Go on, git!"

She flinches sideways, but as the rock skitters off into the dust, she begins to slink toward me again. Her blue eyes haunt me like a distant memory.

You left her behind.

I turn my back, shutting out the image, and keep walking.

At the top of the ridge, I stop and look down into the cove. *Panga* still bobs serenely in the middle of the bay, and Sargo is about halfway down the cliff ahead of me. I hitch my pack a little higher and pick up my pace, glancing back over my shoulder. The dog has disappeared.

Sargo is slinging his pack into the skiff when I catch up to him at the beach. He looks up briefly as he hears me coming, but turns away without saying anything. I stop a few feet from the skiff, chewing the inside of my cheek.

"I'm sorry," I say finally. He makes no indication that he's heard me, so I keep going. "I'm sorry I got worked up over some hair-brained scheme to save some mangey doggerel. I'm sorry I dragged you into my hair-brained scheme to get out of Brume. I'm sorry we're in this mess. It's my fault we're out here with no food and no supplies. You're right. We need to focus on surviving. I sent the dog off, I think. She's gone, anyway."

Sargo finishes coiling the skiff's rope and wipes his palms together.

"I'm sorry too," he says, his gaze on his hands, "I shouldn't've —" He looks up and his eyes go wide. "Bird," he says quietly, "don't move."

I freeze, my skin prickling. "What is it?"

"I'm not sure," he mutters. "But it's big, and it's angry-looking, and it's standing right behind you."

The hairs on the back of my neck stand up as a snarl curls around my left ear. That's not the growl of a dog. That's something bigger.

Much bigger.

Sargo drops to one knee. "Get down!"

I drop to the sand as something enormous sails over my head, so close that I feel my hair ripple. A sandy-colored animal as big as a horse is twisting through the sky above me like a ribbon in the wind. It lands between me and Sargo, spitting and flicking its tail. Some kind of mountain cat, rangy and thin, its coat pock-marked with scars and covered in grime. It eyes me, coiling its powerful hind legs.

Out of nowhere, a flash of brown and white barrels past me from behind, nearly taking me out at the knees. A length of thick chain whips through the dust behind it like a sidewinder as it launches at the cat, hitting it head-on and sending them both tumbling over each other in a cartwheel of claws, chain, and fur.

"Let's go!"

Sargo grabs the side of the skiff. Together we shove it into the water, flinging ourselves into it over the sides as it drifts away from the sand.

I look back just in time to see the cat kick with its hind legs, sending the brown and white animal that I now recognize as the dog flying sideways with a pitiful yelp. She staggers to her feet, limping and shaking the dust from her coat. She's half the size of the cat and skinny as a rail.

My chest squeezes. Ripping open my pack, I shove both hands into it, digging around for something to throw. If I can distract the cat, or even hit it with something, the dog might have a chance to run. I just need to find something big enough—

Two sharp whistles pierce the air.

I look up. Sargo is standing with one foot up on the side of the skiff, two fingers in his mouth. He whistles again and the cat freezes—its belly to the ground, its ears pinned. It flicks its tail like a switch.

"Well, come on then, you big dumb mutt!" Sargo pounds on the side of the skiff. "Get in!"

The dog tilts her head.

"Let's go!" I shout, throwing aside the pack and clapping my hands. "Come on!"

But the dog is hesitant. She puts one paw into the water. The cat prepares to pounce again.

"Swim!" I scream.

In the next minute, several things happen at once.

The dog takes another uncertain step into the surf. The cat, screeching, launches itself at the dog again. And Sargo leaps over the side of the skiff.

"Sargo, what the hell—"

He lands waist-deep and starts wading toward the shore as the cat takes the dog down and they both disappear under the water. Coming to my senses with a jolt, I scramble to flip on the motor, snatch up the tiller and spin the skiff in a circle, aiming it toward the beach.

As I reach the spot where the animals went under, the dog breaks through the surface and paws frantically at the air, her eyes white with fear. I manage to grab the scruff of her neck as Sargo catches up, grabs her, and heaves her over one shoulder. The cat surfaces, swiping at Sargo with a massive paw.

He stumbles, staggering sideways. "Get her in the skiff!"

Grabbing the dog by the scruff of her neck, I help Sargo heave her over the side. Sargo throws himself after her, his wet shirt clinging to his chest and slicking along the curve of his shoulders. *Did he always have those shoulders?* I wonder abruptly.

Something flips over in my stomach and I quickly turn around, grabbing the tiller again and swerving us away from the beach. Sargo rolls onto his back in the bottom of the skiff, breathing hard, wiping water from his face.

"Are you okay?" I cry.

He holds his arms out and examines himself. "I think so."

"Why did you do that?"

"You were right," he gasps, "I couldn't just leave her behind." He pulls himself upright in the bow, shaking water from his hair. Wet, black curls settle in a dripping tangle against his smooth, brown face and my stomach flips over again. I put my gaze firmly over the bow past his shoulder and renew my grip on the tiller.

"Besides," he says, "she did save our lives. Maybe she's good for something after all."

We careen away from the shore toward *Panga*. The dog hunches in the bottom of the skiff and fixes me with a hard-eyed stare, growling. Sargo and I share a nervous glance and both move as far away from her as we can. I surreptitiously tuck my injured hand out of sight. Probably best not to bring that up now.

"I don't think she saved our lives on purpose," I mutter. "I think she just attacks anything that moves."

The skiff bounces over a wave and my stomach lurches as the dog slips toward me, her claws skittering against the hull. I scrunch myself even further into the corner of the stern.

"She's probably just scared," I say, unsure if I'm trying to convince Sargo or myself. "And hungry. I bet if we feed her she'll warm up to us."

"I sure as Salt hope you're right about that," he says under his breath. "I hope I didn't just make a huge mistake. I don't know what I was thinking. We can't afford this kind of...malarkey."

"*Malarkey?*" I scrunch my face. "What is that? Another word from Mama Marlin?"

"No," he says. "That's one of Mama G's. It means 'nonsense.'"

"I know what it means. I just never heard anyone actually use it. What are you, like a thousand years old?"

He curls a lip. "Very funny."

I pull the skiff up alongside *Panga*, kill the motor and stand up to catch hold of *Panga's* deck rail, pulling us closer.

"Malarkey," I repeat, keeping one eye on the dog and rolling the word around in my mouth as I tie up the skiff. "You know what? I like it. Pretty good name for a dog if you ask me."

chapter
thirteen

My assessment that Malarkey is 'just scared' appears to be correct. Once we get her aboard *Panga*, she wedges herself securely under the bunk in the bow and refuses to come out. Whether she will 'warm up to us' remains to be seen—when I toss a chunk of bread under the bunk for her, she thanks me with a snarl.

The discussion about whether we should keep going to Alluvium is a short one. There's nowhere else to go along this desolate and brutal stretch of coast. Going back to Brume at this point seems out of the question; at least, neither of us mentions it.

Sargo is quiet and moody, and even though he eventually came around to my side on taking Malarkey with us, I get the sense he's still pissed. He's probably still stewing about my general recklessness, incompetence, and inability to be a halfway decent person.

I keep my mouth shut and try to stay out of his way, partly because I don't want to piss him off any further, but partly because the image of him leaping out of the skiff to rescue Malarkey, of his dripping black curls and the translucent shirt clinging to his chest, seems to pop into my head every time I look at him. The only way to make it stop seems to be not to look at him.

We leave Naze prepared to sail straight through the next day and night. The wind is good and the water is calm. I secretly thank whatever gods might still be hanging around up there, even though I don't believe in them, because I don't know how Malarkey would fare in a storm. And to be completely honest, I don't know how I would either.

Sargo says we should take turns on watch overnight—four hours awake, four hours of sleep—which suits my insomnia just fine. He rigs up the autopilot so we don't always need to be at the helm. He says it's a common thing to do, but I suspect he just doesn't trust me to steer the ship by myself while he's asleep. Which, to be fair, I probably can't.

Stars wink on two by two, and as I go on watch at 2030, the full, hazy moon throws a great sweeping cone of glittering red light across the black water. Sargo sleeps in the bunk at the front of the boat, and Malarkey is still hiding under that same bunk. I chew my thumbnail and stare at the bloody water. My nails are starting to disappear again.

Snippets of visions drift around my head like leaves. The name Fife. A boy and two little girls. Hard, red earth. I can't seem to hold on to any of it long enough to make sense of it. Are they dreams? If so, I don't know when I dreamed them.

When I'm not trying to grab hold of drifting snippets, I'm ruminating on the blackouts I had before I left Brume.

Blackout. I don't like that phrase. It's so…real.

I blacked out once at a party in Brume. The next morning, I woke up in the skiff wearing someone else's shoes. Sargo informed me that I'd gotten so drunk I spent twenty minutes yelling at him to let me take the skiff for a 'test drive', and when he wouldn't, I apparently took off my shoes and threw them in the Salt. Didn't throw them at *him*. Just…threw them in the Salt. I asked him where I got the other shoes and he said he didn't know. I thought it was pretty funny. Sargo was *concerned*. I never did find out where those other shoes came from.

It seems crazy to me that grog can do that. That you can be walking around, yelling at people, throwing your shoes into the

Salt, and wake up the next day and not remember a thing. Like a...gap in the tape. Kind of scary.

That day I blacked out in the bathroom at Azimuth and woke up at the harbor I had been drinking. Not drinking much, but... still. So is that what happened that day? Is that what happened in the Flats? Like that night at the party. Or was it more like when I space out in sailing class and don't remember who had the right of way? A gap in the tape. A blip.

"Blip."

I say the word out loud. It's certainly more *fun* to say than 'blackout.' So maybe I'll go with that for now. Blips. That thing that happened at Azimuth. That night in the Flats. Where I woke up and didn't remember how I got there. They were blips. Just a gap in the tape. A tiny bit missing from my memory. That's all.

And those weird dreams? Maybe they're connected. It's difficult to say.

I turn my thoughts toward Shale. *He* might know. According to Mama K, he was drinking before he left Brume. Is it possible he was blacking out—sorry, *blipping*—too? Could I ask him about it? Would I even want to? I haven't even told him I'm coming to Alluvium. In all the craziness of leaving Brume and getting to Naze, I never thought to message him.

I tap my right temple to pull up Messenger, but all I see is

>>> *Out of range. Messaging unavailable.*

I've never seen that before. I didn't even know biochips had a range. I wonder what else doesn't work out here? I tap my left brow to pull up a map.

>>> *Out of range. Map unavailable.*

That's...concerning. Didn't we have a map at Naze? I'm sure we had one. I remember Sargo checking it. I hold a finger behind my left ear and hear the familiar static of the radio. So that must work, although I doubt there's anyone out here to talk to.

I look around for my pack and spot it tucked into a corner of the cockpit. Reaching into it, I dig around, pull out my slate, and open the file that contains my expulsion letter from Azimuth. It shows up, no problem. So some things still work.

The words of the letter jump out at me again.

...legitimate threat to her classmates...

Swiping the file closed in disgust, I tuck the slate back into my pack. No point worrying about that anymore.

I go off watch at midnight and Sargo comes up from below deck to take over. The air is damp and chilly, and I'm shivering by the time we switch, my fingers frozen stiff, my skin prickled with goosebumps.

He trips up the three companionway steps as I come down—groggy-looking, his hair tousled, still half-asleep. We squeeze wordlessly past each other on the narrow stairs, both turning sideways, and the brief press of his chest against mine—the closeness of his scent—rouses a heat under my skin that clings to me all the way to the bunk in the bow that we take turns sleeping in.

Rigid with cold, I strip off my damp hoodie and crawl under the thick blanket, pulling it all the way over my head and curling on my side. Sargo's smell is all over the bunk too—the sheets and blanket still warm where he rolled out of them moments ago.

The flush that his closeness aroused on the stairs simmers under my skin as I sink into that heat. His smell. The close, soft brush of him all around me. Images of him float to the surface of my mind. Sargo, soaking wet. The slick, translucent fabric of his shirt adhering to the curves of his chest. His dripping black hair falling around his smooth brown face.

I flip onto my other side.

It wasn't just the way he looked. In that moment, it wasn't just his wet shirt and broad shoulders and beautiful face that rattled me. It was his foot up on the side of the skiff. It was whistling for Malarkey. It was the way he jumped over the side and went back for her. That he saved her. Even though he knew it was foolish. Because she needed help. Because it was the right thing to do.

My skin prickles. Rolling onto my other side, I take a deep breath, but that only fills my nose with the scent of him. It's like he's all over me. More images push their way to the front of my mind. Him lying in this bunk. Sleeping between these sheets.

Doing…what else?

My face turns red hot and I flip over again, quickly shutting the door on that thought.

Or at least, trying to.

But it's in there now. Has he done *that* in this bunk? What does it look like, that thing in his hand? What would it look like in mine—

Nope. Too far, Howsley. Reign it in.

I roll onto my back, shoving the blanket around my hips to let the air against my skin. My breast pebble in the cool rush across the thin fabric of my shirt. I push the hair off my face and draw a long, hard breath through my nose.

"You okay down there?"

The air comes out in a rush. Sargo can hear me tossing and turning. There's no door between us—just the small space of *Panga's* main cabin and the three short steps up to the cockpit, where he now sits on watch. No privacy, ever. I close my eyes and swallow.

"Yeah, fine." The words stick in my throat.

"Seasick?"

"No. Just…" I gesture uselessly in the dark, looking for a lie. *Just thinking about parts of your body that I probably shouldn't be thinking about. Just picturing you naked. Just wondering if you could spare a second to come down here and get in this bunk with me and—*

"Just winding down."

He doesn't say anything else and I shiver and pull the blanket over me again. I tilt my head back to see if I can make out his silhouette in the cockpit, but it's too dark to see anything. I stare into that darkness, across the fifteen feet of space and three steps that separate us, wondering if he can see me.

If he's watching me.

An ache blooms between my thighs. I squeeze my legs together, wishing there was some way to relieve the pressure gathering there. Some way to get these thoughts out of my head without…

Without him catching you.

My blood throbs and ebbs. In my face, in my feet, in my core. Between my legs. My whole body is giving over to that thumping, pulsing heat.

He can't see you, says a voice in my head. *It's too dark.*

As slowly as I can under the blanket, I slide one hand to my breast and squeeze it gently, over my shirt, feeling the hard point of my nipple straining through the fabric into my palm. The ache between my thighs becomes urgent. I hike my shirt up over my breasts.

A footstep on the stairs freezes me. I snap my eyes shut and go still as Sargo steps off the last step into the galley. I hear him making sounds with the kettle. Making tea for his watch.

For what feels like an eternity I lie there, pretending to sleep, my shirt hiked up under the blanket, my breasts taut and aching in my hands. I listen to him running the water, lighting the stove, setting the kettle to boil. Then he goes quiet.

I listen for his footsteps retreating back up the stairs to the cockpit, but don't hear them. He must be leaning against the counter in the galley, waiting for the kettle. I imagine his arms folded, the shape of his shoulders and the cords of muscle in his forearms. The curve of his neck as he fixes his gaze absent-mindedly on the floor. Thinking.

I risk a tiny movement under the blanket, letting my fingers glide over my nipples. A red-hot connection arcs to the burning ache between my thighs. I press my lips together to silence a moan. I am desperate for release. But I can't…do this with him right there.

Can I?

I open my eyes and stare at the ceiling, close above my head.

He can't see you, repeats the voice.

What if he comes in here?

Why would he do that? He respects the watch schedule. He wouldn't disturb you.

My hands wander over my ribs. My bare stomach. They hesitate at the top of my pants. It's so hot under the blanket sweat is sheening on my skin. My hips roll against the bed as my aching sex strains to find some friction. I slip my hand into the front of my pants and go still again, listening.

If he caught me…what would he do?

My fingers slide lower, grazing my thighs, the edges of my sex.

Would he stay quiet and watch me? Get hard watching me?

I sip in a breath at the thought.

Would he join me?

My hand continues its torturous teasing. I imagine him finding me. Unbuttoning his pants, crawling into the bunk on top of me, pinning me down, putting his hands on me. His lips. Grinding his heat against my thigh.

Forgetting where I am, I groan low in my throat.

A small sound in the galley.

Jesus, was that him?

I freeze, listening, until the need to keep going outweighs my fear of being caught and almost without thinking, I slip one finger in and roll against the heel of my palm. The relief is so intense I shudder. But I need more. I *want* him to catch me.

The kettle shrieks.

Nearly jumping out of my skin, I wrench my hand out of my pants and roll onto my side, curling into a ball and pulling the blanket tight around me. Sargo removes the kettle from the heat and pours his tea. My heart beats in my ears as I listen to his footsteps retreat back up the stairs to the cockpit.

For several minutes, I lie there, trembling, twisted into knots, trying to breathe. Then, somehow, my brain finds its way back to the control panel.

Don't be an idiot, Howsley, it says. *Don't make this weird.*

The heat under my skin begins to dissipate. When I push the blanket down this time the cool air is like a welcome slap in the face. I gulp it down and close my eyes. I find my breath, and breathe.

On the afternoon of the next day, the wind starts to pick up. The water stirs like a simmering pot, and the sky darkens with thick clouds, as though someone has closed a lid over us. By early evening, the wind howls, and the Salt heaves like a beast awakening from a deep sleep.

"We need to reef," says Sargo from the helm, squinting at the scudding clouds. His voice, as always, betrays no panic or alarm, but his face is as dark as the sky. "I should have done it earlier."

"Okay," I say nervously, unsure if I remember what reefing is and how to do it.

"I'm going to point *Panga* directly into the wind so that the mainsail will luff," he says. I must look confused because then he says, "Luffing means the sail is loose, flapping, not filled with wind. Right?"

I nod quickly, feeling like I'm back in his class at Azimuth.

"When it's luffing, you go out on the bow, pull it halfway down, and cinch it to the boom. Then raise it again. The sail should be half as big as it is now. Does that make sense?"

I hesitate. "Yes…"

"Are you sure?"

"Yes. We're making the sail smaller, so it won't catch as much wind." I remember this lesson now. "So the boat doesn't get overpowered and capsize."

"Exactly." He eyes me. "It will be scary. The swell is big, and the wind is very strong. It's going to knock us around. And it will be hard to raise the sail again once it's cinched down. You'll need to use all your strength."

"Okay." I try to keep my face from showing my nerves.

"Ready?"

"Now?"

"Yes, Bird, now."

I nod once.

"Okay, here we go."

He turns the wheel, and the boat cuts up through one of the rollers, tipping sideways so that I have to grab the side of the cockpit to keep my balance. As we turn through the eye of the wind, the mainsail loses its full, curved shape and begins to flap, the thick fabric beating thunderously against itself like a monumental drum.

"Now!" yells Sargo.

Gathering my courage with a breath, I climb out of the cockpit onto the slick deck and cling to the handholds, inching toward the mast on all fours, my gut heaving. When I reach it, I grasp around it with both arms and pull myself upright, clinging tightly with my knees.

Facing the stern, I can see Sargo in the cockpit, wrestling with the wheel, trying to keep us pointed the right way. His eyes are glued to me. He looks scared.

Is he...worried about me?

No. He probably just thinks I won't be able to do this. Shaking myself back into focus, I take a determined breath and remove one hand from the mast. Squeezing my knees even tighter, I unwind the main halyard from its cleat and the mainsail begins to drop. I let it fall until the small loop of rope that hangs about halfway up the face of the sail is close enough to grab, then I pull the loop down over a hook in the side of the mast to cinch the sail down. It takes me three tries and all my strength to get the loop over the hook, and by the time I do it, my fingers are raw.

Gripping the halyard with both hands, I pull hard to raise the main up to its new height—but it doesn't move. A deafening crash rattles the whole ship, and a sheet of water dumps over my head as we slam through a wave.

I'm gasping and blinking through saltwater when Malarkey suddenly leaps past Sargo and out of the cockpit. The wave must have spooked her out of her hiding spot. She slides across the deck toward the edge, her paws scrabbling uselessly on the wet wood.

"Malarkey!"

My scream is whipped away by the wind. I'm clinging to the mast and can't do anything to save her. If I move, I'll be over the side too.

Sargo lunges over the side of the cockpit, snatching her by the scruff of the neck and, with some kind of superhuman strength, pulling her to safety. He grabs the helm again just in time to turn us up through a wave, and Malarkey thanks him for saving her life by barking aggressively in his face.

Relief pours through me, until I remember I'm still not done reefing the sail. I grab the winch handle and shove it into the halyard winch. Clinging to the mast with one hand, I crank the handle back and forth with the other, my arm burning as the sail inches its way slowly into its reefed position. Finally, the halyard is tight. I check it with my free hand and blink in surprise.

That's it. Shit...I did it.

Another boom rattles the ship, and another sheet of water crashes over my head. My foot slips and I lurch sideways, clutching the mast with both hands.

"Bird!"

Sargo's shout comes to me from somewhere over the crashing of the waves and howling of the wind. I scrabble my foot around the slippery deck until my toe wedges into something firm, then I drop to my hands and knees, crawl back to the cockpit, and fling myself back into my seat, gasping.

"Are you okay?"

I tilt my head toward Sargo. He's drenched too, still fighting to keep us pointed the right way, his sleeves rolled up as he heaves the wheel around with both hands, arm over arm.

Some kind of snarky retort would be great right now, but all I can think to say is, "Uh huh. Fine."

He takes his gaze off the horizon for a moment and looks at me. In his eyes is an expression I've never seen from him before. Surprise? Admiration? Both?

His eyes hold mine a moment longer. Then he says, "Nice job, Howsley," and flicks them back over the bow.

I sit up, tugging off my sodden beanie and shaking out my hair.

"What?" I try to shrug casually, but my shaking hands and voice probably give me away. "You didn't think I could do it?"

His eyes flick to mine again and he humors me with the flicker of a smile.

Malarkey cowers in a corner of the cockpit floor, gazing up at me with wide eyes that say, "Why have you brought me to this place, human?"

"Sorry, Malarkey." I strip off my soaked hoodie and fling it into a corner of the cockpit. "Perhaps you would have preferred to starve to death?"

"I feel like we didn't rescue this dog so much as kidnap her," says Sargo.

The wind eases overnight, and at some point I must fall asleep because I wake in the cockpit mid-morning, disoriented and sore, my clothes still damp and stiff with salt. I touch my face, testing the pain of my days-old injuries. My eye is no longer tender. I sit up and look around.

Sargo has turned on the autopilot and is nowhere to be seen. Malarkey yawns widely at me from the floor of the cockpit and rubs the side of her nose against her leg.

"You're still here," I say, impressed. "I thought for sure you'd be hiding under your bunk again."

She licks her nose and, astonishingly, doesn't growl.

"Morning."

Sargo's voice floats up the companionway, and I look down to see him standing at the bottom of the steps, holding two cups of steaming tea.

His eyes are sleepy, hair disheveled, and a smattering of stubble is coming in around his jaw. His blue Azimuth button-down is rumpled and faded from being worn two days in a row, drenched in saltwater, and slept in. It's also—I try not to notice—distinctly more open at the collar than it ever was in Brume. I quickly put my eyes somewhere else and take both the mugs, handing his back to him after he climbs up into the cockpit. We sip quietly for a few minutes, gazing over the Salt.

A squadron of archipelicans swoops in front of the boat in prehistoric formation, their long-feathered wingtips and low bellies brushing the surface of the water. One dips its big beak and snatches up a fish, tipping its head back to swallow it in one smooth motion.

"What do you want for breakfast?" says Sargo.

Breakfast is the same thing it has been for two days: chunks of bread slathered with a mixture of diced carrots, scraggly orange things, and greens, because that's the only food we have. We eat in the cockpit as the sun begins to warm the deck.

AS I swallow my last mouthful, I wonder if we'll make it to Alluvium before we run out of food. We've gone through half a loaf between the three of us. We have enough veg for another few days, but that's three long, hungry days, and Malarkey can't survive on just veg.

"I think we should try fishing again," says Sargo, as though reading my thoughts. "I have enough coin to buy food, but there isn't another City between here and Alluvium, and we won't make it there for at least a week."

I don't try to argue this time. My own coin is pitifully low, and

I don't even know how to rig up a fishing pole. I stare between my feet, Sargo's angry words floating through my head again.

Can't even help yourself.

"I'm sorry I dragged you into this," I mumble. "But...I'm glad you're here. You were right. I can't do this on my own."

Sargo stares into his mug for a long time. "I'm sorry I said that," he says finally, not looking up. "I didn't mean it. And you didn't drag me into this. I mean, you did, but...I've wanted to leave Brume for a long time."

I look up but don't say anything.

He shrugs. "I always kind of hoped one day I'd go to Pocosín. See where my family is from. Find my people."

"Did you always think you'd be sailing to Pocosín with a crewmate who doesn't know how to reef and a mainsail that might fail at any moment?"

He gives me a small smile and doesn't respond right away. He sips his tea. Then he says, "Do you know how many things need fixing on this boat?"

I frown and shake my head.

"Hundreds. It's not just the mainsail. There are winches that need servicing, rigging that needs replacing, wood that needs refinishing. I need to repaint the hull, replace the zincs...not to mention all the small projects—restitching seat cushions, building shelves, fixing the leaky faucet in the galley—"

"Okay," I cut him off, "I get it. So basically what you're telling me is this boat is a piece of shit?"

"No, what I'm saying is..." He sighs. "I could spend years finding things to fix on this boat. There will always be things to fix. I've been telling myself I was only staying at Azimuth to help Blenny pay off his debt, but the truth is...I would have sat at that dock, fixing things and trying to make things perfect...for years. But it's never going to be perfect. There's never going to be a right time. At some point, you just have to go. And..." He rearranges his hands around his mug. "Without you I don't know if I ever would have."

His eyes meet mine and my chest squeezes.

He clears his throat, his face suddenly going red. "So, don't be too hard on yourself. Yes, you're a bit...reckless. And okay, you're not a great sailor. You drink too much, and you don't pay attention—"

"You said *don't* be too hard on myself..."

"—but you're decisive. You make things happen. Not always good things. Sometimes terrible things. But...you get stuff done. And...I think you at least *try* to act from the bigness of your heart." He drains the last sip of his tea. "And I guess that's what matters. You just need to slow down sometimes. Think before you act. Take one step at a time."

I drop my eyes. "I know. It's just not always as easy as that."

He sighs, and I sense frustration. "Why not?"

"I mean...I am *trying*. You know? It's like...I don't *want* to be a disaster. I'm not trying to screw everything up and forget things and space out and be a reckless asshole all the time. But sometimes it feels like...like it doesn't matter how hard I try. Like no matter what I do, I always make the wrong decision. Like my brain just takes the helm and I'm tied up in the brig with a blindfold on."

He frowns. "Like you don't have control of your own *brain?*"

I shrug.

He nods slowly. "I guess I don't really have an answer for that."

"Me neither."

"Did you ever talk to anyone about it?"

"There was a counselor at Azimuth. Ms. Parley. But all she ever did was give me breathing exercises and make me talk about my feelings. I don't need anyone else poking around in my brain. I can handle it by myself. I just need to try harder."

He looks at me with shrewd eyes. "Do you really think that's the answer?"

"What?"

"Trying harder."

I skirt his eyes and shrug. "I don't really know what else to do."

I feel him watching me for another long breath, then he sighs. "Well, think about what I said. One step at a time."

I feel a flicker of irritation. "Okay, and maybe you could try taking, like…two steps at a time, every once in a while?"

He shoots me a look, then drops his gaze into his mug again, turning it slowly in his hands. "It's not that easy for me either."

"Why not?"

He sets the mug on the floor. Malarkey gives it a suspicious sniff, then licks the last few drops from the bottom. He watches her as he says, "Okay, fine. You want to know why I'm so careful all the time? Why I work so hard and try to make everything perfect? It's because I can't make a mistake. I don't *get* to screw up like you do. Ever."

"What the hell does that mean?"

"There's hardly anyone else in Brume that looks like me. People that look like me don't live in Brume. People with my last name don't live in Brume. Do you know how much pressure that is? I represent *everything* that the people of Brume know about people from Pocosín. If I screw up, that's all they'll see. They'll think that people like me don't deserve to be in Brume, because we're not good enough to be there."

I frown. "Did someone tell you that?"

"They didn't have to. When I was a kid, people just looked at me differently. If I said something smart, they looked surprised. If I did something kind, they were amazed. They would say, 'You're so well-spoken!' or 'What a polite young man!' But I knew what they meant. They mean, 'For a brown kid.' And I knew…that I would have to work twice as hard as everyone else to be taken seriously. That I would have to be careful and methodical and make sure I never screwed anything up. So that's what I did."

I stare at him, my mind reeling. "Sargo, I—*never* thought of you as a…as—like that. To me, you're just…Sargo."

"But I'm not *just* Sargo, either." His voice rises sharply and I flinch. "Sorry. I know that doesn't make sense. But as hard as I work to fit in, I can't just...pretend like that part of me doesn't exist. I want to feel like I fit in, but I don't want to be erased. I don't want people to notice that I'm different but I don't want to lose the part of me that's different." He sighs. "I don't know. It's confusing. I don't know anything about half of my family. I don't even speak the language. It just feels like there's this whole part of me that's...missing. This part that no one in Brume understands. That *I* don't even really understand. That I can't talk to anyone about."

"You could talk to me."

"You never ask. You're too..." he drops his eyes, "busy with your own problems."

His words hit me like a punch in the gut. *Selfish.* I've been reckless and selfish. Running around, screwing things up. Never even bothering to ask Sargo about his problems. I always liked him because he didn't pry. But maybe I'm the one that should have been prying.

"I'm sorry I never asked," I mumble. "I guess—I thought it was easier not to talk about it."

"Easier for you, maybe."

I squirm, wishing I could disappear into the bottom of my mug.

"I don't know what to say." I force myself to look at him. "Except that I'm sorry and I'll try to do better."

He studies me with dark, thoughtful eyes. Eyes that in the sunlight are flecked with black and gold. Then he smiles.

"Were you really trying to buy me a new mainsail?"

I nod.

He shakes his head. "That was—absolute lunacy, Howsley. But it was...sweet."

Heat floods my face. I feel like I just downed a flask full of grog all at once. No, not grog. Better than grog. This heat makes my hands tingle and my heart beat fast. The knot of guilt in my gut has untied a little, but a new, different kind of knot is tying itself there instead. A nervous one.

He looks away, folding and then refolding his arms as though he can't quite decide what to do with them. Finally, he stretches and clasps them behind his head, leaning back and propping his bare foot on the wheel.

"So what are you going to do when you find your brother?"

I blink. I had almost forgotten the reason I came out here.

"He said he had a job for me."

"A job?"

"Yeah."

"Doing what?"

I shrug. "I don't know. It doesn't really matter, does it? I can't go back to Brume. I don't have much else."

He stares over the water. "So you're going to stay in Alluvium?"

"I guess so. I hadn't really thought about it. But...yeah. I think." I watch his face. "What about you?"

"Honestly...I don't know." He unclasps his hands and rubs the stubble around his jaw. I've never seen him with stubble before; it suits him. "I don't think I can go back to Brume either. But I was thinking...I think I'm gonna keep going south. To Pocosín."

"By *yourself?*"

"Maybe." He shrugs. "I haven't really thought it through."

"*You* haven't thought something through? Wow, I must be rubbing off on you."

"Well, to be honest..." He looks down at his hands as though he suddenly finds them terribly interesting. "I guess I thought you might come with me."

My stomach sways. "Do you...want me to come with you?"

"Sure. I mean...it's much easier to sail *Panga* with two people. To split up watches and stuff. Might be nice to have a first mate."

The sway in my stomach abruptly stops. A first mate. Just someone to help him crew the ship. An extra pair of hands. I choose my next words carefully, hoping the confused feelings diving around inside me don't make their treacherous way across my face.

"I guess...I guess I thought you'd be ready to be rid of me after all this."

He frowns. "Why would you think that?"

"I dragged you out here into a mess of trouble. I barely know how to sail. And...it's not as though we were really friends in Brume. You were my teacher. You only started hanging out with me because you had to."

A cloud crosses Sargo's face. His brow furrows. "Is that really how you feel?" he says to his hands.

I give an almost imperceptible shrug. The air between us feels suddenly very thick.

He sighs and sits up. "Look...at the end of the day, I do think what you did in Brume was pretty stupid, and to be honest, I probably need some more time to let that go. But..." He shrugs and stands. "I'm out here. I'm doing *something*. And I guess I owe that partly to you. For better or worse."

He scoops his mug off the floor and swings himself down the companionway steps into the cabin below.

Malarkey watches him go, then heaves a dramatic sigh and flops sideways onto the floor.

The flecks of gold in Sargo's eyes seem burned into my retinas. I blink hard a few times and try to rub them away.

Just because you suddenly noticed he's cute and has nice shoulders, doesn't mean he feels any differently about you, I remind myself. And who even said I was feeling differently about him anyway? I mean, come on. *You see the boy in a wet shirt one time and completely fall to pieces?*

Get it together, Howsley.

chapter
fourteen

"INCOMING!"

I look up from the half-mended fishing net in my lap and follow Sargo's pointed finger over the starboard bow.

"Uh oh." I grin. "You ready, Malarkey? Here they come!"

Delfíns. A pod that looks to number over a hundred slicing through the water toward us, their fins cutting the surface like knives.

Since we got well south of Brume and Naze, we've started seeing more life on the Salt. Not much, but some. Archipelicans, delfíns. This morning, while the sun was still just a milky white disc slithering over the yellow horizon, Sargo caught a fish.

Yesterday, Malarkey was the first one to spot delfíns, but today they're downwind of us, and she hasn't caught the scent.

The pod falls into formation around the boat, sweeping and diving under the bow, emerging on one side, then the other. One explodes through the surface, twists in a balletic arc, then slices without a splash back through the water's edge.

Malarkey scrambles to her feet. She scrabbles to the bow in a raucous clatter of claws and fur and hangs her nose over the side, her tail spinning.

Sargo shakes his head. "You're not gonna catch them, Malarkey!"

"Do you think it's good for her to chase something she can't catch?" I wonder aloud. "What if it makes her crazy?"

He shrugs and picks up the length of rope he's been working with. "We're all chasing something we might not catch. And she's already crazy."

We've been on the Salt for seven days now. The wind has been strong, frighteningly so at times, but we're making good time. Sargo says we should be grateful for the wind—it didn't always use to be this way along this part of the coast. Before the climate got all screwed up, sometimes you'd sit out here for days with no wind.

We're about five hundred miles south of Brume, still hugging the coast. The dark smudge of the shore is always to our left, and the sun sets to our right every evening. Every night, we find a cove to anchor in, and every morning, we scan the horizon for pursuing sails. But we've seen none since leaving Brume. Neither Sargo nor I have said it out loud, but I think we both secretly hope we might have dodged the Anonymity for good. Or if not for good, at least for now.

I try not to think about my moms. I try not to wonder if I'll ever be able to return to Brume.

The sun is high, and although the sky is not blue, the air is breathable. The days out here pass more quickly than I thought they would. Malarkey is taking to sailing better than either of us expected, and Sargo finds plenty to occupy us during the long hours on the water.

This morning we both sit cross-legged and barefoot on the bow, working on 'boat projects.' Sargo splices a pile of rope with his hands and a knife, bending over his slate and scratching his head every few minutes, I assume reading instructions for something, which I guess must be saved somewhere on his biochip, since we've been 'Out of range' for days now.

I'm mending a fishing net with a length of twine. Sargo showed me how to tie the twine to a small wooden dowel, then pass the dowel over and under the broken strands of the net, pulling them together around the hole. It's another meditative, repetitive task, like varnishing teak, and my mind ebbs gently with the looping of the twine, the rolling of the swell.

My thoughts wander back to Shale. What will he look like after all these years? Will he have a beard? A girlfriend? A boyfriend? What kind of job does he have? How much coin? Does he still get in trouble like he used to? Is he in trouble now? What if the Anonymity—

I drop the net into my lap. I can feel my brain running away with the ship again. I close my eyes and grab at some unrelated thought.

How long has it been since you had grog? says the voice in the back of my head.

Seven days.

So when do you think you'll have it agai—

I toss the net aside and turn to Sargo. "What are you making?"

He holds up the pile of rope in his lap. "It's a harness. For Malarkey. To stop her falling over the side in bad weather. This part goes over her head," he tugs at a small loop near the top, "and this goes around her chest. Then you hook this…" he produces a metal shackle from his pocket and clips it onto a loop at the end of the rope, "onto something in the cockpit."

"That's amazing."

"I'm going to make them for us too." His voice turns serious. "That night we had to reef the sail, you shouldn't have been out on the bow without a tether. It's my fault. We should have reefed sooner when it was safer to do it. I shouldn't have sent you out there."

"Someone had to go," I counter, "and you have to steer the boat."

"I know," he says, "but we have to do better. *I* have to do better. If you went over the side—" He stops and fiddles with the harness, avoiding my eyes. "Well, it would be bad. We have to be prepared, always, for anything. Right now," he gestures around, "sitting here in the sun, it's easy to forget. But the Salt doesn't take it easy, and it doesn't care if you do."

"Well, I think you're doing a good job." I hesitate. "Captain."

The word feels awkward on my tongue and he rolls his eyes, but I glimpse a small smile as he returns to his work.

The deck is warm from the sun and I roll onto my back, letting my limbs sprawl, absorbing the heat like a lizard. Malarkey comes huffing excitedly back from the bow, snorting, and sneezing and carrying on loudly enough to make sure we all know that there were delfíns, and that she got 'em. It's not long before she's shoving her cold, wet nose rudely into my face. She can't seem to resist bugging me when I'm lying down.

"Gods flog-it Malarkey, haven't you ever heard of letting sleeping dogs lie?" I swat her away and roll myself upright, wiping my face with the back of my hand.

The sun reflecting off the surface of the Salt is so bright it makes my eyes water, and I have to screw my eyes up so tightly in order to see, that at first, I'm not sure if the small white shape perched on the horizon is a cloud, a bird, or just a figment of my imagination. I frown, shielding my eyes with my hand, and squint at it harder.

The realization creeps from my gut like a cold, black tide. I try to swallow it down, to shove it away like I've been shoving away my fear for my folks; my fear for Shale; like I've been shoving down the creeping feeling that the Anonymity are right behind us for days now. But the longer I stare at that little white blob, the harder I find it to deny what it is.

A sail.

They've caught us.

chapter
fifteen

"WHAT DO WE DO?"

Sargo is already swinging himself from the stern into the cockpit, shutting down the autopilot and taking the helm.

"We need to pick up speed," he says. "Trim the jib."

I jump down after him and pick up the line that controls the headsail. Doubt flickers through me.

"Should I let it out, or sheet it in?"

"Gods, Bird!" His voice is uncharacteristically harsh. "You know this! Just look at the telltales! I don't have time to teach you right now."

I bite back a retort and stick my head out of the cockpit to check the three little red streamers that run along the inside of the sail. They're sagging, so I pull on the line to sheet the sail in closer to the boat. The telltales catch the wind and stop luffing; they lift and ripple in the breeze. *Panga* heels over a little and we pick up speed.

The muscles in Sargo's forearms pop as he heaves on the main sheet. I sip in air and look away, trying not to let the smooth motion of his shoulders derail my focus as he braces one foot agains the side of the cockpit and leans back on the line.

Now is not the time to be noticing his forearms, Bird. We are about to be chased down and captured by men without faces.

He glances over the stern. The sail on the horizon behind us already looks bigger than it did when I spotted it five minutes ago. They're gaining on us.

"It's not going to be enough," he says under his breath.

"How did they catch up to us?" I cry. "It's been a week! If a ship that fast had followed us from Brume, they would have caught up to us already."

"Maybe they're not from Brume," Sargo says darkly.

"What do you mean? It's not an Anonymity ship?" My stomach flutters with hope.

"I don't know," he mutters, "but I'd rather not find out. Keep your eye on the jib. We need all the speed we can get."

We trim the sails and adjust our course obsessively for the next half hour as the pursuing boat slowly closes the gap. We catch every shift in the wind, snatch every minuscule opportunity to pick up speed. The air in the cockpit crackles as we weave around each other in a tight, focused dance. My palms are raw from handling the sheets, but I'm so filled with adrenaline I barely notice the pain. I'm sailing better than I've ever sailed before.

It makes no difference. Before long, the pursuing boat is so close that I can read the name printed across her hull. *Valkyrie*.

The ship is enormous—at least five times as long as *Panga*, made entirely of metal, with turrets, stacks and pilot houses all over the deck. She has no mast—instead, her three sails are like enormous parachutes that fly over the bow, tied to the deck with thick tethers and managed by the crew like kites. The boat looks like some kind of freighter, or maybe an old military warship converted to run under sail power. Unorthodox, but smart. I doubt they could get their hands on enough diesel to run a motor that size.

Before long, the *Valkyrie* is so close that she towers over *Panga*, her gunmetal gray hull blocking the sun, throwing us into cold shadow. I count the crew on her deck. Five, but I assume there must be more. Desperately, I turn to Sargo. Surely he has a plan, some sailing trick up his sleeve that I don't know about. But his face is ashen. Defeated.

"You sailed well," he says quietly.

"You mean it's over?! We just let them catch us?"

"There's nothing we can do."

My mind races. There must be a way out of this. If we can't outrun them, then we'll have to think of something else. Just because they caught up to us, doesn't mean they've caught us. Doesn't mean we have to go quietly. I set my face in a mask of grim determination and turn to Sargo.

"Do we have any weapons?"

Sargo scoffs. "What do you think?"

There isn't time to bicker, so I ignore his tone and swing myself down the companionway steps into the galley. Hanging above the stove from a loop of leather is a long, curved knife. I take it down and examine the blade. Dull as ditchwater. Probably as useless for stabbing someone as it is for chopping veg.

It'll have to do.

I throw open the galley drawers to look for a second knife, frantically rifling through an assortment of mismatched spoons, forks, a whisk, a ladle. Some of the stuff in here is so old I think it must have belonged to Sargo's great-great-grandfather. I wonder if Sargo even knows what's in these drawers.

My hand closes around a handle and I pull it out a short, slender blade. We've never used it; I'm not even sure what it's for. But it's sharp. I turn it over in my hand then hold it out in front of me, pointy end forward. I feign a couple of stabs in the air with it.

What are you doing, Bird? This is ridiculous.

I've never wielded a weapon before in my life. Am I really about to try and fend off the Anonymity with a kitchen utensil?

Yes. That's exactly what you're about to do. Because you can't do anything else.

What did Sargo say that first night we sailed out of Brume? 'As the Salt, so the sailor.' Well, the Salt is about to get pretty violent. So the sailors are following suit.

When I turn back to the drawer to close it, I catch a glimpse of something metallic, nearly buried under all the junk. Frowning, I dig it out. It's a flask; small, silver, with a woven pattern of knots etched into the face of it. I turn it over. The initials B.F. are clumsily scratched into the bottom. Blenny Farr. I hold the flask to my ear and shake it. A measure of liquid sloshes inside.

A familiar, itchy feeling creeps into my limbs. A feeling I've been pushing down for days. It was easy enough to ignore when there was no grog to be had. But now that it's sitting right here in front of me…

Carefully, I unscrew the lid and sniff. Stinging vapors send me reeling backward with a violent cough.

That's grog alright.

God knows how old this stuff is. But it's not like grog goes bad, does it? I mean, they use it as a preservative for flog's sake. I take a small sip. It burns my throat and starts a fire in my chest. It's a good burn. Familiar.

I finish the flask in three big gulps and take a breath, feeling emboldened, lightness and heat coming into my limbs. I brandish the knife again. Suddenly, it doesn't feel so ridiculous. It feels like a weapon.

Malarkey emerges from her spot under the bunk to see what I'm up to. I hold the knife out for her to inspect. She sniffs it once, then looks up at me.

"You ready?"

She gives me a single, slow wag of her tail.

"Good girl."

Tossing the empty flask back into the drawer and slamming it closed with my hip, I pick up the other knife and climb back into the cockpit with Malarkey beside me. I feel like a soldier about to go into battle with my trusty mutt. A tipsy soldier, sure. But a soldier nonetheless.

The *Valkyrie* is alongside us now. The rush of water against her rusty, barnacle-covered hull is a roar. I hear shouted orders as the crew prepares to board us.

"Here." I hold the two knives out to Sargo. "Pick one."

Sargo looks at me as though I've just emerged from the galley with a second head.

"Bird, this is crazy."

"We don't have time to argue. Pick one. Quickly!"

"Bird, I can't—"

"Sargo!" I fix him with a fierce, grog-fueled stare. "As the Salt, so the sailor! Right?"

He stills. A kind of electricity jumps between us and I see something shift inside him. Wordlessly, he takes the bigger knife.

"We have the element of surprise." I tuck the small knife into my sleeve. "They won't be expecting us to fight back."

The air fills with a sinister hiss—the sound of uncoiling rope. Looking up I see four heavy lines flying over the side of the *Valkyrie*, four pairs of boots jumping over after them.

Here we go.

Malarkey launches herself at the first intruder before he even hits the deck. He gets an unpleasant welcome as her teeth sink into his arm. With a scream that tears my throat in half, I jump after her.

The feeling of grog in my limbs is like gunpowder, like strength I never knew I had. I shove the man hard in the chest and he stumbles backward toward the edge of the deck. Malarkey, latched onto his arm, skids with him.

Sargo must have let go of the wheel, because *Panga* suddenly swerves wildly to starboard, and I realize with a jolt that the man is about to take Malarkey overboard with him. I lunge after them, grabbing Malarkey around the chest and heaving. She releases her jaws as the man teeters backward, and he disappears over the side as I land on my back, Malarkey on top of me, kicking like a mule.

Shoving her off, I stumble to my knees, working the little knife out of my sleeve and trying to get my bearings. A hand closes around my neck from behind, yanks me to my feet, and turns me around. A hideous face, embroidered with scars, fills my vision.

He has a face, says something quiet and distant inside me.

Without thinking, I flip the little knife out of my sleeve and press it against the side of his neck. His eyes widen with momentary surprise, then crinkle with amusement.

"You know how to use that?" he leers.

My nostrils fill with the smell of rancid milk. I push the blade harder against his throat.

"Sure do," I lie.

His grin broadens and he leans toward me until the hairs of his beard are scratching my cheek.

"Go on then."

I take a breath, pushing as hard on the knife's edge as I dare.

"You don't have the salt," he growls.

Panga plunges sideways again, pulling my heart and gut into opposite ends of my body. The man slips backward, his leering face twisted into a comical 'oh' of surprise. At least, it would be comical if he wasn't dragging me with him toward the edge of the deck.

His grip tightens as *Panga* heaves again, and we teeter at the brink, the water seething below us. I feel the inescapable pull of his weight tipping us over the edge and brace myself for the cold, hard smack of the water.

But it doesn't come.

Instead, everything goes black.

chapter
sixteen

"WE WON!"

The girl's brother burst through the hut's flimsy corrugated metal door. He threw his pack at the table where his sister was eating and flung himself into a chair opposite her.

"We won! We're going!" He was breathless with excitement, and with the effort of running all the way home to share the news. His face, beet red, glistened with sweat, and his eyes shone like fire. He sprawled in the chair, heaving great breaths and looking ecstatically at the girl. He looked like a kid again; like he was eight and not fourteen-and-a-half.

"Great," his sister said quietly. She didn't look up, kept her gaze fixed on the bowl of mash she was eating with her fingers.

"Come on, aren't you excited?! We won! Do you know what that means?!"

The little girl didn't say anything. She knew what it meant. If they had won, it meant that Fife hadn't won. It meant they were going without her. It meant Fife had to stay, and she had to go.

She didn't want to go. She didn't want to leave Fife behind. But she also knew that if she didn't go, her brother would go, and she would lose him instead. Angry tears began to well in her throat.

"Are you crying?" Her brother's voice was soft.

She wiped her nose angrily. "No."

His face changed. He came around the table and dropped down on one knee next to her chair.

"Don't cry." He pulled a yellow bandana out of his sleeve and handed it to her. "It's gonna be okay."

She blew her nose and sniffled. "I don't want to go."

"I know. But we have to."

"Why?"

"Because it's a great opportunity. It's better there. Much better. You can have a real life there. Go to school and learn to read. You can grow up and get a job and live in a house. There's nothing here."

"What about Fife? Don't you care about her?"

Her brother was quiet for so long that the girl looked up at him. His face was twisted, as though he was about to cry too.

"Of course I care," he said quietly. "But it's not going to do anyone any good to be sad."

"I guess it must be easy if you don't actually have any friends," said the girl, glaring at her bowl.

Her brother stiffened. "That's not fair. Fife's my...friend too."

"Then why don't you come to the creek with us anymore?" the girl demanded, turning her furious eyes up to his. "Why don't you make fires for us any more? Why don't you care that we're leaving her behind?"

"Because she's a little girl!" he shot back, his voice rising. "You're little girls. You're only eight! Fife is eleven. I'm fourteen now. I can't be hanging around with little girls anymore. There's no one here my age! Do you understand that? This place is a wasteland. There are ten people inside the entire perimeter."

They glared at each other.

"Fife will—she'll be fine," the girl's brother said finally. "The people from Zenith said they do the Lottery every year. I'm sure they'll come back this way before too long."

The little girl frowned at her bowl. "You don't know that."

Her brother didn't say anything. He squeezed her shoulder

too tightly, then stood up quickly. "I'm thirsty. Let's make some brackish."

On the bank of the creek, the boy produced a pot from his pack. It was the same one he had made for himself the year before, well-worn with use now; a special pot with a steam trap inside the lid. He filled the pot with water from the creek while the girl set about gathering twigs and dried grass, collecting them into a little pile near the base of the tree.

"Will you show me how to make a fire?" she asked.

Her brother squinted at her. "You're too young."

"I know. I won't touch anything. But can you explain it?"

Her brother pulled a flat piece of board about three inches square from a pocket in his pack. He set it on the ground.

"This is called the fire board," he said, pointing to the flat piece of wood, "and this," he pulled a long, skinny and very straight stick from another pocket, "is called the drill."

He gathered the dried grass that she had brought into a pile and formed a nest with it on the fire board.

"That's your kindling," he said. "It's the first thing to light." He stacked the twigs and sticks around the nest like a teepee. "And that's your tinder. It catches the flame and makes it grow. You need to make a little house for the fire with the tinder, see?"

He held the slender stick between his palms and pressed the point against the board, directly in the center of the pile of kindling, and began to spin.

"When you spin the drill against the fire board, it creates heat. When you have enough heat, the kindling will catch."

He sawed away with his arms, spinning the tip of the drill against the fire board until a thin ribbon of smoke appeared. Sweat began to bead along his brow and the girl wiped it away for him with her sleeve.

"Blow," he said.

She dropped to her knees, placing her face close to the kindling, and blew a soft, steady stream of air into it. She had to keep it up for several minutes, pausing to inhale and then blowing again, gently, carefully. Spots were dancing in front of her eyes and her head was spinning when suddenly, with a soft *whoomp*, the kindling lit and they had a flame.

The boy carefully fed the single flame until it became two, then three, then grabbed the pot and placed it over the fire. Then they waited. As the toxic creek water began to boil, the steam rose into the lid, where it turned back into condensation and ran down into the steam trap, drip by drip.

After about ten minutes the boy removed the pot from the stand and looked inside. He took off the lid and set it carefully aside, then dumped what was left in the bottom of the pot back into the creek. Then he produced two small cups from his pack, handed one to the girl, and poured the water that had collected in the lid into each cup.

They sat and sipped. The water was too hot to drink, certainly not refreshing in the baking sun, and there wasn't enough of it. When they finished, the girl handed her cup back to the boy, and he put it away in the pack.

"Feel better?" he asked. She nodded, even though she didn't. "Listen, don't be scared about the City. You have to be brave. You have to be brave for Fife. Scope out the scene so you can show her what it's all about when she gets there. Okay?"

The little girl nodded again. The boy picked up his pack and put the drill and the fire board away. They started home, the girl trailing behind.

Normally, her brother was an excellent liar, but this time she could see right through him. Fife wouldn't come. He knew Fife wouldn't come. He was only saying it to make her feel better. Deep down, she suspected she would never see Fife again.

chapter
seventeen

"This is called the fire board..."

I wake with a gasp.

"...and this is called the drill."

The dream is evaporating faster than I can remember it. A girl and her brother, boiling water. Red earth. A creek.

Something cold and wet touches the back of my neck, and I nearly jump out of my skin. The dream is gone.

Malarkey's cold wet nose presses into the back of my neck again, and I hear a couple of slow thumps as her wagging tail beats against something. I open one eye. Something beside me stirs; a rustle of clothes in the darkness. A groan.

Half of my face is against a cold metal floor. My arms are twisted painfully behind me, my wrists lashed together. I can't make out anything but shades of light and dark. The walls around me creak. My cheek presses harder against the floor and then pulls away as the floor tilts one way and then the other.

I sit up, fending off Malarkey's tongue, crane my neck, and squint around. Moonlight lances through a single small window high in the opposite wall, strafing hard orange lines across a stack of crates on the floor beside me. I make out Sargo's profile. He's slumped against the crates, his chin on his chest.

"Sargo," I hiss, "can you hear me?"

"Mmh."

"Are you okay?"

"No."

"Can you move?"

His head lifts slightly and he groans. "Did we get in a fight?"

"I think so."

His head drops again. "How'd we do?"

"Not great."

Curling my knees to my chest, my hands still tied behind me, I manage to get my legs under me and struggle to my feet. The floor tilts abruptly sideways, sending me tumbling. I catch myself with my shoulder against the wall.

In front of me is a thick, metal door with a small, round window at eye-level, large rivets around the edge, and no handle. I peer out of the window.

A set of metal stairs with open rises leads from about five feet in front of the door, up over my head. I'm peering out between the steps; so we must be in a room under the stairs. Some kind of storage room, I guess.

We're on a boat. The metal deck, slick with water, throws up orange glints in the reddish moonlight. There's nothing charming about this boat—no hand-laid teak or lovingly polished stainless steel. Everything about it is functional, utilitarian, ugly.

We must be aboard the *Valkyrie*. So they caught us.

I hear Sargo struggle to his feet. He leans against the wall next to me and puts his face to the window. We watch a couple of crew members wrestling with the thick lines that control the boat's bizarre parachute sails.

"How do they sail upwind?" Sargo murmurs. "Those sails would only be effective if the wind was coming from behind."

I turn my head to gape at him in disbelief. "Really? *That's* what you're thinking about right now?"

He gives a slight shrug. "I guess so."

"Unbelievable."

The boy is obsessed with sailing.

In total, I count five people moving about the deck. I can't make out their faces, but I'm not sure if that's because they don't have any, or because it's too dark to see. The flat, orange disk of the moon is just bright enough to make out some of their clothes. I catch flashes of cleavers tucked into waistbands, knives laced into the ankles of thick leather work boots.

"Sargo," I murmur, "how did we...get here?"

"They caught us."

"Right, but—how did we get *here*? On this boat? How did they get us off *Panga?*"

"You don't remember?"

Things are coming back to me. I remember a chase, a fight, a leering face and rancid breath. But I have no memory of being brought to this boat.

Sargo squeezes his eyes shut and tilts his head from side to side, as though the act of remembering physically hurts him.

"There was one really big guy who cornered me. Malarkey went after one of them. And then I saw you—" His eyes go wide in the moonlight and he looks straight at me. "I saw you go over the side."

Icy horror shoots up my spine. I *did* go over the side. At least— I thought I did. I remember now—the churning water, the grip of the man, pulling me toward the edge, tipping, tipping, and then...nothing.

That guy who had me must have regained his footing and knocked me out. Or maybe we fell back onto the boat and I hit my head. Or maybe I drank so much of that flask I found that I just— blacked out again.

Blipped again. Not blacked out. We're using a fun word for it now, remember?

That seems crazy though. There wasn't *that* much in that flask...

"I...I think I almost did go over the side," I say slowly. "One of them had me. *Panga* went sideways and he lost his footing. I thought he was taking me down with him for sure."

"So what happened?"

I shake my head. "I don't know. I can't—I can't remember."

All I remember is blackness and then the dream: a boy and a girl, and hard, red earth. But how can I explain that to Sargo? More to the point: how can I explain that to Sargo without telling him about the grog?

He's staring at me with a funny look on his face. "I *saw* you go over," he says, with a slight shake of his head. "I saw you...disappear."

I give him a small, apologetic shrug. "I guess...I didn't? I don't know. I'm sorry."

"You really don't remember?"

I shake my head.

He squeezes his eyes shut. "Anyway, I guess it doesn't matter." He tilts his head from side to side again, slowly this time, wincing. "That big guy hit me with a bag of something."

A shout from outside jars me back into myself. I have no idea how I didn't end up dragged to Jones' locker, but at the moment, honestly, we have more important things to worry about. I press my face to the corner of the window again.

The ceiling shudders with heavy footsteps, and a pair of stout boots appears on the top step above my head. They scuff their way slowly to the bottom, then turn in my direction.

I pull away from the door and drop to the floor. "Get down!"

The door opens with a series of clicks, and a shaft of orange moonlight falls across my face, blinding me. Malarkey's cannon-fire bark fills the room, and I sense her massive frame launching through space at the opening. There's a gruff curse, a dull thud, a yelp, and I hear her claws skittering back toward me.

"They're awake," says a thin, high-pitched voice. "What do you wanna do with them?"

I squint at the doorway. The man standing in it is barely as tall as I am sitting down, and appears to be all chest and shoulders. Moonlight from behind him gleams off his bald head, rendering him in silhouette. I can't make out his face.

There's a muffled reply that I don't catch, and then a second figure appears over his shoulder, a wiry skeleton, silver coils of hair like a halo around her head, illuminated from behind by the moon.

"Get the captain," she croaks.

Another creak, the door clicking closed, then the sound of retreating footsteps. Malarkey whimpers. I inch myself toward her, my hands still bound behind me, and press my forehead to hers.

"I'm sorry Lark. We're gonna get you out of here."

Sargo grunts and I hear him shifting to sit against the wall. "I don't think this is an Anonymity ship," he says under his breath. "Those weren't Anonymity members."

"How do you know?"

"The Anonymity hack their chips with malware to hide their faces," says Sargo. "Remember? The guys who came to your house in Brume—you couldn't see their faces. Those two," he nods after the retreating footsteps, "I saw both their faces."

"I couldn't see anything. The moon was so bright."

"I only caught a glimpse. But I definitely saw their faces. They weren't hiding."

"So...who are they?" I ask.

Sargo takes a deep breath and exhales through his nose. "Dead Reckoners."

"Dead *Reckoners?* The people who were supposed to be living out at Île Tor? But I thought—didn't they all die in the pandemic?"

"They looked pretty alive to me."

"What do they want with us?"

"It could be anything. Our boat, coin, food. Maybe they think they can ransom us, or sell—"

Footsteps outside. The door swings open again and a hulking form fills the doorway, blocking the moon entirely. Pants crusty with salt, a stiff coat restraining a bosom like a pair of boulders in a sack. She squats, bringing her hard black eyes level with mine.

She doesn't bother with a mask or bandana; against her weathered gray skin, her lips are a gleaming black bloodstain in the red moonlight.

"Miss Howsley," she growls.

My blood freezes. "H—ow do you know who I am?"

Her lips twist into a grin that's more like a snarl. "I know all about you, Miss Howsley."

I detect the trace of an accent—a softness around the 'how' that makes 'Howsley' sound more like 'Hosely.'

"Well," she continues, "not *all* about you, I suppose. I didn't expect you to put up such a fight." She glares at Malarkey. Malarkey growls. The captain turns to Sargo. "Mr. Paz, I presume?"

I feel Sargo trembling against my shoulder. "Yes."

She leers. "Well, that's grand. Two for the price of one. And with a boat thrown in to boot." She leans toward Sargo and lowers her voice. "She is a beauty. Yours, I presume?"

Sargo nods, tight-lipped. The captain pats his cheek.

"Good lad. And you, Miss. I imagine you're...first mate?"

I nod, tensely.

Her expression slackens into one of derision. "Cute."

She grabs my face in her beefy hand and turns it from side to side, looking at my squashed features down her wide, crooked nose.

"Who are you?" I grunt through fish lips.

"That's not information you need to have, sweetheart."

"Why did you chase down our ship?"

She curls a lip. "Business."

"What kind of business?"

"You could call it freelancing."

"What does that mean?"

Still squeezing my face in her meaty paw, she pulls me toward her and leans her own face close to me. "It means we work for whoever's payin', and today, someone's payin' big for you two."

"Mercenaries," mutters Sargo.

"If you like."

"Who's paying?" I demand.

She lets go of me and stands. "I'm afraid that information is on a need-to-know basis." She wipes her hand on her coat as though I might have contaminated it. "No hard feelings. Like I said, it's just business. You understand."

She turns. As she does, Malarkey, perhaps sensing an easy target, goes for her backside. But the captain hears the approach and counters, slugging Malarkey across the face with the back of her forearm, then kicking her in the ribs as she staggers sideways. Malarkey yelps and I scramble to her as the captain walks away, her boots like a draft horse on the slick black deck.

"Where are you taking us?" I yell.

"All in good time, missy." She waves a hand over her shoulder without turning around. "Close 'em up!"

The door slams shut, plunging us back into darkness. I get to my knees, my heart racing.

"They're gonna take us to the Anonymity." I shuffle blindly to the wall and use it to push myself to my feet. "They're going to sell us back to the Anonymity!"

"Bird," Sargo hisses. "Calm down!"

"Calm down?! We need to get off this boat!"

"How do you plan to do that? We're completely outnumbered! They have weapons."

I don't really register Sargo's voice, as I'm too busy flinging myself at the door, which opens so suddenly I almost fall through it. A wiry pair of hands catch me hard by the shoulders. An old woman's face, so black it's almost blue in the moonlight, razor-sharp, and etched with deep, angry lines, glares into mine. I recognize the halo of silver curls around her head: the skeleton who stood behind the little bald man when he first opened our cell.

"Keep it down, Turf Rat," she says quietly.

"Why don't you make me?" I spit back.

The cold sting of a blade is suddenly against my throat. She grins a nasty grin full of metal teeth as she leans on the point just hard enough to hurt me.

"Careful what you wish for, Turf Rat," she whispers. "I just might."

She pulls away the blade and shoves me back into the room. I glimpse her silver-toothed grin once more before the door slams shut.

"Bird, please try to think," says Sargo as I slide down the wall and sit next to him. "I don't think we're barging our way out of this one."

I hang my pounding head between my knees. My shoulders ache. My wrists, still tied behind me, are raw.

"Okay," I mumble. "So what's the plan?"

"I think we should wait. Observe the crew. Think. We might see an opportunity."

It's not what I want to hear. Sitting around doing nothing is not my preferred way of handling things. But at the moment I can't come up with anything better. I tap my foot on the floor and try to roll the stiffness out of my shoulders.

"Fine," I say finally. "But you're on first watch."

I turn my back and lie down as best I can, wedging myself between the wall and the crates. I hear Sargo get to his feet again and lean his shoulder against the wall by the window.

"Sails! Off the starboard stern!"

A muffled yell from somewhere above pulls me back to consciousness. I open my eyes to the dim cell, now awash with the gray light of early dawn. The ceiling above me shudders with the pounding of footsteps.

"All hands!" someone yells on the other side of the door.

"What's going on?" I hiss.

"I don't know." Sargo is peering through the window. "It sounds like they're trying to gain speed."

As he says this, the room lurches. A thunderous clap that sounds like one of the ship's massive parachute sails launching shakes the walls around us.

"It's Savage!" comes another hoarse shout from the deck.

We lurch sideways again with a gut-wrenching crunch. I hear Malarkey's claws skittering sideways across the floor.

"Flogging Molly!" grunts Sargo, "I think we've been *hit!*"

Scrambling to my feet, I brace my shoulder against the wall and press my face to the window.

"They're boarding us!" comes another cry from above, but a chorus of angry hollers drowns out the last word. The sound of pounding feet multiplies, and pairs of boots begin spilling down the staircase onto the deck.

The air fills with the sizzle of uncoiling ropes and shadowy figures drop onto the deck as if from the sky. The air becomes so filled with shouting and the clang of metal on metal that I can barely make myself heard as I turn to Sargo.

"I think I see an opportunity!"

In the corner of the room is a crate with a crooked nail sticking out of one side, the end of it sharp where a hammer must have chipped off the head. I drop to my knees and begin sawing the rope around my wrists against the point. Sweat is beading along my hairline and running down my spine when the rope finally snaps. My hands come loose with a sudden jolt, and I pull the nail from the crate to cut Sargo loose.

He peers through the tiny window, rubbing his wrists.

"And what's your plan for getting through this commercial-grade walk-in refrigerator door?"

"So salty," I mutter, shoving him out of the way with my shoulder so I can look through it too.

Crusty-looking men and women are slashing at each other with knives, cleavers and clubs as the cold, yellowish light of dawn creeps over the smoggy horizon. I count maybe twelve, total. It's impossible to tell who is part of the *Valkyrie's* crew, and who is part of the crew that just boarded her.

"I'm not being salty," mutters Sargo, "I'm being logical. There's no way we're getting through this—"

I take as much of a run at the door as the tiny room will allow and launch myself at it, landing heavily on my shoulder.

Sargo winces. "Jesus, Bird!"

"It moved! I felt it move." I tilt my eyebrow at him. "And since when do you say *Jesus?* Mr. Polytheistic revolution."

"Since the situation started to call for it," he snaps back. "And that door definitely didn't move. There's no way that door moved. What are you, like a hundred and ten pounds soaking wet?"

"I'm a hundred and ten pounds bone dry *thank you very much.* Come on, help me!"

"Can we just stop and think? I'm sure there's a better—"

"Don't think, just do!" I launch myself at the door again.

"Bird! You're not going to barge your way out of this! Please, just—"

Something in my shoulder torques painfully as I land against the door. I blow a frizz of hair out of my sweaty face and lean against the wall, rubbing it.

"Fine. What's your plan?"

"I don't have one yet."

He presses his face to the window again and I restrain a frustrated sigh. *Typical Sargo.* Doesn't want to go along with my plan, but never has an idea of his own. I let myself slide to a seat against the wall. My shoulder throbs. Outside, the brawl continues. Minutes pass.

As they do, the sounds of the fight diminish. The shouts become less frequent. I make out the sounds of individual blows. I hear someone give an order to 'drop your weapon!'

Can it possibly be over so quickly?

I start to pull myself to my feet, but Sargo drops to a knee next to me, pushing me down with a hand on my shoulder.

"Someone's coming," he says.

"What?"

"Someone is coming!"

chapter
eighteen

I THROW myself onto the floor in the shadows, my back against the door as the brisk *clip-clop* of boots on the metal deck approaches. At the last moment, the sound changes as the boots step onto the bottom step and climb the stairs over my head. They *clip-clop* across the ceiling toward where I assume the ship's helm is, then back and forth for a few moments.

"All clear," a girl's voice shouts. "Let's get to work."

Sargo and I sit motionless, our backs to the door, as the boots *clop* down the stairs and away toward the bow. As they retreat, I feel Sargo slowly unfold himself and get to his feet. Keeping to the shadows, he leans a shoulder against the wall and looks through the window again. I push myself up and lean against the opposite wall, doing the same.

The girl walking away from us is short and well-muscled, with dark brown skin and what looks like a buzzcut. The first rays of the rising sun behind her render enough to see that she wears cargo pants and low-heeled ankle boots, and has a small pack slung around her hips. She walks purposefully, toward a congregation of people at midship, about twenty feet from us.

The group is lit from behind, so it's difficult to make out much detail, but I spot two shapes I recognize: the very short bald man and the old Black woman who came to our cell last night. A third person—a lanky fellow with a shock of frizzy ginger hair lit like a fireball by the sun behind him—casually holds a long-handled ax across one shoulder, standing with one foot propped up on something.

I squint at the thing under his foot. A lump, maybe a sack of something. Next to it are three other lumps, lined up in a row. At the far end of the row, the old woman rests the tip of a cleaver as wide and long as her leg on the last lump. The bald man stands behind her, the top of his shiny head barely coming up to the height of the old woman's waist, a thick, nail-studded club as tall as he is resting in the crook of his shoulder.

"Prisoners up," barks the girl with the buzzcut as she draws level with the group. The lanky figure removes his foot from the lump and stoops, and I realize with a jolt that the lump is a person. The three other lumps stumble to their feet as the redhead yanks the first up by one arm.

"Where's Stark?" barks the girl.

The hulking form and enormous bosoms of the captain who interrogated us last night stumbles forward. Shoving her from behind is a man so large I do a double take. His arms are almost as big around as the bald man's tiny chest. A shock of short, black hair sticks straight up from the center of his head, like a mohawk.

He pushes the captain to her knees in front of the row of prisoners, where she slumps with her head hanging.

"And Savage?" the girl says.

Silence. The big man clasps his hands in front of him and stands over the captain with his feet wide apart, like a soldier.

"Where is Savage?" repeats the girl, irritation edging her voice.

"Right here."

A young man's treble cuts through the still air, and a figure who looks to be about Sargo's height and build hops nimbly over the *Valkyrie's* rail, I assume from a ladder. I squint, trying to make out either a face or a blank void, but he's lit from behind, and all I can see is shadows. Next to me, I feel Sargo tense.

The man—who I assume is Savage—lands lightly on the deck

and pauses, pushing shaggy, unkempt hair from his face and dipping one hand into the pocket of what looks like a peacoat. He withdraws something small and slender and lifts it to his lips, then tips his head back and exhales a plume of thick, white smoke into the morning.

"Is this all of them?" he says. He has an accent I can't place—a kind of twangy drawl. The Black girl with the buzzcut steps forward and nods once, tightly. "Okay, thank you, Fetch. Dismissed."

The girl doesn't move. She seems to pull herself a little taller, as though about to say something, then abruptly pivots and stalks to the other side of the deck. Savage saunters away from the rail toward the group, pulling the collar of his peacoat up around his jaw.

"Mojave Stark," he says, drawing level with the kneeling captain and putting the dart to his lips again. "Didn't think we'd run into each other so soon."

The boulder-bosomed captain drags her gaze up from the floor to meet his.

"Jameson Briggs-Savage," she replies. Her voice is thick, as though she's working the words around blood and broken teeth.

"This is quite the situation you've found yourself in," says Savage.

Stark abruptly turns her face down and spits at his feet. Savage *tuts* and lifts one foot to inspect his boot.

"Mind your manners, Stark." He shoves the toe of the boot into her chest. She topples sideways, bracing her fall with bound hands.

Savage puts a hand into his other pocket and withdraws another item. He flips it over in one hand and a flash of metal reveals the item to be a butterfly knife. He spins it deftly around in his fingers a few times so that it opens and closes, catching the sun, making soft, sinister *snicks* in the still morning air.

"Quite the situation," he repeats. He stops the knife so

suddenly my heart skips, holding it with the point toward Stark. "Find yourself a little shorthanded last night?"

"Go to hell," says Stark.

"I'm sure I will," says Savage cooly. "And I'd be very surprised if I didn't see you there." He flips the knife end over end, a lazy, hypnotic motion. "But I suppose I do owe you an apology. I'm sure it was an unpleasant shock to discover last night that Sterling and Nana here were, in fact, never really part of your crew."

The tiny bald man utters a high-pitched, raspy chuckle and adjusts his stance. The old Black woman with the mane of wiry gray curls sneers and flourishes her cleaver.

Stark wipes her chin with her two bound hands. "No skin off my hide. What do I want with a bald midget and a toothless old hag?"

The old woman steps away from the prisoner she's guarding with frightening speed and shoves the point of her cleaver hard against Stark's cheek.

"Call him 'midget' again," she growls.

"Alright, Nana." Savage holds up a hand. "We need her alive, at least for now."

The old woman doesn't move right away, leaning on the blade until Stark flinches, then drops it with a snarl and returns to her post.

"So, Stark," Savage continues, flipping the knife over in his hand as he speaks, "what's the angle with that little yellow boat you've got rafted up alongside?"

Next to me, Sargo catches his breath. *Panga.* They have *Panga.*

"None of your business," growls Stark.

Savage shakes his head. "I thought you might say that. But that's where you're wrong, Stark. I'm afraid it is my business, because, you see—"

He flips the blade again, catching it by the point, then drops to his haunches in front of her. He raps the handle of the knife against the side of her head.

"—What's happened here is, we've commandeered your ship. Commandeered it with the intention of taking anything and everything that isn't nailed down, I'm afraid. And that *may* include that lovely yellow boat. But before we take it, we'd like a little more information. We'd like to know what we're potentially getting ourselves into, vis-a-vis, kidnapping situations and the like."

Stark glares at him, silent.

Savage raps the handle of the knife against her head again. "I recommend cooperating," he sings. "For the sake of your men here. It's going to make things very difficult for them if you don't."

"I'm not telling you a damn thing," says Stark.

Savage sighs and gets to his feet. "I was afraid you might say that." He rubs something off the blade of the knife with his thumb. "That's what I've never understood about you, Stark. You've no consideration for the lives of your own crew."

In a breath, he lunges, grabs the prisoner standing nearest him by the back of the neck, and uppercuts the knife into the man's jaw.

The man retches, and his eyes bulge as Savage pulls the blade back out, a thick, strangled gurgle and a slick of black liquid following it. The man collapses to the deck, burbling incoherently.

My stomach heaves. I reel away from the window, my hand over my mouth, and come up hard against the wall behind me. Sargo stands frozen, staring through the window, his chest rising and falling rapidly.

"That's one," I hear Savage say.

Swallowing the tide of cold panic crawling up my throat, I force myself to look back through the window. The big man with the mohawk scoops up the convulsing body in his thick arms and dumps it unceremoniously over the side. Savage produces a bandana from the inside breast pocket of his coat and wipes the man's blood from the blade and his hand.

"Fetch!" he barks. The girl with the buzzcut steps forward.

"Shake this place down. If there were souls on that boat, I want to know about them."

"There were," the old woman—Nana—sneers. "They're right over there."

She lifts her cleaver and points it directly at the door I'm standing behind. My blood runs cold. Of course. She knows exactly where we are. She put us in here last night while she and the little bald man were pretending to be part of Stark's crew.

Fetch nods once, then pivots, beckoning the lanky redhead after her with a flick of her wrist. I pull away from the window again, finding Sargo's terrified eyes in the dim light. Wordlessly, we both sink to the floor. I realize my hand is still covering my mouth and pull it away.

Malarkey, apparently sensing our distress, walks a circle between us, her nails clicking against the cold metal floor, until I grab her around the neck and force her into a sit, holding her still between my knees. I realize she's shaking, and then I realize that it's not her shaking, it's me.

Savage is saying something outside, but I can't seem to hear anything over the sound of my ragged breath and the *clip-clop* of those heeled boots walking the deck toward us. Another *glug* turns my stomach, and the muted *thud* of a body dropping to the deck tells me a second man has died. Stark curses.

The *clip-clop* of the boots draws nearer.

Savage says something and Stark curses again. Another *glug*, another *thud*. The sound of my breath creates an off-kilter rhythm with the beat of the approaching steps and the pounding of my heart, until I'm no longer sure which sounds are coming from outside my body, and which are coming from within.

The boots draw nearer. Nearer. They pause outside the door. Malarkey snarls.

The door opens so fast that even Malarkey is caught off guard. Instead of lunging and barking, she jumps and scurries for the back corner as the buzzcut girl and the redhead push through the doorway.

I scrabble backwards on my hands, but the girl is already on top of me. She's shorter than me, but her dark brown hands are hard and strong, and up close I can feel the solidity of the muscle packed around her tiny frame. She pulls me to my feet and shoves me through the door ahead of her. I look back for Sargo, but she grabs the side of my face with her whole palm and forces it forward.

The door slams behind me, Malarkey barking her head off on the other side of it. I stumble on numb legs toward the group; Stark still on her knees, the big man with the mohawk dumping another body over the side, Stark's only remaining living crew member shaking so hard I can see it from fifteen feet away. The old woman leans against the rail with her wiry arms folded, the leg-sized cleaver hanging from her hip, a silver-toothed sneer painted across her face.

Savage has the bandana in one hand and is wiping off the blade of the knife. He looks up at the sound of our approaching steps. "Ah, that's a shame," he says, a pained expression briefly crossing his face. "So it is a kidnapping situation."

Stifled sobbing reaches my ears, and as I draw level with the group I realize it's coming from Stark's remaining crew member. He's just a boy, probably younger than me. Gangly, pale-skinned, with big feet and hands and a face pockmarked with acne. Savage finishes cleaning off the blade while he looks me up and down with sharp, gray eyes.

A tangle of dirty-blonde hair falls around his chin, and a scraggle of scruffy beard, flecked with salt and pepper, covers his jaw. Under the peacoat, he wears a faded black shirt and black jeans full of holes. I note the word HOLD tattooed across the knuckles of the hand that holds the knife. His lean face, white, but tanned a deep gold by the sun and marred with a patina of dirt, is faintly lined, but youthful.

So he has a face, at least. So this probably isn't the Anonymity. Honestly, though, I'd welcome the Anonymity over these guys under the current circumstances.

Sargo stumbles to a halt next to me, his arms pinned to his sides by the lanky redhead, whose skin is so white it's almost translucent, and spattered with constellations of freckles. His wild mane of ginger hair is matched by an equally impressive beard, and he wears an olive-green army jacket and pants. A long-handled ax hangs from a black canvas strap at his hip.

Savage's eyes take Sargo in, then return to the knife. I glimpse the word *FAST* tattooed across the knuckles of his other hand.

"Welcome to the party, my friends," he says. His eyes flick back to my face, and I find myself momentarily caught off guard by how handsome he is; terrifying, but striking. Beautiful in the way a wolf is beautiful, right before it tears your face off. He returns his attention to the knife, wiping more blood from the blade and says, casually, "How much of that did you hear?"

"Nothing," I blurt.

He smirks, shaking his head, and for a fraction of a second, I see something almost like pity flit through his eyes. Or maybe I just imagine that I see it. Maybe I'm just so desperate not to be stabbed in the jaw and thrown over the side that I convince myself I see sympathy in those gray, wolfish eyes.

"They heard it all," says Fetch from behind me.

Savage tuts. "That's a shame."

He swaps the knife into his other hand and tucks the bandana into his back pocket before turning his attention back to the captain kneeling on the deck.

"So, Stark," he says, "what was the plan here? Hm? Take that beautiful yellow boat from these nice young folks and sell it to the highest bidder?" He waves the point of the knife at me and Sargo. "Maybe sell these nice young folks to the highest bidder too, while you're at it?"

Stark hisses through her teeth. "You don't know what you're talking about."

"Well then, by all means, enlighten me, Stark!" Savage cries, his voice tipping into impatience. "I've given you ample opportunity and incentive to explain to me what the hell is going on here."

Stark doesn't respond. *Why doesn't she respond?* Why not just tell him she was hired by the Anonymity to track us down? Why not just tell him she's taking us back to Brume? Why let him kill three of her crew?

Savage sighs and flips the knife over a few times. Then he crosses briskly to the boy, the only member of Stark's crew left standing, and throws an arm around his shoulder. He waves the knife casually under the boy's nose as he leans on him the way a friend might lean on another friend to share a piece of advice. The boy whimpers. I find myself staring at the mesmeric glint of the blade, transfixed.

Savage lowers his voice conspiratorially. "I suppose you can't tell me what it is your lowlife scum-of-the-earth captain is up to here, can you?"

The boy stifles a sob and shakes his head. Savage draws a deep breath and lets it go very slowly. He stops the blade again, holding the knife loosely in his hand. He, the boy, and I all stare at it. My pulse screams in my wrists.

"And you're sure about that, are you?"

"I don't—I don't kn—know any—" the boy chokes down a gulp of air, "anything."

Savage nods, slowly, then pats the boy on the shoulder. "Okay." He pulls away, releasing his grip. "That's not your fault." He steps away and I see the boy visibly crumple with relief. "Fetch!"

The grip around my arms releases and Fetch steps around me.

"See to him," Savage says.

The boy's face goes white with terror. Fetch pulls a crooked knife half as long as my arm from a sheath strapped across her chest. She levels it at the boy. She's at least a head shorter than him, but he withers in front of that tiny, solid ball of muscle, the shaved head, the hard, black eyes.

"Move," she says quietly, and flicks the knife to the right.

It's dawning on me that I'm no longer physically restrained by anyone when the big man with the mohawk steps out of the shadows. The impulse to run and the impulse to freeze fight for space in my limbs as he bears down on me. But as he draws nearer, both impulses are replaced by stupefied surprise as I realize that he isn't a man at all.

She's a woman—a young woman, probably in her early twenties. The muscles in her arms and chest coil like ropes under a thin tank top riddled with holes. Nearly every inch of her is covered in intricate tattoos that weave and knot across her alabaster skin. Her wide, sharply defined jaw and heavy brows are set in a grim expression of malcontent. She carries no weapon. She's the only person on the deck who doesn't. She's so awesome—and I mean literally awesome—that by the time I realize I'm staring and haven't even tried to escape, her hands are around my arms, and I'm captive again.

Fetch has driven the boy over to the rail on the side of the boat nearest the shore. He looks wide-eyed at the distant, rocky cliffs, pounded by the surf, then back at her.

Savage steps in front of me, wrenching my attention back to him.

"Well, Stark," he says, "since it looks like I won't be getting anything useful out of you or any of your crew regarding these fine young folks and their little yellow boat, I suppose there's not much point in wasting your time any longer."

A splash to my right whips my head around. The boy is gone. Fetch slips the knife back into the sheath across her chest and stalks back toward us. I widen my eyes at Sargo, who shakes his head almost imperceptibly. Did the boy jump? Did she kill him and throw him overboard?

Savage flips the knife closed and tucks it into his pocket, then tilts his head at the redhead. The redhead and the woman with the mohawk release Sargo and I and haul Stark to her feet.

"God dammit Savage!" Stark screams as they drag her away. "One day you're going to be sorry you did this."

"All you had to do was cooperate, Stark," Savage calls after her. He puts both hands in his coat pockets and turns to us, his eyes landing on mine. "All you have to do is cooperate."

Suddenly, Sargo's hand is around my wrist. He pulls me sideways and steps in front of me, his familiar scent bizarrely washing over me, disorienting in this nightmare.

Peering around him, I see amusement turning up the corners of Savage's mouth. With his eyes on me, he removes the dart from his pocket again and puts it to his lips. His eyes don't leave mine until he tips his chin up to exhale a thick plume of fruity smoke.

"No need to fight over who goes first," he says to the sky. "There'll be plenty of time to kill you both."

chapter
nineteen

SAVAGE JERKS his chin at Nana and a moment later I feel the iron grip of her bony fingers around my arms. Flanked by Fetch and Name, we follow Savage toward our cell.

Nana chuckles, walking too close behind me, deliberately stepping on my heels and gripping my elbow painfully with one hand. She leans on the point of the limb-sized cleaver she has between my shoulders.

"I call this the Rat Catcher," she wheezes into my ear. "Wanna find out why, Turf Rat?"

As we reach the steps that lead above the cell door, I hear Malarkey scratching and whining on the other side of it. To my surprise, Savage doesn't return us to the cell. Instead, we climb the stairs.

Every step threatens to buckle my knees. I somehow make it to the top, where the upper level is enclosed by a solid steel pilot house with a large window in the front. Savage ducks through a door in the side of it, and we follow him into a sparsely furnished, utilitarian cockpit.

I've gathered that this isn't Savage's boat, but he somehow seems to know his way around—he reaches over his head without looking to tug on a small light in the ceiling.

The light is harsh, and I squeeze my eyes shut against it. When

I open them, Savage has sprawled in the captain's chair, crossing his feet on the corner of the navigation console. His boots are the kind with steel toes and laces; scuffed, and flecked with salt.

Nana releases my arm and slinks to lean against the wall near the filing cabinet. Her wide, calloused toes spread firmly onto the floor like roots. Like someone used to being on the Salt. Someone used to standing on unstable floors that tilt and roll and try to knock you down. She props her blade against her leg, then pulls a sliver of a knife from the breast pocket of a ratty silk cardigan, and begins to pick her teeth with it.

"Do you have to do that in here?"

Fetch, arms folded, stands wide-legged across the open door-way. She's close enough now that I can take in the array of small, silver hoops that adorn both of her ears. A similar hoop pierces one nostril, and a fine silver chain links it to one of the hoops in her left ear. As she turns her head I make out a tiny tattoo on her shaved scalp, just above that same ear—the number *4242*. So small it's almost invisible against her skin.

She looks younger than me—and she's definitely smaller, but I note the veins in her forearms. The muscles in her sleek, velvety biceps. The abs visible through the shirt.

The door is still open. But would I stand a chance of getting through it? Past her?

Savage drags on the dart again and surveys us with mild curiosity, apparently in no hurry to speak. When he tilts his chin and exhales, I see a gap in his mouth where his left canine should be. The tips of the thumb and first two fingers on his right hand—the hand with *FAST* tattooed across the knuckles—are black and shiny. I note almost invisible lines at the corners of his eyes. I can't place his age. Thirty, maybe?

Nana's tiny knife *nicking* softly against her teeth is the only sound in the room. The silence buzzes against the edges of my fraying nerves.

"What do you want with us?" I finally blurt, my voice too loud. *"Why haven't you killed us yet?"* is what I mean to ask.

Savage drags on his dart again. His eyes flick to Sargo.

"That's your little yellow boat rafted up out there."

It isn't a question. Smoke pours lazily from his mouth and curls around his face as his speaks.

"It is," says Sargo carefully.

"Cute," drawls Fetch from the doorway.

Savage looks past my shoulder to her. "Fetch, I'm sure Sterling needs a hand cataloguing the score we're taking from the *Valkyrie*. Would you be so kind?"

Fetch tenses and fixes her steely glare on Savage. "Why can't I stay?"

Silence descends. I stand in the middle of it, trembling in the heat of Fetch and Savage's mutual glares.

From the wall by the filing cabinet, Nana leers. "Go on, girl. Git."

"I don't take orders from you, Nana," growls Fetch, her voice so hard it makes the hair on the back of my neck stand up.

Savage waves a hand. "Nana, why don't you get out of here, too. See if Red and Goliath have finished with Stark."

Finished with her? Finished *what*?

"Maybe she'll have an eyeball left for you to extract," Savage continues. My stomach wobbles and I have the overwhelming urge to sit down.

Nana twists her mouth and grumbles, snatching up the cleaver and laying it across her bony shoulder as she skulks out the door.

Fetch doesn't move. She and Savage glare at each other for another long minute. Then, with a sharp exhale through her nose, she pivots and stalks out of the room, slamming the door behind her.

At the sound of it banging shut, my insides clench. *Is it locked? Is there another way out?*

Savage removes the butterfly knife from his pocket again and swivels it open, casually.

"I need to make a brief imposition on your time, my friends," he says, "in the form of some questions."

Friends. I clench my trembling hands into fists. If he's going to kill us, I wish he'd get on with it already.

He flips the knife again. "You may have gotten the gist outside, but the long and short of it is, I can't for the life of me figure out why Mojave Stark might have taken an interest in a small…underfunded boat, such as yours."

Of course. There would be no obvious reason for a boat like the *Valkyrie* to chase down a tiny sloop like *Panga*. We don't look wealthy. We don't have expensive equipment or cargo, and *Panga* herself isn't worth much. There would have to be another reason. Something to make it worth Stark's while. That's what he's trying to figure out.

That's why he hasn't killed us. The realization hits me like cold water to the face. He's trying to figure out what we're worth. Who's after us. As long as he thinks we're worth something, we might be worth keeping alive. Whatever the redhead and that big woman are doing to Stark right now is probably in aid of finding out how to get their hands on that score.

I wonder how tightly Stark will cling to that information. If she gives it up—if Savage finds out we're wanted by the Anonymity—I've no doubt he'll turn us over to them in a heart-beat for the payout.

My mind races. I suddenly see our position—halfway between the frying pan and the fire. This is an opportunity. With Stark out of the picture, we can stay clear of the Anonymity. And as long as Savage thinks we're valuable, he won't kill us. But how can I make him think we're valuable without telling him why? And can I do it before the redhead and that giant pull the truth out of Stark?

I meet Savage's gaze again, schooling my face into an expression of naive uncertainty, hoping his incisive eyes haven't just watched me work all that out, stalling for time while my brain climbs around inside my skull.

"I—I don't know what she wanted. We were…we were just sailing. She came out of nowhere."

He arches an eyebrow. "Just sailing."

I nod.

"And may I ask where a boat of your size, carrying such an… unlikely crew, might be 'just sailing' to?"

Sargo's voice behind my shoulder is unnaturally hard. "None of your business."

"Now look!" Savage stabs the point of the knife into the arm of his chair with an abruptness that makes me jump. "I'm doing my best to be patient here. But my patience will wear thin very quickly if I don't see at least a modicum of cooperation from the two of you."

His eyes flick back to me as he takes another drag on the dart, leaving the knife sticking out of the chair.

"Why don't we start with some names?"

I say the first name that comes into my head that isn't mine. "Electra—Nation."

"Nation?" Savage cocks his head.

Suddenly I realize what I've just done. I've just told this murderous Reckoner that I'm the daughter of the CEO of Zenith. Even out here, on the Salt, five hundred miles from Brume, people know what that means. The daughter of Axioma Nation, one of the most powerful women in the world. My pulse accelerates.

I just made myself worth something.

"Yes," I say, my brain scrambling to catch up with my mouth. "Electra Nation. This is—" I stumble over a list of possible aliases for Sargo; something that won't be tied to the Anonymity, "— Pitch Starkey."

The name of the first boy I ever kissed. Not sure why that popped into my head.

Savage regards me quietly. "And what, exactly, is the daughter of the CEO of Zenith doing out here 'just sailing' in the middle of the Salt?"

"I was…" My mind spins, pulling disparate threads together into some kind of story that might sound convincing. "We were running away. Pitch and I are…in love. But he's—my family doesn't approve."

Savage turns mildly amused eyes to Sargo. "In love?"

I force myself not to look at Sargo, but every nerve in my body silently screams at him to play along. I feel as though I'm walking an extremely narrow ledge, struggling not to look down. Electra doesn't look anything like me—she looks like someone whose family came from Zhīliú, not like a little white girl from Brume—but apparently Savage doesn't know that.

"Yes," says Sargo, and a strange jolt of elation pierces through my panic. "Yes, we're in love."

The sound of those words is so oddly exhilarating that I almost forget why he's saying them. And that they aren't true. I fight back the heat rushing to my cheeks and force myself to focus on Savage.

"Your family must be worried about you," his drawl is edged with amusement as he turns his attention back to me, "if they were desperate enough to hire someone as unscrupulous as Mojave Stark to find you."

"Yes."

"And I imagine she was to take you back to—Brume, is it?"

I hesitate. "Yes, but…we were trying to get to Alluvium. I have a brother there. If you…if you let us go—"

"Let you go?" Savage's eyes dance. "I don't think I'll be doing that. Not when your family in Brume will be so grateful to see you returned safely. You've found your way to a particularly dangerous part of the world, my friend. I'd be remiss if I didn't offer my services."

"Services?"

"Mojave Stark may be the lowliest Reckoner I've ever met in these waters, but she's certainly not the *only* Reckoner. I wouldn't want to leave you at the mercy of any other unscrupulous types."

"So they are Reckoners," I whisper.

Savage inclines his head. "As am I."

"Pirates," mutters Sargo.

Savage's lips twitch. "We prefer 'freelancers.' But yes, if you like. Pirates who know these waters far better than you do, my friend. I'm willing to bet you don't know about any of the bad weather hideouts in these waters. What would happen if you sailed into a storm?"

"We've been in a storm," says Sargo.

"I mean a real storm." Savage drags on the dart again. "No, my friends, I'm afraid this part of the world is far too unsafe for me to even *think* about sending you off on your own. Not if I'm to continue calling myself an upstanding member of society—which I would dearly love to do."

Upstanding. The murdered man's bulging eyes flash through my head. I try not to let the image panic me; try to think. Savage just wants coin. He wants a reward. If I can't convince him to let us go, can I at least convince him not to take us back to Brume? Can I buy us enough time to figure out a way to escape?

Another realization hits me: Savage can't just show up in Brume with the daughter of Zenith's CEO and demand a ransom. Zenith would overpower his crew and probably lock him up for the rest of his life. He's got to play this carefully. He probably doesn't want to deal with Zenith at all. If he thinks it'll be safer for him to deliver us to Alluvium, he might be inclined to take us there instead of Brume.

I take a breath. "Please—just...not Brume. Take us to my brother. In Alluvium. He'll pay."

Smoke curls from Savage's nostrils. I see calculations happening behind his eyes. "Alluvium's a long way from here. Your brother would have to make it worth my time."

"He will," I lie, breathless. "Whatever you want. I swear." I'm digging a hole I have no idea how to get out of, but at least we're alive.

He leans forward and pulls the knife out of the arm of his chair.

"Here's what we're going to do," he says. "My crew and I will escort you to Alluvium, where you will explain to your brother

that we—an upstanding crew of fine women and gentlemen—
rescued you from a gang of murderous pirates. Your brother will
be so overwhelmed with gratitude that he will pay me—" he
waves the knife, "—let's say...seventy five thousand Ubicoin.
There will be no further inquiry into who we are, and no attempt
will be made to contact Mojave Stark or the *Valkyrie*. You will not
mention what you witnessed this morning, nor will you mention
my name, the name of anyone on my crew, or anything you might
happen to see between here and Alluvium."

"What about our boat?" says Sargo.

His eyes narrow. "The boat you can keep."

I fight to keep the breath from leaving me all at once. He
uncrosses his boots, stands, and extends the hand with *FAST*
tattooed across the knuckles. Cautiously, I take it. His palms are
rough with callouses, his grip firm. His eyes hold mine with an
intensity that makes me want to look away, and I can feel myself
turning red.

"Fetch can help you get your boat back in the water," he says.
"Then you'll follow us south to Alluvium."

I keep my face from showing my surprise. *Follow us?* He's
sending us back to *Panga* now? He's practically handing us a
chance to escape. Either he's stupider than he looks, or I'm
missing something here.

He drags on the dart and fills the room with sweet, fruity
smoke.

"And it should be obvious that if you do anything that tests
my generosity," the blade flashes as he spins it closed, "there will
be swift renegotiation of terms."

He indicates the door with the knife, and I take it that the
conversation is over.

chapter
twenty

"THAT WAS PRETTY QUICK THINKING, HOWSLEY," mutters Sargo under his breath, as Fetch and Nana steer us down the steps from the pilot house to the *Valkyrie's* main deck. "But what the hell are we going to do when we get to Alluvium and you don't have a rich, grateful brother to bail us out?"

"I don't know," I whisper back. "I haven't gotten that far yet."

Fetch helps Sargo and I loose *Panga* from where she is tied up alongside the *Valkyrie*. We retrieve Malarkey from the cell and leave the metal warship to board our little yellow sloop.

As my feet touch the familiar planks of her deck, I almost collapse with relief. My hands shake so hard that I can barely ready the lines to set sail. From *Panga's* cockpit, we watch Savage and his crew depart the *Valkyrie* in a skiff and board their boat, the *Kingfisher*, an enormous, navy blue sailboat.

"You read me?"

Fetch's terse voice buzzes into the radio channel inside my head. At Savage's request, we've tuned our chips to an open radio frequency, like we used to do in sailing class, so the *Kingfisher* can communicate with us. I press my fingers to the spot behind my left ear.

"I read you."

"Copy that."

She buzzes out.

"She's chipped," mutters Sargo.

"What?"

"Fetch. She's chipped." His brow furrows. "From what I always heard, Reckoners aren't, or weren't. Zenith never had the resources to chip anyone outside Harbor Cities."

I furrow my brow back at him. "O—kay. Is that...something we should be worried about?"

He shrugs, shaking his head slowly. "I don't know. I don't think so. It's just...weird."

We raise *Panga's* sails and take stock of the deck, then follow the *Kingfisher* into open water. As the wind fills the sails and the familiar tilt and roll of the swell begins to gently rock us, exhaustion overwhelms me. I sink to a seat in the cockpit, my arms heavy, my legs like water. Sargo collapses behind the helm, his eyes empty.

We sit like that for several minutes, until I find enough of my voice to croak, "The first chance we get, we run, right?"

Sargo whips his head up to stare at me. "Run?" His eyes are incredulous. "No way."

"What do you mean? They let us come back to our ship. They practically handed us a chance to escape!"

He sighs, rubbing his face with one hand. "We can't escape, Bird. We can't outrun ships like that. We're not big enough, we're not fast enough. You think they would have just let us come back to *Panga* if they thought we stood a chance of outrunning them? They know we can't get away."

"So we just...do what they say? We're not actually letting these guys take us to Alluvium, are we?"

"I don't think we have a choice." He shifts on his seat and adjusts his grip around the helm, putting his gaze over the bow. "Look...Savage is obviously dangerous and I feel like he talks a lot of shit, but something he said in there stuck with me. We *are* in dangerous waters. If the *Valkyrie* chased us down that easily, I've got to think there will be more ships out there that can. The Anonymity. Other mercenaries. People who might not be as willing as Savage to cut a deal with us. And what he said about the storms...what we've seen so far is nothing. If we get caught in something big, I don't know if we could handle it. And my chip won't even pull up a map out here, what about yours?"

I open my mouth to argue, but he goes on.

"Why do you think they call these guys Dead Reckoners?"

I blink. Actually, I have no idea why they call them that.

Sargo sighs at the blank look on my face. "Because that's how they navigate. Dead reckoning. Did you really learn nothing from my class? The Net doesn't work out here. Chips are basically just radios. Most Reckoners don't even have them. There's no GPS. They use math, and the stars, and landmarks along the coast to estimate their position. It's ancient stuff. Stuff we aren't prepared to handle on our own. And if we hit weather—I mean *real* weather —we're as good as dead. If someone goes overboard in bad weather, forget it. They're gone. They would never find you."

I gape at him. "So you want to put your faith in a bunch of... pirates? Aren't you the one who's always telling me to think before I act?"

"I am thinking. I'm thinking that without this Savage guy, we might not make it to Alluvium."

"He murdered people in front of us!"

"I know Bird! I was there." His chest rises and falls. "We just need to feel this out. Keep a low profile and wait for an opportunity. Observe."

"What the hell are we going to do when we get to Alluvium and he finds out I'm not Electra?"

"I don't know, Bird. That was your brilliant plan."

Hot fury slashes through my veins. "I didn't see you coming up with anything in there."

"I'm sorry...I didn't mean that. It was quick thinking. I just..."

He shakes his head again. We lapse back into silence, him staring at the *Kingfisher*, me staring at the floor.

The morning meanders into afternoon, hot and still as we follow the *Kingfisher* along the coast. Two hours roll slowly by. Sargo puts on the autopilot and staggers below to sleep, and even though my bones ache with exhaustion and my frazzled nerves are hanging by a thread, I let him sleep and I take watch, because his face is hollow and his hands are shaking and I can't stand to see him like that.

I've been on watch for an hour or so when Fetch buzzes into my ear again.

"Some nasty-looking storm clouds coming up behind us."

There's an edge of urgency to her voice that makes me sit up out of my drowsy half-sleep. I glance over my shoulder. Black thunderheads rise out of the horizon like a dark, ominous city. I hadn't even noticed them.

I touch behind my ear to radio back. "What do we do?"

"There's a cove not far from here that we've used as a storm hole before. It's well-protected. We can make it there before the worst of the weather hits."

"Okay."

"We're tacking that way now. Close your hatches. It's gonna get rough. Over and out."

The clouds skate over the horizon so fast that by the time I've woken up Sargo, they threaten to swallow our stern. A warm wind surges through the air, whipping the Salt into a frenzy of white peaks, carrying with it a choking, yellow cloud of particulate. A smog storm. I pull my bandana up to keep the burn of sulphur out of my nose and squint through my lashes as grit and dust sting my eyes.

Sargo pulls his own bandana on and takes the helm.

"Do you see the cliffs?" he asks.

"Not yet."

He reaches down with one hand to flip open the top of one of the cockpit's bench seats and pulls out Malarkey's half-finished harness.

"Put this on Malarkey." He hands me another length of line. "And put this around your waist. Tie it to something in the cockpit. It's not a proper harness, but it'll be better than nothing."

Before we know it, the storm is on us. The Salt rolls like a bag full of jackrats. Waves rise like mountains around us, so tall that the tops disappear into hazy, swirling dust. They climb, dwarfing tiny *Panga*, and then crest, their ridges shattering, white water tumbling down their faces like landslides. Hot wind lashes my face, kicking up sheets of spray.

Sargo, his face half covered by a gray bandana, is almost a silhouette against the rapidly darkening sky. He cranks the wheel to port as we crest another wave, then fights to keep the bow pointing forward as we careen down it. I lean out to check the sails. Despite the lashing wind and rolling waves, they're holding fast.

"Don't panic!" Sargo screams over the wind. "This is what the boat was built for!"

The particulate in the air is so close and so thick I can barely see beyond the bow. As we come to the crest of another wave, a gust of wind rips across the surface of the Salt, parting the smog like curtains. In that brief moment of clarity, I spot the cliffs.

"There!" I yell, taking one hand off my handhold to point. "There they are!"

As I let go, the bow tips forward. It crashes into the face of the wave, and my other hand slips. I lose hold of the boat completely and my blood runs cold as I feel *Panga* drop away beneath me. Suddenly, I'm floating in space, no part of my body making contact with the deck.

Time slows. The sound of the wind seems to quiet. Inside my head, I hear Sargo's voice.

"If someone goes overboard in bad weather, forget it. They're gone."

Another gust of wind whips the curtain of smog away and for a second, the full expanse of the Salt flashes before my eyes. It's enormous; bottomless. An endless plane of pitching black water. How long could I survive in there? How long until someone found me?

They would never find you.

The line around my waist yanks taught, jarring me back to reality. I have a tether. I'm attached to the boat. I'm not going over the side. The world goes upside down as I slam back onto the deck. We're plummeting down the face of the wave, carving a rooster tail into the wall of water behind us.

I scrabble to gain a grip, managing to grab the rail as a sheet of water crashes over the front of the boat and cascades down the deck toward me. I don't have time to catch my breath; all I can do is close my eyes and turn my head as the water hits me like a brick wall.

"Bird!" Sargo's voice gurgles to me from somewhere, muffled, faint.

I emerge, gasping and choking.

"Bird!" Sargo's voice again, clear now. "Howsley! Get up, Howsley!"

My limbs move automatically, one numb hand finding a hand-hold, one foot gaining traction on the deck. I push myself upright and propel myself toward his voice. Blindly, I tumble back into the cockpit and land on my side, gasping.

"Are you okay?" Sargo yells. I wave a shaking hand at him, nodding, unable to speak. "Good," he shouts, "because I need you to get back out there and help me find this cove!"

"What?! Are you serious?"

"As the Salt, so the sailor," he yells.

My ears are ringing, my nose and eyes stinging with salt water. My head, hips, and shoulders ache from being clobbered against the deck. My hands are shaking so badly I can't imagine using them for anything useful ever again. My nails sting with salt water. But there isn't time to recuperate.

As the Salt, so the sailor.

I take a deep breath and sit up, holding on tight and leaning out over the side of the cockpit. The cliffs loom ahead, and behind us, waves tower like a monumental city. We're caught between two walls that threaten to crush us. We've lost sight of the *King-fisher*. Squinting through the swirling spray, I spot a nook in the cliffs.

"There!"

"I need you to get out there and guide us through the rocks," Sargo yells, "I can't see them."

"You mean…on the bow?!"

"Yes! Now!"

It takes everything I have to step back out of the cockpit onto that slick, deadly deck again. I check my tether and cling to the rail with both hands, the boat bucking below me like an animal. The entrance to the cove is frighteningly narrow and snaggletooth rocks jut from the waves.

"Come to port!" I scream, throwing my arm to the left to indicate the direction. We narrowly miss a jagged rock shooting up out of the water. "Now to starboard!"

The gap between the cliffs is so slender as we careen toward it, that for one terrifying moment, it looks like we're going to wreck. I hold my breath and grip my tether with white knuckles, closing my eyes in spite of myself.

Sargo must have turned us in the nick of time, because I feel *Panga* swerve to port, and suddenly the world becomes still. The quiet is so abrupt it takes my breath away. I open my eyes.

We're inside a tiny cove, surrounded by sheer, towering rock on all sides. The water is flat and the air is calm. The cliffs block all the wind and swell from outside. The only gaps are the nook at the entrance behind us, and, high above my head, a small circle of stormy sky. In the center of the bay, the *Kingfisher* sits serenely, her anchor already set.

"You made it," Fetch's voice crackles into my ear.

I radio back with a trembling hand. "Yeah."

"Get your anchor set," she says. "The captain wants to see you. Ten minutes." She buzzes out before I can respond.

I sit down heavily in the cockpit, my ears ringing. I want nothing more than to get out of my soaking wet clothes and crawl into bed for three days. What could Savage possibly want?

"Savage wants us to come aboard," I croak. Sargo's face is white and his hands still clutch the wheel. He stares straight ahead and doesn't appear to have heard me. "Sargo?"

He blinks. "What?"

"Let's set the anchor. Savage wants to see us."

Sargo nods slowly, still not looking at me. "What do you think he wants?"

"I don't know."

"Okay." He takes a deep breath. He sits up. "Okay." A note of his usual logical calm creeps back into his voice and the fist around my heart unclenches a little.

"Maybe we should…arm ourselves. Take those knives," I offer.

"You mean the knives Mojave Stark's crew took when they captured us? Savage probably has those now. Besides, it's not like they did us much good last time." He shakes his head. "No. I think it's better to keep our heads down and play along. Savage made it pretty clear what would happen if we tested his generosity."

I shiver, wrapping my arms around my soaking torso.

"I think there are some dry clothes below," he says quietly.

I almost reply that it's not the cold or wet making me shiver. But the look on his face tells me he already knows that.

I find the clothes stuffed in a locker below deck while Sargo drops the anchor. They're Sargo's clothes, and I hesitate before putting them on. It feels intimate. Weirdly so. But they're dry, and I don't have much choice but to wear them unless I want to sit around damp and shivering all night.

I dry myself as best I can with a dish towel from the galley, then pull the clothes on slowly, my breath catching at the overwhelming scent of Sargo in them. I knot the button-down shirt around my waist and roll the sleeves all the way up, then cuff the ankles of the pants until I can walk without dragging them on the deck.

When I climb back up into the cockpit, Sargo's eyebrows lift. "Suits you."

I roll my eyes.

His gaze drifts to the few inches of bare skin left exposed between the bottom of the knotted shirt and the too-big waistband of his pants hanging too low on my hips. I feel his eyes stick there, watch them follow the curve of my hip like he's forgotten I'm watching, and my face heats.

"Keep it in your pants, Paz," I snap.

My voice comes out more angry than I mean it to—it's enough to make his eyes shoot up. He whips around and heads for the bow to ready the skiff. I stare after him, the skin on my stomach prickling like it was his hands on me and not his eyes.

I shouldn't have said that. *Keep it in your pants, Paz?* Too harsh. I was flustered. Now he thinks I'm mad that I caught him looking at me, when actually…I kind of liked it.

As we silently lift the skiff off the bow and drop it into the water, Sargo seems to be very busy finding lots of places to put his eyes that are obviously nowhere near me.

Malarkey, who had been curled in her hiding spot under the bunk, ventures up to the deck as we climb over *Panga's* rail and into the skiff.

I ruffle her ears and give her an apologetic smile. "Not this time." She cocks her head to one side and puts a paw through the rail. "Sorry, Lark. These guys are bad news. If we get murdered it's one thing, but if they got you, I'd never forgive myself."

Malarkey's forlorn face tracks us all the way across the bay as we motor the skiff over to the *Kingfisher*. Above our heads, the sky still shakes with thunder. We pull up alongside and tie off to a cleat on the stern.

The *Kingfisher* is big, sleek and expensive-looking. The kind of yacht that super-wealthy people used to take on vacation, back when people still did that kind of thing. She looks worn, but well maintained. A dark blue fiberglass hull, trimmed with white, polished to a shine. The teak deck is graying but clean. Every piece of metal gleams. I wonder where she came from. Stolen, would be my guess. Lifted from some charter company in the Med when their economy tanked during the pandemic. A lot of boats went missing around that time. A lot of blood was shed.

My stomach knots with sudden trepidation.

What are you doing here, Howsley?

chapter
twenty-one

As I PULL myself over the transom and onto the deck, Fetch steps out of the cockpit. Her knife is still strapped across her chest.

"Good evening," she says.

Sargo steps up beside me. His voice is careful as he returns her, "Good evening."

We stand watching each other, my heart beating in my ears. Then Fetch motions for us to follow her, and disappears down the companionway.

The boat's interior has long since been converted for utilitarian purposes, but the rich fabrics, expensive wood, and careful attention to detail betray a fading luxury. Compared to *Panga's* single cabin, dimly lit by portholes and so low that Sargo's head brushes the ceiling, the *Kingfisher's* opulence is difficult to comprehend.

Fetch crosses the cabin and leads us down another short set of stairs to a corridor. Doors line either side; I imagine they must be the crew's quarters. *Panga* has just one berth—the tiny, triangular bunk in the very front of the bow. This boat has…at least six.

We follow Fetch to the end of the corridor and enter a long, narrow room with a single metal table stretching the entire length of it. Two metal benches run along either side of the table. The galley. Compared to *Panga's* nook, which is barely big enough for one person to stand in, it feels enormous.

A rich, spicy aroma wafts from a pair of swinging doors at the far end of the table. Fetch motions for us to sit.

I don't move. "What's this about?"

"About?" Fetch gives me a withering look. "It's about dinner, Alluvium." She folds her arms, a look of extreme displeasure twisting her features. "Not my idea. Captain's orders. Sit."

Dinner? I glance at Sargo, who shrugs minutely. This morning we watched Savage efficiently and violently dispatch the *Valkyrie's* entire crew. Now he's feeding us?

Is he planning to poison us? No, that wouldn't make sense. Savage wants his coin. It's in his best interest to get us to Alluvium. But dinner?

I sit at the end of the table. Sargo squeezes in next to me, sitting close enough that his shoulder and thigh touch mine. Even through both of our clothes the heat of his skin against me makes me warm all over.

"Sorry," he murmurs under his breath, "just trying to keep up the illusion."

I blink. "What?"

"We're supposed to be in love, remember?"

My stomach swoops. *Jesus, I forgot I said that.*

"What do you think the angle is here?" he mutters. "Feeding us."

I keep my eye on Fetch and my voice low.

"I don't know, but...I think Savage must be as wary of the Nations as we are of him. He seemed pretty adamant that we didn't mention anything we saw this morning to anyone. I bet if Zenith wanted to, they could make his life pretty miserable. He's probably trying to butter us up. Make sure we have only good things to say about our saviors."

Sargo nods. "We keep a low profile, okay? Don't give them any reason to be suspicious. We'll have time to come up with a plan later."

The doors at the end of the table swing open, and Nana staggers through them backward, barely upright under the weight of the enormous, steaming pot she's carrying. Sweat beads on her forehead. Her gray coils are piled high and secured with a handkerchief, wisps escaping at her temples and the nape of her neck.

She sets the pot in the center of the table, shoots us a surly glance and slinks back through the doors without a word.

Fetch turns to the wall behind her, where a large copper bell hangs, green with rust. She gives the fraying rope tied to the clapper a single, decisive tug. The bell's harsh clang has barely subsided when the sound of voices turns my head and the rest of the crew falls in.

There are surprisingly fewer of them than I expected: the redhead, the awesome tattooed woman with the mohawk, the tiny bald man, and a skinny boy with deep brown skin and a head of tightly coiled black hair. He looks to be no more than seven, and flashes me and Sargo a gap-toothed grin as he squeezes himself onto the bench between us, clutching a metal spoon and bowl. I try not to let disappointment show on my face as the warmth of Sargo's shoulder is pried away from mine. Savage, I notice, is conspicuously absent.

Nana shoulders her way back through the doors, her arms now laden with three baskets of crusty bread rolls and a bag of apples. She slings the baskets of bread around the table and sets the bag of fruit on the floor in the corner.

Fetch sits opposite me, wordlessly sliding a couple of small metal bowls across the table. As I reach for one, Nana sits at the opposite end of the table, glaring at me with undisguised hatred, and mutters something to the tattooed woman. I hesitate, my hand hovering.

Fetch follows my gaze. "Ignore her. She's just a crotchety old woman with an ax to grind. Eyes to yourself, Nana!"

She stands and reaches to the pot in the center of the table, dipping her bowl right in the middle of it, filling it to the brim with thick, dark green soup. I spot chunks of meat and white potatoes, and my mouth begins to water.

"It'th nopal!" squeaks the little boy next to me.

I jump and look down at him. "What?"

"The thoup. It'th made of nopal. *Thopa de nopal*." Without waiting for me to respond, he sticks out a small brown hand, his eyes shining. "I'm Fid!"

"Uh, Electra." I shake his hand, surprised at both the strength of his grip and the delicate feel of his tiny bones. "What's nopal?"

"It's cactus," interjects Fetch. "In Pocosín they call it 'nopal'."

"Did you come from Pocosín?" asks Sargo cautiously, reaching to dip his own bowl into the soup.

Fetch stares at him silently, then turns her attention to her bowl as though she hasn't heard him. He glances at me and I give him a minuscule shrug.

As I stand up and reach to the center of the table to dip my bowl in the soup pot, a hush falls over the room. Glancing around, I find the eyes of every single crew member on me. I freeze, my hand hovering over the pot.

"Relax," growls Fetch, glaring around the table with her mouth full. "She's just some rich asshole's kid, not the flogging queen."

I quickly scoop up a bowlful of soup and sit, trembling. Fid pushes a basket of bread rolls in front of me with a sympathetic smile. As I gratefully reach for one, I hear Sargo's voice.

"Are those bolillos?"

I blink and look up at him. "What?"

He's staring at the basket of rolls, his face oddly alight. He reaches into the basket and pulls out a roll.

"Bolillos." He holds it up.

"Yup!" says Fid.

Sargo's eyes flick to mine as he tears off a chunk and sticks it in his mouth. "Mama Marlin used to make these."

"They're from Pocothín," says Fid. "Nana got the rethipe when she wath there waiting to infiltrate captain Thtark'th ship."

"Fid…" Fetch says in a low voice. "What have I told you? We don't share our business outside the crew, remember?"

"Oh. Right." Fid's face darkens and his turns his attention back to his stew.

I tear off half my bolillo, dunk it into the soup, and pull it out, soaked through. Dipping my face close to the bowl to keep drops from spilling, I cram the whole chunk into my mouth. The soup is too hot to eat, and the crust is so hard it cuts the roof of my mouth. I can't remember the last time I ate something so good. Or...anything at all.

"Drinks?"

The hunger in my belly turns to ice as Savage's voice cuts through the murmur of conversation at the table. He stands in the galley door, a massive brown jug in each hand.

"For our esteemed guests."

He produces two mugs from inside his coat and hands them to Sargo and me. I take mine with numb hands and Savage decants a slog of amber liquid into it with a flourish. He passes one jug to Fetch and the other to Sargo, who serve themselves and pass the jugs along.

"Friends," Savage raises his glass and the room falls silent, "and honored guests," he tilts his mug in my direction, "I'll keep this brief."

A few jeers. Fetch, stuffing a chunk of bread into her mouth and pointedly not looking at him, rolls her eyes. Savage holds up a hand for silence.

"Congratulations on another job well done. Sterling has been kind enough to do the math and divide the *Valkyrie's* haul for us."

He tilts his mug toward the short, bespectacled bald man, who smiles graciously as the rest of the crew raise their mugs to him too.

"You'll each be entitled to your share when we make port," continues Savage. "Incidentally, as I'm sure you've all heard by now, our next port of call will be Alluvium Bay, where we will deliver our esteemed new friend here into the arms of her waiting —and very grateful—family."

My face flushes as another jeer goes up. Savage waits for it to quiet before continuing.

"I expect everyone here to be on their best behavior and show our guest the utmost courtesy and respect. I shouldn't need to remind you all how incredibly valuable her company is."

Soft snickers from Nana's end of the table.

"For now," Savage continues, "eat. Drink. Get to know our new friends. We'll be spending a considerable amount of time together in the coming days."

A chorus of "cheers" quickly dissolves into a rumble of talk, which dims to a low murmur as everyone digs into their food.

I examine what's in my mug. It's not grog, but it smells vaguely boozy. When I sip, it's mild, bubbly, and slightly bitter. The anxious knot of fear in the center of my chest loosens just a hair. I may not be able to trust any of the people at this table, but I can at least depend on the contents of this mug.

My eyes fall on Savage, making his way around the outside of the room. He claps the redhead on the shoulder, then sits, crossing his feet on the corner of the table. He tilts his ear toward Nana as she mutters something to him, then throws his head back and barks a rich, musical laugh. I can't help but notice the way the blonde hair shakes back from his face, even as the image of his knife going into a man's jaw flashes through my head.

"Who's she?" I hear Sargo ask. He's indicating the muscular, tattooed young woman with the mohawk at the other end of the table.

"That'th Goliath," I hear Fid say. "And it'th *they*, not *she*."

Savage drains his mug and produces a flask from his inside pocket. It catches the light as he unscrews it, and suddenly, it's as if everything else in the room has been shut behind glass. I try to put my attention back on Fid, but the corner of my mind can't pull itself away from Savage. From that flask.

"They're from the north," Fid is saying. "Or eatht. Or....northeatht."

"Fid…" Fetch's voice is low and threatening. "What did I just say? Not outside the crew."

Savage swigs from the flask and stands. He looks around the table and I drop my eyes quickly as his gaze lands on me. When I peek back, he's watching me, and as our eyes meet, he lifts one eyebrow. I stare at him for a long moment, my face growing warm under that wolfish, dangerous gaze. Then he tilts the flask in my direction, winks, and slips out through the swinging galley doors.

"How long have you been on the *Kingfisher*?" I hear Sargo ask. He's turned away and is talking to Fetch.

I try to pull myself back to the conversation, but I still feel as though I'm watching through a pane of glass. For seven days, the thought of grog barely crossed my mind. Now, suddenly, it's all I can think about.

I scan the table, trying to gauge whose mug is empty, and whose is full. There are seven of us, not including Fid. If we all had one so far, how many jugs is that? One? Half of one?

"A while," I hear Fetch say.

What if it's all gone? What if there's none left? Am I allowed to have more? Should I wait for Fetch to have more first?

"Where were you before this?" Sargo asks.

Fetch shrugs and sticks the last bite of soup-soaked bread into her mouth, wiping her fingers on her shirt. She chews in silence, giving no indication of answering the question.

Just reach over there and pick it up, says a voice in my head. *You're an esteemed guest. You can do whatever you want.*

A shiny red apple comes flying at my head. I barely register its trajectory in time to pull myself out of my mental calculations and catch it. Goliath stands at the other end of the table, holding the fruit bag and chuckling.

Sargo presses Fetch again. "How often do you go down to Pocosín?"

Fetch picks up her mug, still chewing, looks into the bottom of it as she swirls around the dregs, then tips her head back and throws down the last gulp. She wipes her mouth and turns to Sargo, stone-faced.

"Look," she says, "the captain obviously didn't tell you this, so I will: we don't ask those kinds of questions around here. We don't want to get mixed up in your business, and we sure as Salt don't want you mixed up in ours. This isn't a sleepover. It's a transaction. As far as I'm concerned, you're cargo." She stands. "Now if you'll excuse me, I've got a lot of sleep to catch up on. Red will show you out when you're ready to leave. 'Night Fid— try to keep your damn mouth shut around the guests please?"

Her boots *clip-clop* briskly out the way we came in.

"'Night!" Fid calls after her.

I turn my attention back down to my bowl. Next to me, Sargo stands.

"Where's the head?" he asks.

"End of the corridor outside," says Sterling, gesturing over his shoulder. "Back the way you came."

Sargo squeezes behind me, putting his hands on my shoulders. He stoops close to my ear and says in a low voice, "I'll be right back."

My pulse quickens. "Where are you going?"

"Just using the bathroom."

"You're leaving me here?" I glance around the table. Surely these people won't just let Sargo walk out of the room right now? Unguarded? Are they really so unconcerned about us getting away? Isn't someone going to stop him? Jump him? Stab him?

But nobody even looks up as Sargo steps around me and out of the room. I watch him go, breathing in slowly, and out carefully.

Nothing's going to happen, I tell myself. *Calm down. They want you alive. You're the daughter of a rich asshole, being escorted to Alluvium, not a panicked little nobody who's been kidnapped by pirates. As long as they think that, you'll be fine. So think: what would the daughter of a rich asshole do in this situation?*

My eye falls on the brown jug in the center of the table.

Have another drink to settle her nerves?

I call out to the redhead sitting on the other side of the jug. "Excuse me?"

"He can't hear you," pipes Fid. He sets his bowl down, waves his arm over his head to catch the redhead's attention, then makes some swift, complicated gestures at him.

"Red Bread ith deaf," he explains.

I blink. "Sorry—did you say Red *Bread*?"

"Yup."

"Not…Red *Beard*?"

Fid grins. "When Red joined, none of uth thpoke Thign. He had to write hith name down for uth. Turnth out he'th not a great thpeller. We never let him live it down."

"So it's a…typo?" I frown. "How does he feel about having a typo for a name?"

"Why don't you ask *him*?" Sterling interrupts, a little tersely. "He's sitting right over there." He glares at me then turns back to his plate.

"Oh…" I can feel my ears going red. "I don't…speak Sign…"

Fid signs to Red Bread, who hands over the jug. I smile meekly and give him a thumbs up across the table.

"Like thith." Fid tugs my arm. He touches the fingers of his right hand to his lips and then extends his palm toward Red Bread. "Thank you."

I mimic his movement. Red Bread returns the gesture.

"It meanth 'thank you' and 'you're welcome'," says Fid.

I pour myself a drink, feeling the knot in my chest loosen a little. With Fetch no longer right next to me, I feel slightly less anxiety about being in a roomful of murderers.

Fid signs something else to Red Bread, who signs back. Fid grins.

"Red thayth at leatht hith name ithn't thomething you tell a dog to do."

"You mean Fetch?"

Fid nods, still grinning, and swings his legs.

"The word 'fetch' actually referth to the waveth that the wind maketh on the Thalt," he says, with the precociousness of a seven-year-old who knows what they're talking about. "*We* all know that. But we thtill give Fetch shit for being Thavage's retriever. Jutht like we give Red shit for being a terrible thpeller and deaf ath a potht."

My eyebrows jump. "Are you...allowed to say that?"

Fid frowns at me. "Thay what? Shit?"

"Well...yeah, but also...you can't give someone shit for...being deaf."

"We give *everyone* shit here." He points down the table, listing things off on his fingers. "We give Nana shit for being old and mean, and we give Goliath shit for having a terrible haircut and complicated pronounth. Thavage geth shit for being a preten-tiouth, inthufferable alcoholic, and Therling geth shit for being a midget."

I can't help but feel my mouth drop open, and I glance at Sterling to see his reaction to this. He just tilts his bald head toward Fid and says in an exaggerated whisper, "You're supposed to call me a 'little person'."

"It'th like they alwayth thay," Fid says, grinning, "If you can't take a joke, you shouldn't have joined!"

I narrow my eyes at him. "What about you? Does anyone give *you* shit?"

"Yup!" he says, proudly. "I'm a wee, motherleth bathtard."

A surprised laugh trips out of me. "Is that so? Well, for a wee, motherless bastard, you're pretty good at Sign."

He nods, digging into his bowl with his fingers. "I learned when Red joined."

"You learned it just for him?"

"Of course he did," Nana snarls from the other end of the table.

I look up, suddenly realizing the room has fallen silent. Every pair of eyes at the table is on me. How long have they been watching me talk to Fid?

Nana glares at me as though I've just asked the world's stupidest question. "We all learned it," she says. "How else would we talk to him?"

I shrink against the wall, scoop up my mug, and duck my face low over it.

"Careful Turf Rat!" Nana sneers. "Drink too much and you're like to fall overboard."

Goliath chuckles.

"I think I'll be alright, thanks," I mumble.

"Alright with what?"

Sargo squeezes behind me to sit on the other side of Fid. He glances around the table as everyone returns to their food and the low murmur of chatter resumes. His eyes fall on the mug in my hand.

"How many is that?" he says in a low voice.

"Excuse me?" I fix him with a defiant glare. "Is that really what you're worried about right now?"

"I didn't mean...never mind." He scoops up his own mug and begins to turn toward Sterling, but I catch his elbow, irritation flickering in my chest.

"Never mind what?"

"Nothing!" He leans toward me, his voice hushed. "Just—now is not a great time to be getting drunk, is it?"

I stare at him. "Of all the situations where having one-too-many drinks to settle your nerves is perfectly understandable," I hiss, "I think 'kidnapped by pirates and threatened by a murderous old hag' is near the top of the list."

"Come on," he whispers, "just...you know how you get."

"How do I *get*?"

I can hear myself speaking too loudly, feel heat rising in my cheeks. Glancing down, I notice Fid watching us. I drop my voice.

"I'm not a child. I don't need you to tell me when and when is not a good time to do something."

"Okay. Sorry. Just drop it."

"Why don't *you* drop it?"

Sargo opens his mouth, then pauses, glancing at Fid. "Can we take this outside?"

I wordlessly sweep my arm toward the door.

"Lovers' spat?" Nana sneers as I follow Sargo out of the room.

The hallway outside is dark and cool. I press the backs of my hands to my cheeks. Away from the low din of voices and dinner, the rumble of wind and thunder creep back into my ears. Sargo walks halfway along the corridor, then leans against the starboard wall, his arms folded.

I lean against the opposite wall and glare at him in the dark. We're close enough that my feet are planted on either side of his.

"Well?"

He glances over his shoulder, and says under his breath, "I followed Fetch."

"You *what?*" My voice rises and I glance over my shoulder too. That was not what I expected him to say at all.

"When she went to bed, I followed her. Just to...I don't know, get some more information."

I gape at him in the dark. "You *followed* her?" My mind spins. "What if she had caught you?"

"She didn't."

"What happened to keeping a low profile? You're getting on *me* about having too many drinks and meanwhile you're off tailing murderers?! What if Savage had seen you? You don't think he'd consider sneaking around his ship in the middle of the night 'testing his generosity'?"

"Bird—"

"Electra!" I look back at the door to the galley. "I'm *Electra*, remember?"

"Okay, sorry, Electra—"

"And we're supposed to be...you know—*together*." My face flushes and I'm glad he can't see it in the dark. "How are we going to convince anyone we're in love if you abandon me in a room full of murderers at the drop of the hat? We need them to think we are who we say we are until we get to Alluvium."

His voice edges above a whisper. "And then what? When we get to Alluvium, then what?"

"I don't know! I haven't gotten that far yet."

He scoffs. "Yeah, exactly."

Angry tears prick my eyes. Angry, drunk tears. "That's not fair. I saved our lives."

"No, you saved *your* life."

"What does that mean?"

"Come on," he says, folding his arms and eyeing me in the dark, "your deal with Savage? The one where you're the daughter of the world's most powerful woman? Who am I in that again? Oh that's right: nobody. I'm just your boyfriend. The brown kid your family doesn't approve of. A prop."

"I—" My mouth drops open. *The brown kid your family doesn't approve of?* "That's not what I meant when I said that."

"Well what did you mean?"

"I don't know! I was—panicking. I wasn't—"

"You weren't thinking." His voice is hard. "Right. Well whatever you meant, it doesn't do me a lot of good, does it? I'm expendable. Did you notice nobody even batted an eye when I just got up and walked out of the room? They don't care about me. You're the valuable one. What incentive does Savage have to keep me alive?"

"I'll—I'll make him keep you alive."

"Sure." He shakes his head. "I need to look out for myself."

"Where is this coming from? An hour ago we agreed to keep a low profile, and now…you're following an armed Reckoner around a boat you don't know, in the dark, alone?" I lower my voice. "*We* need to look out for *our*selves! We can come up with something. We just need to keep our heads down and wait for an opportunity, like you said."

He laughs a short, bitter laugh. "So *now* you want to wait for an opportunity? For once in your life you want to stop and think? Where was that level-headedness a week ago in Brume?"

Fury sparks in my chest. "What about *you?* Suddenly you're a risk taker? Where was that attitude when *you* were in Brume? Mr. 'One Step At a Time.' *You* said we should keep a low profile. *You* said we should observe. Now you're sneaking around after murderers? Doing *recon*? Why? What happened? Did you get tired of being the kind of person who sits on a dock fixing shit for years and years and never makes a move? Did you get tired of being the person who never has a plan or anything to contribute—"

"Alright, *enough*!" His fist comes down sharply on the wall behind him.

A shadow falls across the square of light spilling from the galley door and Goliath steps into the doorway. They fold their arms and lean against the door frame, and before I've even clocked that the reason they are standing there is to keep an eye on us—that our raised voices must have made them suspicious— Sargo closes the gap between us, pinning me to the wall with his chest and bracketing my head with his forearms. His scent floods my nose and my breath goes still.

"What are you doing?"

He puts his lips against my ear. "Pretending to kiss you. We're arousing suspicion."

A bolt of electricity shoots down my spine. I look at the door out of the corner of my eye. Goliath's massive frame still leans against the frame, and though they are just a silhouette in the shadows, I'm sure they are watching.

"Well…" I whisper, "I don't think they're buying it. Maybe you should—"

He pulls back to look at me in the near dark and his eyes narrow. The small space between us goes irresistibly taut.

"Maybe I should what?" he says. His voice has a huskiness to it that turns my insides to liquid.

Maybe you should kiss me for real.

In the corner of my eye, I sense Goliath's silhouette straighten and move out of the doorway. A sliver of light returns to the corridor.

Neither Sargo nor I move. Our eyes are still locked, our faces inches apart. His breath seems as short as mine; I can *feel* it on my lips.

A vision sears itself across my mind—not just an image but a vividly rendered imagining that grips all my senses: smell and taste and touch. His hands around my wrists, his warm, hard body crushing me to the wall, smothering me with that intoxicating smell of sand and sweat and salt. The harsh, desperate sound of our breaths. His teeth on my neck, his hands on my breasts, on my hips, fumbling with my pants, lower...

He steps back.

"I'm leaving," he announces.

The heat and air leave my body in a confusing rush. "What?"

"You can find your own way back."

"You're *leaving* me here?"

He has his back to me, walking away. "Why don't you have another drink?" he says without looking back. "If you get into trouble, you can always come up with another shortsighted plan to save your own ass."

The simmering, furious heat of the grog returns to my chest, rises into my face, boils over, and brims onto my lashes. *Asshole.*

"Great idea!" I spit after him. "Why don't you go back to *Panga* and keep a low profile? Maybe six years from now, you'll have a plan too!"

He waves a frustrated hand over his shoulder as he rounds the corner and disappears. I claw a breath back into me and drag my hands across my eyes. Something about watching him storm off like that feels familiar. *Naze.* He stormed off just like this and left me in that veg patch in Naze. Last time, I went groveling after him because I was scared of Malarkey.

Not this time.

He's right. I *am* valuable to the crew of the *Kingfisher*. And as long as I am, there's no reason to be afraid of them. And as long as I'm not afraid of them, I'd rather go back in there and have another drink than deal with with whatever...*that* just was.

I turn on my heel to stride back to the galley, but the sight of Goliath's imposing form stepping back into the doorway stops me short.

"Am I really going back into the roomful of murderers just to spite Sargo?" I mutter to myself

No, my self retorts. *You're going back into the roomful of murderers just to have another drink.*

Goliath steps aside as I stalk through the door. Nana, Fid, and Sterling have gone. Red Bread lays along one of the benches, his hands behind his head. Goliath steps around me and seats themself wordlessly at the far end of the table, and Red lifts his booted feet and crosses them in their lap.

"Mind if I sit?"

If Goliath is surprised by my request, they don't show it. They gesture wordlessly to the empty bench opposite them. I sit and indicate the jug in the middle of the table. Red Bread raises one hand above the edge of the table and signs to me.

"He says is empty," Goliath rumbles. Their voice is deep and thickly accented, their tone surly. I sigh and let my back fall against the wall. "You want drink?"

Goliath is scowling at me. Their question seems less like a friendly offer and more like disinterested obligation. Like a Zenith peace officer asking if you need help with directions. Probably Goliath's attempt at 'best behavior.'

"Sure," I say, carefully.

They reach into the front of their coat, produce a small silver flask, and hand it over without looking at me. I lift my eyebrows.

"Thanks."

Goliath doesn't acknowledge me, just leans against the wall, folding their big arms. I unscrew the cap, and a blast of acrid fumes rakes the inside of my nose. The smell is so overpowering, and so eye-wateringly familiar that I actually laugh out loud—a laugh of relief that dissolves into a fit of coughing. When I pull myself together enough to sit up, I'm met by Goliath's deadpan stare.

"It's grog!" I choke, waving the flask.

They look nonplussed, completely unmoved by my revelation.

"Grog?" I repeat, pointing to the flask.

They shake their head. "Is hooch."

I frown and sniff the open neck. "Nah," I shake my head and take a sip, "this is grog."

"Hooch!" Goliath's hand comes down sharply on the table.

"Whoa, okay." I flinch, holding out the flask. They snatch it back. "Okay. It's hooch."

Red Bread sits up and signs something to me. I stare at him helplessly. He sighs and shakes his head.

"I'm sorry," I tell him. "I guess I don't speak either of your languages."

He gives me a small, exasperated shrug and lies back on the bench. Goliath angrily swigs from the flask and then shoves it back at me.

Surprised, I take it.

Crossing his boots in Goliath's lap again, Red Bread signs something to them. The flicker of a smile crosses Goliath's hard face.

"Your boyfriend leave," they grunt.

"He's not my boyfriend," I almost say. Instead, I grit my teeth and say, "Yeah."

"He not worry about you? Leave you here?" Their eyes are faintly amused.

I hesitate. "What about you? You're not worried about him? What if he escapes?"

Goliath snorts and signs to Red, who chuckles. "He won't."

One mostly silent hour later, I find myself staggering out of the galley. I've learned how to sign "hooch," "boat," and "rain." Red Bread was more amenable to teaching me his language than Goliath was theirs—apart from the comment about Sargo leaving, Goliath said next to nothing.

I don't remember finishing the grog, but Goliath is tucking the empty flask into their back pocket, so I suppose we must have.

Red Bread slips his hand into the back of Goliath's waistband and the two of them stumble together down the hallway toward the crew's quarters.

"You sleep in galley," Goliath slurs over their shoulder as they disappear through one of the doors.

Sleep in the kitchen? I don't want to sleep in the kitchen. I want to go back to *Panga*. I rub my already aching head and vaguely remember that Sargo left in the skiff.

How are you supposed to get back now, genius?

The question is too difficult for my sloshy brain to even begin to unravel, so I decide to focus instead on the immediate and much more important problem of finding somewhere to pee. I take a few hesitant steps down the corridor toward the crew quarters. Where did Sterling say the head was?

Something catches my toe and I stumble, instinctively throwing out a hand to steady myself on the wall. Unfortunately, however, the wall isn't there. I've put my hand through an open doorway.

My feet trip over themselves and I get a brief, sideways glimpse of a room stacked with crates full of apples. Before I've even hit the floor, though, everything is turning black, darkness swallowing the edges of my vision, tunneling the light to a pinprick.

It's happening again, says the voice in my head. *You're blippin*—

chapter
twenty-two

"WE WON."

The girl sat in the shade of the saltnut tree, twisting a leaf off a branch. She tossed it half-heartedly toward her hemp sack. It missed the sack and fluttered away in the wind. She didn't bother going after it. She was supposed to be stripping leaves for mash, but her heart wasn't in it. The afternoon sun was low, beating its dark orange rays straight across the land.

"I know," said Fife quietly.

"I don't want to go."

"I know."

"Shale says you'll come. Next year maybe?"

The girl tried not to let hope creep into her voice, tried not to peek over at Fife to gauge her reaction. If her brother believed Fife would come *and* Fife believed it too, then maybe it would be true.

Fife paused. "Maybe."

"I'm gonna miss you."

"Nah." Fife nudged the girl with her shoulder. "There'll be lots of new people in Brume. You're gonna make tons of friends and forget all about me."

"I won't."

"Promise?"

"Promise. I don't care about stupid kids in Brume. They're probably all a bunch of stray sonsofbitches."

Fife laughed. "Better not go using language like that 'round there. They're gonna know you're a Settler straight away."

"I don't care. I want them to know. I don't want to be a Citizen."

She crossed her arms and sat back hard against the tree. They sat side by side, not speaking, for a long time.

Finally, Fife stood and held out her hand. "Come on." She pulled the girl to her feet. "It's dinner soon, we'd better get back."

The girl stood but didn't move. She clung to Fife's hand, tears suddenly choking her. She tried to hide them, but Fife saw. Fife always saw.

"Don't cry," Fife said. "You'll make me cry."

The girl stuck out her bottom lip and screwed up her face and put all her eight-year-old strength into not crying, but it was no use. The tears rolled down her cheeks. She wiped them away furiously and looked back at Fife.

Fife's eyes blazed clear blue and bright as the defiant stars, and they were rimmed with trembling tears. The tears seemed to enlarge her eyes; amplify them. The tears turned her eyes into something bigger; they pulled a magnifying glass before the eyes and said, "Here! Look. Here it is. The sadness."

But there was something else in those eyes too. Behind the tears. Behind the sadness. Something more permanent, something...harder.

Anger.

The little girl didn't recognize it as that, because she didn't know this kind of anger. The anger Fife felt wasn't the childish anger of being left out of a game or told to blow her nose when she didn't want to. It was the real, grown-up anger that comes from powerlessness. The anger of being left behind. Of being forgotten. Of being given no chance. Fife knew this anger now, and it was consuming her. She knew what was coming to her. Or rather, she knew what was *not* coming to her. She wouldn't go to

Brume. She would never leave the Settlement. It was likely that she would die here, and not necessarily as an old woman. Fife knew all this, and her eyes reflected that knowledge.

"I'll miss you, Fife," said the little girl.

"I'll miss you too, Bird," said Fife. And even though she was angry, she meant it.

chapter
twenty-three

"*I'll miss you, Fife.*"

I blink my eyes open. The sun barges through them, followed almost immediately by the hangover. Some kind of insane, lousy hangover worse than I've ever felt. My ears ring and spots dance before my eyes. My mouth is filled with a sour taste, like the tang of metal, or blood. That's new. I never tasted my hangover before.

I squint, covering my face with my arm.

"*I'll miss you too, Bird.*"

Bird. *Me.* The little girl in the dreams is me. And the boy—is *my* brother. Shale.

And the other little girl? Fife?

The dream is fading. I clutch at the evaporating images, but they disappear like fog, burned away by the sun.

I sit up, propping myself up on my elbows, and look around. Malarkey licks her nose and fixes me with a reproachful stare. I'm in...*Panga's* cockpit.

How the hell did I get back here?

Closing my eyes, I squeeze my head between my hands. Sargo stormed off. I remember that much. What were we even arguing about? *Oh, right.* Me being a drunk, reckless asshat, of course. Well, I guess he's got me there. Here I am again, waking up hungover *again*, not knowing how I got here, *again*.

I remember going back to the galley. I remember Red Bread and Goliath were there. I remember we polished off Goliath's flask. And then—

You blipped.

I shut my eyes.

It's time to stop using the cute word, I tell myself. *You drank too much, and you blacked out.*

This is no longer cute. This is a problem.

Am I turning into a grog blossom like Sargo's uncle Blenny? Am I going to start forgetting things all the time now? Waking up in strange places, shambling around in my pajamas?

I stand up and lurch down the companionway to the galley, expecting to find Sargo making a cup of tea, but he isn't there. I squint across the cabin to the small cabin in the bow. He's kneeling on the bunk, facing away from me with his head down. A shaft of fear goes through me. Is he sick? If he's sick, I don't know how I'm going to sail *Panga* on my own.

Then I see what he's doing. My view of his hands is blocked by the angle of his body, but I know immediately by the sound. It's a sound I've never heard, and yet somehow, I know exactly what it is: the rhythmic sound of his fist, beating against his hips. The short, ragged breaths he is trying to take quietly.

My chest goes tight. I feel like I just stepped over the edge of the world and am free-falling into nothing. I should turn around and go back to the cockpit. I should pretend I haven't seen this.

Instead, I take a step closer.

He sits back on his heels, his knees spread wide in front of him, his arm moving in long, lazy strokes. I dart out of sight around the corner that separates the bunk from the main cabin. I imagine his pants, unbuttoned and pulled open. An ache twists deep in my core. I wish I could see him properly. Step around the corner and get a closer look.

Don't do that, Bird, says a voice in my head. *That is a very bad idea. That would be pretty flogging stray.*

He stifles a breath, and I slip to the very edge of the doorframe to peek around the corner as though pulled by that sound. He's so close to me I could reach out and run my finger down the back of his neck. I imagine him shuddering under my touch, the arch his neck would make as he tilted his head.

Pressure grips my core like a fist around my center. I take a trembling, silent breath, holding it at the top, afraid to exhale. Slipping my hand under my shirt, I cup my breast, imagining his hand instead, large and warm and calloused. I flick my thumb over the nipple, and as I do, he tilts his head back and groans.

I cover my mouth to mute my own moan, pressing my burning forehead to the wall.

His breath starts to come faster and heavier, like he's having trouble controlling it. I keep my eyes closed and my forehead against the wall, afraid to look around the corner again, because the ache between my thighs is becoming unbearable and if I look at him again I won't be able to stop myself from doing something about it.

You could still walk away, says a voice. *You can pretend this didn't happen.*

I peek around the corner.

His head is down and his shirt is hitched up in the front, like he wanted to take it off but thought better of it. Or like he wanted a better look at himself. What does his stomach look like? What would it feel like against mine, skin to skin? My hand drifts to the waistband of my pants.

His hand is fisted in the sheet in front of him and he leans on that fist, his weight braced on it, head down again, like he's focusing. Like he's working.

Unable to hold back any longer, I slip my hand into my pants and stroke one finger from the base of my sex to the tip, shuddering. His hand pumps in harder, steadier strokes. I stroke myself again. And again.

A bead of sweat appears at the nape of his hairline, rolls down his neck, and disappears into the collar of his shirt. I almost moan, imagining my tongue following it, the taste of him—sharp and salty. The sound he might make when I put my mouth on him.

He hisses and his hips begin to buck, his fist working faster, his breath coming harder. I grind into my hand, matching his pace with my fingers, until I'm aching. Until I'm so close I have to stifle my whimpers against the wall.

Unfisting his hand from the sheet, he reaches overhead to brace his arm against the low ceiling. Whatever decorum it was that was keeping him quiet has vanished—his breath comes in harsh gasps and the sound of his forearm slapping against his hips is brutal and hypnotic. There is nothing careful or cautious about him now—he is lost to his need. Animalistic. Thoughtless.

He mutters something under his breath and then he comes, his head rolling back, ribs shuddering under his shirt. He thrusts his hips into his hand over and over, and for one delirious moment, I imagine him thrusting into me, wild and senseless and unhinged. Something in me comes undone and I come too, quivering, smashing my lips against the wall to stifle the desperate, grateful sounds of my relief.

For minutes afterward, we heave staccato, intertwining breaths. Gradually, they grow longer, then quieter, then calm. Then I hear him move. Hear a zip and the rustle of sheets and creak of the mattress. I wrench my hand out of my pants and dart away from the wall and back up the stairs to the cockpit, flushed and sweating.

I lie down on the bench seat in the cockpit and close my eyes while downstairs, his footsteps come into the galley. He runs the water, then begins making the sounds that I know mean he is brewing tea.

In the aftermath of my pleasure, a wave of guilt washes over me. He'll know—there's no way he won't know. He must have heard me, or he'll smell it on me, or something. And how am I supposed to sleep in that bunk again now? There's no way I'll ever be able to lie between those sheets without picturing him kneeling over me, stroking himself, and growling under his breath.

What was he *saying?* That's the thing I'm never going to be able to get past. What was he muttering under his breath before he came? Was it romantic? Filthy? Incoherent? I open my eyes and stare at the sky. Suddenly, escaping the Anonymity, making it to Alluvium, finding Shale...all of it becomes unimportant.

The only thing I want now is to find out what Sargo Paz says before he comes.

Eventually, I stand up and climb back down the companionway into the galley. Sargo is there, making a cup of tea. He doesn't acknowledge me, and I remember with a jolt that we are fighting. Or at least, that we were fighting last night. I reach silently around him for the kettle, blushing as I remember the way he pinned me to the wall last night. Wondering if that moment had anything to do with what I just saw. If he was affected by it too.

The galley is not big enough for both of us: the air is thick, the silence of us ignoring each other deafening as we go about preparing our tea, bumping into each other, reaching over each other, stepping around each other. Finally, unable to stand it any longer, I set my mug down with a bang and turn around.

"Look, I'm sorry. For what I said last night. I didn't mean it."

He stills. The curve of his neck lengthens as he drops his head, his hands flat on the countertop. His shoulder brushes mine as he turns to face me, the faint scent of his sweat rousing a nervous flutter from my stomach. He observes me quietly.

"How did you get back?"

I avoid his eyes and lie. "Goliath brought me."

He nods. "I'm sorry too," he says finally. Quietly. "Being cooped up on this boat is making me...a little crazy. I know you didn't come up with that plan just to save your own ass. You were thinking quickly."

"I didn't mean...the thing you said, about being the brown kid my family doesn't approve of. I didn't mean...I don't know what —to say."

He draws a long breath. "I know."

"I'm sorry. That I made you feel that way."

We stare at each other in silence.

Are we going to talk about what happened after the argument? Are we going to talk about the fact that we maybe very nearly kissed? That you were maybe as turned on by it as I was?

He sighs. "I'm sorry I hassled you about—drinking. It's not my business. I just..." His eyes dart around my face. "I worry about you sometimes."

My chest squeezes. My skin stretches against the air, hot and tight, like the feelings inside me are too big to be contained. Nervous anticipation. Breathless excitement. And also...anger. Frustration.

"If you're so worried about me, why did you *leave* me there?"

"I—" His mouth sticks open. He scratches behind his neck. "I shouldn't have done that. It's just—hard to be around you when you're...like that."

Like that. Right. There it is again. He feels bad for scolding me but he doesn't even *know* how bad it is. He doesn't know that I've been blacking out and waking up in unexpected places. That I have no idea how I got back here last night.

I hesitate, feeling the pressure of those hot, tight feelings solidifying inside me until they start to become words. Until the edges of them are so sharp that I have to get them out.

I take a deep breath. "Sargo, I—"

"Heading out," Fetch's voice crackles into my ear. "Be ready to haul anchor in ten."

Sargo jumps and taps behind his ear. "Copy that."

He looks at me a moment longer, as though he's about to say something too, and in that moment I want to tell him everything. Not just about the grog. All of it. That last night, I *felt* something in those few tense inches between us. That right now, in this moment, all I want is to close the small gap between us and fold myself into his arms. That he's right to worry. That I'm not okay. That I hate myself for ever making him feel bad.

But I'm too afraid. If he were any other person—even someone I had feelings for—I wouldn't care. But he's *Sargo*. What if I tell him my feelings and he doesn't feel them too? What if I tell him about the grog and he's...disappointed? Or freaked out? Or disgusted? I wouldn't just be losing a person I have feelings for. I'd be losing my friend. My *best* friend. At this point, let's face it, my *only* friend.

So I just stand there, staring back at him, the pressure of a thousand unspoken words and the heat of a million unresolved feelings pressing against the inside of my skin like the air inside a balloon.

Then he turns, picking up his tea, and steps out of the galley.

———————

We follow the *Kingfisher* down the coast as the bright morning sun tracks across the sky. As it reaches its highest point, beaming hot and white, obliterating shadows, Fetch buzzes into my ear again.

"We're making a stop. Phreatic. It's a small bay about a mile from here. Follow us in, drop anchor, and wait for instructions."

The shape of the bay of Phreatic reminds me of Brume. A small horseshoe set back into the lee of a gentle point. The entrance to the bay is protected by two enormous rocks, which we navigate carefully, yesterday's harrowing journey still fresh in our minds. A beach of black sand lines the water's edge, and red hills slope away from the bay into the desert beyond.

The shape of the bay is where the similarity to Brume ends. There's no lush, green blanket of trees covering the sloping hillside. No fog. No city. No harbor. No solar panels, or fog traps; no windmills ponderously turning in the distance. Phreatic is just a single row of about eight small, brightly painted wooden houses lining the beach.

For the first time since leaving Brume, we find other ships already anchored in the bay. I eye them as we glide past. Three boats, one at least as big as the *Kingfisher*. It flies a blood-red flag with a set of yellow fangs stitched into it. Across the stern is painted the name *Beowulf* in dark red letters. Another boat—*Tomahawk*—flies a tattered black flag with a large red *X* slashed across it. The very names are enough to make me uneasy.

We find a spot as far from the menacing ships as possible and drop the anchor. As we stand on the bow, watching it set, the sound of a motor reaches my ears, and I look up to see a skiff pulling away from the *Kingfisher*.

I shield my eyes with my arm as it arcs across the bay toward us, the forms of Goliath, Fetch, and Red Bread visible in it. They pull up alongside the bow, Fetch standing wide-legged, and cross-armed in the front. I notice that she's trimmed her hair. The buzzcut coils are even shorter today than the last time I saw her. She must do it all the time to keep it looking so crisp.

"We're going ashore," she says. Goliath produces two lengths of thick rope from inside a large sack slung over their shoulder.

"What's that for?"

"This is how we're going to ensure you don't do something stupid while we're gone," says Fetch.

She takes a rope from Goliath in one hand, grabs hold of *Panga's* rail with the other, and swings herself nimbly over the side. Malarkey's deep, booming bark issues from somewhere below as she lands on our deck.

Fetch advances, pulling the rope taut between her hands, while Goliath heaves themself over the rail behind her.

"We can't risk you two going rogue while we're conducting business on shore," Fetch says. "If you cooperate, we won't have any problems."

Malarkey barrels past me as if from nowhere and launches herself at Goliath. It happens so fast I barely have time to step out of the way. To my horror, however, Goliath is ready for her. They duck sideways, simultaneously throwing out a massive, tattooed arm to catch Malarkey around the neck, and wrestle the eighty pound dog into a headlock, one knee on the deck, their face stony.

"Sorry dog. I no like to hurt you. Keep still and will all be fine."

I glare at Fetch. "So, what? You tie us up and leave us here?"

She sneers. "Obviously not. We tie you up, take you back to the *Kingfisher*, and lock you down below, where Nana and Sterling will keep an eye on you."

I step back, shaking my head. "No way."

Fetch sighs, drawing the knife from the sheath on her chest. "Don't be stray, Alluvium. I don't want to have to do this hard way."

"Take us to the captain," says Sargo, abruptly. Fetch stills and looks at him. "Take us to the captain," he repeats, "or we'll have to tell our families about the poor treatment we received while we were your so-called 'guests.'"

Fetch steps hard toward him, opening her mouth as though about to argue, when Goliath stops her with a hand across her chest, bends to Fetch's ear, and mutters something I can't hear. Fetch's jaw sets while she listens to Goliath, then she looks to Red, who signs, shrugging. Fetch glares at Sargo. Then, with a huff, she sheaths the knife.

"The dog stays here," she growls.

Savage sits behind the *Kingfisher's* helm as Sargo and I climb out of the skiff and board the massive sailboat, the point of Fetch's knife firmly between my shoulder blades.

Something about Savage's profile seems different. He doesn't have his boots jauntily crossed on the edge of the instrument panel; he sits with his elbows on his knees and his head hanging, sipping delicately from a small flask.

At the sound of our footsteps he looks up and I almost do a double-take. His skin is sallow and gray, his eyes sunken, and his cheeks hollow. He looks tired. Beyond tired; exhausted. Weak and frail. He looks as rough as I felt when I woke up this morning. A pair of mirrored darx lays on the cockpit floor by his feet, and he quickly picks them up and puts them on as I draw level with him. He doesn't get up. He cranes his neck to look up at me, the darx obscuring his eyes.

"Yes?" There is no trace of the cruel amusement or machismo I saw in him yesterday. His voice is thin and clipped.

Fetch digs her knife into the spot between my shoulders as she says, "They're not cooperating."

Savage sighs and scratches his lanky blonde hair with a tired hand.

"Don't make this difficult, Alluvium. My crew and I need to go ashore to take care of some things. Naturally, we can't have you and your boyfriend wandering off while we're gone. It will only be for an hour or so."

I shake my head. "You're not tying us up."

He waves a hand. "Fine. Nana and Fetch—"

"I'm not staying here with that woman." I try to shrug the point of Fetch's blade away from my shoulders, but it stays firm.

A grimace of impatience flickers across Savage's tired face. "Then what would you propose, Alluvium?"

"Take us ashore," says Sargo. "You can keep an eye on us there."

His voice is so firm it startles me. I peek at him out of the corner of my eye. I don't know what he's thinking, but something tells me it's along the same lines as what I'm thinking: that we stand a better chance of getting out of this mess as long as we're not tied up and locked aboard the *Kingfisher*.

Savage draws a long breath. "As much as I would love to take you both on a tour of all the fascinating places that Reckoners inhabit, this particular location is one I'm afraid I can't share with anyone who might disclose its location to Zenith."

"What does Zenith have to do with us?" I demand.

Sargo stiffens. Behind the darx, I sense Savage's eyes narrow. "Aren't you the daughter of the CEO?" he asks cooly.

My blood goes cold as I realize my slip-up. *Shit.* I'm Electra. *Shit shit shit.* I scramble to cover my mistake.

"Yeah—but....that doesn't mean I care about Zenith. Just because my mom is the CEO, doesn't mean I agree with her."

"Is that so."

"I don't give a shit about her stupid company. I hate her. Why do you think we're running away?"

Savage's eyes behind the darx are inscrutable. I stare at my own reflection in the lenses, wishing I could see even a glimmer of what he's thinking. I decide to take a chance and play the only piece of leverage we have.

"Look, you can threaten and intimidate us all you want, but I know you're scared of my family and what they can do to you. And you're right: I could tell them about everything I see if you take us ashore. I could tell them the name of every boat in this anchorage. I could tell them everything I know about you and your crew. I could tell them how I saw you murder two of the men aboard the boat they hired to find me, and that I'm pretty sure you tortured that boat's captain for information about me. And I don't know much about the law, but I'm willing to bet that none of that stuff is going to put you on the right side of it. So if you want to get your coin, and you *don't* want me to tell them any of that, I suggest you do what you said you were going to do, and treat us with courtesy and respect. And that means not tying us up and locking us in your boat."

Next to me, Sargo exhales softly. Savage glares at me. Then he takes a slow, deliberate sip from the flask, carefully caps it and tucks it into the breast pocket of his coat.

"Okay, Alluvium," he says. "You've made your point." He stands. "Fetch, take our fine young friends here back to their boat so they can prepare to come ashore."

The point of Fetch's blade digs even more painfully into my shoulder blades.

"Captain," her voice grinds into my ear through gritted teeth, "I don't think—"

"That's an order," he says smoothly. A beat goes by as he stares at her over my shoulder. Then Fetch withdraws the point of her knife and sheaths it.

"You heard the captain," she growls. "Back in the skiff."

I stumble out of the cockpit on weak legs, my hands and feet tingling, Sargo tripping ahead of me.

"Oh, and Alluvium…"

Savage's voice stops me as we reach the edge of the deck. I turn. He steps out of the cockpit behind us and crosses to me, stopping so close to me that when I step back to create space, my heel slips over the edge of the deck. He dips his face and speaks next to my ear, smelling of grog and pineapple dart smoke.

"That was a very eloquent speech," he says quietly. "But don't forget that your argument hangs on me thinking this whole ordeal is still worth my time."

His hand dips into his pocket.

"You may recall, when we first came to this little arrangement, that I asked you to please not do anything to test my generosity. I'm a fickle man. When things test my patience, I tend to change my mind about them. And if I decide that taking you and your boyfriend all the way to Alluvium is too much trouble to be worth the coin, well…"

The hand withdraws from his pocket and the butterfly knife whirls open with a flash. He lays the cold blade against my cheek.

"I'm afraid there won't be much sense in keeping you around then, will there?"

Back aboard *Panga*, Sargo and I prepare to go ashore in tense, terrified silence. He neither commends me for standing up to Savage, nor berates me for getting us deeper into our hole. We wrap bandanas around our faces and despite the heat, I pull my hood over my head and my collar all the way up, as if they will somehow protect me.

Into my pack, I stuff a canteen of water and the nox. I fashion a leash for Malarkey out of rope. I'm done leaving her behind for her own protection: we have no weapons; we may need her massive jaws to deal some damage. Finally, we drop the skiff into the water and load ourselves into it.

The beach is already littered with other little boats, and we land as far away from them as possible. One I'm sure must have come from *Beowulf*, because its hull is painted the same shade of blood-red as the ship's flag. Some look as though they haven't moved in years, with peeling paint and splintering hulls.

We pull our skiff out of the tide. Malarkey leaps over the side of it and bounds up the beach as though she's never seen land before. She throws herself down and rolls in the sand like she's afraid she might never see it again.

I shake my head, a speck of amusement drifting around the edges of my discordant nerves. *Drama queen.*

Fetch, Red Bread, Savage and Goliath land the *Kingfisher's* skiff right behind us. Red Bread and Goliath hop out into the ankle deep water, each carrying a lumpy duffel bag over their shoulder, which I assume are filled with weapons stolen from the *Valkyrie*. As they haul the skiff up the beach, I note the lethal-looking ax hanging, unconcealed, from Red Bread's belt.

Savage sees me eyeing it.

"Only for show," he says, slithering over the side of the skiff and landing on legs that look ready to buckle. Whatever's in that flask he's been sipping on clearly isn't helping his hangover.

"You have to let 'em know you're serious in a place like this," he says. "But don't worry. Disagreements rarely come to blows."

I narrow my eyes. "How rarely?"

With a slight chuckle and a knowing look, he sets off up the beach toward the row of houses. Red Bread swings the ax from his hip and points it at me. He flicks the head in the direction of the houses.

"He say 'walk'," says Goliath, shoving Sargo hard in the chest.

Following Savage up the beach, I try to put what I've sussed out about the crew so far into some kind of order in my mind. Fetch appears to be doing most of the work. But she listens to Red

Bread and Goliath. Goliath *looks* like muscle, but I suspect there's more to their role than that.

The fact that Savage is even more hung over than *I* am this morning makes me wonder if he's much use for anything except drinking, making speeches, and stabbing people.

"Does Savage look...different to you?" I mutter to Sargo.

"He looks like he had a rough night."

"Yeah, like, a *really* rough night. He left dinner early. What do you think he was doing?"

He shrugs. "I don't know."

"Aren't you curious?"

His voice takes on an edge. "I think we've pushed the limits of what we can get away with far enough today, don't you? Maybe now's not the time to be asking questions. Maybe it's time we actually started keeping a low profile."

I gape. "Are you *kidding* me? After last night? *Now* you want to keep a low prof—"

"Quiet," barks Goliath.

Savage stops at the beginning of the row of huts and leans against the trunk of a lone, anemic-looking tree. I drop to a seat in the dirt and brace my elbows on my knees, wishing I had brought more water. My hands and face are already coated with red dust and my mouth feels bone dry.

Studying the row of houses, I note that each one is painted a different bright, pastel color, and each has a small, well-tended garden. I frown.

A garden?

I look for a water source, but see none. Which is weird. How do they have gardens but no water? In Brume we have fog traps. Even the Settlement at Naze was working on building a desalinator. But there's no indication of any fresh water here at all, not even a creek.

A creek.

Some scrap of memory or fragment of a dream floats by me. Hard red earth; a creek. Two little girls and a boy. Me and Shale.

I'm sure the boy is Shale now. I recognize the eyes. In my dream I saw him bending over a fire, tending a small pot. Making...brackish.

What is that word, 'brackish'? Just something I dreamed?

"Hey," Sargo's voice pulls me out of my thoughts, "do you notice anything weird about this place?"

I blink, letting the image of young Shale fade, and turn my attention back to the row of houses.

"Yeah, they don't have a water source."

Sargo frowns and studies the houses again. "You're right. Good eye, Howsley. I was going to say—doesn't it seem kind of...empty?"

I scan the row of huts again. Apart from the veg gardens, there's no sign of life anywhere. The one closest to us has boards across the windows.

"That's weird," I murmur.

"Right? How are the gardens so well-maintained if there's no one here?"

"And how are they watering veg with no water?"

Fetch, who hung back to secure the *Kingfisher's* skiff, strides up from the beach and joins the group at the tree. She reaches into the small pack around her hips and takes a couple of swigs from a canteen.

I squint up at her. "What's the deal with this place? Where is everyone? Where's the water?"

She wipes her mouth on her sleeve and doesn't respond, then tucks away her canteen and pulls Savage aside. The two confer in hushed voices. Fetch looks over her shoulder at me and Savage shakes his head. She glares at him, then turns and stalks back to the rest of us.

"Circle up."

Goliath and Red Bread drag Sargo and I to our feet and we form a semi-circle around Fetch. She signs for Red Bread as she speaks.

"Captain thinks we'll draw too much attention if we handcuff the prisoners—"

"Guests," Savage interrupts, falling into position in the semi-circle.

Fetch grimaces. "*Guests*. So we'll need to stick together to ensure we can prevent them from doing anything—" she eyes me, "—stupid. We'll get the score on the haul settled first. Then pick up some provisions. Everyone clear?"

She looks around the group. We all nod.

"Let's get in and get out," she says. "One hour."

As terrified as I am of her, I have to admit that something about Fetch is extremely impressive. She's got to be all of seventeen, and she's basically running this crew. Where did she learn to command that kind of respect?

She turns briskly, marches up to the first house in the row, and raps smartly on the bright green door. A hatch in the door slides open, and Fetch stands on tiptoe to speak through it.

"*Kingfisher*," she says, then she lowers her voice and mutters something I don't catch.

The hatch slides abruptly closed. After a moment of clicking and jingling, the door swings open. Fetch beckons us with a single flick of her hand and steps across the threshold. Savage goes first, and Goliath and Red Bread shove Sargo and I through after him.

The air inside is stuffy, and my clothes immediately stick to me. I peer around in the dim light at a single room, sparsely furnished with an old sofa, a low table, and a chair. On the table is a slate and a mug, half full of brew. The walls are bare. Mobiles made from sticks, shells, and feathers spin lazily under the ceiling.

Red Bread hooks his ax back onto its leather loop, but the look he gives me as he does so tells me that to take that as an invitation to try anything would be very foolish.

A small, gray-haired woman with ivory skin locks the door from the inside. She hobbles past us to a second door in the far wall, which she opens with a large rusty key. *A key.* Where did she get a key? No one uses those anymore.

Fetch leads the way as the old woman gestures us through,

pressing something into the woman's hand as she passes her. I crane my neck to look over Savage's shoulder, and through the door I see a set of stairs disappearing down into darkness.

As we descend the stairs, the air grows cool, and a crisp, familiar smell fills my nose. We're going underground. The smell of damp earth and stone is so reminiscent of the forest of Brume that I'm transported back to my room. I'm looking out of my window at the trees, shrouded in fog.

I hope my moms are okay. I hope the Anonymity hasn't come for my moms.

I shove the thought down and focus on putting one foot in front of the other.

At the bottom of the stairs is another door with a sliding hatch in it. Fetch gives the *Kingfisher's* name again, and drops her voice to mutter something I don't catch. A password, I assume. As the hatch snaps shut she turns to Sargo and me.

"Welcome," she says, with a grim smile, "to Reckoner's Row."

chapter
twenty-four

THE FIRST THING I'm hit by as the door opens is a wall of sound.

A hubbub of voices, punctuated by shouts, laughter, and the occasional strike of metal on stone. I'm sure for one surreal instant that I even hear the bleat of a farm animal. Music drifts above it all, a jangle of strings and percussion carrying a clear, earnest voice. The air smells of grilled meat and baking bread, of brew and tea, and has a pungent, fishy undertone.

Stretching ahead of us is a wide tunnel with a ceiling just a few feet above the top of Sargo's head, so long that it disappears into darkness. It's packed with people. The walls on either side are crammed with stalls and tables. A hodgepodge of string lights, lanterns, and bare lightbulbs hang from the stalls, throwing a kaleidoscope of colors onto the cinder block walls and bare earth ceiling.

Goliath, Savage and Red Bread flank me and Sargo, as Fetch pulls a slate from her hip pouch, pressing two fingers to her brow. Sargo nudges my shoulder. I watch as Fetch swipes through the air, reading from the slate, I guess checking some kind of provisioning list on her biochip. I squint again at the tattoo on the side of her head. *4242.*

Sargo says a Reckoner being chipped is unusual, and I wonder if the tattoo has something to do with it. I never heard of anyone being tattooed when they got chipped, but I guess it's possible. Neither Goliath, Red Bread, nor Savage does anything to indicate that they're chipped, but it seems there's definitely more to this crew than meets the eye—or at least, there's more to Fetch.

She tucks the slate back into her hip pouch. "Ready?"

Without waiting for a reply, she ducks into the crowd. A stern look from Goliath is all I need to stumble after her, clutching Malarkey's leash and pulling her close to my side. We follow Fetch; Goliath, Savage, and Red Bread close behind, the crowd pressing too tightly around us to even think about trying to escape.

We pass a band of musicians—four people crammed into a tiny doorway, thumping away on their instruments with broad smiles and bright eyes. I spot tables full of slates, others laden with tomatoes, greens, apples and other veg, and still more covered in spare parts, scrap metal, toys, clothes, shoes, and more semi-precious stones than I would know what to do with.

There are carts laden with fly-covered raw chickens, or hung with whole pigs, flayed open to reveal the ribs, blood pooling in the dirt below; others bow under pounds of fish and oysters. The rich smell of warm yeast emanating from a stall piled high with loaves of flatbread is so strong it stops me in my tracks.

"Impressive, eh?" says a hoarse voice in my ear.

Savage's partially toothless leer greets me as I whip my head around. I recoil, my eyes darting around his face. He hasn't removed the darx, even though we're deep underground and the space is barely illuminated.

What is he hiding? The multicolored lights from the various stalls reflect off the lenses, and I stare into my own wide-eyed reflection as he steps around me. I counter, taking a step back, my chest facing his as he circles me, the crowd jostling against us.

He smirks, and even in his haggard state, the smile is disarmingly handsome. "Are you afraid, Alluvium?"

Next to me, Malarkey snarls. Savage's eyes flit to her as my back comes up against something firm. Sargo is standing right behind me, his eyes fixed on Savage.

Savage chuckles and eyes me again. "I see you brought *both* your guard dogs today." His hand dips into his pocket and I imagine him fingering the handle of the butterfly knife I know is in there.

"Do you think if I wanted to kill you, I would do it in the middle of a crowd like this?" he says. "No, Alluvium. I'm not going to do something as stupid as that. But," his eyes move over my shoulder to Sargo, his grin broadening, "I might make him do it."

Sargo sucks in a sharp breath. "What?"

"What do you say, Son? Get yourself out of this mess she got you into? Trade her life for yours? I could use another strong sailor on my crew."

My heart begins to beat in my hands and feet.

"What would make you think I would do something like that?" Sargo says in a low voice.

Savage shrugs. "A hunch. Maybe you're starting to feel like you need to look out for yourself. I can't have been the only one who's put two-and-two together and realized her little plan doesn't offer you much insurance."

"What about your coin?" Sargo says, his voice so close to my ear I shiver. "If she's dead, you don't get anything."

"Perhaps I've decided she's no longer worth it. Perhaps I've realized this whole gambit is just a little more work than I'm willing to do. Perhaps I've realized that I can't guarantee that *both* of you will make it to Alluvium."

No, I think. *He's bluffing.* He has to be. He wouldn't throw away seventy-five thousand Ubicoin like that. No way. This is just intimidation. He gets some kind of twisted kick out of trying to scare us. Plus, Sargo would never go for that.

Right?

His words from last night ricochet through my head.

"I have to look out for myself."

Savage leans in closer and I shrink against Sargo. My cheeks heat; I have no reason to believe that Sargo wants me this close. But there's nowhere else to go. I'm trapped between Savage's dangerous leer and the edge of the chasm of unspoken words separating me and Sargo.

Then Sargo's hands close around my shoulders, and I swear I feel him pulling me tighter against him. His grip is firm. His heart beats hard against my back. And even though I can feel his fear through that heartbeat, something about it empowers me.

I glare into Savage's eyes. "You're bluffing. You're just trying to scare us. It won't work."

"And I'm not interested," says Sargo, his voice a low growl that rumbles through me from deep inside his chest.

Savage shrugs with a lazy grin. "Suit yourself."

He removes his hand from his pocket, shoulders past us, and disappears into the crowd.

"Move," says Goliath.

We weave through the throng and stop in front of a nondescript door. Fetch raps on it smartly. When it cracks open, Goliath and Red Bread heave the two enormous sacks that they carried from the *Kingfisher* across the threshold. Fetch and Red Bread slip through the door and it closes behind them, leaving me, Malarkey and Sargo standing between Goliath and Savage.

Goliath clasps their hands in front of them and adopts a wide-legged stance with their back to the door, while Savage sits heavily on a crate against the wall, rubbing his eyes under the darx and pulling the flask from inside his coat.

Goliath's glare settles on me. "We wait."

My hand tightens around Malarkey's leash and my eyes flick to Sargo. Surely now, with just two of them to deal with, and Savage obviously in rough shape, is the time to run. I can't help looking over my shoulder at the crush of people. It would be so easy to disappear in here.

"Don't get any ideas, Alluvium," says Savage. "Even if you manage to lose us in this crowd, there's nowhere for you to go.

The place is locked from both sides and guarded. You need a password to get in or out."

I glare at him, wondering if what he says is true, or if he's just trying to scare me again. Dissuade me from trying something.

"Would I have brought you down here without handcuffing you if I thought you might be able to get away?"

He leans against the wall and stretches his legs in front of him, crossing his boots. As he does, two words are revealed on the side of the crate he sits on: *Zenith Biotech.*

I frown at them, my mind not fully grasping the significance of seeing those two familiar words, here, so far from Brume. What the hell is a crate of Zenith merchandise doing here? I look around, becoming aware of more stacks of crates and boxes. Many are printed with the same two words. Others are marked with the names of the other Big Four companies. *Spindrift Hydrosolutions. StarNet.*

"Black market goods," mutters Sargo. "This whole place is full of stolen parts."

Savage grins at me. "Not exactly a place your mom would approve of."

"I can see why you wouldn't want Zenith to know about it," I say carefully.

"It is rather special." He uses the flask to gesture around us. "One of the few spots along this coast that didn't burn during Fire Season. When Reckoners figured out this cove was big enough to anchor in, they started coming here to trade."

He sips from the flask, and coughs.

"The people here were running out of water, so they were happy to trade their fish for Reckoners' desal. Eventually, all kinds of stuff started coming through here. This tunnel used to be basements for the houses above, but the market got so big they knocked through the basement walls and made this."

Goliath steps away from the door as it cracks open and Fetch slips through it, Red Bread behind her. The sacks are gone. Fetch nods to Savage, who tucks the flask back into his pocket and pulls himself to his feet.

"Shall we?"

We continue along the Row. After so many days on the water with no one but me, Sargo, and Malarkey around, being in a tight, fully enclosed space with so many other people is jarring. Even more off-putting is that no one but me and Sargo is wearing a mask or bandana.

An old woman gives me a hard-eyed stare as we pass, and my skin prickles.

"People are looking at us," I whisper.

Sargo glances around. "Probably the bandanas. If these people are dealing in black market goods, I'm guessing they don't put much stock in Zenith's policies."

"Should we take them off?"

He says nothing.

"We're trying to keep a low profile, right?"

He tugs the bandana away from his face and I see that his jaw is clenched.

"So now I'm playing a character who is such a hardcore Zenith dissenter that I'm hanging out, unmasked, at the black market?" he mutters.

I forgot that Sargo is actually pretty serious about his support of Zenith. I guess maybe because his moms had some kind of tie to Electra's family back in the day. Or maybe because when he was a teacher at Azimuth, he was technically an employee of Zenith. He used to quote the slogans at me all the time. *'Brume pride.' 'Put on your own mask first.' 'The most good for the most people.'* He's always been a fan of rules and policies and order.

I've never really paid much attention to what Zenith do. I mean yeah, it's cool that they ended the pandemic, and that they're all women. But I can't say I've ever called myself a supporter.

"Probably best to keep your moral compass on the down low

here," I say in a low voice, removing my bandana and tucking it surreptitiously into my back pocket.

"Yeah, obviously," he replies tersely, tucking his own bandana away. "I just don't like it."

Fetch halts in front of a stall loaded with veg, bread, and canned goods. "You lovebirds need any provisions?" She gestures at the stall. "Here's the place to get them."

We are actually very low on food, so I fill my pack with greens, apples, a couple of loaves of bread, a hunk of cheese, and a few dented cans of meat for Malarkey. I hold the cans out for Malarkey to sniff before tucking them into my pack and she snorts, evidently not impressed. As I reach to swap one can out for a less dented one, I bump into the man next to me.

He eyes me sharply. "Watch where you're putting those elbows."

"Sorry."

I flash him an apologetic smile. He's a tall, well-dressed young man with a ponytail and fastidiously groomed beard. As our eyes meet, something flickers across his face. A look of recognition, almost.

His brow crinkles ever so slightly. "Do I know you?"

My blood freezes. Is it possible the Anonymity have distributed my picture on the Net? I don't know what kind of people frequent a place like this, but I'm willing to bet that being recognized by one of them won't lead to anything good. I quickly turn my face away, bending to examine a piece of fruit.

"I don't think so," I mumble. "I just have one of those faces."

I feel his eyes on the back of my head, then he pays for his purchases and moves away. When I straighten up and look around, he's gone. But the specter of the Anonymity lays across my mind like a shadow. I had forgotten about them.

The next time Fetch stops, we're in front of a table covered in scrap metal and spare parts. The names of Big Four companies are printed on almost everything. As Fetch haggles aggressively with

the guy behind the table over a part that Red Bread apparently
needs for the *Kingfisher*, my eyes fall on something I recognize.

I pick it up. "Is this a desalinator filter?"

Sargo looks over my shoulder. "Yeah." He takes it from me.
"Actually, it's the same size as the one we gave to those settlers at
Naze." He turns it over in his hands. "I could use another one."

"See if Fetch will get it for you. You can transfer her the coin."

As he continues turning the filter over in his hands, the name
of a Big Four company is revealed: *Spindriff Hydrosolutions*. His
hands still. He sets the filter back on the table.

"I don't want it."

"You just said you needed—"

"I said I don't want it!" he snaps. He begins to walk away, only
to be stopped by Goliath's enormous hand on his chest. He growls
and tries to shake them off.

"I'm not going anywhere! Your captain made that pretty clear."

Goliath removes their hand and folds their arms across their
chest. Sargo shakes his head with a frustrated sigh and retreats to
lean against the wall. Goliath takes up what I'm beginning to
recognize as their trademark stance: wide-legged like a soldier,
hands clasped in front, eyes on Sargo.

I carefully step around them, and lean against the wall next to
him. "What's going on?"

"It's nothing," he says. "It doesn't matter. Forget it."

"Clearly it matters."

His jaw ticks. His chest rises slowly and falls hard. "I just—"
He glances at Goliath and drops his voice a hair. "I just...don't like
being here. That's all. The flogging black market?" He looks
around darkly. "This is not a good place."

"Look," I take a breath and work hard to keep the irritation out
of my voice. "I get that it's hard for you to be here because you
used to work for Zenith. I get that you support them and you
have ties to the Nations and you don't like going against their
policies or being around all this stolen shit. But...can't you just—
let it go? For now? Just...pretend like you don't care? We're on

pretty thin ice with Savage. He literally said he doesn't want anyone in here that might talk about this place to Zenith."

Sargo stares at the ground in front of his feet. "It's not that."

"Well then what is it?"

"I mean, yeah, you're right. I do support Zenith. I think they do good work, and their policies keep us alive, but…"

He leans the back of his head against the wall and delivers his next words to the ceiling.

"In Brume, the black market is run by the Anonymity. They steal a lot of stuff from Zenith and sell it on. That's how they make their money. To fund everything else they do. Like dealing drugs. Dragging people like my uncle into debt. Killing…my moms."

His eyes close slowly as he takes a breath.

"Most of the stuff the Anonymity steals in Brume probably ends up here. I just feel like…if I spend my money here, I'm giving money to the people that killed my moms. It's stupid. But—"

"It's not stupid." I put my hand on his arm, guilt knifing me. "You're right to care about that. I'm sorry. I didn't know."

His eyes flit to my hand. Suddenly, the feel of his bare forearm beneath my fingers is electric. I blush and pull my hand away.

"Just trying to keep up the illusion," I mumble.

I lean my back against the wall next to him and watch Fetch arguing with the spare parts guy while I mull his words around in my head. I've been so worried about Savage and his crew that the Anonymity had slipped to the back of my mind. Now, those faceless heads creep back into my consciousness. The high-collared jackets; the broad calves straining at polished boots.

The parts look good, the little man had said. *Could be sold separately.*

Nausea sweeps through me. Suddenly, the hubbub of the Row is too loud. The lights too bright. The crowd too close. *The parts look good.* Somewhere here, I realize, behind some door, there is a stall selling human body parts. Those could have been my body parts.

Fetch's sharp bark snaps my head up. "That's it crew. Back to the boats."

She pulls out her slate while Red Bread tucks the spare part into his pack. Goliath snaps their fingers at me and Sargo. Numbly, my head spinning, I trip back to where Fetch and Red Bread are standing.

The parts look good.

If the Anonymity run the black market, they could *be here*. That guy with the ponytail...I can't help glancing over my shoulder, scanning the faces in the crowd for creepy, blurred smudges.

Sargo's voice cuts through the noise of my thoughts. "Where's Savage?"

I look around. Savage is gone.

That's twice now that he's mysteriously disappeared since taking us prisoner—during dinner on the *Kingfisher* last night, and now here. What could possibly be so important that he would leave his crew shorthanded while guarding us? The Anonymity drifts to the back of my mind again as I scan the surrounding stalls for his lanky blonde hair and mirrored darx.

Fetch tucks the slate back into her pack. "The captain's taking care of something. It's none of your concern." She eyes me. "Don't get any ideas."

Goliath shoves me hard between the shoulders and I stumble forward, tightening my grip on Malarkey's leash as Fetch turns to lead us back along the Row.

Sargo falls in step to my right. "I heard the password," he whispers.

"What? What password?"

He speaks quickly and quietly, his eyes fixed on Fetch, his mouth barely moving. I can hardly hear him under the racket of the market.

"When we came in. Fetch gave a password at the door. I think I know what it is."

"*What?*" My voice comes out a harsh whisper.

"Quiet," growls Goliath from behind us.

My pulse accelerates. Savage said the way in and out was protected by a password. If we have the password...with Savage gone, if we can lose Fetch, Goliath and Red Bread in this crowd, make it back to the door we came in through...

"Even with Savage MIA I don't think our chances are very good," mutters Sargo. He nods at Fetch then glances quickly over his shoulder at Goliath and Red Bread. "These three are the ones we need to worry about."

"But if we did get back to *Panga*, it would give us a head start, wouldn't it?" I whisper back, my voice barely audible even to me. "They'd have to wait for Savage to show up before they could come after us. It might give us time to get a lead on them."

He doesn't move his eyes from Fetch. "Maybe."

"Okay. So what's the plan?"

Out of the corner of my eye, I see him shake his head. "I don't know. This is crazy."

"Just...run. Go sideways. I'll go left, you go right. Get into the crowd and try to get back to the door."

"It sounds pretty risky," he says.

"Yes, it does," I agree. "Got anything better?"

We lapse into tense silence again, both of us watching Fetch. We walk for another five minutes, shuffling our way slowly through the crowd, until Fetch stops so abruptly I almost run into her.

"God dammit," she mutters. She pulls the slate from her hip pouch and taps her temple, flicks through her list, then turns and addresses Goliath over my shoulder.

"We didn't go to the Shaman. Nana needs her meds." She eyes Sargo and me briefly, and then signs to Red Bread as she speaks. "Can you go? Goliath and I will get these two back to the skiff."

Next to me, Sargo tenses.

Red Bread apparently acquiesces, because Fetch nods, then digs into her hip pack and pulls out a small pouch. She hands it over my shoulder to Red Bread and I glance back as he pockets it and ducks into the crowd, heading back the way we came.

When I turn back to Fetch, she's eyeing me with a flinty, narrow glare.

"Don't worry," I say, "I'm not getting any ideas."

Fetch drops her gaze to tuck the slate back into her hip pouch. As her eyes leave mine and become preoccupied with her pack, I feel Sargo's hand grab me around the wrist and squeeze hard. I don't need any more signal than that.

I duck to the left, dodging between a stack of boxes and a large, plastic barrel full of ice and fish heads.

"*Alluvium!*"

Fetch's angry snarl follows me. I let go of Malarkey's leash, trusting her to follow me, not even looking back to see where Sargo is as I sprint down a short passage and lunge to the right, behind another stall.

Popping out on the other side of it, I find myself shoving through a tight throng of people carrying bags and baskets. Daring to glance behind me, I spot Goliath on the other side of the main row, head and shoulders above everyone else. They don't appear to be coming my way; must be following Sargo. Fetch is nowhere to be seen, but I know that's only because she's too short to stand out amongst the crowd.

There is no thought in my head except that I have to somehow throw Fetch off my track. I push sideways for a few steps, then lurch between another stall and a rack of weapons. Malarkey appears at my hip, tail high, startling the woman beside me so that she stumbles out of my way.

I duck my head and keep pushing, diving and bobbing, weaving around people, elbows in my ribs and shoulders in my face until, up ahead, I see the end of the Row. A familiar head of close-cropped sable hair emerges in the crowd ahead of me.

"Sargo!"

He doesn't hear me; he's shoving people out of his way with a callousness I would have never expected from him. Angry shouts recede into the hubbub as I make my way through the wake of people he's thrown aside.

"What's the password?" I gasp as we reach the door. Over people's shoulders I spot Goliath about forty feet behind us, their eyes darting wildly, searching. I pull my hood over my head. They'll know where we're going; they'll be coming this way, but they haven't seen us yet.

Sargo hammers on the door and a small hatch opens at eye level.

"Red sky!" Sargo cries.

My heart is pounding like a drum. We're almost out. We might actually make it.

The eyes on the other side of the hatch narrow. "Wrong door," says a voice.

My heart stops. "What?"

"You can't get out this way."

"What do you mean, we can't get out?" yells Sargo.

"This is the entrance. You need to go to the exit." The hatch slides shut with a bang.

The world seems to fall out from under me. I step back, staring at Sargo. He shakes his head slowly. A tidal wave of cold panic rises in my chest.

"Alluvium!"

Fetch and Goliath emerge from the crowd, boxing us into the corner. I flatten my back to the door. Fetch's eyes are black and murderous as she pulls the knife from the sheath across her chest.

Malarkey launches herself at Goliath and this time, Goliath isn't ready for her. Malarkey's massive paws land squarely in the middle of their chest and the two tumble backward, Goliath grabbing at the scruff of Malarkey's neck.

In the same moment, Sargo bolts. But as I lunge after him, a tight grip closes around my wrist. Fetch yanks me backward and slams my back against the door, bracing her forearm hard across my chest, the knife in her hand pointed backward into the side of my throat.

I choke on my breath, unable to cry out, as Sargo disappears into the crowd. Over Fetch's shoulder, I see Malarkey twist herself free of Goliath's grip and bolt after him. Goliath leaps to their feet and starts to follow Sargo, but Fetch yells over her shoulder.

"Leave him. We can look for him later. Nation is the priority."

She presses her forearm against my windpipe, lowering her voice and bringing her face close to mine.

"As far as ideas go," she snarls, "that was one of the stupidest I've ever seen."

chapter
twenty-five

THE SUN IS SO bright it stings my eyes as we emerge from a door at the top of a basement staircase at the other end of the Row.

Disoriented, my eyes watering, and my hands bound in front of me, I stumble into the sand. We're on the back side of the row of wooden houses, facing away from the water. Ahead of me, rolling red hills covered with gray scrub slope infinitely toward the horizon.

Fetch presses her knife into the small of my back as she steps through the door behind me, and I arch away from the feel of the sharp point against my spine.

"Keep walking, Alluvium."

Red Bread and Goliath fall in next to Fetch. We walk along the row back toward the beach, the white sun blazing directly overhead, the sound of the bay reaching me through gaps between the houses to my left.

When we come to the last house—the same one we entered the Row through earlier—we turn left. Black sand stretches down to the sparkling blue water of the bay, and my heart sinks as I scan the water.

Panga is gone.

Sargo must have found the exit while Fetch and Goliath were

tying me up and rendezvousing with Red Bread. A confusing mix of relief and despair settles in my bones. He got away.

He left me.

"I guess your boyfriend bailed on you," Fetch sneers over my shoulder. "Smart."

I grit my teeth against tears and say nothing.

Red Bread and Goliath push the *Kingfisher's* skiff back into the water. Fetch flicks the tip of her knife at me.

"In."

I glare at her, not moving. "Where's Savage? You're just going to leave him behind?"

"Why don't you let me worry about my captain, Alluvium. *In.*"

With my hands tied, I scramble over the side and fall clumsily into the bottom. Fetch hops in after me to start the motor as Goliath and Red Bread push us into the surf, then swing themselves over the sides.

We motor back to the *Kingfisher*, where they wordlessly usher me out of the skiff, through the cockpit, down the stairs and through a sturdy wooden door into a storage room next to the galley. Tripping across the threshold, I turn just in time to see the door bang shut behind me, plunging me into total darkness. With my bound hands, I feel my way to a wall, put my back against it, and sink to the floor.

I don't know how much time passes while I sit there, staring into blackness. The room is stuffy and smells overpoweringly of garlic and too-ripe fruit. Multiple pairs of boots scuff back and forth on the deck overhead. I hear muffled voices, snatches of shouted orders. I can't make out any words, but we're not moving, that much is clear. They must be waiting for Savage to get back. At some point, the skiff starts up and pulls away.

Eventually, the drone of the skiff motoring back across the bay reaches me, growing gradually louder. I hear it pull up, hear boots stepping out of it onto the deck above me, then Savage's unmistakable drawl. Fetch's voice replies and the boots make their way across the deck.

Minutes pass as I strain to hear, strain to pick up the sound of Savage's voice again, blinking hard against the darkness, until, suddenly, I clock the sound of the boots at the end of the corridor outside. The sound grows closer as they stride briskly down the hall and stop in front of the door.

When the door swings open, Savage's rangy silhouette stands on the other side, the collar of his coat turned all the way up around his jaw, shaggy hair falling around it. Behind him, I see the unmistakable silhouettes of Red Bread and Goliath.

"Well, well, well." He steps across the threshold and pauses. "You know, there's a light in here."

A wash of yellow light floods the room and I squeeze my eyes shut. When I open them, Savage is leaning casually in the doorway, loading a cartridge into his dart.

He looks...the picture of health. Handsome, even. His eyes are no longer hidden behind dark lenses. His skin has lost its pallor and returned to a radiant—albeit somewhat dirty—golden brown. An air of dangerous shrewdness has returned to him. It's in the energy of his posture; the keenness of his gray eyes. Whatever he disappeared to do at the Row, it apparently did him a world of good.

He regards me cooly. "What did I tell you about things that try my patience, Alluvium?"

I say nothing.

"If I recall, I believe I told you that when things try my patience, I tend to change my mind about them."

He finishes loading the cartridge, clicks on the dart, and takes a long, slow drag.

"Fortunately for you, you are a very valuable commodity, and for that reason," a thick cloud of smoke settles into the air between us as he exhales into the tiny room, "I've been willing to put up with more than the usual amount of shit."

He waves a hand to disperse some of the smoke.

"But enough is enough. That reckless little stunt was a pretty serious breach of contract, as far as I'm concerned. Evidently, you can't be trusted. And as none of my crew can find neither hide nor hair of your boyfriend or his little yellow boat, it appears that you're unfortunately without transport."

I force my face to retain a neutral expression, even though the pain in my chest makes me want to cry.

"So," continues Savage, "you'll be making the rest of the passage to Alluvium aboard the *Kingfisher*, where my crew and I can keep a better eye on you."

"You can't do that. I'll tell my family you kidnapped me. They'll come after you."

"Ah, Miss Nation." He tuts and shakes his head. "You don't seem to have grasped what's going on here. Your boyfriend is *gone*. If you don't come to Alluvium aboard my ship, what are you going to do? Hm? Stay here at the Row? They don't really welcome outsiders. Go back to Brume? How? On whose boat?"

He gestures with the dart in the direction of the shore.

"Or perhaps you'd like to take your chances out there alone in the Turf? To date, I haven't heard of a single person that's survived it, but you are fairly scrappy, so who knows? Maybe you'll be the first."

He drags again on the dart and lets another slow cloud of smoke trail from his mouth as he turns, sauntering out of the room.

"The way I see it, Alluvium," he says over his shoulder, "I'm doing you a favor. In fact, I think my generosity might even be sufficient to warrant an increase in the gratitude displayed by your family. Shall we say...another fifty thousand coin?"

He steps through the door and turns, bracing one hand on each side of the doorframe and leaning back across the threshold. "Call it a handler's fee."

The next six days blur into one continuous string.

The crew move me out of the storage room and lock me in a spare cabin, so at least I have a bed to sleep on, a head, and a porthole to look out of. Through the tiny round window, I can see that we've left the coast. We're still heading South, but Savage must be taking us offshore to find better wind.

The color of the sky changes. The air grows warmer and more humid. Day by day, the thick brown soup of smog and ash that hangs along the coast south of Naze incrementally clears.

My nails become short, then ragged, then bloody with constant, anxious gnawing. I wake with one question on my tongue and fall asleep with it going round and round inside my head:

What the hell am I going to do now?

Short of getting kidnapped by yet another crew of Reckoners, or actually having a rich brother in Alluvium who can pay Savage over a hundred thousand Ubicoin for my ransom, I can't see a way out.

What happens when I get there and Savage doesn't get his coin? It's a question I try not to let worm its way into my head too much. Because I already know the answer.

I fall asleep every night to the creak and roll of the ship as it plows through the Salt, and wake every morning to the same disorienting motion. We don't drop anchor overnight anymore—I guess Savage must be in a hurry to get me to Alluvium before I make any more reckless escape attempts.

Honestly, though, his fear is misplaced: I'm too miserable and defeated to even contemplate an escape. Where would I go? He was right. I have no one out here. I'm alone.

Sargo is gone.

Thinking about that makes my chest ache worse than anything I've ever felt, so I try not to do it. He did the right thing. Since that day I showed up at his house in Brume, his life has only gone from bad to worse. He was right to look out for himself. Savage would have killed him eventually. I just hope he made it somewhere safe. I hope he has Malarkey.

One night, I dream about him.

I'm lying on the bunk in the bow and he's kneeling over me, a knee on either side of my hips, his pants unbuttoned. Kneeling like he was that day I watched him. When I try to move, the weight of him pins my hips to the bunk. A thick rope is around my wrists.

My eyes find his. "Why am I tied up?"

His hair and shirt are wet. A smattering of dark bristles paints his jaw, and his eyes blaze with a fierce, savage heat. They take in my bare legs, the sliver of skin exposed on my stomach, my chest, my lips. I'm wearing his shirt, I realize. His blue button-down. And nothing else.

"You watched me," he says, and a shaft of heat goes through me.

"Yes," I breathe.

He reaches into the front of his pants, where a bulge is already twitching, growing. "Did you like watching me, Howsley?"

"Yes."

My eyes are fixed on his hand, freeing the bulge from his pants. The spot between my legs is already hot and tight. I pull against the rope, twist under the weight of his hips.

"Sargo, why am I tied up?"

"Look at me," he growls.

I flit my eyes up to his, suddenly afraid in the airless room. His eyes remind me of his eyes that night on the *Kingfisher*. I'm not sure if what I see in them is anger or desire. I wonder if he knows himself.

"You shouldn't have done that," he says.

"I'm sorry," I whisper.

"Sorry isn't good enough." He pulls the hard, throbbing length out of his pants and my eyes go wide. "We're going to have to even the score."

"What...do you mean?"

"I'm going to watch *you* now, Howsley."

My blood runs so hot it seems to freeze. "Watch me?"

"Show me how you touch yourself."

"I...can't."

He reaches over my head with one hand to free one of my wrists. "You can."

My mouth hangs partly open as I watch him wrap his fist around himself and stroke slowly, once. An exhilarating torrent of heat and nerves pulses through me.

"Do it now." He strokes himself again. And then, his voice cracking, "Please."

Our eyes lock and I don't seem to be able to tear mine away as I begin to undo the top button of his shirt with one hand. Beneath it, my breasts are bare, the fabric brushing my nipples so gently that I squirm as I slowly make my way down the front, undoing each button. I can smell him in that fabric. Smell him on me.

His eyes track my fingers as his hand continues its long, deliberate strokes. As I reach the last button and push the shirt all the way open, he groans, pumping himself harder, his eyes taking in my belly, my hips, my breasts with a hunger bordering on greed.

Under his gaze, my nipples ache to be touched. I pinch one and tug it until I gasp.

He echoes my gasp with a groan. "Does that feel good?"

"Yes."

He hisses and his fist beats faster. I feel his hips rolling against mine. I writhe under him, wishing he was between my legs, desperate to feel him against me. "Is that how you like it?" His voice is husky. "Is that how you make yourself come?"

"No..."

"How do you make yourself come?"

"I touch myself. Lower."

"Show me."

He raises up on his knees and I shove my hand into the front of my underwear, plunging my fingers into myself, grinding the aching spot at the top of my sex into the palm of my hand. My eyes close, my head tipping back as I moan, arching off the bed.

"*God*," he growls. I hear his fist beating hard and fast against his hips. "God that's so fucking hot."

"Do you want to touch me?" I hear myself say, and my voice is not my own.

"Yes," he groans. "I'm going fucking crazy not touching you."

"Do you want to fuck me?"

"*Yes*. I've wanted to fuck you for weeks."

I open my eyes to find his—and a pair of hands grabs him by the shoulders from behind. A pair of thick, tattooed arms wrap around his chest and drag him, thrashing and swearing, backward off the bunk and through the cabin door.

"*Sargo!*"

I wake, crying out, the sheet twisted around my wrists, my hips bowing off the bed.

On the morning of my sixth day captive on the *Kingfisher*, I wake to a sharp *ping*, and a text alert slides in front of my groggy, half-open eyes.

>>> CONNECTION REESTABLISHED. MAPS, MESSENGER AND THE NET READY FOR USE.

I sit bolt upright. My biochip is back online. I hadn't used it in so long, I had forgotten I even had it. Suddenly, the prospect of sending a message becomes a reality, and with that new reality comes a rush of hope. I can send a message for help.

But to who?

The Zenith Peace Force is so overtaxed I doubt they'd even get to my message before the end of the week. For the CEO's daughter, sure, a swift response would be assured, but for just some girl from Brume? Not to mention a girl who was recently expelled and is likely accused of the theft of an expensive necklace? No chance.

My moms are too far away to be able to do anything in Brume, and Sargo is probably still offline somewhere along the coast.

Then it hits me. Shale.

I may not have a rich brother in Alluvium, but I do have a *brother* in Alluvium. Surely he can help me. He must know of some kind of local law enforcement. Maybe not Zenith law enforcement, but something?

My fingers are halfway through composing the text when the door of my cabin slams open and Fetch strides through it. I crawl backwards on my elbows into the corner of my bunk, but she grabs me by the ankle and yanks me down onto my back, swiftly climbing onto me, planting one knee in my chest, grabbing my wrists in both hands and pinning them over my head against the bed.

"Stop what you're doing," she growls.

"What am I doing?"

"Don't play dumb. My chip just came back online. That means yours did too. If you're thinking about sending a message to your boyfriend or your family, you'd better think again." She climbs off me. "Let's go."

I push myself to my elbows as she steps back from the bed. "Go where?"

"You're with me now. Need to keep tabs on you. Can't have you trying to get in touch with people." She folds her arms and pins her eyebrows to her hairline. "Quickly! Up!"

Trembling, I throw back the sheet and stumble to my feet. She watches as I pull on shoes, then produces a length of rope from inside her hip pack and binds it around my wrists, wrapping it so that my hands are sandwiched together as if I'm praying. Which is convenient, I suppose, as I probably soon will be.

"Move your fingers," she says.

I try. The very first knuckle of each finger barely wiggles.

She gives a brief, satisfied nod. "Follow me."

Up in the cockpit, she ties my hands to a cleat in the back corner, the rope so short that I have to sit cross-legged on the floor. She calls Fid over.

"Watch her," she growls. "She so much as moves a pinkie, I want to know about it."

The whole crew is on deck. I spot Sterling and Nana uncoiling lines on the bow, Red Bread managing the headsail, and Goliath preparing to drop the anchor.

To my left, Savage stands behind the helm, for once not wearing his trademarked peacoat—I imagine because of the stifling, muggy heat. His short sleeves reveal a wealth of new tattoos decorating his arms—a turtle, an anchor, a girl in a grass skirt, a five-pointed star. His face is taut with concentration and he continually checks a small instrument in a panel to his right.

"What's going on?" I murmur to Fid.

"Alluvium!" he chirps. "We're here."

Twisting around as best I can with my hands tied to the cockpit floor, I look over the port side of the boat at the shore as the bay of Alluvium comes into view.

From the water, the city is a jarring mix of wealth and dilapidation. A row of unfinished concrete hotels with exposed rebar and gaping, empty windows lines the rocky breakwater. A row of finished hotels gleams like a jeweled necklace next to it. Corrugated tin roof shacks covered with graffiti are squeezed between elegant homes surrounded by high walls. A spiderweb of telecom wires criss cross between rooftops. The domed tops of grain silos puncture the skyline at random intervals.

Everywhere, there are trees. They stick up between buildings and crowd the sand. The structures interweave so intimately into the foliage that the trees seem to be part of the city. At the northern tip of the bay, a lush estuary comes almost to the water's edge.

"This place looks crazy," I murmur.

"It ith crathy," says Fid.

"I thought it would be like Brume."

A frown crinkles Fid's tiny forehead. "No. People in Brume are rich."

The bay is not well protected from swell or wind, and the *Kingfisher* bounces through chop, making her way toward the northern shore, where a massive whitewater surf break crashes into the sand. We anchor in a small cove out of the way of the chaos and I watch from the cockpit floor as the crew puts the sails away. It takes them over an hour to furl the sails, coil all the lines, tidy the deck, and jot down readings from the instruments.

Plenty of time for me to get my bearings, remember why we're here, and start to panic.

———————

Fetch swerves the skiff away from the *Kingfisher* and toward a channel mouth that will take us up a river to the city docks. The channel is narrow, lined on either side by lush, bright green vegetation that grows straight up out of the shallow water on slender, twisted roots. The air is muggy, the surface of the water perfectly still but for clouds of tiny flies.

At the top, the channel opens up and as we make our way across a wide lake, we pass every manner and class of boat. Tiny fishing vessels to super yachts like the *Kingfisher*, to rotting heaps of what I imagine used to be sailboats. Skiffs zip around us like gnats. Music floats through the air from at least three different places, coagulating into a weird, off-kilter mashup. The rich smell of grilling meat wafts into my nose.

Savage hasn't told me where he's taking me. Some kind of safe house, I assume, where they can arrange the handoff. I tried to convince Fetch that it would be better for me to message my brother myself, let him know what was happening, tell him where to bring the money.

"It might take him a day or two to come up with it," I lied in a panicked voice, as she untied my hands from the *Kingfisher's* cockpit floor ten minutes ago. "If you just tell me where you're taking me, I can tell him where to bring it. I can tell him how much he needs to bring so he can start getting it together now. Then you won't have to wait. You can get the money sooner. Isn't that better for you?"

Fetch just leveled me with one of her withering stares. "Nice try, Alluvium, but we're perfectly capable of tracking down your family."

Fetch squeezes the skiff in at the busy public dock, and Goliath and Red Bread haul me out by my elbows. The set my unsteady feet down on planks that radiate heat and smell vaguely sweet: soft pine, baking in the sun.

Savage takes the lead, with Fetch right behind him and Red Bread and Goliath flanking me. Feeling as though I'm right back at Reckoner's Row, I follow them through the harbor.

The piers are swarming with people. Russet-skinned sailors, ruddy and flecked with white sun spots. Fishermen hauling nets of fish that reek and stare into the sun with vacant, jellied eyes. Reckoners carrying canvas bags full of God-knows-what across their backs. Vagrants sprawled in doorways and on corners.

As we round the corner from the public dock and step onto the harbor's main walkway, a man steps between Fetch and me. I run into the side of him, rebounding and stumbling sideways, feeling Goliath catch me under the arm.

The man shoots me an impatient look as he straightens his jacket.

"Watch where you're goi—" He frowns, his eyes sticking on mine with a look of surprised recognition. "It's you again."

I blink. "Excuse me?"

Ahead, Fetch and Savage have turned, Fetch registering the interaction with impatience. Goliath tightens their grip on my arm and pulls me sideways around the man.

"Let's go!" Fetch barks.

"No, hold on." The man puts his hand out, stopping my shoulder. "I know you. I've seen you somewhere before."

His brow is knitted quizzically, his blue eyes narrow, scrutinizing my face. He looks to be in his mid twenties, with thick, chestnut hair gathered into a ponytail at the nape of his neck and a sleek, well-groomed beard, also streaked with chestnut, and styled with wax. He wears an expensive-looking jacket and a crisp linen shirt, buttoned all the way up, despite the heat.

I *do* recognize him, I realize. It's the same man I bumped into at the veg stand in Reckoner's Row. I had been afraid he might be a member of the Anonymity, or someone who had seen my picture somewhere and knew I was wanted by them. Suddenly, I don't care if he is or not: he's a human who recognizes me. He's a human who might be able to help.

"She don't know you," growls Goliath, pulling me by the arm. "Now move."

The man doesn't remove his hand from my shoulder. His eyes dart to my bound hands, then back to my face, then to Goliath.

"Everything okay here?" he says in a low voice.

A sharp voice cuts through the noise of the crowd. "Everything is fine."

The man turns as Fetch and Savage press in behind him. Fetch's hand lays casually on the handle of the knife sheathed across her chest. The man looks back at me, then up at Goliath and Red Bread, who have moved closer, boxing him in.

He carefully removes his hand from my shoulder. "Okay, no problem." He takes a slow step backward, maneuvering himself around Savage. "Didn't mean to interfere."

His eyes dart back to mine. Fetch's hand is slowly closing around the handle of her knife, and behind me, I hear Goliath crack their knuckles.

Help me, I try to telegraph with my eyes. *Please.*

Something in the man's face shifts. Suddenly, something clicks, as though whatever he was trying to work out about where he knows me from has just fallen into place. His brow un-furrows, and his mouth falls slightly open. For one long, hypnotizing breath, he just stares at me, a look of bemused disbelief unfolding across his face.

Finally, he blinks. He shakes his head once, as if to clear it, and says, "Bird? It's me. Shale."

chapter
twenty-six

My body goes dead still.

Pieces of the face in front of me start to swim into a new arrangement inside my head. The bright blue eyes. The quizzical brow. The thick, chestnut hair and a beard I would recognize better as a weedy patch of scruff. In my mind, I see a boy in a tree. Making brackish. Starting a fire. This is him. This is Shale.

"She's not who you think she is, buddy."

At Fetch's icy reproach, Shale's eyes dart around the faces of the four Reckoners surrounding us. This is not the time or place for a tearful family reunion. My brother and I are surrounded by bloodthirsty pirates who all think I'm someone else. Someone important. Someone they think is worth a hundred thousand coin. In the corner of my eye, I see Savage's hand slide into his pocket.

Oh God. My stomach turns as a cold, black realization settles on me like a shadow. They'll kill him. If Shale doesn't walk away, they'll kill him. He can't save me. I have to save *him.* I have to make him walk away.

I bury the voice inside me screaming for Shale to help me and take a breath.

"I'm sorry," I say, "you have me confused with someone else."

His face creases. "What? Birdie—"

"She doesn't know you, friend," growls Savage, so close to us now that his face is inches from the side of Shale's. Fetch's hand remains tight around the handle of her knife. All around us, oblivious people stream like a river around rocks.

"I'm going to ask you once more," says Savage, low into my brother's ear, "to kindly take a step back, and leave the young lady alone."

Shale's eyes meet mine again and hold them for a long moment. Then, to my absolute horror, without breaking my gaze, he says to Savage, "And what if I don't?"

In a flash, Savage has the butterfly knife out of his pocket and against Shale's ribs. A woman walking past tucks her head as she scurries on, pretending she hasn't seen.

"Well, then I'd have to cause a scene," Savage says. "And that would be a real problem."

"It *would* be a real problem," says Shale carefully, his eyes still on mine. "You're already calling more attention to yourselves than I bet you'd like to." He inclines his head ever so slightly to the right. "And harbor patrol is right over there. Where are you going to run to in this crowd?"

A flicker of hesitation crosses Savage's face. His eyes flit to the stream of people going by.

He has no intention of causing a scene here, I realize.

He can't risk being caught with me before he gets me to my family. He must have been counting on Shale being scared enough of his empty threats to drop it. Apparently, though, my brother is not so easily intimidated.

"Now look," Shale continues evenly, "clearly there's been a misunderstanding. Whoever you think this person is, I can assure you, you're mistaken. This is my little sister, Bird Howsley. If you'll let me—" He raises his hands very slowly, palms facing out, until they are on either side of his face. "I can find you a picture." He taps his temple with one finger. "Is somebody here chipped?"

Savage's jaw tightens. He grips the knife harder, twisting the point against Shale's ribs as his keen, gray eyes calculate. Then he withdraws the blade and tilts it toward Fetch.

Fetch lets go of her knife and steps forward, tapping her temple. Shale presses two fingers to his brow, then slides them through the air toward Fetch, initiating a file transfer. She taps her brow to open the file.

Her eyes unfocus briefly as she looks at the image inside. "It's her," she confirms.

Savage turns his steely glare to me. "That doesn't prove anything. So he has a picture. Anyone could have a picture of the Nation girl."

"The Nation girl?" Shale's face cracks into an incredulous smile. A *smile*. Here. Surrounded by Reckoners, with the point of a knife barely removed from his ribs. "Electra Nation?" He shakes his head and his smile widens. "Did *she* tell you that?"

My heart is beginning to beat fast. Shale is either very brave, or very stupid. Either way, he's taking the threat posed by these Reckoners very lightly. If they find out I'm not Electra, that they wasted over a week and sailed over a thousand miles for nothing...

I swallow and glance at Savage. Behind his eyes, I can see the realization dawning that he may have been lied to, the rage beginning to bubble.

Shale taps the side of his head again and gestures briefly in the air, then transfers another file to Fetch.

"*This* is Electra Nation."

Fetch receives the file with a suspicious, sideways look and opens it. Her eyes narrow.

"It's not her."

Savage's eyes dart to mine and an eternity passes as I absorb the fury in them. Then he rounds on Fetch.

"Are you sure?"

"Yes!" Fetch taps her brow to close the file and glares at me. "The Nation girl looks like she came from Zhīliú or something. Plus she's blonde. She doesn't look anything like this chick."

Savage seems to hang suspended in time, vibrating, his hand

clenching and unclenching around the handle of his knife. Then he grabs Fetch roughly by the shoulder.

"How did this happen?" he snarls. "How did you let this happen?"

Fetch seems totally unfazed. She glares back at him with eyes as hard as his. "We've been offline since we picked her up," she says. "How was I supposed to verify? Besides, this was your scheme."

Savages shoves her away in disgust and she stumbles into a man walking by. A few cries of surprise go up around us. Several faces turn our way. People are starting to notice us. Savage notes it. He flips the butterfly knife closed so fast I hardly see it and tucks it into his pocket.

"Grab them," he says quietly, his eyes turning to Goliath and Red Bread, "and take them to the ship."

Goliath's massive hands close around my wrists and my stomach drops into my feet.

"No!"

I twist to my left, but I'm impotent in their iron grip. Red Bread throws an arm around Shale's chest.

"Wait a minute!" Shale cries. "Wait a minute! I have coin."

Savage stills. He holds up a hand to Red Bread, who loosens his grip on Shale. Shale wrenches himself free, straightening his jacket and smoothing his ponytail.

"That's what you want, isn't it? Some kind of payout?" He nods at me and lowers his voice. "That's why you kidnapped the girl you thought was the daughter of Zenith's CEO."

Savage regards him with hard eyes and says nothing.

"Now, I can't promise you I've got anything like the amount of coin you might have gotten out of the Nations," Shale says under his breath, "but seeing as how you're not going to get *anything* from the Nations at this point, it seems like we should be able to make some kind of deal."

My eyes dart between Savage's face and Shale's as the two size each other up. Savage tilts his head to one side, his eyes shrewd.

"Twenty-five thousand Ubicoin."

"Fifteen," says Shale. My eyes go wide. Does Shale *have* fifteen thousand Ubicoin?

"Twenty-three," says Savage.

"Seventeen."

"Twenty."

Shale pauses. The two stare at each other for a long moment. Then Shale holds out his hand.

"Done."

My legs turn to water. Twenty *thousand* Ubicoin? How the hell does my brother have twenty thousand Ubicoin going spare?

Savage drops Shale's hand and steps back. "Fetch!"

Glowering, she skulks up to Shale, and she and Shale do the transfer. She checks something on her slate, then looks up at Savage and nods once.

Savage smiles. "Well, what do you know?" His eyes slide to me, the smile twisting into a leer. "I guess you had a rich brother in Alluvium after all." He extends a hand to Shale again. "Pleasure doing business with you, friend."

Shale takes his hand, not returning his smile. "The pleasure was all mine."

Savage drops Shale's hand and motions to Fetch. He doesn't so much as look at me as he pulls the collar of his jacket up around his jaw and shoulders his way into the crowd. Fetch, Goliath and Red Bread push around us and follow him.

And just like that, they're gone.

I follow Shale in a daze through the busy harbor to the gate that leads out to the City. He walks fast, not attempting to make conversation or even look back to make sure I'm keeping up.

"We should probably get out of here," was all he said to me after Savage and his crew left. I barely had time to register that the transaction was over before he was dodging through passersby toward the harbor's main entrance.

The scene outside the harbor is madness. There is no street, just a shallow, black swamp with a series of low footbridges stretching across it.

The buildings around us are made of shipping containers, closely packed, raised out of the muck on teetering wooden foundations. Dense-population living. A Zenith project that started here but never got off the ground. Recycling old junk to make homes for the influx of refugees. Grain silos, shipping containers, that kind of thing. By the time the Big Four started implementing those kinds of programs, it was way too late to make a difference. I think this was the only place they ever built them.

A crush of people shuffles across the bridges, which all converge at the base of a wide metal tower in the center of the swamp. Strafing my eyes to the top of the tower, I feel my jaw drop.

The tower appears to be a hub for a network of bridges—towering, cabled monstrosities at least sixty feet above the ground. They are wide, packed with people, shaking with the weight of thousands of footsteps.

I tuck myself behind Shale, letting the crowd carry me forward as more people fill in behind us. Black muck caked onto people's shoes above drips onto our heads. My arms are pinned to my sides as the surge of people squeezes us across the swamp on a narrow, wooden footbridge, and then up a spiral staircase inside the tower.

At the top, we pop out onto a wide platform that completely circles the outside of the tower. Six bridges all converge around the platform, and I follow Shale to the right one.

We're so high that I can see the land stretching from the shore to my right, to the distant horizon on my left. It's flat. Very flat. The city sprawls, seems to exist where it can, with large expanses of swamp separating densely packed hubs of buildings. Each hub is connected to the others by bridges.

We make our way across several of these bridges to a wealthy-looking neighborhood by the beach and descend by another tower onto a wide, beachfront promenade. It's almost deserted, just a few people wandering along the breakwater.

Like Brume, I assume the majority of activity and life in this city is centered around the harbor. The empty beach is covered in trash, windswept and somewhat bleak, the surf breaking furiously against the dark sand and making the air hazy with spray.

On the other side of the street from the breakwater is a row of walled homes. They give off the impression of having been expensive at some point, but even behind their high walls, I can tell that they are in disrepair.

Shale stops in front of a large wooden gate set into a towering stone edifice and taps his left brow. The gate clicks and swings open.

I tilt my chin back to gaze up at the wall. "This is your house?"

"It is."

He steps through the gate. On the other side of it is a large plot of bare, rocky earth with a few scraggly scrubs and some patches of dry grass dotted about. A path of concrete slabs leads to the front door of an enormous, crumbling mansion that looks only half-finished, as though whoever was building it stepped away for lunch one day and never came back.

Inside, the house is dimly lit and sparsely furnished. The curtains are all drawn, I assume to keep out the heat of the blazing sun during the day. The living room smells faintly of mint and dart smoke. It feels like the room of someone who has a lot of money and not a lot to spend it on. Or the room of a boy who never quite grew into a man.

Shale releases a long breath as the door closes behind us and I find myself triggered to do the same. He turns to me as though about to say something, but then he just stands with his mouth open, his brow furrowing, eyes taking in my face, my filthy

clothes, my borrowed shoes. The shoes Sargo threw to me the day
we fled Brume. It feels like so long ago now I wonder if it actually
happened at all. Did I really make it? Am I really here?

Shale spreads his hands and shrugs with an awkward smile. I
offer the same smile back. A long moment of silence hangs
between us.

"You look like hell," he says finally.

"You finally managed to grow a beard," I retort.

He barks out a sharp laugh, then smoothes his ponytail and
nervously adjusts collar of his jacket.

"I guess I don't really...know what to do in this situation," he
says.

"Me neither."

"Do you want...a cup of tea? Or something?"

I shrug. "Okay."

In the expansive and mostly empty kitchen, Shale sets a small
black kettle to boil on the stove while I sit at an island in the
center of the room. Through the floor-to-ceiling window domi-
nating the west-facing wall, I can see the beach. The *Kingfisher* is
still anchored across the bay. I flick my eyes away, breathing
through a jolt of fear. They're gone. They can't get me. I'm safe.

I stare at the back of Shale's head as he scoops loose leaves into
a teapot. I want to tell him that I can't believe I'm here. I want to
tell him that I can't believe he's alive. I want to ask him how he
pulled twenty thousand Ubicoin out of his ass like it was nothing,
and how he could possibly have a picture of me when we haven't
seen each other for almost ten years.

Questions are free-falling through me like water from a ledge,
as though they've been building up behind some dam inside my
mind for the last two weeks and are now cascading through me
all at once.

Why did he leave Brume? Why did he message me? Does he
really have a job for me? What kind of job? And why? Why me?
Why now?

But I can't find my way around any of those questions well

enough to see a way inside. I find myself retreating, sidestepping, recoiling from them and seeking out something easier. Something smaller. Something less intimate.

"Nice...place," is what I land on.

The kettle whistles. Shale decants the boiling water into the teapot, filling the room with the scent of peppermint.

"Thanks. It's an abandoned prospector home, I think."

"Prospector home?"

"Prospectors were the people who came here to make a profit off the population boom. Before the pandemic." Setting a steaming mug in front of me, he pulls up a stool on the other side of the island. "Alluvium is one of those weird little micro climates that stayed temperate. Too far south for hurricanes, too far north for lightning. And they have the estuary, for water."

"Kind of like Brume."

"Well...yeah. But Alluvium was a backwater. Tiny little town. Not a lot of resources. Then people started coming in droves. Climate refugees, mostly, but other people too. People with money. They started building hotels and buying up real estate. You couldn't do that in Brume—property was too expensive. Everything there was already bought up. Plus you had the Big Four people pricing everyone out."

"So what happened? Why is everything...half-finished?"

"The pandemic. Everything stopped. The people with money left. Or died. Mostly died. This city is full of places like this. Empty lots. Half-built houses. Vacant hotels. Just...a lot of shit that was going to be great and never ending up getting built."

"Why don't you finish it?"

"Me?" He looks around as though the thought had never occurred to him. "I don't know. I guess I kind of like it this way."

We sip our tea in silence.

"You live...alone?" I venture at last. He nods. "You must be... doing well?"

He shrugs. "It's much cheaper to live here than it is in Brume.

But yeah, business is good. I've got a lot of irons in the fire right now. Big things on the horizon."

Twenty thousand Ubicoin big? I think. But I don't say it out loud. It feels rude and ungrateful to ask him that.

Instead, I say, "Thank you. For…I don't know what. Saving my life, I guess. If I hadn't run into you…"

He takes a slow sip of his tea. "Let's just be glad that didn't happen."

"I…saw you at the Row, right?" I ask cautiously. "Reckoner's Row. What were you doing there?"

He chokes, tea apparently going down the wrong way, and sets his cup down, coughing. He waves a hand as he fights to speak.

"Just—business. Research."

He pulls a yellow bandana from the pocket of his coat and coughs into it until he recovers enough to straighten up and pick up his tea again. He wipes his eyes with the bandana and tucks it back into his pocket.

"What were *you* doing there?"

The *Kingfisher.* The *Valkyrie.* Stark. Savage's blade. Malarkey. The Anonymity. The brutes in Brume. The necklace. Sargo. The pictures came so fast that I can't stop them, as if someone flipped a switch and the reel is just spinning in front of me. I shut my eyes. When I open them, Shale is watching me.

"Savage stopped the *Kingfisher* there to trade some stuff they looted from another ship."

He strokes his beard thoughtfully. "So that was Savage?"

"You know him?"

"I know *of* him."

"Kind of a scumbag."

He shrugs. "Guys like him are usually just after coin."

I fiddle with the handle of my mug, staring into the murky inch of green tea at the bottom of it. "But that was…a lot of coin."

Shale waves a hand. "Like I said, business is good."

"I don't know how I'm going to repay you."

Silence suddenly squeezes me from all directions. I feel a slow minute tick by as Shale repeatedly tries to say something, fails, picks up his mug, sips from it, and tries to say it again.

"Well, actually—" he says finally, "I wasn't going to bring it up right away, but...I'm assuming you're here because of my message?"

An odd, panicked excitement grips my chest. "Actually...yes."

"For the job?"

I hesitate. It feels like so long ago that I was sitting in the girls' bathroom in Brume, toasting to failure and deciding to embark on this crazy journey. Now that I'm here, in light of everything that's happened, it feels so trivial to have come all this way for a job. But he's right. It is why I came.

"Yeah. I guess I came for the job."

He grins. "Stellar, Birdie. That's stellar."

"*Stellar?*"

"Is 'stellar' not cool anymore? What do you say now? Wicked? Bad?"

I lift an eyebrow. "Cool?"

He makes a face. "Okay. 'Cool.' Whatever you like. It's good."

"So you...actually want to give me a job?"

"Sure do. And we can figure out a repayment thing." He shrugs. "If you take the job."

"You're serious?"

"Dead serious, Birdie! That's why I wanted you here."

"But...why?"

"Like I said, a lot of big things are happening. I need people around I can trust."

I frown. "But...you barely even know me."

"Know you? Of course I know you, Birb. You're my sister. You're family."

My heart thumps so hard in my chest that I have to drop my gaze into my mug again. "So...what's the job?"

"Why don't you come see for yourself? Tomorrow morning. I'll take you to the shop."

I peek up at him. His eyes are bright, expectant, hopeful. I nod. "Sure. Okay."

Shale grins, tips the last of his tea back, and wipes the corners of his mouth. He stands and takes his mug to the sink, rinses it, sets it to one side, then turns and folds his arms, leaning against the counter, surveying me.

"I'm assuming you don't know anyone else in the city?"

I shake my head.

"So you probably don't have anywhere else to stay?"

Again, I shake my head.

"So you should probably stay for dinner? And the night? At least."

Tears prick the backs of my eyes and I pour the last of my tea down my throat to hide them from Shale.

After dinner, I follow Shale up a spiral staircase to a guest room and washroom. He digs a towel and a pair of pajamas out of a cupboard and bids me goodnight.

I turn up the shower so hot I can barely stand under it and emerge from it feeling reborn. Wiping fog from the mirror above an elaborate stone sink, I step back to examine my reflection for the first time in two weeks.

I've never been very curvy or exciting to look at, but two weeks of little food and hard sailing have left me even skinnier than I was when I left Brume.

Not exactly the kind of shape that keeps men awake at night, I think to myself.

Oh? And who is it you're hoping to keep awake at night? my self retorts.

Tears twist in my chest like a knife. I brace my hands on the sink. *Nobody*. At least, not anymore. He left. He had to. He had to look out for himself.

I close my eyes and let my head drop, drawing a deep, difficult breath. Then, with my eyes still shut, I tap my temple to open Messenger. My fingers hover in the air for a long time. Finally, I write

>>> *I* HOPE YOU'RE SAFE. AND...*I* MISS YOU. *I* CAN'T BELIEVE YOU'RE GONE. *I* SHOULD HAVE TOLD YOU THAT *I*

Then I delete it all and replace it with

>>> HOPE YOU'RE OK. LMK IF YOU GET THIS.

I gesture to send it, then open my eyes and stare at myself in the mirror.

What would have happened today if Sargo had been with me when I bumped into Shale at the docks? Would Shale have been willing to fork out another twenty thousand coin to buy Sargo's life as well? Would Savage have even brought Sargo off the *King-fisher?* Would he have even let him *live* after what happened at the Row?

No, I decide, firmly. It's better he got away when he did. With any luck, he and Malarkey are on the way to Pocosín right now. As long as *Panga's* mainsail is holding out. I hope it is. I hope he makes it. I hope he finds his people. That's why he came out here, after all.

I force a grim smile at myself in the mirror then push his face out of my mind and examine my face instead. My skin has tanned and my face has thinned. My hair is streaked with blonde from days in the sun, and the saltwater has thickened it, turned the frizz into a tangle of curls. I reach up to touch it.

A curve in my arm I've never seen before stands out under the hard bathroom light. My brows shoot up. Is that a *muscle?!* Flexing my arm, I turn sideways. Shadows define more muscles in my stomach. My thighs. I smile at myself in the mirror again. A real one this time.

A hundred-and-ten pounds soaking wet, but getting stronger.

The towel Shale lent me is well-used but soft, and the pajamas, which are just a pair of boxers and an old tank top, are warm and smell faintly of lavender.

I pad down the cool hallway on bare feet and open the guest bedroom door to another vast, nearly empty room with a floor-to-ceiling window in one wall. Faded, dusty, floor-length curtains hang either side of the window, and upon approaching it I discover that it's actually a pair of French doors that open onto a small balcony.

Outside, the air is warm and sticky; the sound of surf from the beach below a constant, soothing drone. I leave the doors open and collapse into bed, barely finding strength to crawl under the thin sheets before the hum of the surf and the caress of the breeze slip around me, pulling me into deep, welcome sleep.

chapter
twenty-seven

After breakfast the next morning, Shale and I head for his shop.

The air is wild, the breeze whipping the bay into whitecaps and pulling sheets of spray off the crashing surf across the street. Despite the heat, I pull my beanie on and try to stuff my hair into it to keep it from whipping around my face. We pull bandanas up over our noses.

The footbridges near the harbor are packed with citizens making their morning commutes, faces covered by masks, scarfs, and bandanas despite the warm air. Shale walks fast, like a person with somewhere important to go. I try my best to keep up.

We take the bridges toward a central hub and descend toward the crowded, sodden ground-level. An enormous hexagonal platform, raised a few inches above the swamp on stilts, stretches before us.

"Main square," says Shale. "Well…hexagon, I guess. This is kind of the center of the city. Lots of the outer hubs are uninhabited now, but it's still a pretty crazy place. Way bigger then Brume; way more diverse."

He points things out to me as we cross the platform. A cart with an enormous leg of meat turning on a skewer. The vendor hacks off chunks, folds them into small, round flatbreads, sprinkles them with diced onions and some green herbs, and distributes them to customers. A bike with a cooler strapped to the back, laden with fruits of every color, sprinkled thickly with chili and salt. Racks of hats, tables piled with slates and jewelry; stalls that smell of brew and tea.

We stop in front of a wide tree tucked between two teetering half-finished cement buildings. A set of wooden steps spirals around the outside of the trunk and disappears into the branches.

"Is this your shop?" I ask.

Shale scoffs and shakes his head. "Brew!"

At the top of the stairs, my mouth drops. A sturdy wooden platform has been wedged into the massive branches, and chairs and tables are scattered across it, filled with chattering people sipping brew and sharing sweetbreads.

Shale strides to the back of the cafe, where a counter is crowded with people yelling over each other and shoving each other out of the way. A short, wiry girl with skin like Sargo's and a shock of iridescent purple hair appears at Shale's elbow as if from nowhere. She's drying a cup with a rag, nudging a second cup to the edge of the counter for a customer with one elbow, and opening a cupboard below the counter with her foot.

Shale produces two small thermoses from inside his coat, which she fills from a steaming pot behind her.

"That your girlfriend?" I tease when he returns.

"Ellie? Nah, she's just a friend." And he's halfway down the stairs before I've even turned around.

Back on the street, Shale ducks and weaves through the morning commuters so skillfully that I can barely keep up.

"Good brew, right?" he calls over his shoulder, gulping from his cup.

I take a tentative sip from mine. It's so hot that I can barely put my mouth on it, and I don't understand how Shale is downing his so quickly. I've never had brew before. It's bitter and gritty.

"Yeah, it's good," I lie, picking coarse black specks off my tongue. "I've never had it."

"Never?!" Shale's face, as he looks back at me, is gleefully incredulous. "I drink it every morning." He bobs around a tiny woman staggering under an enormous stack of boxes. "But I can't keep it in the house, otherwise I'd just drink it all day and never sleep."

"I guess I prefer tea."

"What?" He's further ahead now, and my voice is overpowered by the crowd and gusting wind.

"I said I guess I prefer tea!" I call, shouldering past a girl my age and doing a double-take as the scarf around her neck raises its head and looks at me. "Was that a snake?!"

"Probably," Shale says, not bothering to look back, "I'm telling you Birb, this place is nuts!" He grins over his shoulder at me. "If you stick around a while you'll see."

We ascend to the footbridges again and I watch different neighborhoods of the city pass under my feet as we walk to an industrial area on the far side of the harbor. We descend to ground level and Shale disappears down an alley between two warehouses. I dive after him, spilling my brew and cursing.

"Here we are!" Shale stops abruptly, and I almost run into him. I notice a red door in the wall next to us, almost completely obscured by stacks of empty boxes.

"This is your shop?"

"This is it!"

"How do people know it's here?"

The footbridges criss-crossing above us are completely devoid of foot traffic, and as far as I can tell, Shale and I are the only people in this part of town. It hardly feels like the same city; it feels distant, like another world. I can't imagine anyone finding their way down here by mistake. The warmth of the sun is obscured by the shadows of the surrounding buildings and I shiver, feeling suddenly isolated.

"Ohh...word of mouth." Shale waves his hand, tapping the side of his head and shoving open the door with his shoulder as it beeps.

As I follow him through it, my eyes adjust to the dim, unlit space of a high-ceilinged warehouse. Every possible square inch of the floor is filled with stacks of boxes, save for a cramped walkway that's been cleared down the middle.

Shale flips on a bare lightbulb and sets down his empty thermos, simultaneously picking up a sleek white slate from on top of a crate. I've never seen a white slate before. It looks crisp and expensive. Like Shale and his waxed beard; his clean, white shirt.

He reads silently off the slate, making quick check mark motions with his finger in the air as he winds his way slowly between the stacks, opening lids, checking labels, making notes on his slate. I follow him, trying not to trip on things.

"Like I was telling you yesterday, Birb, business is good," he says over his shoulder. "I want to bring you in. Not just to the business, to the whole organization."

"What will I be doing?"

The path between boxes is so narrow I have to turn sideways to wedge myself down it. He lifts the corner of a lid to check the contents, then makes a little check mark motion in the air. I try to glimpse what's in the box, but he closes the lid too quickly for me to see.

"Oh, little of this, little of that. It's the perfect time for you to be coming in," he continues. "Some really exciting things are in the works. Stuff that I think...well, I think you're gonna play a big part in."

I frown. "*Me?* A big part in what?"

He pauses, turning his gaze back to me. "Something is coming, Bird. Something big."

"O—kay." His eyes are so intense they make the hair on the back of my neck stand up. "What kind of thing?"

Folding his arms, he turns and leans a shoulder against the nearest crate. He looks at me for what feels like minutes, his eyes quietly calculating. The back of my neck continues to prickle. Something about this is weirdly unsettling.

"Tell me," he says finally, "have you been getting the blackouts?"

My heart seizes. "How—did you...know about that?"

Smiling grimly, he gestures to a box beside me. "Sit down, Birdie. This is going to take a while."

I perch on the edge of the box, suddenly realizing I'm still clutching the mug of brew Shale bought me. I had forgotten I was holding it.

"What's the earliest memory you have?" Shale asks, leaning against the crate opposite me. "As a kid," he continues. "Me, for example. What's the earliest memory you have of me?"

Setting aside the brew, I frown, digging through my mind, trying to picture Shale as a kid. But weirdly, all I can find is the image from the dream. A gangly thirteen-year-old in ratty clothes, standing on red earth, about to get a jackrat down the back of his shirt.

"I guess I mostly remember you from when you were older— fifteen, maybe? I remember you were...popular. Happy. Good at school. You loved it. You loved Brume. Then you—"

Died.

"—left."

Shale nods slowly, watching me. "What about before that? Do you remember what it was like being a little kid in Brume?"

I shake my head. "I don't remember much about being a kid. I don't think most people do, do they?"

He shrugs slightly, saying nothing.

"Also...I forget a lot of stuff. It's kind of a problem. I have a stupid brain; I space out a lot. Mama K used to call it a *blip*. That could be why I don't remember a lot."

At the mention of Mama K's name, Shale's eyes go hard. Just for a moment, then it passes. "I remember that word. Your blips." He takes a breath. "I'm going to tell you something, Bird. And what I'm going to tell you is going to sound…maybe crazy."

He hesitates, as though weighing some stack of words against some other stack of words.

Finally, he says, "You don't have any memories of growing up in Brume because we didn't grow up in Brume. Brume is not your home."

I stare at him.

"We were born in Naze. Some flog-forsaken climate Settlement shithole down the coast from Brume. When I was fourteen, Zenith came out there. They were running a competition, like a lottery, and they relocated us to Brume. I guess you would have been…eight?"

I interrupt him, too loudly. "Is this a joke?"

"A joke? No, Bird. I'm telling you what's—"

"Because all this stuff, what you're telling me…I mean, I've *seen* this stuff. I—I dreamed this stuff."

He looks at me for a long moment. "Those weren't dreams. They were memories."

"I don't—"

He holds up a hand. "I'm trying to explain it to you. If you just listen, I promise it will make sense."

I open my mouth to protest, but then realize I don't even know what I'm protesting.

"When I was sixteen," he continues, "this was *after* we came to Brume—I started hanging around with some people I probably shouldn't have been hanging around with. Older kids. I used to drink with them down at the harbor. Sometimes we would get pretty wasted, and when I blacked out, I would see things."

I feel as though I'm standing on the edge of something massive, willing myself not to jump. "What kind of things?"

"Little kids. Some kind of desert. I figured it was from the grog. But my friends were all drinking it and it wasn't happening to any of them. Everyone kind of blew it off when I asked them about it, except for one guy. He had a dad who used to work for Zenith, and when I told him what was happening, he seemed really interested. Said his dad wanted to meet me.

"His dad was...an interesting guy. He hated Zenith; a real hardcore dissenter. And he told me about this lottery that he heard Zenith was doing. Not something Zenith advertised or anything. A secret program. Every year they would pick a family at random and pull them out of a settlement. Move them to a nearby Harbor City. Set the parents up with jobs, get them all chipped. A new life. Which was crazy, because according to everything we had been taught in Brume, everyone in the Settlements died during the pandemic."

Outside, the wind howls through alleys between warehouses, rattling tin, but the room is deadly quiet. I watch Shale's face carefully.

"Okay. So you're saying Zenith picked us for this lottery?"'

He nods.

"And we moved?"

He nods again.

I feel weirdly unsurprised. Partly because of the dreams I've been having, but also...I feel like some part of me knew this already. Like something in me was just waiting for someone else to corroborate it. I never felt like I fit in in Brume. I always felt like something was...off about me. Like I was wrong somehow. It's actually kind of a relief.

I shrug. "Okay. I guess I can believe that. But...why don't I remember any of it?"

A smile begins to creep across his face. A cold, sinister smile that doesn't reach his eyes. "Because they didn't want you to."

"Who didn't want me to?"

"Zenith."

"Why?"

"You think a company like Zenith runs a program like that out of the goodness of their hearts? The organization whose slogan is

'*Put on your own mask first*'? You think they go around helping families get out of the Settlements and start a new life, for free? No. There's a price."

"What price?"

"Us, Bird. You and me. We're the price."

A gust of wind shrieks down the alley outside. I swallow. "What do you mean?"

"These chips?" He taps the side of his head. "Zenith put them in us when we won the lottery and came to Brume. But they aren't regular chips. They're not like the chips that everyone else in Brume has. There's experimental tech in them. Zenith is developing something."

"Experimental tech?" I frown. "That sounds a little...dystopian."

"It is."

"Okay..." I narrow my eyes. Something has changed about him. I can't quite put my finger on it, but a light has come into his eyes that wasn't there before. A cold, unsettling light.

"They're developing something," I repeat. "What?"

He presses his lips together, scrutinizing my face. "I don't know for sure," he says finally. "But if you want to know what I think? Teleportation."

A sharp laugh barks out of me. "*Teleportation?*"

The word rings into sudden silence, sounding so alien and ridiculous that all I can do is gape at Shale with my mouth open in a confused half-smile.

Shale just looks at me. "Every time you black out, do you wake up somewhere else?"

The bottom half of my face keeps smiling, but my brows come together.

When I blacked out—blipped—in the Azimuth bathroom, I woke up at the harbor. Blacked out in that club in the Flats and woke up on the beach. When the *Valkyrie* chased us down and that guy from Stark's crew almost dragged me over the side...I never hit the water. And when I blacked out on the *Kingfisher* after drinking with Goliath and Red Bread...

I shake my head, my mouth still open.

"And it's immediate?" Shale says. "It happens right away?"

"I don't...know. Sometimes I wake up right away. Sometimes not for a while."

He nods thoughtfully. I continue to stare at him, my mind spinning. *Teleportation?* No, it was grog. It was grog making me black out and forget what I did. Grog that made me wake up in weird places. Grog that made me blip.

Wasn't it?

"You think..." I watch him carefully, the words coming slowly. "You think Zenith is testing experimental teleportation technology on *children?*"

He nods. "The other Lottery kids—the kids that Zenith picked in the years before us? Got chips that malfunctioned so badly they were electrocuted. Thousands of kids. Fried from the inside out. Burned the eyes out of their heads."

The light in his eyes is becoming frightening. Dangerous. It raises the hair on my arms. Something deep and primal inside me tells me to sit perfectly still under those eyes. Something else tells me to run.

"Just black holes," he continues, leaning almost imperceptibly closer to me, "charred. Blood coming out of their noses. Ears—"

"Shale—"

Panic is simmering in my throat. Those eyes don't look like my brother's eyes anymore; they are the eyes of a person I no longer recognize. A person, I realize, who threw twenty grand at a Reckoner to buy my life without batting an eye. A person who's been living alone for ten years in a crumbling mansion in a city thousands of miles from home. A person who thinks the world's most powerful corporation is putting teleporters into the heads of children.

A crazy person.

Almost unconsciously, I glance over my shoulder. The door we came in through is closed.

I work hard to keep my voice level. "Come on. That doesn't make sense. How would Zenith get away with that? Year after year? Kids dying?"

"Think about it!" His voice rises over mine. "Desperate people! Families with no choice. Kids who won't be missed!"

"But *thousands* of kids—"

"Zenith lures destitute families in with the promise of getting out of the Settlements. A new life in the City! Relocate, get a job, put your kids in school, get chipped—for free!"

"Zenith's policies keep us alive," I say, the words coming to me from some deep, unconscious place of rote memorization.

He scoffs. "Who's 'us'?"

"Shale, this is crazy. There's no way our moms—"

"Our moms *knew*! They knew, Bird. That's why I left. Not because of the Lottery, or the chips, or the flashbacks, or any of that stuff. I left because...because I couldn't trust my own moms anymore."

Silence.

I suddenly feel very alone. Very far from my moms. Very far from home; very far from anyone I know; very far, even, from the safe, busy center of this strange new city. Alone. Trapped. I check the door again.

"Anyway," he says quietly, "it doesn't matter now. What matters now is that you're here. You're here, and now you know everything. You're ready to join the organization."

That primal fear prickles me. *There's that word again.*

"What...organization?"

He sits up, setting his cup aside.

"That guy I met in Brume, the Zenith dissenter who told me about the Lottery—he was involved with an organization. He brought me in to meet some people there. The more they told me, the more it made sense. They didn't have any proof, but it all made sense. All the stuff about Zenith, about the Lottery kids. I started hanging around there a lot, talking to people. Eventually, they got tired of me asking questions and told me if I wanted to keep hanging around then I needed to work. Said they could bring me on board and give me good money for dealing haar and doing black market deals. Been working for them ever since. They brought me out here."

A chill is crawling up the back of my neck like a cold shadow stretched by the sinking sun. *Black market deals.* I only know two types of people who make black market deals: Dead Reckoners, and the Anonymity.

And Shale sure as Salt doesn't look like a Reckoner.

I open my mouth, hesitate, close it again. *The Row.* What was Shale doing that day at the Row? When I manage to speak, my voice is a whisper.

"What's—what's the name of the organization?"

His eyes answer me before he does. "The faction I lead here in Alluvium is called Ardent," he says. "But in Brume, people still call them the Anonymity."

chapter
twenty-eight

THE ROOM TILTS. Shapes blur. I stand up and stumble sideways, knocking my brew cup to the floor. For the first time, I note the words printed on the crates stacked all around me. *Zenith Biotech. Spindrift.* Black market goods.

It's a trap.

The thing I've been running from is here. All this time I thought I was running away from it, and it's been here, waiting for me. I was so preoccupied with Savage and his crew that I stopped paying attention.

I try to swallow my pounding heart. "The Anonymity is here?"

Shale smiles. "The Anonymity is *everywhere.*"

My eyes dart around the room. The only way out is behind Shale, through the door. Did he lock it behind us when we came in? Why wasn't I paying attention? Am I strong enough to fight my way past him? *Where is Malarkey when you need her?!*

A ping ricochets through my head and a message alert slides before my eyes, disorienting me as I struggle to keep my wits. Instinctively, I raise my hand to open Messenger, but Shale snatches my wrist in a vice-like grip.

"What are you doing?"

I swallow. "A message—answering a message."

He shakes his head. "Don't do that. We're talking."

Focusing briefly on the text of the alert, I can see that it's from Sargo. I twist my arm but my wrist remains trapped.

Shale raises his other hand in a placating gesture. "Let me explain. Close the message, and let's finish talking."

I take a step back and my heel comes up hard against the wall. I can't run. I can't fight my way out.

But maybe I can keep him talking. Maybe I can keep him talking long enough to think of something. I stare into his eyes, feeling sick, and nod. Smiling, he lets go of my wrist. I tap my temple to close the message.

"I know what you're thinking," he says. "I know you think you know what the Anonymity is. But you don't know everything."

I try to keep my voice steady. "What do you mean, I don't know everything?"

"In Brume, all the Anonymity was known for was dealing haar, and selling black market shit, and dragging people into debt."

"And murder."

"But listen!" His voice rises over mine. "It's *Zenith* that regulates manufacturing so tightly that people are forced to trade for parts on the black market! It's *Zenith* that's luring people out of Settlements with false promises. Turning people into lab rats. Killing children! The Anonymity has been working against Zenith for years. Running the black market so settlers can get parts for desalinators and solar panels. Getting kids like me out."

I stare at him with my mouth open. This is lunacy. Unhinged nonsense from a guy corrupted by dangerous radicals. He was only *sixteen* when these guys started filling his head with these ideas. For ten years he's been isolated, absorbing their propaganda.

He stands, moving imperceptibly closer to me. "And now we're ready to expose them. That's why I *need* you, Bird. It's why I brought you here. You're proof. *We* are proof. I can't do it by myself. By myself I'm just another angry dude with an ax to grind at the Fat Sallies. But you... you're sympathetic. You're a kid. You're a girl. People will believe you."

I gape at him. "Is that why you paid Savage twenty thousand Ubicoin to get your hands on me? Because you needed me to—to be a mouthpiece for your extremist group?"

"To tell your story! To expose the lies—"

"I thought you cared about me. I thought you were going to give me a job."

He takes another step toward me. "This is a job! This is the most important job you can do!"

Even as my mind clouds with panic, I note that he didn't try to clarify that he does, in fact, care about me. His eyes betray a powerful, unstable energy, like a star that's close to burning out. He's close enough now that at any moment he could reach out and grab me. My eyes dart to the door. What if this 'job' isn't something I can turn down? How far would he go to convince me to take it?

Keep him talking. Keep him talking and think.

"If I'm so important to the Anonymity, how come they sent thugs after me in Brume?" I demand, pulling back my beanie to reveal the scar above my eyebrow. "They almost beat me to death. They threatened to kill me."

He shakes his head. "Those weren't my guys."

"What do you mean?"

"The faction of the Anonymity that's working on this plan to expose the Lottery is...only a handful of us. The rest of the organization—they just want to do business as usual. Those guys that came to your house...they were business as usual guys."

A realization goes through me like a bolt of lightning. "But... you knew about them. You knew they came after me."

His face goes taut. His eyes register a mistake, a slip-up, and suddenly dart away from mine.

"Shale? Did you know they went after me?"

He touches his fingers to the slate sitting on top of the crate. He fiddles with the edge of it. Picks it up. Puts it down.

"I'm going to tell you something," he says, carefully. "Please don't flip out."

I stand very still, watching him. "Why would I flip out?"

More calculations happen behind his eyes as he looks sideways at me. "You're right. I knew."

My jaw drops open, but he puts up his hands and continues before I can say anything.

"A few days after I sent you that message about the job, I got word through the grapevine that some Anonymity members in Brume had been hired by a high-ranking Zenith official to track down a thief. Something about a stolen necklace. They had a picture of the primary suspect. Well, I don't need to tell you who that was…"

My stomach turns over. The picture he showed to Savage. That's how he got it.

"I saw…an opportunity."

"What…kind of opportunity?"

"Bird, you have to understand: this thing I need you to do, it's…it's so important. I *needed* you to come. I couldn't tell you anything because Zenith monitors everyone's biochip conversations—"

"*What?* No they don't."

"—and I wasn't sure if offering you the job would be enough. You're a kid, you live at home. There was a high chance you just wouldn't leave Brume. I thought you might need—more incentive. And when I heard the Anonymity had been hired to find you, I saw…a way to incentivize you."

"*Incentivize* me?"

"I knew the Anonymity guys would only be after the necklace. Maybe they'd shake you up a little. But as long as you gave it up, that would be it. They'd get their coin, and you'd go on your way."

"Only I didn't have the necklace when they found me."

"R—ight. Because I called in a favor to a buddy of mine. You probably don't remember him. When we were kids, he went by Five. These days everyone pretty much calls him V."

The air leaves me. The image of a man standing in a doorway, tipping his hat to me, swims before my eyes. The man who drugged me and stole Electra's necklace in the Flats. The man who destroyed my future. I put a hand on the crate behind me to steady myself.

"But...how? He messaged me. The forum. It could have been anyone..."

"Ah." Shale smiles and the cold smugness of it makes my skin crawl. "Actually, that was a bit of luck. I *could* have simply put him in touch with you myself. But that might have made you suspicious—a message from out of the blue. You made it much easier, posting on the Net. Volunteering information. Opening yourself up as a target." He regards me somewhat disparagingly. "Not your proudest moment, Birdie, I have to say."

My voice is hoarse. "You turned me into a fugitive."

He scoffs. "Don't be dramatic. I needed to get you out of Brume and I know how the Anonymity operates. I knew that if they caught you, and you didn't have the necklace, they'd give you a pretty short list of...options. The kind of options that would likely force a person to—well, run."

"What if I hadn't run?"

"I know you better than that, Bird," he says dismissively. "I knew you would run."

"You *know* me?" I gape at him. "Who *are* you? I don't know you at all! What if they had caught me?! What if I had died on the Salt? Jesus, they sent mercenaries after me!"

I sit down hard on the crate. My head is spinning. I want to run. I want to throw up. This man with the crazy eyes is not my brother. He turned me into a fugitive. He sent criminals after me. He forced me to risk my life on the Salt to find him. And for what? To use me in some delusional plot to overthrow the most powerful corporation in the world? Because he thinks they're building a *teleporter?*

He reaches for me and I recoil. "Don't touch me!"

In a heartbeat, the fire in his eyes extinguishes. Two flinty slates glare at me from under his hard, unfamiliar brow.

"Bird, I don't think you understand what's happening here."

His voice is low and deliberate. In his cold eyes, I suddenly see the faceless voids of the creeps that came after me in Brume. Members of the same organization Shale works for. A final realization crawls up my spine: my brother works for an organization that kills people. *My brother kills people.*

He takes another step toward me. "I'm trying to be patient," he says quietly. "I'm *asking* you. Don't make me *make* you, Birdie. Don't make me force you. We're family."

An ear-splitting *bang* shatters the quiet.

Dazzling light pours into the room, and a moment later a collision from behind sends Shale stumbling into me, clutching clumsily at my shirt. He drags me to the floor, both of us stunned and scrambling, hands clawing hands. I throw my knee into his stomach and roll out from under him, get to my feet first, my eyes struggling to adjust, scanning the room wildly. Then I see her.

Malarkey.

She pins Shale with her bear-like paws, wraps her massive jaws around his ankle, and shakes. He screams, and under the shrill of it, I hear the *snap* of splintering bone. Behind her, daylight pours through the open door. A familiar silhouette steps into the rectangle of light.

"Howsley!"

"*Sargo!*"

I don't think. I leap over Shale, grab Malarkey by the neck and drag her through the door.

"*Run!*"

We barrel down the alley, tumbling over crates and boxes, ricocheting off the walls, skid around the corner at the end and plunge into the empty street then up the tower to the footbridges.

I don't look back until the bay comes into view, glittering and white-capping in the clear morning sun. The wind howls around me as I scan the water and spot *Panga* bucking and bobbing on her anchor, her yellow hull shining like a beacon of hope.

Sargo shoulders people out of the way as we barge through the harbor gate and sprint for the skiff. He kneels to untie the lines as Malarkey leaps over him into the boat, then he hops in after her and turns, reaching out a hand to me.

Without thinking, I take it.

Our eyes meet and the world drops away. The chaos of the docks, the sunlight on the water, the wild, stinging wind, the escape from Shale. All of it disappears.

He came back for me.

My heart stumbles, flustered, against my ribs and Sargo smiles. Like he can *see* it. See right into me. My stumbling heart, the falling away of the world. Everything. It's a smile I've never seen from him before—confused but curious. A question. Like he's seeing something he doesn't understand yet, but can't wait to figure out. Heat blooms across my throat as I realize I'm returning the same smile.

He tugs me into the skiff and his chest is against mine. The scent of him—of fogwood trees, of petrichor, of sand and the Salt —overwhelms me. I'm transported back to Brume. To the dark, ponderous spires of the forest and the mist winding through it. To the fresh salt spray of the surf; to the soft crunch of wet sand beneath my feet.

Home, I realize. He smells like home.

His arm loops around my waist, pulling me closer. "Te tengo, mija," he murmurs against my hair. "I got you."

I shiver. Suddenly, I want to take him down, right here in the skiff, in front of everyone. Shale and the Anonymity be damned. They can have me when I've finished with him.

He holds me for a second longer, then steps back, finding my eyes. "You good?"

I try to think of something clever to say; I try to think of anything at all, but my brain has turned to mush. All I can do is nod.

He grins. "Just trying to keep up the *illusion.*"

Winking, he steps nimbly around me to the stern, kicks on the motor and snatches up the tiller, spinning the skiff around in a bank of spray and shooting us away from the dock. My hair dances wildly around my face as we speed across the water, making a beeline for *Panga.*

"How the hell did you find me?" I gasp.

He shakes his head, grinning, and points at Malarkey. "*She* found you. Or...it was a joint effort."

"But—at the Row. You escaped."

He grimaces. "I didn't mean to leave you...I...didn't realize you weren't behind me until Malarkey and I got to the exit. And I figured..."

He shakes his head, looking pained.

"I wanted to go back, but...I just didn't see how I would be able to help you. Not with all of them in there. I knew I had a good head start because I guessed the *Kingfisher* would have to wait for Savage. So I got *Panga* out of the bay and started heading for Alluvium. I figured Savage would go offshore to find faster wind so I stayed close to the coast so he wouldn't spot me. Even with a head start, the *Kingfisher* beat me here; I arrived this morning and saw them in the anchorage, so I figured you must already be somewhere in the City. I tried to message you but you didn't respond. When we got to the dock, I thought we had no chance of finding you. But *this* one," he grins at Malarkey, "just put her nose on the ground and started walking. She led me right to that warehouse. All I did was follow her. Well..." He shrugs, looking modest. "I also kicked the door in."

The pressure of tears wells behind my eyes like a dam close to bursting. "You came back."

Our eyes lock. "Of course I came back, Howsley. You're my first mate. I need you."

Something pulls so tight in my chest it hurts. His face is alight with that same inquisitive smile that I *know* means he is looking right inside me. I wonder if he's always been able to see my heart aching for him, even when I couldn't see it myself.

A wave tilts the boat sideways and I lurch out a hand to steady myself. He drops his eyes, readjusting his grip on the wheel. "Anyway, Malarkey's *useless* as a first mate. Can't pull a line or anything. She doesn't even have thumbs."

I grab Malarkey's big dumb head in my hands and smash my face against it, half to thank her, half to hide the tears spilling out of my eyes. She waves her tail ecstatically and washes my head with her tongue.

"So...what happened, exactly?" Sargo asks. "With Shale?"

I dig the tears out of my eyes with the heels of my hands and stumble through the events of the morning, struggling to turn the shitshow that was my conversation with Shale into something coherent.

Sargo's eyes grow wide. "So he's a terrorist?"

"A terrorist?" I frown. "No, I don't think—"

"He sounds like a terrorist."

"He's just..." I wave my hands with my mouth open, struggling to find a better word, "...passionate."

Sargo scoffs and shakes his head. "He's a terrorist."

I turn my gaze back over the stern, watching the crazy, mismatched skyline of Alluvium grow smaller.

"You think he'll come after us?" Sargo asks nervously.

I chew the inside of my cheek and say nothing. I'm almost certain that he will. He didn't seem like the kind of person who just lets something go.

We come alongside *Panga* and haul ourselves aboard, weighing anchor and setting the sails in record time. I put Malarkey below while Sargo steers us toward the point at the top of the bay. As we pitch over the restless chop toward open water, I realize with a jolt that I have no idea where we're going.

"So what now? Where are we going to go?" Low-grade

anxiety begins to pulse in my temples. "We can't stay here. We can't go back to Brume."

Sargo says nothing, his thoughtful eyes on the water. Then, to my amazement, he smiles again. A calm, logical smile that somehow grounds me, plants me in the eye of this hurricane.

"Pocosín," he says. "Come with me to Pocosín."

My heart skips. "Really?"

"Yes, Howsley. I don't want to go without you."

My heart swells again, and all I can do is nod. His smile broadens into a grin, and he turns the wheel to set a new course, putting his eyes back over the bow toward the horizon.

In less than a heartbeat, his expression changes. His face falls.

Following his gaze, I see a black, angular speedboat flying around the point, its hull skimming over the water like a stone. I don't have time to question where it came from. It's moving faster than anything I've ever seen, and it's coming straight for us.

"Bird, tack!" Sargo yells.

I scramble to grab hold of the jib sheets, wrench the port sheet free and shake it loose, catching the starboard sheet in my other hand. Sargo grabs the main sheet with one hand, spinning the helm with the other. *Panga* begins to bank to starboard, out of the path of the oncoming ship.

"Help me with the mainsail!" Sargo yells.

I scramble to him and he hands me the main sheet.

"When I say 'now', let it out—slowly!" He peers up at the sail as the boom begins to tack across the deck. The boat pitches so hard that I have to brace myself to keep from falling. "Now!"

The next few moments seem to happen in slow motion. As I ease the boom into position, another gust of wind comes up behind us, catching the sail the wrong way. It flaps like the wing of a struggling bird, making great, heart-stopping cracks against itself. The sheet wrenches from my hand, and the boom slams hard all the way over to starboard with a monstrous crash.

The unmistakable screech of tearing sailcloth rends the air.

chapter
twenty-nine

THE MAINSAIL HANGS NEARLY in two. The ragged pieces, shredded from foot to head, flap viciously in the wind. Through the raw edges of the sailcloth, I catch fleeting glimpses of the clear blue sky.

I stare up at it with my mouth open, hope, anger, and even the rush of adrenaline leaving me. It's over.

If you hadn't stolen that stupid necklace...if you hadn't been so reckless...if you had listened to Sargo...if you hadn't made him sail this boat when he knew *it wasn't ready* —

"Bird! Take the helm!"

Sargo's voice floats to me over the howling wind like something out of a dream. I stare at him. *Take the helm?* Sargo's never let me take *Panga's* helm in my life. The only time I've ever been at the helm is in sailing class, and that ended with me almost wrecking two boats and getting expelled.

"Bird, come and take the helm!" he yells again. "Stay with me! We're still sailing here! I don't have time to tell you everything twice!"

I stumble to the helm. Sargo steps aside and I take the wheel, noticing, even in the chaos, a lingering warmth where his hands had been. I close my grip tight around it, as though Sargo's hands are holding mine through the wheel, galvanizing me.

"Just keep us steady," he says, laying a hand on the small of my back and pointing out over the bow. "Point us out past that sandbar. I'm going to deal with the mainsail." He climbs out of the cockpit and onto the bow.

Even with the mainsail gone and just the headsail still up, the wind is strong enough to heel *Panga* so far to starboard that I feel like I'm standing on a wall. I brace myself and cling to the wheel, fighting with all my strength to keep us pointed the right way. On our port side, the black boat starts to turn.

"Sargo, they're coming this way!" I yell.

"Keep us steady!"

He stands forward of the mast, hauling down the shredded mainsail hand over hand. I feel as if I'm watching him through a curtain of fog. The thoughts plummeting around my head are all I can focus on.

This is your fault, says a voice. *This is how it ends, and it's all your fault.*

What will Shale's Anonymity faction do with Sargo? They don't need him. He isn't part of their plan. Would they send him back to Brume? Bury him in debt like his uncle? Force him to sell haar? Kill him?

Stupid brain. Stupid Bird.

My Moms. I'm never going to see them again.

Stupid brain. Stupid—

"Bird! Bird, what the hell are you doing?! Pay attention!"

Sargo's voice snaps my eyes up. The black boat is dead ahead, and we're about to plow right into her.

I crank the wheel hard to port and *Panga* turns so sharply I have to cling to the wheel to keep myself from falling sideways. We narrowly miss the black ship, and regaining my balance, I let the wheel spin back through my hands to center, pointing us toward the other end of the bay. Glancing over my shoulder, I see the black boat heading in the opposite direction. Relief pours through me like cold sweat.

"It's okay!" I yell, looking back toward the bow. "We—" The words die on my tongue.

Sargo is gone.

Panicking, I turn around and scan the water. He's fifteen feet behind the boat, face down in the water, unmoving.

"*Sargo!*"

Panga lurches over another wave and I almost lose my grip on the wheel. Suddenly, the full realization of what's happening hits me. Sargo is in the water. He must have fallen over the side when I made that crazy turn. I'm alone. *Panga* is completely under my control. *Barely* under my control. I don't even know how to engage the autopilot. I have no idea what to do.

You've killed him. You've killed—

"Think, Bird!" I shout out loud over the unhelpful voice in my head. "What would Sargo do?"

I glance over my shoulder again to check Sargo's position. The black ship is circling him, drawing closer. Horrified, I watch as a tall figure, clad head to toe in black rubber, climbs atop the boat's deck rail and dives into the water. He swims to Sargo in three brisk, powerful strokes, gets his arm around him, and drags him back toward the boat.

"No…"

Helpless, I watch as a second man appears on deck and reaches out to help Sargo's captor haul Sargo out of the water. In less than a minute, they've hoisted him aboard.

They've got Sargo. They've got Sargo and—

The boat revs its motor and swings toward me. A bank of spray shoots into the sky.

They've got Sargo and now they're coming for me.

The motor roars again and the boat hurtles toward me. It's faster, more nimble, better manned. There's nowhere for me to go.

Unless…

I glance over the side. *You're going to have to jump.*

Letting go of the helm, I step up onto the edge of the cockpit, clutching the rigging, the wind whipping my hair across my face as *Panga* bounces out of control over the swell.

The black boat chews up the distance between us and spits out spray behind it. I can see the face of the man behind the helm now, his black eyes trained on me like a predator chasing down prey. I cast one more desperate glance around at the choppy water, at *Panga's* flapping sails.

Then I let go of the rigging and jump.

But I don't hit the water.

Instead, I disappear.

chapter
thirty

THE ZENITH TRANSPORT vehicle squatted on the hard, red earth like an enormous, shelled creature, its knobby tires baking in the sun, emanating the pungent smell of hot rubber. One door stood open, revealing the vehicle's dark, cool interior.

Even from ten feet away, Bird could feel the cool air from inside the vehicle blowing on her face. She had never felt cool air before.

"Shut that door!"

A tall, pinched woman strode past her, a small, stone tablet tucked neatly under her arm. "You think coolant is free?"

Bird watched as a second, smaller woman scurried around from behind the vehicle and slammed the door shut. The tall woman stood next to the vehicle, surveyed Bird and her family briefly, then pulled the tablet out from under her arm and tapped the side of her head. She made a few quick, nimble gestures in the air with her fingers, then seemed to become very interested in the tablet.

Bird felt the grip of Mama Kestrel's hand tighten on her shoulder.

"Gods, what if they change their mind?" Mama K's voice was thin, high-pitched, and tense. Bird could feel her trembling through the hand on her shoulder.

"They won't, Kes," said Mama Jade, with a hint of irritation. "Just relax, please? You're frightening the children."

"No, she's not," chirped Shale.

He had an enthusiastic look on his face and was peering all around at the activity around the transport. He was taller than the Moms by now, with a few scraggly hairs on his chin making a brave effort at being a beard. But that day he looked like a kid again, practically standing up on his toes, craning his neck to see.

The last two days had been a blur of check-ups and questions. Zenith women produced all kinds of equipment from that van, which had been parked outside the perimeter of the Settlement for so long that Bird had almost forgotten it was there. They weighed the family and measured them—not just their heights but the length of their arms, the size of their heads, their feet, hands, even fingers. They poked and prodded and stuck things in their mouths and went "Mm" and tapped the sides of their heads and consulted their little stone tablets.

"It's routine," Mama K said. "They want to make sure we're all healthy."

"When do we get our chips?" was all Shale wanted to know.

"Will we come back and visit?" Bird asked Mama K. Mama K got a strange expression on her face and squeezed Bird's shoulders so tight it hurt.

"No, sweetheart," she said. "People don't leave Harbor Cities."

Once Bird knew that, that her worst suspicion was confirmed, that they were never coming back, that she would be trapped in Brume forever, that she would never come home or see Fife again, all the fight went out of her.

She sleep-walked through the physical examinations, allowing herself to be propelled, manipulated, positioned, and prodded without objection. She felt like a leaf, blown around in the wind.

Now, the day had finally come. The day she had been dreading for weeks. Today was leaving day.

She twisted her neck around and peered through Mama K's

legs. The whole Settlement had come out to see them off. People stood around in twos and threes outside their huts. Some murmured to each other and pointed, watching with unabashed interest.

Pathra, Mama J's best friend, brought her a little wrapped package, and when Mama J thanked her she burst into tears and wrapped her so tightly in her massive arms that Bird thought she would crush her. Bird remembered the day Pathra had carried her home from the creek. The day she, Shale, and Fife had found the old man drinking the creekwater.

The image of Fife, standing by the creek, went through Bird like a bolt of lightning. She squinted against the blinding sun.

Where was Fife?

"Okay Howsleys, time to go."

A woman's sharp voice pulled Bird back to the scene around her. Mama K's grip tightened so hard on her shoulder that she yelped.

"It's Howsley and Shorbe," said Mama J to the woman. "We aren't married."

"Jade, for gods' sakes she doesn't care about that," Mama K hissed.

"Of course. Howsley and Shorbe," said the Zenith woman with a quick smile. "My mistake. You can get into the transport now."

"When do we get our chips?" Shale asked.

The woman gave him the same brief, tidy smile. "Soon."

"Okay Birdie, in you go." Bird felt the grip on her shoulder loosen, a hand gently propelling her toward the van.

She stumbled, looking desperately over her shoulder. This was all wrong. Where was Fife? She should be here, she said she'd be here!

"No!" Bird twisted away and lunged out of Mama K's reach. "No!"

She ran blindly, her heart in her ears. She plunged toward the small crowd of people gathered at the edge of the Settlement. She had to find Fife. She had to say goodbye.

Something big and soft collided with her stomach and she felt herself lifted off her feet. She tipped sideways, the ground falling away from her, as she was tucked tightly between a massive arm and a familiar bosom.

"Come on little Bird," Pathra's warm voice vibrated through her bear-like grip. "Time to go."

"No!" She kicked her legs and thrashed like a jackrat in a kill sack, but it was no use. She could see nothing but the ground moving beneath her as Pathra carried her back to the vehicle. She felt like she was six all over again.

Pathra turned her upright and set her on her feet in front of the open door. "Door's open, little Bird," she whispered. "All you have to do is walk through it."

"Come on, Birb." She heard Shale's voice behind her, felt his hand on her shoulder. "It's gonna be okay."

"I don't want to leave her behind," she wailed, tears streaming down her cheeks. "I didn't get to say goodbye."

"Fife will be okay," Shale said. "She's coming. Don't worry."

But the way he said 'she's coming' made Bird think he might be trying to convince himself as much as he was trying to convince her.

"She's not," Bird sobbed. "I'm never going to see her again."

"You'll see her again." Shale took his hand off her shoulder, knelt in front of her and held it out to her, palm up.

Bird glared at him, snot pouring from her nose. She wiped it on the back of her hand and sniffed. She looked back over her shoulder one more time.

Why wasn't Fife here? Of all the times for her not to be here, why now? A new feeling stabbed sharply inside Bird's chest. Something she hadn't felt before. Not sadness. Not fear, longing, or helplessness. Something different. Something…harder.

Anger.

Her jaw tightened. *Fine*. If that's how Fife wanted it, that's how it would be. Bird didn't need her. She glared at the crowd gathered around the perimeter.

You don't need anyone, she told herself.

She took a deep breath and touched the two middle fingers of her left hand to her forehead, bowing her head deeply. The crowd returned the gesture. She turned to face Shale. His eyes crinkled.

"Ready?" he said. She nodded. He held out his hand again and this time, she took it.

She stepped up into the cool darkness of the transport vehicle and didn't look back.

chapter
thirty-one

I WAKE, tumbling head over heels.

Everything is water; my mouth and nose are full of it, my eyes stinging with it. I inhale without thinking and suck water down my throat.

All around me, the world is dark and murky and blue. Through my feet, I see the sky through the water's surface, warped by fractured, rippling sunlight.

Another crazy, spinning rotation and my head breaks the surface. I gasp air that burns my throat and squeeze water from my eyes. The sun reflects in shattered pieces all around me. A wave crashes over my head, sending me spinning into the gurgling blue madness again.

My foot touches something firm and I push off it.

As I surface for the second time I glimpse white sand. I pull myself toward it, feeling a current lifting and pulling me too, finally making sense of what's happening. I'm in a surf break. These are waves. That is the shore.

Dragging myself onto the sand and throwing myself down on my knees, I cough and gasp and snort saltwater until my breath returns. I roll onto my back and close my burning eyes against the hot, white sun; breathing, grateful for breathing.

I dig water from my ears with my finger. As I do, silence is replaced by a cacophony of shrieking—a raucous, deafening din. I open my eyes.

Birds. Thousands of them. Circling overhead, their forked tails starkly painted, black against the blinding sky. They dip and swerve, chase each other and dive, their shrieks and cries filling the air. I wonder vaguely where they've come from. What they're doing here. My chest rises and falls. Thoughts dip and swerve through space, chasing each other, diving in and out of my consciousness.

They've got Sargo.

I sit bolt upright.

They got Sargo.

And you forgot Malarkey.

Pain opens up my chest like a knife. Malarkey was still down below when I jumped. Where is she now? Where is Sargo? Where am *I*? I look around, tears springing to my eyes. A beach. Some kind of beach somewhere. Where's *Panga?* What the hell just happened?

My head spinning, I stare back out at the surf tumbling onto the shore. The churning, ceaseless motion drags a big, slick glob of nausea up from my belly. I roll onto my side and vomit into the sand. My eyes close.

———

"As the Salt, so the sailor."

I wake with a gasp, clawing my way out of some dark, damp nightmare. My face feels tight and hot. Sunburned. I turn my head, feeling cool water at my cheek. The tide has risen. The sun has moved and the air has cooled. The smell of feathers and bird shit and vomit invades my nose. It wasn't a nightmare. I'm actually here.

Sargo's voice floats through my head as fragments of sleep recede. Sargo, face down in the water. Sargo, being dragged aboard the Anonymity's boat. Sargo, holding me, his lips against my hair.

"*Te tengo, mija.*"

I shrink into the sand, as if physically moving will help me dodge the pain of those words going through me.

I got you.

He did have me. Always. Had my back. Had my heart. And I couldn't keep my shit together long enough to do the one simple thing he asked me to do. "*Keep us steady,*" Sargo said. *That's all you had to do.* Keep us steady.

I close my eyes. I didn't mean to do this, it isn't my fault. It isn't fair. I *tried*; I'm *trying*. I didn't ask for this stupid brain. I didn't mean to make these stupid decisions.

I can't change who I am.

"*You can't change the wind,*" says Sargo's voice in my head. "*You can't change the waves. You can only change yourself and your ship. You have to find a way to make it work.*"

I don't want to find a way to make it work. I want to give up. I want to disappear. I want to drink until I can't stand up and lie here in bird shit and vomit until the tide rises and the water overwhelms me and the Salt drags my useless body down to Jones.

You know you can't do that, Bird, says a voice, and this time, it isn't Sargo's voice. *This is your wind. These are your waves. These are the conditions you've been given. You have to find a way to make it work.*

As the Salt, so the sailor.

I struggle to my feet.

Shielding my eyes with my hand, I turn a full circle. The beach behind me disappears into a mess of scrubby, tangled trees. A wide stump sits at edge of the scrub, hollow inside and as tall as I am, its craggy points white with feathers and bird shit. Behind the scrub, a hill rises steeply, and at the top of it, a swarm of birds circles endlessly.

There's no sign of the docks, of the bay, or of Alluvium. I take a few shallow breaths to quell my rising panic while I turn to gaze out to the unfamiliar horizon. Two enormous rocks thrust into the sky like monuments just beyond the surf break, their twin tops shrouded by matching carousels of birds. Behind them, it's empty all the way to the edge of the world.

Don't panic, I tell myself. *Think.*

Don't tell me what to do, my self retorts. *Why don't* you *think?*

Maybe there's a map.

I press a finger to my brow. Static screams through my head like a hurricane, like a trillion needles drilling against the backs of my eyes, inside my ears, against the inside of my skull. I wrench my hand away, blinking away white spots, my ears ringing. The sharp, rusty taste of metal or blood floods my tongue.

What the hell was *that?* Am I out of range?

I touch my brow again. Static. I pull my hand away. That wasn't anything like being out of range. My chip must be broken.

Wonderful.

Squinting around, I look for some kind of landmark. But even as I do, I know it's pointless. What am I going to recognize? I have no idea where I am. Even if I'm still near Alluvium, I was in that City less than twenty-four hours. The only parts of it I saw were the docks and the footbridges to Shale's house.

Okay. Stay calm. Don't panic. There's nothing you can do but start walking. The sooner you start walking, the sooner you'll know where you are.

I turn to my right and find myself squinting into the sun. So I turn left. I'll put the sun behind me. I'll walk along the beach until I find someone to help me get back to Alluvium. Then I'll find

Shale and make him tell me where they took Sargo. And then I'll break his flogging legs.

Sounds like a plan.

The sun warms my back as I walk and steam begins to rise from my clothes. I ignore the thirst beginning to crinkle the back of my throat and try to guess the time—1400, maybe 1500? I have nothing to go on except the angle of the sun. I wish I could remember how to read it.

Sargo could do it. He can tell you the time down to the quarter-hour just by looking at the sun. I can't help but laugh, bitterly. Why didn't I ever pay attention to anything he tried to teach me? All that shit would be so useful right now.

I walk for what feels like hours, the drone of the surf and the racket of birds underscoring the rhythmic crunch of my footsteps. I pick my way around nests and through piles of feathers, expecting at some point to come to the end of the colony, to see a thinning of the flock, some other form of life. But it just goes on and on. There's nothing else. Nothing but me and the birds.

The sun sinks and the air gets cold. I try to ignore the fact that I still haven't seen anything that resembles a City. I try not to think about how much I would love to just sit down and drink an entire flask of grog. I try not to bite my nails. I focus all my energy on walking because it's the only productive thing I can do. I create a rhythm out of my breath and steps—two steps in, two steps out, two breaths in, two breaths out—repetitive, meditative, endless, until suddenly, ten feet ahead, I see footprints.

Another person. Suppressing a small whoop of excitement, I hurry to them. They stretch ahead of me, a single, long line of tracks in the sand. Maybe they go all the way back to Alluvium. Maybe I just need to follow these—

I frown. Actually, these footprints look very familiar. They almost look like…

I slowly lift my foot and place it into the first footprint. It's a perfect fit. These are my footprints.

That can't be. The back of my neck prickles as I gaze ahead at the path of the footprints, snaking away from me along the beach until they disappear. I turn and look behind me. The same prints track toward me out of the rapidly falling darkness.

Turning away from the water, I look up the beach. At the edge of the tangle of trees and scrub, sneering at me like a craggy, toothy face, is the hollow stump I started from. I've gone in a circle.

I scream and scatter a cluster of nearby birds with a savage kick. How did this happen? How did I get turned around? I walked next to the water, I never changed direction. I couldn't have gotten lost, I've only been going one way. I look desperately up and down the beach at my footprints stretching off in both directions, as a harsh and inescapable realization dawns on me.

The only possible way I could have walked in a full circle is if this beach forms a complete circle. And the only way that could be true…is if this is an island. And if this is an island…then I am well and truly lost.

The next morning dawns damp and muggy, the sun hot on my face before I even open my eyes. My mouth is dry, my clothes stiff, and my skin itchy with dried saltwater. I smell earth, wood, and sand. And sweat. Mostly sweat, in fact.

I roll onto my side and sit up. The cries of birds and the musty reek of shit and molted feathers are immediately overwhelming. I'm inside the hollow stump at the edge of the scrub. I slept here.

My stomach growls. I haven't eaten since breakfast yesterday. *Yesterday.*

Yesterday comes rushing back at me so fast I actually lift my hands in front of my face to stop it. Yesterday feels like a lifetime ago.

This time yesterday I was sitting at Shale's kitchen table, looking through that big window, watching the sun come up over the bay of Alluvium, filled with hope. I had a brother. I had a job. I had a future.

I shut my eyes against yesterday.

Standing up, I scan the beach. Still full of birds. No surprises there.

My rumbling stomach becomes acutely more noticeable as I watch the birds preening and flapping their wings. They don't look particularly fast. Most of them seem reluctant to leave their nests. It would probably be pretty easy to grab one…

And then what would you do? Have you ever killed a bird before?

The image of me with my fist around a bird's neck paints itself across my mind. I shudder and turn away.

The trees in the scrub behind me are short and skinny, their white, brittle trunks and spiny branches twisted, their leaves dry. There's enough space between them to walk, a carpet of dead leaves and feathers covering the ground below.

There are trees here, says a voice in my head. That means there must be water on this island somewhere. I lick my parched lips. If I don't find water soon, there isn't going to be much point in killing birds. An empty stomach gets your attention, but it's not so swift and deadly as the sneaking specter of thirst.

I need to find that water. I climb out of the stump.

Wait. Think for a second.

I want to be smart about this. I don't want to get lost. I don't want to go recklessly plunging into the woods without thinking, in classic Bird fashion, and realize in two hours' time that I have no idea where I am. I need to leave a trail so I can find my way back.

I cast my eyes about the sand at my feet. I need some kind of marker that I can leave as I go, something recognizable.

There are no stones to be found, so I opt to create a symbol out of sticks. It takes me a few minutes to come up with a suitable symbol: two sticks, stuck into the ground to form a right triangle, the bottom corner of the hypotenuse indicating the direction I should go.

Standing back to admire my handiwork, I smile. It kind of looks like a sail.

Feeling somewhat buoyed, I take a breath and step into the trees.

It's immediately unpleasant. Everything is armored with tiny spines and needles; they tear at my clothes and scratch my face and arms. The birds in the trees are big and black. They puff bright red throats like balloons and click their beaks as I pass beneath them, spreading their wings and shaking their feathers as if to say, "You shouldn't be here."

The way rises steeper and steeper until I'm climbing on all fours up a slippery bank of loose soil. My palms collect needles, and my face mars with dirt and sweat every time I wipe it on the back of my arm.

Suddenly, my foot slips, plunging into the soft soil of the bank. The branch I'm holding tears out of my hand, and I'm tumbling backward in an avalanche of dirt and leaves. I roll down the bank, head over heels, my arms scrabbling, until I land hard on my shoulder, the side of my face buried in mud.

Gasping, I heave myself onto my knees and sit back on my heels, clawing mud from my eyes and hair. I've fallen into a small clearing, come to rest against the side of a large log in a squelchy, soupy mess of sludge. One side of my torso is black, my shirt sticking to me, my feet and legs completely soaked.

Soaked. Soaked means water.

The realization propels me to my feet. I spot the source of the water: a tiny trickle seeping almost silently from between two rocks. Thirst returns savagely, and I throw myself down in front of the little stream, making a cup with my hand and slurping with chapped lips.

Almost immediately I gag and spit it out. *Salt*.

I wipe my mouth, staring at the trickle of water in disbelief.

How can it be salty? How can all these trees be here if the ground-water is salty?

Because they're Saltnut trees, Genius.

I stare at the trickle of saltwater, willing it to be something else. *Anything* else: freshwater, or oil, or blood, or grog, or just…nothing. I'd rather have nothing. I'd rather have never seen water at all. I sit very still, breathing deeply, concentrating all my energy on not letting rage at that deceptive trickle of water consume me.

Finally, I wipe my face and do what I can with my clothes. Then I pick myself up and begin to climb again.

Little by little, the undergrowth thins, and through the trees above me I feel the heat of the sun on the top of my head. A breeze shifts through the canopy, showering me in leaves. It catches my clothes, pulling them away from my damp skin, and I hold my arms away from me, relishing the cool air. Up ahead, I can see the crest of a ridge, and above it, the sky.

When I reach the top, I can see with an unsettling mix of vindication and dismay that I was right. This is an island. A very small one. I shade my face and look out at the Salt in all directions. There's not a lump of land on the horizon or a single sail on the water.

For flog's sake, where are you, Bird?

Sitting on a rock, I rest my elbows on my knees and stare at the water, thinking back to the moments before I jumped from *Panga*. I jumped but I never hit the water. I blacked out. I saw the red desert, and the girl and her brother again. I saw me and Shale, leaving the Settlement. I blipped.

You teleported.

That word—'teleported'—squats in a shadow in the corner of my mind and I ignore it, because it's insane and ridiculous. But it's there. Like a shard of glass in the bottom of my foot. Try as I might, I can't dislodge it.

What if Shale was right? Whatever a 'blip' is—whatever I *thought* it was—it doesn't explain this. It doesn't explain how I woke up with a broken biochip on some flog-forsaken island in the middle of the Salt. This was not just a blackout. This was... something else.

The knife of hunger twists in my stomach, bringing me back to the world in front of me. White sky. Black birds. Endless, endless, endless miles of gray, miserable Salt.

An impossible heaviness settles in my bones. The desire to give up and sit in the shade and drink until I'm dead hasn't gone away. The only thing that's preventing me from doing it is the fact that I don't have any grog.

With some effort, I push the itch for grog to the back of my mind, along with the ridiculous idea of teleportation. I need to focus on what's happening *here. Now.*

One step at a time. As the Salt, so the sailor.

I stand up and take one last look around the island, taking stock of everything, trying to fix a mental map of the place in my mind.

Then I carefully make my way down from the ridge and begin the long climb back down to the beach.

chapter
thirty-two

I AM UNBELIEVABLY, viciously thirsty.

My tongue and throat are so dry they burn. My lips crack when I move them. I'm hungry too, but it's nothing compared to the thirst. The feeling is like dry rot in my bones. Light in my head. A hollowness.

I lay on my back in the sand by the stump, my arm over my face, the white sun burning a hole through my spirit. Even the itch for grog, which has been a constant, gnawing presence at the back of my mind for days, shrinks away from the thirst. The idea of drinking grog is repugnant. Just thinking about it makes me thirstier. I need *water*.

"I guess it must be easy if you don't have any friends," said the girl, *glaring at her bowl. Her brother stiffened.*

Another fragment of a dream. I try to wave it away with a tired hand.

"That's not fair," he said, *"she's my friend too."*

Pieces of the dreams are coming back to me all the time now. Memories of my life before Brume, I guess, if I'm taking Shale's word for it. It's like the blip in Alluvium Bay opened some kind of floodgate, and my brain is pummeling me with a deluge of information about my childhood in the Settlement.

A deluge of information about my childhood in Naze isn't

going to quench my thirst though. An actual deluge, like, of water, would be great.

"Will you show me how to make a fire?" the girl asked.

Her brother squinted at her.

"You're too young."

I pound on my forehead with my fist. *Come on, Bird, concentrate!*

I can't seem to stop the memories from coming. It's making it nearly impossible to think about a solution to the water problem.

"I know, I won't touch anything," said the girl. *"But can you explain it?"*

What I do have is plenty of saltwater. If I could figure out a way to get fresh water from saltwater—

"Come on," he said, *"I'm thirsty. Let's make some brackish."*

I sit up.

Brackish.

My stupid brain isn't just flooding me with useless memories. It's putting the answer right in front of my eyes. With fire, I can boil saltwater and trap the steam to make brackish. Young Bird knew you could do that.

I struggle to my feet, dizzy, but invigorated.

Young Bird knew how to make a fire.

It takes me a long time, but eventually, I assemble a small pile of leaves and grass and choose a flat, sturdy log to serve as my fireboard.

A warm, offshore breeze passes through my camp, causing some of the leaves to flutter away, and with a *tsk* of irritation, I corral them back, nesting them into a small pile on top of the log and pressing the pile together with my palms.

"When you spin the drill against the fireboard, it creates heat," says Shale's voice in my head. *"When you have enough heat, the kindling will catch."*

I place the slender, round stick I've chosen as my drill in the center of the pile, sandwich my palms together around it, inhale deeply through my nose, and begin to spin. The motion immediately re-opens all the cuts on my palms that I sustained while climbing around in the scrub yesterday. I grit my teeth and squeeze my eyes shut against the pain.

The drill slips. It shoots out from between my palms, tearing a chunk of skin from my thumb as it does. The tip slides abruptly off the fireboard, scattering my pile of leaves and grass, which are caught by the wind, lifted, and blown across the sand like tumbleweeds.

"No..."

I drag myself to my feet, hopelessly snatching at them as the wind chases them away, far too nimble for my sluggish, tired body. A wave of lightheadedness makes the ground rise in front of me and I stagger to a halt, falling to my knees, watching in despair as the work that encompassed the last hour of my life skitters away down the beach.

Do better, says a voice in my head, and at this point I'm no longer sure if it's my voice, Sargo's voice, Shale's voice, or someone new entirely. *You have to do better. This isn't a joke, Howsley. For once in your life, take this seriously. As the Salt—*

Yeah, yeah, yeah...

Heaving a sigh of resignation, I get up and begin scouring the sand for kindling again.

When I have a pile of it assembled, I dig a small pit to stop the kindling from blowing away while I light it. As I'm digging the hole, I start to wonder what else I could improve about the process.

I wash my hands in the Salt and wrap them with tough leaves to protect them from the drill. As I'm doing that, I wonder if there's anything else I could do.

I spend the better part of an hour carefully peeling all the bark off the fire board to make it smoother and easier to manage. Finally, with all my preparations made, I kneel at the fireboard and place the drill between my palms.

I lose track of how long I spin the drill. An hour, maybe? I mutter a mantra under my breath. I don't know for how long. It becomes rhythmic, meditative, picking up the rhythm of the drill, the rhythm of my breath, focusing everything into a single, cohesive beat.

"As the Salt, so the sailor. As the sailor, so the Salt."

A tiny flame leaps into life. I bend my face close to it and blow as it sputters and trembles and then, timidly, starts to grow. It catches and crinkles the grass around it, rapidly turning the small pile of debris into ash. Terrified that I'll lose it, I grab a handful of leaves and carefully feed the flame until it becomes two flames, and two become three, and three become a fire.

My heart soars. *I flogging did it.*

A tremendous clap of thunder ruptures the sky, and a torrent of water unlike any I've ever felt comes down on top of me.

I watch in horror as my fire is extinguished. My little pile of kindling is drenched and then swamped, the water pummeling the delicate grass, pooling on the branch, picking up the leaves, and swirling them away. Everything is soaked.

In disbelief, I turn my face to the sky. Storm clouds completely obscure the early evening stars—I hadn't even noticed them rolling in.

I snatch up the drill and hurl it into the trees, screaming, the sound barely reaching my ears over the barrage of the downpour. The tears I've been repressing for days finally erupt and I sink to my knees and sob.

I was trying. I'm *trying.*

I heave gasping, furious, devastated breaths. It doesn't matter what I do. It doesn't matter how hard I try. I can't change. I can't do this on my own. I can't even help myself.

My face is so thoroughly soaked with water that I don't even feel the tears running down it. The rain running into my mouth is oddly sweet on my parched tongue.

And then it hits me. Rain is water.

You can drink this, Idiot.

Rain. The first rain I've ever seen. It's so alien to me that I hadn't even realized what it was. I was so blinded by my anger that I couldn't see the gift that was falling from the sky. I couldn't see the water for the rain.

I stretch my hands out in front of me in a daze, watching the water pour through my fingers like liquid silver, then cup them, and let them fill.

When I bring them to my lips, the rain is like a poultice on my rage. It's like nothing I've ever tasted: cool, and sweet, and clean. It pours through my head like a soothing light, driving away the headache that's been clanging there for days.

My clothes become heavy, stick to me, and without thinking I tear them off and fling them on the sand. Days of salt and sweat and muck pour off me. I throw my head back again and open my mouth, letting it fill until it overflows, water spilling over my cheeks and running down my chin. Grog never tasted like this. Nothing ever tasted like this.

If I ever make it off this island. I'll never drink grog again.

I need to capture it. Store it somehow. My legs move on their own, propelling me to the edge of the scrub, the downpour so thick I can barely see through it. Tucked amongst the small, spindly trees with their brown leaves and white bark squats a dark green shrub with big, waxy leaves. In a frenzy, I gather the leaves until my arms are full.

With renewed determination, I return to the beach. I drop to my knees and start to dig. I dig a hole about six inches across and tuck one of the big leaves in it to create a small bowl. The rain begins to pool inside the leaf. I dig another, then another, and another, until I have about fifteen little pools, all lined with leaves, all filling with rain.

I can't help but laugh, imagining the sight of myself, naked, stumbling around in the rain, digging holes in the sand. I laugh so hard it winds me. I laugh until I collapse, overcome with exhaustion, soaked to the bone.

I wake the next morning with a snort, face down in the sand with my ass in the air. I sit up and look around.

The pools I dug last night are still full. A few have drained, but I count about twelve still full of fresh water. They glitter like jewels in the sand. They might be the most beautiful thing I've ever seen.

Kneeling at the one nearest me, I put my face in it and suck it down. The water is warm and has a faint, leafy taste.

I stand up take stock of my camp. Everything is still soaked from the deluge, my clothes included, so I throw on underwear and hang the rest in the branches by the stump.

One thing at a time.

I'm alive. I have water. Today I will make another fire.

The morning is overcast, damp, and muggy. The air, bitter with petrichor, seems to cling to me, and the sky is close with low-hanging clouds. At some point, the sun emerges, blazing hot, drawing steam from the beach. By late afternoon, the scrub seems dry enough to attempt another fire.

It takes me the better part of three hours, but I manage it. As soon as the fire is stable enough to be left, I venture into the bird colony to steal some eggs. I don't feel great about it. But I feel better about than killing birds.

I crack the eggs into one of the big, waxy leaves and set it over the hot coals near the edge of the fire. I cook them until I can't wait any longer then pour them down my throat. They're rubbery around the edges, cold in the middle, slimy, and very salty. I chase them down with warm, leafy water.

I can't remember a better meal.

I wake many times during the night. Every time I wake, I panic. I feed the fire and struggle to keep my eyes open, watching it. By morning, the roaring pyre has turned into a pit of glowing coals, and I scramble to feed it before setting out into the scrub to gather more wood.

For the next three days, scarcely another thought occupies me but the fire. There is an immediate and undeniable need to keep the fire going at all costs. I wake, feed the fire, eat half-cooked eggs, drink from the pools, and fight my way through the scrub, gathering wood.

Every morning the fire has dwindled down to embers, and by every evening I've built it back up. I watch the weather like a hawk.

On the morning of day four, I see rain clouds. I move the fire inside the hollow stump and cover the stump with leaves. It rains, and the fire stays dry. I dig more pools and collect more rain. After several failed attempts, I give up on making brackish; I just don't have the tools. Instead, I focus on collecting rain, and I begrudgingly thank whatever gods might be watching for their help with that.

"I hope you're all enjoying the show."

My life is tending the fire. I live moment to moment, always focused on the task at hand. Thoughts of blipping, of Shale, of finding Sargo and Malarkey, are crowded out of my mind by the ever-present hunger of the flame. I don't even think about leaving the island. I don't even think about grog.

So it's with no small amount of shock that I wake on the morning of my seventh day to see a sail on the horizon.

chapter
thirty-three

I STAND with my feet in the surf and one hand over my brow, watching the approaching sail with a sickening sense of dread. The ship is too far away to make out in detail, but there's little doubt in my mind about who's coming after me.

The Anonymity.

Suddenly, being rescued from the island doesn't seem like such a high priority. Not if Shale's going to take me back to Alluvium to join some insane terrorist organization. I'd rather stay here. Anyway, am I not doing fine here? I have a fire. I have these eggs. It'll probably rain again at some point…

Don't be insane. You can't stay on this island. You're panicking. It's probably just some fishermen or something.

Just some fishermen or something. Is that the kind of luck I usually have? Anyway, even if it's not the Anonymity, what are the odds it's someone friendly? How many friendly people have I met out here so far?

So proud of my stupid little fire.

Way to go, Bird.

It's too late now to put the fire out; they've seen the smoke. They know I'm here. I'll have to hide. At least until I know who they are.

There's a rocky outcropping tucked in the trees that I discovered on a wood-gathering mission two days ago. It looks down on the beach and gives me a good view of my little camp at the stump. If I can get up there I'll have a good vantage point to watch them land.

I fly back up the beach, snatching up and pulling on my clothes and stuffing the drill into my back pocket. I kneel by the pools, almost all empty now, and tip the last of the water from them down my throat, then run to the edge of the scrub.

Wait. Stop and think.

If I go into the woods here, they'll be able to follow my footprints right from the beach. I should try and throw them off my track.

I shuffle back to the stump, kicking sand over my footprints, then run down the beach in the other direction, towards another opening in the trees, leaving a long trail of footprints. Then slowly, carefully, I creep back along the edge of the tree line, being careful to walk on the carpet of leaves below the trees so as to leave no prints.

I fight my way up to the ledge I discovered two days ago and tuck myself behind a rock. For what feels like a lifetime, I wait.

I can't see the water from here, but I can hear the dull hum of a motorized skiff approaching, then shouts and splashes as the crew land the skiff and drag it up the beach.

The first of them comes into view. He's tall and wearing a hood. The wind flips a corner of his coat open, and something metallic at his hip flashes in the sun. He's followed by a small, nimble-looking fellow, and an absolute giant of a man. They scuff around my camp, turning over branches with their feet.

The little one points something out to his partner. My footprints leading off in the wrong direction. The tall one starts to follow them, but the little one stops him. They confer briefly, and then to my horror, the little one points to the exact spot where I entered the scrub.

If they saw through my trick that easily, it won't take them long to find me here. Moving as silently as I can, I turn and jump from the outcropping.

My sleeve snags on a branch. It snaps as I tumble to the ground, an explosion of squawking filling the air as a giant black bird launches out of the tree, scattering leaves and swelling his big, red throat.

I hear a shout from somewhere below me. Stumbling to my feet, I run. I bob and weave around branches and logs, spines tearing at my face and clothes, someone crashing through the trees close behind me. He must be faster than he looks because he's gaining on me.

Somewhere up ahead of me is the embankment I fell down on my first day in this forest. I reach it and teeter on the edge, casting one wild glance back over my shoulder before I jump. I slide and tumble down the slope of loose dirt and roots, finally coming to a stop against a log. Rolling onto my belly, I wedge myself under the log, holding my breath and lie still.

The crashing behind me has stopped. I hear a shout and a grunted response. The sound of big footsteps tromping through the undergrowth at the top of the bank. The footsteps stomp around for a couple more minutes, then recede. I hear another shout, another grunted response, but muffled, further away this time.

Exhaling softly, I inch out from under the log on my forearms.

"Stop right there."

I freeze, my chin in the dirt. The cold point of a blade is against my cheek. I sense rather than see a booted foot firmly plant itself inches from my head.

"Come all the way out, slowly, with your hands up."

I slither out with my hands over my head, stand, and turn to face my pursuer. My jaw drops.

"*Fetch?*"

The scrappy Black girl with the buzzcut does a double-take.

"Alluvium?"

I begin to drop my hands.

"Keep them up!" she snaps, pointing her knife at me.

I jerk them back up. "What are you going to do, stab me?"

"I might."

The sound of something enormous crashing through the trees draws my eyes away just in time to see a hooded figure burst into the clearing. He wrenches off his hood to reveal a thick, black mohawk and an alabaster neck covered in tattoos, and I realize he isn't a man at all.

"Goliath!"

Goliath stops, their eyes darting to Fetch with her knife drawn. "Who is?"

Fetch replies without taking her eyes off me. "You don't remember our friends from the little yellow boat? What happened, friend? Lost your way?"

The lanky figure of Red Bread stoops under a branch and steps into the clearing, the long-handled ax in one hand. He takes in the scene, then quietly hooks the weapon into the canvas loop on his belt, walks up behind Fetch, and puts a hand on her shoulder.

Fetch stiffens, tightening her grip on the handle of her knife, then with a *tsk* of frustration, she sheaths it.

I slowly lower my hands, glancing from Red Bread, to Goliath, to Fetch, who stands with her hands on her hips, looking me over.

"You look like shit," she says.

"I've been stranded on a deserted island for a week," I retort. "What's your excuse?"

In a breath, she lunges at me, one hand flicking her knife back out of the sheath across her chest, but I'm prepared for her attack and lunge back, raising my fists.

A new, powerful energy burns in my veins. I just survived a week on this God-forsaken shithole bird farm of an island. I'm not just some pathetic, naive nobody anymore. I'm sick of being intimidated by this little...*stray*.

Red Bread wedges himself between us, driving us apart with a hand on each of our chests.

Fetch glares past him at me. "So where's your boyfriend, and that big dumb dog?"

"He's not my boyfriend."

"Search the area," she calls to Goliath. "They could be hiding in the trees."

"They're not."

"Oh yeah?" Fetch glares. "Why would I believe that?"

I hesitate. How much do I want her to know? How much can I tell her without having to explain the Anonymity? If Savage and his crew find out how valuable I am to Shale and his insane faction, I'll be right back where I started. They'll turn me over in a heartbeat. And Shale would probably pay Savage whatever he asked for.

Red Bread shoots a look to Goliath, who mutters into Fetch's ear.

Fetch glowers. "I'm not taking her anywhere near the captain."

Red Bread removes his hand from my chest and uses it to sign something.

"Is Captain's decision," Goliath says in a low voice. "She have rich brother."

Fetch sheaths her knife with a sharp exhale. "You're lucky these two are such bleeding hearts," she says. "If it were up to me you'd be getting a knife in the neck."

"Guess it's a good thing it's not up to you," I reply.

She narrows her eyes as though preparing to lunge at me again. Then she whirls around and stomps across the clearing into the trees.

Savage observes me from the chair behind the helm in the *Kingfisher's* cockpit, his steel-toed boots propped, as ever, on the edge of the instrument panel, the butterfly knife turning lazily over in his hand.

"That was some stunt you pulled, *Electra*. Made me look pretty foolish."

His voice is casual, but I sense the dangerous undercurrent just beneath the words. He flips the knife abruptly at the floor, where it sticks in the wood with a sharp thunk. It stands on its point in the deck, vibrating.

"I don't like to look foolish, Alluvium."

My hands are bound in front of me with the itchy rope that Fetch insisted on tying me up with before she, Red Bread, and Goliath loaded me into their skiff and brought me out to where the *Kingfisher* is anchored. Every wave that rolls in toward the island tips us sideways, and I have to constantly readjust my feet to steady myself.

"How were those eggs?" Savage clasps his hands behind his head, his eyes glinting. "I've heard they're almost inedible. You know there are fruit trees on this island?"

"No," I say warily, "I didn't."

"What I don't understand," says Fetch, "is how you came to be on this island in the first place."

She leans with her arms folded in the doorway, the side of her head with the 4242 tattoo on it propped against the doorframe.

"I had to abandon ship," I say. "I jumped overboard and hit my head. I must have drifted out into the Salt and washed up here."

"From Alluvium?"

"Guess so."

"Alluvium is almost a thousand miles south of here. You're telling me you drifted a thousand miles, unconscious, against the prevailing current? In less than two days?"

I try to keep the shock from showing on my face. *A thousand miles?*

"You abandoned ship?" Savage cuts in, genuine curiosity cutting through his usual visage of malice. "Why?"

"We lost our mainsail. It tore in half. Sargo—Pitch—uh, my... friend...went overboard, and I jumped in to get him back. I don't remember what happened after that."

It's not entirely a lie.

Savage and Fetch are silent. I try to return Savage's incisive gaze without looking like I'm hiding anything. Finally, he uncrosses his boots and swiftly stands. He stoops to retrieve the butterfly knife.

"Well, it sounds to me like that rich brother of yours is probably worried about you."

"I'm sure he is."

He swivels the knife. It *snicks* quietly as it opens and closes in his hand.

"So what are we going to do about that?"

I keep one eye on the knife. He hasn't used that knife on me yet. And he won't as long as he thinks he can get more money out of Shale.

"I guess you'll just have to take me back to him."

I have no intention of letting him do that, but if I can get to Alluvium, I can figure something out. I know the city now. I'll be prepared.

He watches me carefully. He knows I'm up to something. Or at least, he suspects I am. Of course he does. But I don't think he knows what. And for some reason, I'm not afraid.

For some reason, Savage and his crew don't feel so threatening to me anymore. Maybe it's because I dodged them last time. Maybe it's because I dodged the Anonymity too. Maybe it's because I just clawed my way through a week of Hell on a deserted island, alone. Death felt inevitable in those first few days. Something about escaping it makes me feel like escaping Savage and his crew might not be so difficult. On the island, I had nothing, and I made it out. Here, I have tools. Options.

"How do I know this brother will be so generous a second time around?" Savage says, still swiveling the knife. "Twenty thousand is a lot of coin. Your family might be tired of your... shenanigans. I know I am."

I glare at him. I don't have time for this. Just take me back to Alluvium so I can escape, already. "Trust me. He'll pay."

He stops the knife, holding it with the point facing me. "Trust you? Why on earth would I do that?"

"Because if you want the coin, you don't have a choice."

His eyes narrow. He flips the knife closed and tucks it into his pocket.

"Fetch, see to it that Alluvium here gets a berth in the crew quarters. We're going to treat her a little less...delicately this time around. She's not royalty, after all."

I frown. "What do you mean, 'delicately'?"

"Since I have no guarantee that your brother will cough up the coin for you a second time around, I think it's only fair that you earn your passage back to Alluvium. Plenty of things need to get done around here that my crew, frankly, are tired of doing. It'll be nice to give them a break from all the menial, degrading tasks. They surely will appreciate it."

Savage flashes his teeth as Fetch unties my wrists and takes hold of my arm to steer me out of the room.

I shake her off. "I've got it, thanks."

She rolls her eyes and motions for me to follow her. As we reach the door, Savage's voice stops us.

"Oh, Fetch—"

We both turn. His expression is serious as he watches us from behind the helm. My stomach twists. What now?

He leans an elbow on his knee and points a stern finger at Fetch.

"See to it that there are no shenanigans this time."

———————————

I eat with the crew at the same long table in the galley that Sargo and I sat at just two weeks ago. It feels like so long ago it may as well have been a dream. Sargo and I argued that night. Stupid. So pointless, in light of everything that's happened. He was right. He was always right.

I eye the big brown jug of drink in the center of the table. Last time I was here, that jug so thoroughly consumed my attention that I could barely pay attention to what was going on around me.

Tonight, I decline the jug when Red Bread passes it to me, and even though it makes me itchy, it also feels good. I'm so grateful just to be alive—and I'm still so *thirsty*—that just to have *water* feels like a miracle. I told myself when I was on the island that if I ever made it off, I would never drink again. I'm sure it won't always be so easy to say 'no', but tonight, at least, I've proven that it's possible.

Later, I stand on deck as the *Kingfisher* sets sail, watching the island recede into darkness. As my eyes adjust, I hold up my hands and crook my knuckles to look at my nails in the dull orange light of the moon. I haven't chewed them. Not since I started tending the fire. There wasn't space for that on the island. Just like there wasn't space for grog or spacing out or getting myself twisted into knots. There was only space for the next five minutes. There was only space for one thing at a time.

A cold gust kicks the sails open. Wrapping my arms around myself, I put my back to the island and gaze over the bow toward the dark horizon.

A faint, high-pitched ringing in my ears reminds me that my biochip is broken. More unsettling than remembering that, though, is remembering that it broke when I inexplicably blacked out in Alluvium bay and somehow wound up on an island a thousand miles away. When I somehow *blipped* a thousand miles.

When I...teleported?

"Alluvium!" Fetch's bark snaps me out of my thoughts. "Go help Red clean up dinner."

I nod once and head for the steps below deck.

Malarkey and Sargo are gone. I might have escaped the Anonymity, overcome my fear of Reckoners, and survived a deserted island, but my work is far from over. I saved myself; now I have to save them.

The enormity of that task feels overwhelming, insurmountable. But I think I'm beginning to see the way to go about tasks like that: thoughtfully. Carefully. Thinking before I act. Taking it one step at a time. Changing myself and my sails to suit the conditions I've been given.

As the Salt, so the sailor.

I pause at the top of the steps, casting one last glance over my shoulder to the island, no more than a shadow now, receding into darkness. I inhale the night. Exhale my fear. Then I head below to join the crew.

get the next book

It is not the Salt we conquer. It is ourselves.

When Bird learns that Sargo has been kidnapped and taken to a city eight thousand miles across the Salt, she realizes she has only one choice if she ever wants to see him again...

...undertake a dangerous voyage to get him back. *Alone.*

Desperate but determined, Bird sets out to rescue the friend she may be falling in love with. But the closer she gets to Sargo, the close she gets to the truth about the people that took him...and about herself.

"Crack. That's what this is." - Amazon Review

"I am, yet again, amazed by how much adventure is packed into this book." - Amazon Review

free novella

LIZSHIPTON.COM / NEWSLETTER

Join my mailing list and get a FREE prequel novella to the
Thalassic Series

The world has ended. The virus took everything. Heron Howsley and her cat Zig Zag flee the tornado-ravaged Alley for a better life in Naze, a climate refugee camp on the West Coast.

Heron has just two rules: don't make friends, don't get murdered. But when she spots a lonely hitchhiker on the side of the road, she breaks Rule One and stops to pick him up.

That simple act of kindness sparks a chain of events that forces Heron to reconcile with demons both old and new: a past she thought she'd left behind, a sister she thought was dead, and a future she may not be a part of.

social media and stuff

acknowledgments

As an indie author working primarily on my own, I don't have a big team to thank. However, there are a few people who have been incredibly supportive throughout this process, and without whom, this book would not be what it is.

In no particular order, those people are

My writing group JOSELINA REIS, TARA BRODBECK, CAROLYN VIOLET, and KAREN MARKS for showing me how to be a better writer

SAM STOKES for beta reads, ARC reads, reviews, and general unbridled enthusiasm

MY TIK TOK CREW for ARC reads, support and being amazing

GEOFF SHIPTON for dad jokes

TREVOR HOPE for steering the ship and fixing everything all the time

ALOY BONESNATCHER MCGEE for being the world's most legendary dog

about the author

PART-TIME AUTHOR  FULL-TIME PIRATE.

HI! I'M LIZ. I'm a freelance writer, indie author, and full-time, off-grid, live-aboard sailor. I'm currently sailing around the world with my boyfriend and my dog, turning my real-life adventures into Sci-Fi and Fantasy books.

I love incorporating the incredible experiences, beautiful places, and fascinating people I encounter on my travels into my work. Many parts of the world are underrepresented in fiction, particularly speculative fiction, and I feel grateful to be able to explore them.

I also use my books as a means to explore themes of mental health, addiction, technology, climate change, and the looming collapse of society (but, like...in a fun way.)

When I'm not penning novels about the impending apocalypse, I work as a freelance content writer specializing in articles about code, music theory, and off-grid living. On the rare occasion I'm not writing, you can find me swimming, hiking, telling my dog I love her for the bazillionth time today, or watching Taskmaster.

Printed by BoD™ in Norderstedt, Germany